LIFE CYCLES

The work of the spirits,
Truth and Love.

Love

MIGUEL SOTO

Book's Cover: Provided by book designer.
Other graphics, images, and artwork by the author.
Book ISBN printed version: 978-1-7347532-0-2.
ISBN book digital version: 978-1-7347532-1-9.
Book printed in the United States of America.
Other books written by the author, Miguel Soto.
Misterios: Amor, Luz y Vida.
      Page Publishing, Inc. de New York, NY
      ISBN 978-1-64138-085-0 (printed version)
      ISBN 978-1-64138-087-4 (digital version)
      Printed in the United States of America.
Project Information Manager, Vol. 1 Pre-construction phase.
      Copyright 2017 Miguel Soto, first edition.
      Page Publishing, Inc., New York, NY.
      ISBN 978-1-64027-075-6 Hard Cover.
      ISBN 978-1-64027-076-3 (Digital).
      Printed in the United States of America.
Angels in My Way.
      Copyright 2010, Miguel Angel Soto Flores, author and Publisher.
      ISBN 978-0-578-07196-1 first edition.
      Published and printed in the United States of America.

CONTENTS

Dedication

Dear Reader,

I dedicate this book to you and to those who seek the truth, knowing that the truth will free you from improbable beliefs. Nothing is more rewarding than knowing that what we know is true with the highest certainty. But we know our level of knowledge does not allow us to reason beyond our understanding. Prudence prevents us from thinking and acting based on false assumptions; and makes us aware of the limitations of our knowledge. The theme of this book will fascinate you, and the evidence presented can open a window to the dimension of spirits, including your soul. Your mind can see life from another perspective of your reasoning.

The author.

Ride on Winged Horses

Close your eyes, my dear friends,
and feel the fresh air caressing your lips;
sense the warmth of thoughts about
journeys that started but have no ends,
and follow the hints and tips.
for which your heart cries out.
Let the wild spirit within you
ride on winged horses: your choices.
Let them jump the hurdles of your shell
and explode your wishes long due.
Lead your emotions, as did Moses,
but to the promised gardens you smell.
Live life for life that only once comes,
the same that each day by sunset is gone.
Let your time not go by as an empty day
but fill it with passion, not crumbs;
fill it with glorious love in deeds done,
while placing yourself as you may.
Only then your soul will be realized
out of the unbearable exhaustion you felt
when the love you long for once melt
by rules and laws, you abide.
In the wondrous journeys we take,
our spirits let, with persistence
each day, our tireless minds know
there is, oneness. And for love's sake,
let in this generous existence,
the endless Life Cycles we undergo.
Life is short; so, ride your time through
on winged horses of challenging stature.
But the spirits and feelings are always true
in this physical world, by nature,
Love always waits for you.

PROLOGUE

Shadows of souls come out when humans reach deep mental absorption. They unleash moorings that keep human egos tied to themes, emotions, and material problems. Your mind reach higher thoughts while in that trance-absorption. Soul awareness is the shield that protects the human body and filters emotions, problems and issues that can disturb its absorption state. The ego sleeps while the mind remains alert. Existence is reality and unreality in its domain. And your mind sublimates consciousness of reality, as in a dream; enjoy seeing the world behind a glass window. It's a fantastic state! The mind reaches omniscience in the spirit dimension and sees creation in its entirety. What a beauty that is!

I'm on the street, "Arroyo Seco Parkway." That street passes over California Highway 110. I've finished my part-time work, and I'm going to downtown Los Angeles. I walk this street, and I stop at this overpass every day: I love watching the hectic road under the bridge. The vehicles rush in both directions, in and out, under the bridge, winding through the traffic lanes. And I ask, what happens in the minds of drivers when they travel home after a day of work? The mystery of knowledge haunts my mind. Traffic is heavier on weekdays than on weekends; but today, for an unknown reason, the road is empty. It's only 4:30 pm. this Friday, it is as if people have left town. It's a spooky afternoon, scary as Halloween. I'm falling into that state of deep absorption this afternoon. The weather is cloudy but warm, somewhat windy and humid, which increases the unsettling feeling. Thinking of dread, I finished reading the book–Misterios, Amor, Luz and Vida–by Miguel Soto. He says that light–knowledge–is what drives the universe, and the purpose of existence;

it is love, suggesting that with knowledge and love humans can live with love, for love, and to love. His writing inspires me.

When I finish my university studies of English, I will write on the secrets of the spirits; this issue is fascinating! And I will write my book as a thesis, with the evidence available. First, I'll present the premises and methods, tracing the topic and then my conclusions. My mind darkens, I'm confused. Where was I? Yes, I was thinking of the book. What? Look, it's impossible, I'm done writing that book. How and when did I do it? I don't know, my mind worked beyond reality, I can see that, and I present my thesis in the prologue, proposing that spirits are energy; we can neither create nor destroy it. Each spirit is a molecule of a global spirit. The spirits exist, no new ones. Spirits enter human eggs at the moment of fertilization; and this spirit becomes the soul of the body. Humans believe that spirits return in other human bodies. Is it possible? Yes! One for each new creature, although energy is finite in the universe. Free spirits interact with souls in humans, and souls interact from human to human; these interactions are real and occur often. If we cannot see or touch the spirits, we can study the existence and or their behavior. Get involve, my reader, and look for signs of encounters with spirits inside and outside your being.

Wait, I hear heavy engines. Wow, look; that guy on the motorcycle chases that car. He's got a gun and he's shooting at the car. They must go over a hundred miles an hour, driving over the highway's shoulder; they meander through the traffic lanes. They're approaching the overpass where I am. Oh, my God, they crashed. Oh, oh, what's happening? Oh, my head hurts. I cannot feel anything; I can't see. Everything is dark; everything is quiet, floating, as if time stopped or was in slow motion. I woke up. The daylight is bright as I have not seen it before; I have no pain, where am I, where am I? I am fainting; my mind is blank. Silence is deep. Time stood down; the world stopped; that's weird. I can see and hear everything with my mind across time. That's crazy! I feel strange, my mind. I hear and see this at the same time. It's like in a movie I can go backwards or forwards. I see the commotion, and I'm a part of it. Tell me, reader, am I dead or am I dreaming! I feel nothing, I just perceive and think.

CHAPTER 1

Premises and Approach

Abstract

If I asked, have you ever seen a spirit, heard or spoken to it? Your answer is probably, "No, I haven't," and I would understand. Most humans don't talk about their encounters, because they know that people make fun of these stories. But are you right to mock these experiences? No. And if I said, I saw a spirit crossing in front of me; or I heard a voice that told me something that's about to happen; or, a spirit stopped me before I set foot on the street, kept me on the sidewalk, just as a vehicle flew by. What would you say? Maybe you'd assume I'm making up the stories. But these events can happen; I have many examples, I can tell. The question is not what you experience, or what I went through; the question is how to test these encounters with the spirits. They are entities of another dimension, intangible and invisible; and humans can't capture images to prove their encounters. Human beings have few or zero evidence to prove their brushing with spirits. In my mind, perhaps humans can plan a proposal and find ways or methods to base their contacts with spirits. I have thought about this subject for a long time; and the author came up with a suggestion he tries to explain: it's the hypothesis of my book.

The Premises.

Humans are so used to the real dimension: here they are born; here they live and die–but they exclude the unreal dimension. Is there an unreal dimension? perhaps, but humans are not sure, or positive, and this truth is why they are eager to discover. The subject of the behavior of spirits and souls is difficult if not impossible for humans. Humans don't even know where to start. They need a guide or route; but also, a map, and an action plan: the premises, the themes and the method, which can logically lead them to the finish line. So, let's get started. But not so fast, my friend, not so fast. First let's list the premises, which we need to study and document, for which humans need to have credible explanations. For the author these premises, concerns or questions, are as follows.

Ten key questions:
Are there spirits?
If so, where?
Do we have a spirit in the human body?
So, how do spirits enter the body?
-And if that happens, what are we, humans?
What happens while a spirit is in the body?
When and how does a spirit leave?
Where do spirits go after the body dies?
Do they come back?
Is there contact with spirits and humans?
Can they go out and re-enter the human body?

These challenge the existence of spirits. And we'll study them in this book. Have these assumptions as we pass through the chapters and episodes of the book. How can we study the questions and produce answers to give credible conclusions? How can we answer them? We need a plan and a procedure or a method to do this study and repeat it as often as necessary. Any experiment we suggest or do must be repeatable and produce the same result. If not, the study is not valid as all deductive or inductive inferences.

Method - What does it require?

The nature of the topic requires specific procedures. However, we do not have real tools or procedures to see the invisible and grasp the intangible. We may not study the existence or behavior of spirits; unless we enter that unreal dimension and study the spirits right there. But how can we get into that dimension, we need a procedure? But a procedure–or method–that includes at least the following.

Six necessary actions:

> Define the dimension of spirits;
> Define life cycles:
> > Integration of spirits;
> > Separation of souls;
> Establish the nature of the human;
> Identify the spirit in the human;
> Describe the behavior of spirits, and;
> Describe the encounters of the spirits.

A nine-step sequence.

One–sequence. explains the separation of spirits from the human body. Two–we studied the inflection of spirits in human eggs. Three–we describe the birth process and the interactions of spirits. Four–we describe encounters with spirits while in human bodies. Five–we explain the life of dual beings. Six–we give evidence to support the author's thesis. Seven–we explain the structure of spirits and the management of the spirit in the human. Eight–we explain encounters with the spirits. And nine–finally, we give end notes that support or complement the author's thesis. The author explains the purpose of the existence and nature of the spirits simultaneously. The book also features a play, "Life Cycles": A Dialogue of spirits and humans. And while the order of explanation jumps from topic to topic, the discourse addresses the six elements and the nine fundamental steps. Well, we take at least five assumptions as the basis of the theory; without them, it is difficult to address the issue.

Five basic assumptions.

One–spirits exist and ghosts may not. We are hoping spirits exist to validate the need to develop the thesis. If the assumption is impossible, the study ends, and the spirits are vain and null, or we cannot study them.

Two–spirits exist in a dimension of their own. That we cannot see or touch the spirits leads us to assume that they are in a dimension where we cannot enter easily.

Three–the dimension contains everything that is unreal, or not real. If we assume that spirits are in a dimension of their own, let us say this dimension has all that is unreal, invisible and intangible. Anything that is not material is not real.

Four–spirits are energy, and energy can interact with matter. But if we assume that spirits are energy, we also add to themselves that they move in space and time. And as energy, they can interact with matter, and become matter in the universe.

Five–spirits have mind; minds have intentions and purposes. People believe that spirits come and can contact humans, but not the other way around. But beliefs are assumptions that might not be true. So, if spirits contact humans, they have their own minds, purposes and intentions. There is a possibility that humans can connect with spirits whenever they want. We assume that spirits live in an unreal dimension, and we must establish their existence and behavior at the beginning of this study. The two dimensions, real and unreal, occupy the same space of the universe and, therefore, they are in contact. These contacts are paranormal events that humans might perceive; or maybe they don't understand them. We cannot explain these events–paranormal–we have no tools or methods to capture them. [1]Because of these difficulties and the lack of gnosis of the subject, let us carry out a deductive-inductive study in this method. Let's

----

[1]   https://en.wikipedia.org/wiki/Paranormal

start with observable paranormal phenomena applying the universal law of cause and effect that says, (paraphrasing), *"The universal law of cause and effect holds that for each effect there are definite causes, and for definite causes, there is a definite effect"*. But the law of cause and effect involves causal events.[2] A sequence of events is because an event depends on one or more completed events.[3] With this law, we can build chains of events to walk back from a paranormal event to its origin. The law of cause and effect allows us to reconstruct the source of final results. Therefore, we can reconstruct the reality of life, returning step by step to its origin. We have evidence to reconstruct the road. The universe hides nothing; knowledge is available to those who seek it. The universe and its content behave in patterns that follow the laws of existence. The content includes what is material, and what is not; for problems, objects and creatures. The author responds to the ten premises of this book, which may serve as the basis for further research. There is no better method for teaching than letting students have their experience. We then inject and record the physical, mental and or psychological stimuli that exalt the five brain waves; such as the Alpha and Theta waves.[4] The first wave induces relaxation and calm in the mind; and the second elevates the mind to the state of deep relaxation and visualization. In this condition, the mind synchronizes reality with unreality; and handles both worlds well simultaneously. The order of life of living entities is to be born, to live, to reproduce, to produce and to die. Who cannot stop or reverse these stages? No one can; these stages are infallible and irreversible in the half-life cycle for all living creatures. Which of these is more important than the others? none; all are equally important and necessary. Each is part of the chain cause of events in the life cycle. And this is one of life's mysteries.

Why are we born and why do we die, what is the reason for living and what happens before we are born or after we die? The separation of the soul from the body at death is a mysterious event,

______

2   https://blog.iqmatrix.com/law-of-cause-effect
3   https://en.wikipedia.org/wiki/Causal_chain
4   http://www.brainandhealth.com/brain-waves

at least for humans. Humans long to know how they can stay in touch with a loved one who died. Loved ones remain longing to be in touch with those who leave forever. The author considers, perhaps you too, that we must first study what happens during death. And then we study where and when a spirit enters a human egg. Which human wouldn't like to know what happens when they die? Would you like to know? There must be an easy way to explain this event with physical means.

This book presents a live theatrical play in your mind–as a reader–to explain its theory. The author creates an audience for you to see the play, "Life Cycles". The cast includes spirits, except for a few humans added to connect with the physical world. A soul freed from its body comments on the actions of the spirits until it realizes that it must return to the body from where it came from. Another spirit-guide moderates the actions of spirits within the play; and other spirits discuss details of the side of the spirits and their journeys to the material dimension. Everything happens in the reader's mind and while reading this book.

The play is part of the study's method. Six characters play the role of spirits that migrate from their dimension. Other spirits dance to the music of the mind; the mystical music of the five waves that human brains transmit and receive; it is the sublime music of enchantment. Spirits act their mysterious way of life in the spirit dimension. Ah, everything is peaceful and quiet, reflecting a life full of love, which calls souls peace. The theme of the work focuses on human lifestyles and discrepancies between rich and poor. The script points to the social and economic inequalities that create migrations and flows from the poor to rich countries; masses traveling from threatened regions to safe lands. People walk long distances, escaping poverty and hunger. America is the largest, most powerful and richest nation on earth–a beacon of hope. It was on Wednesday, October 12, 1492, that Christopher Columbus discovered America, a vast new continent, opening a route and a door for immigrants to flow to America. No one should claim to be a true American, only the natives living here before people from the old continent invaded these lands.

You know something? Humans are good souls; but many selfish and greedy individuals changed the true purpose of life, a long time ago. Today, a handful of individuals–the rich and powerful–control the lives of most of the world. Is this a fair situation? No, it isn't. This situation does not reflect the purpose of life: that it is to care for and share with our fellowmen under the power of love. All humans may preserve their lives, their thoughts, decisions and actions that aim to achieve that purpose. It is a mandate of the existence and mission of the universe. To support this truth, the United States of America offers opportunities that migrants want and seek. In other parts of the world, particularly third-world nations, the living situation is not like in the United States. A person's life at risk is a fatal drama; fear of death is a reality strewn with drug and human trafficking cartels, such as the Sinaloa cartel. In the spirit world, this situation does not exist. There is true equality, and every spirit is for every spirit, and everything is for all spirits. There is true justice and equality for all in its dimension.

The work tells how spirits travel to earth and embed in human bodies. The body and soul then travel together in the physical world for a life until the body loses its presence. The book has eleven chapters organized in an order contrary to the life cycle. In chapter one (Premises and approach), the author opens the discourse on the presence of spirits in the world. You may have many questions on this subject; but the author only presents ten around the appearance of the spirits. Do you think there are spirits around us? True, they not only exist, but they are within our bodies. In this chapter, we study why we think they are with us all the time. In addition, we confirm their existence and behavior while they are on earth. But we need to make basic assumptions before we start our analysis. You don't think it's just a flicker and you're smart, do you? Maybe it isn't; it's a difficult subject. Spirits are the love that comes to help human consciences in their fight against evil. Evil is in the immoral egos of men. Even if the ego is part of the soul within them; so, the fight is against the human ego. However, the author shows the human situation in chapter two. But in chapter three, we expose the mystery of the life cycles.

Do you know what life cycles are? Yes or no? Well, don't worry; we can discover with the laws and logic of the universe. I am sure that the truth is splendid; and we will reward us. So, stay with me, and we can both discover the truth together. Are you curious? Well, in chapter four we witness the birth of new souls, and also their struggles to survive. Life is difficult after all; because nothing is free. We always pay for everything we get with our efforts. You know, very few give a hand to people in poverty. The poor live at the mercy of their God, if it is true. Do you believe in miracles? In chapter four we witness miracles, but we have to pay attention when they happen. Spirits are souls when they live in a human body as a normal human or what we are used to seeing every day. We see how they behave in chapter five. Is there a devil who tempts us? Well, if you're a religious person, you can say there is. I don't blame you; it's your belief. I don't think there's one; because spirits work to preserve life, for and with pure love. Spirits are the love that comes to help human consciences in their fight against evil. Evil is in the egos of evil men. Even if the ego is part of the soul within them; so, the fight is against the human ego–Chapter 6. Chapter Seven presents potential evidence and valid conclusions of spirit experiences. Humans have the potential to communicate with spirits in the spiritual dimension. It's good to open your mind to understand other people's beliefs–Chapter eight. Thus, we verify the validity and solidities of our own beliefs. I did it and discovered that religions are similar and evolved into similar paths. Beliefs are not important, but their truth we can prove with evidence–Chapter 9, Evidences, in the universe. There are five major religions in the world, and these religions support the author's theory. Perhaps the evolution of man's knowledge comes from the omniscience. This book shows how spirits become souls of human bodies. The author reveals the structure of the soul that manages a human; and describes encounters with the spirits in chapter ten, noting signs of their presence in the world. In this chapter, the author shows that humans are dual beings. But the most important thing is to recognize that we have a mind, a conscience, and an ego. And although we cannot see or touch these elements with high certainty, we are not material beings but spiritual beings. The author puts out this theory and tests it in this book. Humans are dual beings in the dimension of reality; our soul comes from the dimension of spirits. And that soul sets up and manages the material organism we know as a body. Souls, invisible and intangible, need the body, matter, to exist in a real, tangible and visible world. The situation is complex for spirits. Humans carry a small part of the global spirit of existence, their soul. And this soul thinks and directs the human body's actions. That's why the human situation is even more complex, confusing and mysterious. The great premise of the author's theory is the purpose of existence, which we can merge into a single question; why is there life in the universe? Yes, the universe is a large space full of energy and matter. Matter and energy would have no importance if they were just to fill the universe. But, in reality, energy and matter cannot create life. The laws of existence control the circumstances and conditions and specify the requirements for different life forms. Any form of life only appears when the scenario's conditions meet the requirements of life. This is really the purpose for creating life, with love for love. This is the situation of life.

The Point.

*When reality is confused
in the intense heavenly light,
and the attachment to material;
slowly defused,
the soul transcends the bright
world and returns to the ethereal,
the infinite existence,
to the embrace of deep love.
There, life does not end,
it remains blessed in its persistence.
There again in goodness drove
love to germinates and send
the only reality, which inscribes
in every action, in every endeavor.
The care or share that drives
life not death; and in this fatality,
the real point is the unreality.*

CHAPTER 2

• • • • • • • • • • ● • • • • • • • • • •

The Human Situation

A spirit energizes the existence and its two worlds, invisible and visible. And they pour out love, light, and life upon objects and creatures in the material dimension. The universe and the earth contain only invisible energy and tangible matter. And living creatures of two forms of a substance we cannot create or destroy. An eternal spirit exists in two forms in this reality. And the spirits of life roam the earth for a bit of a time of existence; but spirits and human entities never die. Human life is a pulse of transient time at a small point in space. Our spirits come and go and come back as often as they need, randomly. And every time they enter a different body it's a journey with new experiences; the same spirit with the same purpose, the spread of love, and establishment of oneness. The endless journeys to planet earth, and that we live forever in the spiritual dimension, are tangible proofs of the Life Cycles. There is no reincarnation, and I write, thinking of humans' immortality.

The questions that fly in our minds are the voices of the spirits? Maybe they want to connect with us on sleepless nights. And those ideas that jump into our minds when we face daily problems can be messages that spirits send us. And in quiet twilight hours the shadows we perceive could be spirits saying they are with us; and remind us we are not material. You know, it's strange, but knowledge, feelings, emotions, and thoughts are not physical. They are in, and come from, a world we can neither see nor touch. It's the spirit world. We are not physical beings, but we have material bodies. We are *"mentaurs":* a creature with a soul that lives in the dimension of the spirits and body of a physical beast dwelling on earth. Where do we come from, or better yet, how does a soul merge with the beast? We don't know. We only recognize that we live, but are we sure about that? Do we know where we're going when we die? We still don't recognize that, but maybe we'll do it in time. There are problems and things we do not understand; but given in causal events that allow us to trace events back to their origin. That's why we say *something happens for a reason,* and this may be true. Each event has a set of unique requirements to make it happen; but we don't have control over all the requirements. If the conditions do not meet the requirement set, the event does not happen, at least as it should. This applies to all events that occur in the physical world. It would be a dream to control all those conditions, wouldn't it? What is the meaning of all this? It means that the event occurs if the environment gives the conditions; otherwise, it doesn't happen. It's that simple! The *mentaurs* we perceive fit a typical case. Integrating a spirit and a body is a great strange and mysterious event. It's an event we may not understand. And we speak of spirits as evil entities inclined to hurt us; but is this true? Perhaps, but this notion may be a fabrication of the human mind; which, to be fair, can be a misconception. Man has lived with these concerns for centuries. It took millions of years for his mind to evolve. While humans lived indefinitely, the soul trained the mind and configured the human brain. We live, right, and yet we misunderstand life and death. We realize that we may die, sometimes without notice; however, we avoid the idea or concept of death. We fear death, but is it death itself or leaving everything on earth? Death is the end of our lives, but are we sure of that? Perhaps we do not know what death is; or maybe we don't know that the Life Cycles never end.[i] Death is a terrifying idea. Are you afraid of death? It's an experience we live, but we shut up and decide not to tell anyone. We leave this physical world, leave our family, friends and belongings. But perhaps what we love most is not life itself, but a delusive status of fame, wealth, and power. We love that status that our stubborn egos create in our weak minds. It seems we don't know or don't care what happens after we die. Think! Do we have a spiritual life after death? Maybe so, but not like humans think. We're confused. Aren't we going to continue our material life after death? No. Humans create symbols to represent problems, object themes, and live with them. Soon after, we associate with these symbols and give them values higher than they represent. We assume that symbols are the true elements, forgetting what they are–simple symbols. Each living object and creature has a unique truth and value. But we create concepts and situations we want to be true. Our attitudes toward life are those false truths; since the man's inception. And we, perhaps we can no longer change, cannot understand our role and purpose in life. I say, *"there are those who do not create false realities; because they have no illusions of possessing or pursuing fame, wealth or power"*. Humans become fond of materiality, ignoring that purpose; truths for what money and power make our lives enjoyable. All of that is material; nothing belongs to us except life. And we work to be rich, famous and powerful. There is a price for everything we get that is minimal or nothing, compared to living conformed, grateful and satisfied with what we have, looking without urgency to improve the situation. This must be the reason for our life in the real world. It is glorious to be born, but death is terrifying; those are the two moments, the beginning and the end of a life. Humans experience this strange contrast in the ways of their lives. We all cry at birth and our parents and relatives celebrate our arrival; then we become disenchanted, wishing to leave this material life. And we weep. By then, we are tired of suffering unnecessary conflicts and tribulations. Birth, life and death are three phases of the Life Cycles. And love is a mystery of existence. The material world is not for spirits, but what we can see and touch, do you see? For living beings there are Life Cycles, and nothing else; but we do not interpret it well; and for most humans, life is only their presence on earth. We can blame no one for fearing death, not understanding Life Cycles. One aspect is clear; the whole cycle of life is only for spirits. The bodies of living creatures, such as those of humans, only take part once in a life cycle–and only–in half of the cycle. Spirits return to a different body in each cycle. And we are not what we were before; this is sad, isn't it? Maybe it's not. But it is not true that a person who dies and returns to material life. The spirit can return to a new body, but it is a different person; it's a different human soul and mind. It also does not seem workable there will be a final judgment during which all humans who live or have lived will face a trial. Let us only think. If so, the spirits would have as many identities as the number of bodies they stayed in. The final judgment is a paradigm–a creation of religions. It's a trick to influence fear, to dominate the human minds.

We could overcome the fear of death and accept it as reality, reasoning our individual beliefs. We may discover who will help us prove or confirm that every life is new and is not the continuation of a previous life. But we're not aware of that. Maybe we tell no one for reasons of personal protection. We know that we cannot prevent our deaths; we are born; we live for a short time, and we die. This is the physical truth; the evidence we live in these continuous cycles; endless life cycles; but don't frighten. Your life results from causality, cause and effect, over which no human being has control. Spirits do not choose bodies where they become souls. A spirit randomly enters a human body and is the brother of other spirits housed in other bodies; are obvious, and without questions or arguments, or doubts about it. Everything is complex! Who could have established that routine if not a global intelligence; for what purpose? There is evidence that life is spiritual; that spirits enter human bodies and remain in our material dimension for a short time. What do you think, is it possible? Why not? We have that a spirit lives within each of us and that it will, or enter, Shangri La, heaven, Nirvana, etc., when our bodies return to inert matter. Our lack of understanding, and or the whims, ties or bonds of our egos attach us to this material world. And so we don't want to see that other side. For our egos, this life is the most wonderful, the only experience, living creatures can have. But living creatures may not take their form and material substance out of this real world. People think we're going to a purgatory–an undefined site–after death. But our material bodies return to earth to serve in the food cycle–and this is certain.

In purgatory, souls cleanse their sins before going to heaven–religions teach. But will it be true, why do spirits need purifying? We don't have a truthful answer to this question. And it can be a failed notion from the beginning. If you need cleansing before you come back, does this mean that only pure spirits live in that world? It makes sense to think that's the case. Well, when a spirit returns to a human body, it must be a clean, pure spirit. Therefore, it comes clean and leaves clean; this means that any deterioration or contamination on earth remains on earth. Spirits live in their own dimension in the universe. Why not; but if spirits sin in their world, then they use humans to purge their sins in the Life Cycles. What sins are those? Makes little sense, does it?

Spirits are pure before entering human bodies. And they leave clean or enter a purgatory to cleanse their sins before they leave. Only pure spirits inhabit the spirit world, and purgatory is on earth. Spirits don't sin. But the human ego does. And if the spirits sin in their dimension, they come to the material dimension as punishment, then the material dimension (the earth) is the reformatory, and the human body is a prison cell. This idea is not correct; it's not fair to the world or for the humans in it. This idea does not fit with the behavior of the universe we perceive. Do living things deserve such treatment? No, I don't think so; No, okay. This book theorizes the truth; study, explain, or try to clarify this problem. Are you with me? Well, then let's study this issue more. What sins do spirits commit in the spiritual dimension? We understand that humans commit sins while spirits remain in this material life, the earth. That's funny, isn't it? Our selfish attitudes are sources of sin; our egos live for material objects and/or subjects, and their general attitude is to blame the soul. How could souls be sinners? The omnipotence of the spiritual world is enough to cleanse the spirits. Why not? I don't see why not? Is this material life the purgatory that people talk about? Our egos need cleansing on earth. But this could also be a belief. Perhaps Dante's tales put concepts of fear, doubt, and belief into people in the 14th century. Reality is what we feel, and nothing exists forever here.

Non reality is what we do not perceive, but anything is possible despite how illogical it may seem. Nothing is tangible in that dimension; that's why our whole life is spiritual. Our thoughts, feelings, and emotions belong to that world. Physical actions take place only in our physical world. They divide everything. Love, for example, is a spiritual feeling, an emotion. We are sorry and express it; but only the resulting expression is physical–what we do or stop doing.[5] The human splits into what is material and spiritual. But we cannot create or destroyed them. Humans are matter and energy; thus, no one can destroy the humans. What do you lose? The appearance of the living being disappears. But is the earth where spirits come to purge their mistakes, or use a human body? If so, why? The spirits need no purging. Our ego sins while the soul is on earth. Why do we blame the soul? It is not just and we should not punish our souls for the sins of the ego. I must hold us accountable for its decisions and actions. Believing that spirits must pay for their sins implies that spirits are corrupt; and they send them to earth to learn from this material life and to suffer tribulations. Is the earth what people call hell? If so, what is the use of life for humans and what is their role on earth? It does not seem logical that the human body is only to harbor a soul in repentance. It makes little sense. It is not logical for souls to use a human body as tool to purify their evil deeds, on earth. Why are souls so corrupt that they need to purge their sins if they belong to a pure kingdom? This belief contradicts what we think of absolute love. But if that were true, it would imply that our bodies are not corrupt and are cleaning toys or tools that souls used to clean themselves. Let us think; if initially souls were pure, before their first journey to the material dimension, how they corrupted? where? We can't accept all that as true, can we? Maybe these are all religions ideas to manipulate humans. My theory is the fault is in the intrinsic structure of man's mind having an ego with his free will. The sins we commit are the product of capricious acts of the ego while using their freedom of choice. Perhaps this experiment is to fuse spirits with material bodies, in a long-term process; but it is a

---

[5]   Work by Dante: Inferno, Purgatory and Paradise.

failure within our short life. Here, only humans go through purgatory. Other living beings do not go through a purgatory stage. The intelligence of humans differentiates them from non-humans on this planet earth. We can perceive, conceive, think and reason reality, as no non-human being can, on earth. I sense a global equality applies uniformly in the universe, and could consider a law of equality, applying to all the problems, objects, and or living things. Therefore, what was given and applies to earth applies to other place in the universe. In this context, if there is life on earth, there may be life in other places in the universe; beings who may have greater or lesser intelligence than us. So, show us we have a soul, how and why do they come to earth? Spirits can enter living things for various reasons. They could come to learn what life is like living with limited skills; and to drive, manage, or guide the lives of living beings. But why should spirits learn if they have omniscience? If the first way is true, the soul cycle is a cruel process, using living beings to train a soul; there is no gain for living things. And if the second form is true, our theory is true. I suggest that souls come to occupy human bodies for a definite purpose; this is the improvement of all dual beings. The purpose is to perfect the functions of the mind, optimizing the integration of human spirits and bodies. Humans must improve the behavior of their egos until our selfishness is the least. This point is when we achieve a sustained balance, and or the harmony with the universe. At the moment, all this seems false; and we are our own enemies. Our selfish attitudes lead our ego to seek material things like wealth, power, and fame, using any means and way. If we cannot discipline our attitudes, how can handle our desires? Perhaps we can control the most negative ones, such as ambition. Could you dominate or suppress greed, hatred, greed, prejudice, egotism, and envy? Is this an experiment or a game? Humans, and all living things, are only tools. It may not be ones, the possibility is. But it doesn't seem because the law of cause-and-effect shows that an event has causes for support. Fortunately, the information on each path remains in the universe. We can discover what an event requires taking place; we study the nature of the results, themes, objects to get to their beginning. We can walk back the path of truth, from observable results to the origin of the event. Spirits enter human bodies, not for fun, they know the consequences. They come for a specific purpose. The evidence of this lies in the growth of our knowledge and understanding; and in the evolution of humanity since man appeared on earth. Are the existence and the universe deterministic? It seems so, except for events that happen at random. For example, the causal events law shows that the expected supports happen for an event to occur; otherwise, the event does not occur. Therefore, any purpose planned is not a random experiment. Souls enter human bodies with a purpose; it's not an experiment. The human ego blocks this goal; is that the failure of purpose? No, it's not, justice and absolute fairness follows its long-term plan, besides, the human ego may choose. We have evidence that the universe coerces no person to act against his will. The purpose implies an intention, an established goal to go from one point to another. The causal law is final. Events happen that way. All events occur according to the circumstances and conditions of time and space, and in no other way. Human capital improves daily as we age; and that human capital is every human's knowledge, skills and experiences. Let's think; humans left the caves not so long ago, but they've walked long enough to understand that we have to take care of each other. They have advanced their moral values, the values of their consciences. Freedom of choice sets traps for those eager for wealth, power and fame, and our egos fall easily into them. There is no tangible and visible matter in the dimension of spirits or souls. Spirits do not bring matter into the human body when they come or do not take matter from their bodies when they leave. [ii] Do you agree with that? No one but ego sins because of its attachment to things and material matters. The journey of spirits to living bodies has a purpose; integrating a spirit and a body–human in our case–into a perfect entity. That is oneness: *The state in which a spirit and a body become a being in both dimensions.* It can take a long time, perhaps many centuries, to reach that state. There is only one substance in the universe in two forms; energy and matter. No human creates or destroys this substance–we know that. Besides, almost everything we perceive of this substance is in its material state; but we cannot see or touch this substance in its energy form. Energy converts into matter, and vice versa. The quantities of these two forms is constant and finite in the universe. The caveat is that humans have a spirit (energy) and a body (matter); and the theory of the conversion of energy and matter to the speed of light squared also applies to our spirit and body. The laws of existence apply to the universe and all its contents in the same way. What's the difference? Well, we can't touch the energy, as we can't touch the spirit; but we can touch and feel the matter, just as we touch and feel the body. So, our body and soul, energy and matter, we cannot create or destroy. Therefore, spirits and body never die; they are eternal; the body change its material appearance. The difference is that when organic matter loses its spirits (dynamic energy) it becomes inorganic matter. The shape and presence of the body is the only thing that disappears, but it remains in the mind of those who lived with its presence. All human bodies live forever in the material form of the universe; like dust. Thus, the matter of human bodies will prepare for its next life cycle. And souls return to the dimension of spirits to await for their next mission in the universe. So, life is eternal because or no one can destroy its energy (the spirit) and matter (the body). Why we are afraid to die if we don't die? It is a frightening thought to know that our physical presence ends: the end of our appearance as a human form. Human beings and all living beings are eternal. Death is but the end of a life cycle; is the separation of the soul and the human body. Humans do not understand that they live forever; have not reached the mental framework, knowledge or conscience to accept that. Our minds generate decisions; decisions provoke actions; and actions produce work. We cannot see or touch the energy that thoughts and decisions create; but this energy generates actions, which we experience at the end of that process. Cycles are mysteries of life; why did they create and implement these cycles? If we understand them, we may understand the goals of the universe. Could it be that souls and bodies integrated into dual beings can live in two dimensions simultaneously? Two entities in the oneness of a harmonious state of soul (energy) and body (matter) of a dual being. Can humans ever attain this state of oneness? Human beings can come to that state, but they need to gain a greater understanding of the life cycles and their purpose. What could humans do to get such a state? Maybe humans have the answer in their decisions and actions to manage consciousness. They could be different and peaceful if they had different attitudes towards others. Spirits are beings of light, love, and truth. The soul that is a spirit housed in a human body is also light, love and truth. And so are minds and consciences. But the ego, though it is light, is neither love nor truth most of the time. Let's see our awareness. We are born and bring nothing into this material world. We take nothing with us when we get out of here. People remind us of the good deeds we do for them and human society. We are a small part of a global spirit. And this spirit enters and lives in our bodies, and also this spirit can return in another body at random. Our souls connect with the global spirit, because they are parts of that spirit. Thoughts come from a mental dimension we cannot see or touch. Our souls connect with other souls who live in other people, and in a certain way connect with each other through the minds' functions. We create words in that mental dimension, and we produce them with sound–physical codes–that other people can perceive or decipher. How could humans talk to another human, from mind to mind? The caveat is that they do not configure our brains to tune waves from the brains of other humans. I mean, our telepathy still doesn't work; but we have two notions in our minds. Our lives are mental. [ii] The other, good news, is that we can change our attitudes towards others. We are all souls, part of the global spirit; we are brothers and sisters even if our form and physical appearance are different. Our lives are a flicker in infinite time. Similarly, human presence is only an insignificant point in infinite space.

Our life, sometimes over a hundred years, is nothing compared to the millions of years that living beings–like humans–have been on earth; the universe is over thirteen thousand seven hundred million years old. But existence is not the universe; existence includes it. We perceive space, energy, matter and time; and existence is more than the universe. Everything we know is in the universe, but we don't know everything is in the universe, or existence; is this all we'll know? Humans have enough evidence to show we are spiritual; we are not material. For example, we mention in this book that the five elements of the soul are functions that generate energy in human bodies to act and work. And we don't know all in omniscience. The two dimensions of spirits and matter both occupy the same space, and souls and bodies mix in the same space. How can they exist in the same space without interfering with each other, because nothing is outside of the infinite space and everything that is not matter has no weight and does not occupy space? We know that terms concern perception. But if we can't see or touch something, we say it doesn't exist, because we have no evidence to prove it. On the one hand, if something is invisible is not that it does not exist, maybe there is no matter to reflect the light; therefore, we don't see it. Notice, although we do not see or touch electromagnetic, electrical, etc. forces, they produce movement and work. In this sense, thought generates bodily action. And the mind, part of our soul, produces thoughts, feelings and emotions that we perceive neither. The above results from the soul, nothing physical, and we live with them peacefully. So how do we say something exists if we don't see it or touch it? Maybe we can prove that with physical actions. But let's not say they don't exist just because we don't recognize them. The key to suppressing physical awareness admits that we have many other possibilities. Have you felt love? We don't see it or touch it, but we feel the emotion. Love is a force of the soul that generates action (work). That's right; all we perceive is just the evident reality, the material things we perceive. But we lose that reality behind perception, the latent reality. The evident reality depends on physical presence and human perception. An entity in these two worlds depends on its state of being. When a material body is well and alive, it has a soul; and the soul manifests itself through that body. But when the soul leaves the body, the body decays, and returns to the land from which it came; while the soul returns to the great dimension of spirits.

The separation of the soul and body takes a few hours; it's not instantaneous. When the body ceases its functions, the soul expects the separation process to end; the soul returns to its state of mind, instantly. Spirits never become a matter because the soul only coexists with the body during its life. And when our material form disappears, our souls do not travel distances to reach their permanent place. Souls cross a thin film–between perception and non-perception–or a barrier separating the two dimensions, leaving behind the material substance. And when they abandon the material world, they become invisible and intangible, but they remain in the same place, in a different dimension. The dimension of spirits is a strange phenomenon, but there are examples in this world, or material dimension. A live sports game like football or basketball on TV is a good example of what happens to spirits. The baseball or football games we watch on television are also good examples. Well, let's see; this is not magic or mystery; given by the physical laws of the universe. The light is invisible and we only see it if reflected on particles of solid matter. Light cannot reflect on something without matter; it can't reflect on emptiness. Spirits do not carry matter with them, but spirits carry thoughts, emotions or feelings. And all these exist behind the light. Material conditions and laws of the universe establish visibility. There are many dimensions and lights in the universe, and we perceive some of these here on earth. We do not see or touch the electrical and electromagnetic force of motors; and similarly, the radio waves or frequencies that exist in space are invisible and intangible. But the spirits see us from the other side. We don't see them, they're over there. Thus, we cannot alter, influence, change the game, its outcome or conditions beyond our minds' control. Life is material, rigid and has only a short presence; we know that, but we lose the causal and random conditions and situations that come to form our thoughts and actions. Feelings or emotions, feelings, and thoughts are mental attributes that are parts of the soul. Existence has only one space, and the dimensions, spiritual and material, share this space. We have a soul who can freely roam in the dimension of spirits. And the soul in our bodies communicates with souls in other human bodies and with free spirits in that dimension. Free spirits see us and hear us through the dimensional barrier; but we rarely perceive them. The humans create mysteries of what they don't understand. These unknowns test our intellect. We create beliefs and faith to answer and explain these mysteries. Minds do not create knowledge; knowledge belongs to the universe. We only discover knowledge that already exists; therefore, if you think you are intelligent, stop, think you only borrow knowledge from your environment and the universe. What is the situation of our environment? Each of us is the center as in the graph, immediately attached. The concentric circles in the image are spheres. What do they represent? They are concentric influences on the living creature that occupies the center; everything else is around you. And only you are with your knowledge, and your skills and experience–your human capital. With this human capital, you buy your lifestyle–your way of being.

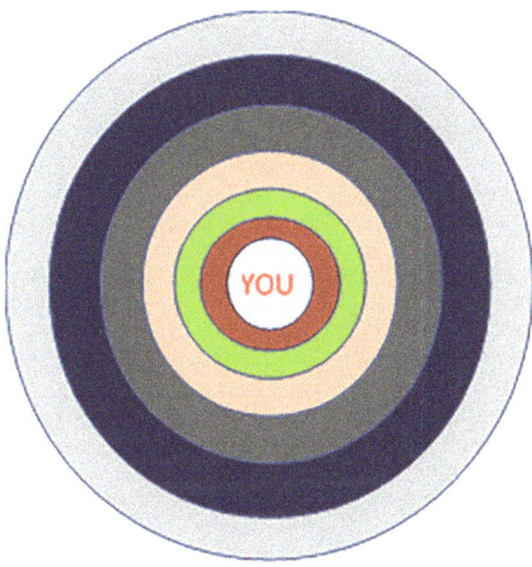

Figure 1: The Seven Environments

These spheres are virtually bubbles of influence in our bodies and minds. We live, think and act as the conditions and situations of these spheres of influence permit.

The singular intensity of influence varies directly proportional to distance. The combined influence is the product of influences of all spheres, divided by the resistivity that a being puts to each influence. Realizing that you are an individual at the center of your environment helps you to know that your life is just you and your environment; therefore, it is not up to others. Really, your life depends on your self-reliance, in all cases. Can you get out of your environment, no, you can't leave. However, if you change position, those spheres move and your perspective changes according to your new position. The laws of the universe fix and control these bubbles;

the conditions and situations of bubbles influence your thoughts and actions. However, when the bodily functions cease, we leave them all. You live in the white sphere, as you appear in the world of reality. You are the center of the universe; and everything else is around your body and mind. Every living creature is the center of the universe, just like you. There, you are alone, only with your human capital, even if there are other humans near you. The first sphere of influence on you is the red one; this bubble is your family and the conditions and situations of your home–your intimate sphere. The second sphere is the light green bubble; this sphere is your immediate environment; This bubble includes your places, your friends, schoolmates, coworkers–this is your personal sphere. The third sphere is orange; it is the community or city where you live–this sphere is your communal environment. This is the beginning of the neighborhood. Remember that the further away a bubble, the weaker its influence and less contact you have in that bubble. This third sphere has all other people. But these people can have different backgrounds, languages and or cultures. You may not know these people, but they're in your neighborhood every day. You notice their culture and behavior; habits and attitudes; everything that influences your mental state. The fourth sphere of influence is the dark green bubble; this sphere represents your country or your state with all its laws, regulations and people–this sphere is your home state environment. Maybe these people are there for a short time. The blue sphere of influence is this world planet earth. The outer sphere, the gray blue, is the entire universe. You are part of the system; and what affects the universe affects you too. We, body and soul, are nothing; all these spheres surround each of us. The space of the universe is infinite, and possibly it is only one. The situation is always each of us against the rest. These spheres of influence made the way we are on earth; we have no other reality, tangible and visible. What is this process? Our senses collect data and information from our environment; the brain makes images; and the mind creates thoughts, and of what is outside these spheres of the existence. Just think of this; the observable diameter of the universe is 93 billion light-years. Let's see it now on the opposite side; the mind rearranges these images and analyzes or synthesizes them and creates new concepts. [6] Amazing, simple, isn't it? Well, it's amazing, but not simple; it's a complicated process. This process is critical and necessary for the mind to think and guide the human. Thoughts, decisions and or actions do not happen if the mind does not get adequate data and or information. That is our life, and our minds drive it; but our minds are parts of souls, and the spirits of humans, the whole process is spiritual. This is the point. Do you understand? We are souls, not material beings; without the soul, no human exists. In addition; without souls we are lost, we are dead. Let's go over this concept, okay? Close your eyes and visualize in your mind the world you perceive now. Think about the things you've done, what you're doing and want to do. Travel to places you've been or places you want to be. Build or do things and the world or whatever you want it to be. What is not seems to be a perfect state; and always present. Anything is possible! For agnostics, the unreal has no meaning; it is a product of imagination. For them, non-reality is nothing more than an illusion, and or an absurdity. But non-reality and reality has these two extremes. And existence is like a great puzzle composed of infinite pieces, where each piece is a gnosis. This place is the omniscience of existence, where all pieces, or gnosis, exist in a disordered state; in the mind of those who intend to mix them. The puzzle is in omniscience, and spirits in existence; the image of reality we perceive has no logical meaning in our minds. Parts do not have images on their undersides; and if all the pieces were upside down the board would be blank; is when the mind loses its consciousness or reason. Normally, the pieces fit and show a part of the big picture of reality. And in the mix, you can't see real images in adjacent gnosis. But all knowledge is in omniscience; yes, all knowledge of the universe is there, including evidence of its origin. The board presents the universe out there, including evidence of its origin; the pieces of an overview are in chaos. All the images that can appear are part of the great image of unreality. Nothing is here, and

---

[6]   Bing.com – (October 2018) – ¿What the size of the universe? The diameter of the observable universe is estimated of about 28 thousand million light years. A light year is a unit of length equal to, more or less, 10 billion de kilometers or about 6 billion miles.

the mind can form the resulting images as part of your imagination. Therefore, this mixture of pieces is imagination directing the hands that stir the gnosis; and the images on the board after each mix are in the illusions of the mind. The total image of existence is available; but souls in humans don't see it. One goal of life is for humans to gather the full picture, while studying and learning reality. Styling the puzzle pieces, or gnosis, continues; and as more pieces fit, the observer sees the big picture. All this happens in the mind of those building realities, while the exercise continues. Then the glorious day of reality finally comes. And the mind sees, for the first time, the image of total reality; and stops to reflect on the greatest achievement of existence. It's an incredible result; they have to put the gnosis together. But that total image is not available to humans. A pair of hands, space and time, shuffle these pieces finally, reality arises from chaos in a unique truth. It comes out of that state of non-reality; a state of confusion, of imagination and illusions of the mind. Reality comes second, but before the first living creature appeared reality was already available. Our minds work in a pseudo cybernetic process and our retro perceptions feed reality in the brain, not all knowledge of omniscience. The product of these processes are mental images that the brain stores in its neurons. Everything that happens in our minds is the product of soul functions. These functions are not material; they are not of the human body. We learn, and our knowledge accumulates as we study, allowing our minds to conceive of new evidences of hidden realities; including the dimension of spirits. We need to have basic knowledge, at least; or our mind does not work. Awareness of reality and knowledge drive life; and the more knowledge we have, the easier life is. Notice that all your knowledge is part of the knowledge of omniscience. It existed before you gained the knowledge you now have. Existence manages the knowledge hidden in it or deployed in the visible universe. The life of every living creature evolves as its knowledge grows; but humans do not create the reality or the conditions of their existences. We live in reality; we do the best we can and according to the conditions and situations of the environment. We see reality and its imbued logic, and we settle for it; that is the logic of the physical world. We ask, is there life because of knowledge? No. There are other factors, but knowledge is the force that drives it. Is there prior knowledge? It's embedded in gnosis we know and don't know. We have prior knowledge to handle new situations we face every moment. We know what we know, but there is more we have not learned, or no one has yet taught us. For example, we must have known of the equation of a parable and the balance of forces, to throw a stone and hit the head of a running deer. We must have learned the concept of balance to walk upright. There must be knowledge of the principles or laws of the universe that regulate our perceptions and conceptions such as depth and speed. We know our strengths and weaknesses; which matches our capabilities with the environment to succeed. Success extends life; living beings fight for their survival. Now open your eyes and see the world in its physical reality. This world is the material dimension in which we live. Everything here is binary, true or false. But we have a spirit within us; and our mind connects us to spirits in their dimension. It's a different world than the one you keep in your mind. It's all a mental or cyber process. In that dimension the spirits have no attachment to, nor restrictions of matter. [7] Spirits have total freedom in their dimension. But the souls of humans must deal with the physical conditions and the content of their environments. Fortunately, they have specified the combinations and or permutations of living objects and creatures in the universe, past, present, or future. Your knowledge is of omniscience. For spirits, living in a body is not a simple project; it's complex. Souls find conditions and situations they do not have in the dimension of spirits. The consciousness of the soul must deal with its rebellious ego. Humans, the soul and the body couple, may not reach the universal order of oneness. It doesn't matter how often a spirit passes through a human body. The purpose of life cycles is to help humans gain oneness; this is the condition of the soul and body, so they live in harmony with the universe, in both dimensions. The laws of existence specify that all living beings have a

---

[7]   Merriam-Webster, Definition of cybernetics: the science of communication theory and control that deals especially with the comparative study of automatic control systems (such as the nervous system and brain mechanical electric communication systems).

soul, or spirit, guiding the improvement of living beings, until they reach oneness. This is not a short process; it's a long, long process that can take centuries. We may not harvest the fruits of our efforts; but think our good deeds help humans get closer to oneness. Looking into the evolution of humans, we see their reality. Now open your eyes; see the world in its physical reality. It's a different world from the one you have in your mind. Here everything is the knowledge that drives the growth of life. It all started about two and a half million years ago; when the wise-man appeared in Africa. Human knowledge was nothing more than its biological instincts, barely understanding and guessing or knowing the basic foundations of existence, life and logic. He only cared for surviving food and shelter. This was the beginning of practical logical reasoning, when man reasoned and wondered about the purpose of existence and its life on earth, at least—the question about existential issues and the discovery of the latent reality in the universe. Thus, reasoning began about two hundred thousand and five hundred years ago, when the man-wise evolves in Northeast Africa.[8] Another reliable source places the appearance of the human-wise being near the time we mentioned; the wise man appeared almost eight hundred thousand years ago. [9] And his knowledge has taken time to develop; and nearly four hundred years the human achieved the industrial revolution. Today we are in the age of instant communication; we talk to others anywhere in the world, using Facebook, Twitter, Google, Instagram, WhatsApp, etc. We said humans can neither create nor destroy knowledge; we can only learn and apply what we learn, and we have a long way to go. Each object and or creature brings its own information. This information tells us about each. It tells us about their nature; why they are present; what role they play in the universe; and what their purpose is in life. Nothing is in vain in the universe; everything has a role and a purpose, or it doesn't exist. The forces, matter and energy of the universe, are always in balance. And each part provides the portion of its energy, matter, and work to keep the

---

[8]   https://herenow.com/common/sapiensbriefhistory/1.html

[9]   https://en.wikipedia.org/wiki/Timeline_of_human_evolution

universe in balance. Each party shows only its evident reality. For example, a grain of sugar salt carries more information than its white aspects and obvious flavors. They have physical and chemical knowledge we don't perceive on their surface. This information is invisible and intangible. This knowledge has existed since the beginning of the universe. And this knowledge has been available to curious and intelligent people to discover all the time. An important point is that only the mind has the power to think, reason, and meditate. The mind is the driving force that commands the body to act. We do not understand the mind; it is invisible and intangible; it's a function of the soul. If we understood, we would realize that humans are spiritual, non-material beings. Spirits transformed into souls live in our bodies. The soul never dies, and the body only changes its form from flesh to dust, and from the earth other living creatures are born. The material body is a vehicle that the soul uses in its journey through material life, and returns it upon leaving material life. The soul is once again a free spirit that can return to the material world in another body. The cycle of spirits is complete and closed in infinity. But matter, in any form, also has its purpose; it is a purpose not given by matter but by the existence throughout the universe.

Have you thought why or what makes a tree grow upwards, or why it avoids obstacles to follow its growth? How does a tree know when to bear fruit or lay its roots to withstand the forces of the winds? The mystery of life is that every matter carries within its own intelligence. Where does this intelligence come from? Souls can only be in living beings in this world and only for a short time—more than a hundred years sometimes. Our souls return to the dimension of spirits when the human form ends. It is the life cycle of human; souls use living bodies as vehicles to live in this world. And they develop an awareness of the material dimension while guiding human bodies. Let us understand this well, we are souls in material bodies for a while, and we return to our dimension when our mission ends. Birth, life and death are three stages of a material life for humans. We have mentioned that a spirit enters our body, becoming a soul to manage the behavior of our human. Souls leave the world or material dimension when bodies fulfill their function.[iv] These are the life cycles, entering and leaving the material dimension, that deals with the fusion of spirits (not materials) and human bodies (materials). The entity that comes out of this process is a dual being, a soul and a body integrated when a sperm fertilizes an ovum. The dual being is the human we are used to seeing in life. Souls, or spirits, cannot live in the tangible world alone; only when they are within material living beings. Humans need an optimization process for as long as it can take. They must conform to the order of harmony of the universe. And souls can go through as many life cycles as necessary; but neither the soul nor the body needs perfection, but the human ego. How can we understand this if we attach to materialism? We must abandon selfish attitudes; and live for truth and love. Perhaps in this way we can live in harmony in the two dimensions of spirits and of matter. Oneness, the order of harmony of the universe, must be the goal of humans.

Can we talk to the spirits? Maybe yes, but why not; If we look at our surroundings, we may find people empowered or able to contact and communicate with the spirits. And because we cannot verify the truthfulness of such contacts, we assume that neither spirits nor spiritual life are true; and we deny such a possibility. [v] Those who have had experiences like these are silent, avoiding taunts. We must study their encounters; how, when and where they happened. The author theorizes how spirits enter human bodies; how they behave in a life cycle; how they separate from their bodies. The book tells the story of how spirits immigrate into human bodies. The book talks about how spirits communicate with each other while they are on earth; how they communicate with others from the spirit dimension. Is it a fact? Maybe not, but it's solid evidence; and because we have spiritual components in us, the original questions are true. I ask where we come from and where do we go when we die? We need answers. [vi]

I was on the overpass with my thoughts focused on my book. I was walking away when my day was dark and my mind became brighter. Now I'm across from an old theater, the *"Million Dollars"* Theater on Broadway Avenue in downtown Los Angeles. The theater has 1,200 seats down and 800 seats on the balcony. When or how I came, I did not know; I just know I was there on the bridge. Now

I stand in front of the billboards and the canopies that shows with neon-colored lights the opening of the play, Life Cycles. My name is in the marquees; it is the production of my book. I found a seat–no one asked for my ticket.

The human life that abruptly ends in the universe opens the curtain that separates the two dimensions. The soul passes this curtain and waits on the other side until it becomes a free spirit again. And from the ethereal dimension, the spirits continue to contact the souls of humans still living on earth. This happens after passing the screen separating material and spiritual dimensions. Spirits are eternal energy. There are issues I still don't understand; why I'm in the theater and also outside of it simultaneously. Am I or am I not a real person? That's my question. Perhaps I find the answer in the existence's life cycles.

CHAPTER 3

Life Cycles: Inflection of spirits

Abstract

Every day someone is born and someone dies; and we ignore the purpose. The laws of existence regulate the universe, and we ignore the origin. Existence has absolute knowledge that can neither be created nor destroyed and we do not know the reason. Energy, knowledge and laws, together are the spirit of existence. Infinite molecules of this spirit visit the universe. A molecule of that spirit becomes a soul as it enters a human body, and under the control of the soul begins a life. And so, they also enter the bodies of other living beings, and they leave when they all die. How do they get in and out? We are born, we live; we fight, fall and rise and die; but we don't know the reason, what is the true me, will it be the soul that I carry inside? We live in cycles, back and forth, of spirits but ignore the goal of existence. And when the body dies the soul becomes a free spirit again and return to the material world in another human body. This process is continuously repeated. But why and how long? This book hypothesizes the mystery of the life cycles.

The separation of souls.

LIFE CYCLES
"The work of the spirits:
Truth and Love"
December 21, 2018

Figure 2: The Theatrical Play

It's Friday, December 21, 2018. The orchestra plays instrumental background music harmonizing the brain waves Alpha, Delta, and theta; it's a creepy music to the rhythm of military marching. People are still entering the theater, and the lights are still on in the audience area. The stage is dark; but the steps rings behind the curtains. The rays of light project three lines on the purple curtains, a title, subtitle, and time appear from top to bottom sequential order, repeatedly. My mind turns, and I feel dizzy, as if I am falling into a big, absorbing funnel, like a vortex, faster and faster. Curtains open and a light mist creeps on the stage floor. Dark shadows cast on the ground are visible to the public. They are shadows of spirits in the spirit dimension. The stage is a part of the spirit dimension, and people can perceive from the audience. Music plays an arrangement with the waves in the brain.

The fog rises into a curtain, giving the stage a murky view, but the silhouettes are still visible through the fog. Spirits wear garments that shine in the twilight light of the stage; are ghostly human silhouettes of young people, men, women and children. The spirits dance the "Ballet of Existence" dressed in transparent white, light pink and heavenly blue garments. Spirits rise, appear, and disappear in the fog that looks like clouds. Spirits dance on stage in two concentric circles. Equal number of spirits dance in the two circles. The inner circle rotates clockwise, and the outer circle rotates in the opposite direction. In the background there is a sanctuary in the center, above the ground, and the spirits in the outer circle stop to worship an image. The music continues to play in the background; it's a creepy, unsettling music. The dancers in the outer circle kneel when they pass in front of the sanctuary in the background. But when they pass by the edge of the stage, they dance facing the audience. The circles rotate twice and when a drum strikes, a spirit exits the outer circle, after passing in front of the audience. In the east (front-right of the stage), a spirit of the outer circle comes out of the dance and a spirit of the inner circle moves to replace the spirit that comes out. A new spirit rises and crosses the outer circle, enters the inner circle on the east side (front-left of the stage) and follows the dance. This dance is birth and death in the life cycles. The circles get smaller, but the dance continues. The dance ends when all the spirits on the stage rise and fall once. Ballet is as if spirits appear on the east side (stage-left) dance through life in the middle (stage-center) and disappear on the west side (stage-right). It is a strange ballet dance, not specific, but the life a forward order given by the turn of the universe. Everything runs on paths created by the actions of the forces of existence. The dance and music end; but some spirits enter the stage, wandering aimlessly. A spirit, standing on a small platform, summons others to gather in the center of the stage; the spirits walk smoothly and randomly and sit on the floor around the spirit that has called them. The convening spirit begins a secret talk (the public cannot hear what they say). Lightning under the ceiling illuminates the stage; and a thunderous sound breaks the peace of the theater. The summoning spirit signals to others, rises in the center of the stage, looks in the audience's direction and says, in a deep bass voice that sounds as if it came from a resonance chamber, above the ceiling of the theater.

Summoning Spirit.—*We have transported you back to the past to Friday, December 15, 1989. The global spirit gave you in this audience the ability to see and listen to the spirits on stage and in the auditorium, but only while you are in this theater; spirits can hear their thoughts. We are celebrating the glory of being part of this perfect system, at the dawn of a new life on earth. This is existence and the universe. The intelligence that created the plans and specifications has an infallible knowledge from before building this system. Every being, or thing, inert or alive, carries the knowledge of how and when they came, and which not only describes* *but also sets the rules of their behavior. This creative intelligence is what religions call God; the energy or soul of existence that fills the space of the universe, a person, and of every object and or living being in all parts of the universe. This is the power of existence, energy and matter that we cannot create or destroy, and from which omnipotence derives. Supreme intelligence is the soul of all living beings and inert objects in the universe. Spirits on stage are integral parts of the global spirit; because nothing exists if it is not a part of this spirit. The mandate of spirits is to spread truth and love and preserve life in the universe. Within this mission, they join a material human body and work to turn them into one being. The goal is to achieve "oneness". Many spirits have gone through complete journeys, but others have never been here on earth, within a human body. From the dimension of spirits, we know what life is like on earth.*

The laws of existence are critical and important; no matter how small they appear to be. But for material life, existence has three very important laws. The laws of cause and effect and that of random events that regulate all events that can happen in the universe, in synergy with the law of combinations and permutations. And the conditions and circumstances that support an event follow all these laws. Combining themes and things produces a unique result, which might allow an event to occur. Existence is to fuse spirits with the bodies of living beings who must follow these laws; this makes life in the universe intriguingly unique and exciting. The fusion of spirits has a goal to lead them to "oneness." The spirits called to serve on earth follow a perfect plan. [vii]

The spirits walk around themselves and around others, drifting and randomly, as in a deep meditation, but they stop to speak.

Spirit two.—*The space that humans see, or do not see, is the main scenario of existence. That space is the continuum in which large and small sub-scenarios form; that's the life of the universe. The main stage has two parts, an unreal part and a real part. The sub-scenarios are singular and unique; and their contents define the way they work within their limits, especially in relation to living beings. The universe is the real part of the existence; apparently it also divides the two parts, unreal and real. There's no division. The universe is a continuum; goes from the unreal end to the real one without breaking. Humans can see and touch the splendid reality part of the universe, but not the unreal part;*

not with physical means. Reality is the essence of all observable scenarios; and reality limits everything living in there. Humans observe, think, and do whatever they want within these limits; you can't observe or do that freely outside these limits. Humans may think the unreal part is the dimension to imagine, dream, or have illusions of beings, objects and themes. Humans, or living beings, are prisoners of the reality of their scenario. But that is not the case in the dimension of spirits; and humans are just not ready yet to live on the other side. Now, can you see what the difficulty is? The universe is the work of art that only super systems engineers and or architects can create.

Why do the spirits say this? But all of that is true anywhere in the universe. Scenarios are prisons for living beings from birth; we are prisoners for life, in prisons of reality: in our bodies and our environments. Thank you, scientists! Thank you for getting us out of ignorance. We now know that fourteen billion years is a long time; but that's the life of the universe. Man's time is short compared to the lifetime of the universe. And there must be a reason for a man's life to be short. Perhaps omniscience knows what a man's ego can do—the damage that ego can do to itself and to the entire universe. And they prevent it early. Humans are already suffering the consequences.

—Humans have discovered laws and rules of existence and how they apply them in the universe. The laws are in force and active to make the life of the universe a reality. Laws establish the methods and requirements for creating the universe and the content that humans perceive. These laws and rules review and manage the actions and reactions of the universe's content.

Were these laws ready before the universe? Either they established these laws earlier or while the universe was forming. The right sequence is the first of this great question; What are these laws?

—The laws of this set are the law of permutations and combinations; the law of proportionality; the law of balance and or equilibrio; and others. Scenarios and all conditions and situations guide, or limit, how actions, activities, and events occur within scenarios.

Spirits dance on stage in an orderly but chaotic mix pattern, crossing each other as they exchange the things they carry in their hands. Their actions suggest a purpose of helping and sharing.

Spirit three.—*Humans may well ignore the total set of components; elements, and or parts of the universe, or the world. But those who engineered and or designed the universe specified the laws that regulate it; and created reality.*[10]

Four television screens hang on stage and show images of the universe, stars and galaxies. Why? Do spirits control these electronic devices? Are they trying to say something? Yes! And scientists realize that universal space is full of energy and matter, and nothing else.

Spirit four.—*Humans know their bodies are matter and have a soul in them. Do humans recognize why they are part of spirits and part material?*

Who cares? Humans only live once and have no clear communication with their spirits after their bodies die. Therefore, you do not see the relevance of this topic and say.

—I call, and I call, but they do not listen or maybe they ignore me. But spirits have a mission they can't leave. Its purpose is to integrate living beings into dual beings capable of living in both dimensions; one spirit and the other of matter. Therefore, we unite energy (a spirit) and matter (a body) into living beings and humans.

All spirits.—*Honor the order of oneness; honor the order of oneness; I honor the order of oneness. Live in the state of oneness.*

Spirits strike the stage floor with their right feet every time they say the word honor; they clap their hands once for each word, ignoring a pulse of the rhythm, and half the time the syllables of harmony sing. The echo of the depth of the universe repeats the song of the spirits, filling the total space. Spirits dance, emulating the meaning of this story. Spirit one returns.

Spirit one.—*The architects expected that humans would need time to learn and attain "oneness". Oh, yes! They included this topic when they specified perception; conception; knowledge; intelligence; and the free will for advanced living beings. Humans are out of step with the spiritual order of the universe. Freedom of choice given to the ego of humans breaks the order of "oneness." Thus, when spirits infiltrate fertilized human eggs,*

---

[10] Read more in chapters 9, 10, 11—Evidence, Structure of spirits, Interaction with spirits, ahead in this book.

spirits come to manage the egos, consciences, wisdom and will of humans to redirect the purpose of their lives.

Yes, that's right. Existence, spiritual immigration, the functions of spirits and life are mysteries that humans need to learn and understand, the sooner the better.

Spirit Two.–*But we have a standard system implanting an optimized process called life cycles. They wrote, spirits in living beings, including humans, are parts of the global spirit. They transform into souls to manage beings is humans. Their mandate is to guide humans to follow the order of harmony of the universe–oneness. It's all part of a main plan we can't alter.*

What? This spirit says we are not who we think we are, but that we are robots driven by souls.

Spirit three.–*That is right; humans know that souls come and go, and even feel the spirits, have visions of them and of the spirits speaking. But they still cannot identify that their mission on earth is to achieve "oneness" –the order of the harmony of existence.*

That's fantastic!

Spirit four.–*Knowledge of existence, omniscience, is the soul of the universe; it is omnipresent but not omnipotent, and it is a resource. Knowledge is essential to create, build and maintain the universe and all lives there. The universe is accurate! The structure and synergy, the laws regulating its performance, suggest that a large-explosion did not create the laws and rules of this world.*[11]

Who did that, a big explosion or a higher intelligence?

The laws of existence, for this universe and everything in it, are the work of a higher intelligence; these laws existed before the universe. Many people think that's the way it is. Most religions, except Buddhism, believe that a creator did everything, including humans. The wonder of the universe, order and purpose, implies a supreme intelligence deliberately created the universe–it is the great explosion that scientists have seen.

---

[11] The Universe: The universe we observe, or not yet, is composed of only energy and matter.

—The world is accurate and thrifty; it has no excesses or waste. Humans misunderstand this or ignore it. When you get there, put this notion in your soul. Keep this in mind. Humans may think the above is false a speculation or assumption. That's normal; they only understand what's within their current knowledge. And ask for proof or evidence to support those premises. Evidence, or proof, appears in the organization, and in the harmony; at least in the part they perceive, in integration and synergy: "something is to affirm everything else, and everything else is there to maintain that something—so that everything exists or all disappears".

Christians believe, suspect, or accept that God, a higher intelligence, created the universe, the earth, and man. Is that true?[viii] The belief that God created every living creature is not correct; and could be a direct consequence of the law of conditions and situations that support life. Existence sets the conditions for living beings to exist anywhere in the universe. Omniscience is the soul of life, organic and inorganic; and the laws of existence apply to itself and its content. Therefore, existence is omnipotent, omnipresent, and has all knowledge; and nothing less than that. The universe is the physical representation of existence. The energy, the substance (the *"anima mundi")* that generates life and movement in existence is the creative force; and, they can transform it into the subject of its own creation. Oneness is the concept and unity itself; as being outside, in and around each object or being a living person. The spirit within humans is part of the supreme spirit, as in all living beings and inert matter; and the energy and matter are two states of a single substance. Spirits in human and living beings are cases of unreality in the dimension of matter. Dual beings, humans, do not yet coordinate with the order of the universe; humans don't respect their environment. Knowledge of existence extends throughout the space of the universe, maintaining universal synergy, balance, and in place. This is the order of oneness of the universe. For humans, the order of oneness comes when spirits and bodies integrate into a seamless being. This is the state of oneness for humans.

This is amazing! God did not create us, and we are a product of environmental conditions. They say energy is the spirit of life, and I understand it. But I cannot accept that creators and creation are one thing simultaneously. I am part of creation and from what they say, I am part of the creator, too. We have a soul; but I thought my soul was my spirit, independent and not a part of a global spirit. I agree and accept that humans don't worry or don't care about their environment. And I also agree that we are not in sync with the order of the universe. I accept this. But being an integrated being, soul and body, in a state of oneness I do not understand it. What is the meaning or message of the spirits?

Spirits.—*Greet the order of oneness. This is the state of "oneness."*

They sing the word oneness three times. The depth of the echo of the universe repeats the war cry of the spirits, filling the space; hit the stage floor with their right foot every time they say honor. And when the spirits are about to wrap up and leave, a spirit enters the group, raising his arm to talk.

Spirit five.—*On another subject. Humans borrow knowledge from the global spirit's omniscience. They know reality, but they are only present at one point. Their presence is material, visible and tangible in the physical dimension; and for a short time. Humans do not know how to enter the spirit dimension when they reach "oneness."*

Not bad. We can't be in two places simultaneously. All right, I agree they only live a few years. Let us understand, humans borrow knowledge of omniscience. I thought humans learned from their environment. Existence specified why, how, when, and where of all things and beings before making the universe and its content. But what is it that regarding not knowing how to achieve "oneness"? Another spirit, who was listening to the conversation, finally comes and says.

Spirit six.—*It's true. Let us explain the life cycles to the public. May the mystery of darkness and the splendor of light capture your minds, so you may observe the matter at stake. Humans can read this script from wherever they are, because they now have the power to feel more than they normally feel in mortality. Let them see us and hear us as spirits. Let us bring humans into our revolution, marching toward our purpose and victory—oneness.*

Other spirits enter the stage through the right and left, like flocks of birds; and continue dancing, synchronizing their steps and movements with the tempo of the spirits' voices. Thunder and lights flash on stage musically. The voices of the spirits bounce off the deep echo above the heads of the people in the audience. Every detail of the stage and the performance follows perfection. And as the spirits dance, they stop at the center of the stage to speak to the audience. What? Now humans can recognize what spirits say. But before I saw them and I heard them. And what's the problem, the cycle of life they mentioned? It's getting more complex rather than simpler. A spirit standing a few steps from the group now speaks to the audience and me.

Spirit two.—*Pay the utmost attention to acts and episodes; and you'll better understand the mysteries of the spiritual dimension. Let your mind fly. Seek the truth; because it will increase your awareness and understanding. The mystery of the night, of the invisible and tangible, opens the power of your sensible soul. We are about to carry your minds into our minds through time to the year 1990; that is when our journey begins in the endless space of existence.*

My body is shaking, it scares my mind. What's going on? Are they taking me to the spirit dimension? Are they kidnapping me? I can't resist; because I can't even run. I see a spirit running towards the group, interrupting and pushing away the spirits of the group. What's going on?

Spirit three.—*Humans can interact with spirits in both dimensions of spirits and matter this time. What you will experience on this journey is part of the spiritual dimension. They can't get in flesh there, even if they had special attributes. But these experiences remain in their minds, because their minds share roles of spirits. Their beings, spirits and bodies need to evolve more; our mission is to help them become better individuals. They have free will, and we do not interfere with their thoughts, decisions, and actions.* [ix]

Okay, but we have to check.

Spirit five.—*Existence has a purpose; it is to create perfect humans, integrate souls with living bodies and guide these beings to "oneness." Oneness is the state in which humans are in harmony with the order of the universe. As they are, humans have the mental power to conquer oneness; but they must learn how to use their mental abilities more efficiently. It's a project that can take many more centuries.*

All spirits.–*Please, let your minds repeat with us: I honor the order of oneness; I honor the order of oneness, oneness, oneness. Welcome to the state of oneness.*

I realize that we are not perfect beings, having many faults; but I never thought we should live and work to win the universal order of harmony. This is a need That I do not understand; at least not yet. Spirits strike on the ground with their right feet in rhythm every time they say 'honor'. The echo of the depth of the universe bears the war cry of the spirits, filling the total space. Singing stops; and the spirits groan as if they expect dwelling, raising their arms to the ceiling as if begging for mercy. They march on the way out of the stage, scared. They lean forward as they kneel with their arms outstretched when they are in front of the back of the stage. The lights on the stage of the theater flicker, and the spirits come out of the stage scared. The curtains close and the stage darkens. The global intelligence has all knowledge in the universe. This absolute knowledge maintains all gnosis, and omniscience is the library of existence. The spirits said that the universe, and the creator and creation are the same, at the same time.

Follow the laws of the universe every instance of life; and understand these laws are the will of the soul that fills the universe. Nature's events show that something happens for something that will happen ahead in time. The event's dependency warrants that an event occurs only when the preceding events occur. Because of this causal sequence, the universe is thin and has no surpluses or excesses. Everything has a useful purpose in the universe, or it doesn't exist. This is the order of harmony of the universe. Every object or living being must contribute just what the universe requires. An object or living entity maintains the excess of its production in energy, or matter forms.

How souls separate from their bodies.[12]

The noises of a muscle car and a heavy motorcycle, running on the street, break the peace of the night. The echo of the night

---

[12] Final note vii

enhances the noises of those squealing wheels, such as when they spin in corners. The roaring engines of that car and motorcycle as they change gears are so clear that we could feel the speed of the air and the vehicles. The echo repeats the sounds of gunfire in the theater, and the cries of a woman on the street. A big blow from an obvious accident paints in the public minds images of a car bouncing off the street. People and spirits in the theater hear another collision; but this time, it sounds like it was against something solid and hard. The deep silence that follows that sound increases the suspense. The accident sounds like it's happening right in front of the theater. It all happened so fast that the public didn't have time to react or run to the streets. But they would have seen nothing because the accident took place miles away from the theater. The accident happened under the Arroyo Seco Parkway overpass. I'm here and I watch the whole event. A deep silence and dread filled the theater. They're strange phenomena. In the dimension of spirits, time can compact by mixing yesterday events with the events of this moment—as in dreams.

Forced separations.[13]

The audience side in the theater is still dark, and the curtains open slowly. The public can see the accident on stage, as if a large window opened to the street, far away. Dimmed lights turn up in intensity; and the public sees a car and a motorcycle demolished, which does not even resemble a car or a motorcycle, the results from the accident. On the road a twisted human body lies bathed in blood, and another body next to the road still shaking. A third body, that of a young woman, lies on the road in a strange figure with her limbs dislocated a short distance ahead of the car. A piece of white cloth flying like a flag on the windshield of the car, as if waving the leaving souls goodbye. The scene suggests that the woman flew through the windshield.

Five spirits forced out of their bodies.[x]

---

[13] Final note v

The sports car impacted a small, stranded car off the road, just before reaching the overpass. Ahead, about sixty feet from the small carriage on the sidewalk, was the body of an older woman in her sixties. The body of a child, about five years old, was on the pavement near the old lady by the curb. The child's body was still shaking with spasms of its coming death. The front of the sports car show signs it stroke that old lady and the child. The sports car ran them over while standing by the side railing along the shore, about twenty feet from the overpass entrance. The old lady covered the child's eyes with her hand, preventing the child from looking at the ugly scene. Dismembered corpses lie on the street and sidewalk, but the old woman and child avoid looking at the accident as they move away from the site. The silence in the audience is profound; while, on stage, the rear wheel of the motorcycle continues to spin, and the smoke and flames rise from the two vehicles.

A man in his thirties and a boy, about eighteen years old, observe the consequences of human attitudes, standing on the side of the road: That fatal race. Smoke coming from the burning car fills the space under the bridge. A few minutes later, the car explodes, while the motorcycle continues to burn. The smell of raw gasoline fills the space. On the opposite side, a nearly five-year-old boy and an elderly woman slowly walk away from the crash site.

The boy.–*Grandma, that car hit us hard. It threw us forward against the pavement. I'm scared, and my body hurts; when are we getting home? I want my mom.*

The boy cries.

The old lady.–*Yes, dear, we're going home, don't cry, we're going home, now. It'll only take a little while before we get there, when all your pains go away.*

The old lady picks up the little boy, embraces him lovingly, kisses him, and says.

–Soon we will be at home my child, both of us. So, don't cry my baby; we'll be home in a little while.

The old lady also cries as she hugs and kisses the child and disappears into the dense smoke. I was still on the overpass watching the accident. A man and a teenager are on the road, watching the accident, at a distance behind the destroyed vehicles; he says.

The man.–*Son of a bitch; this was an accident, fast and brutal. Did you see how the car flew against the overpass wall?*

The boy.–*No, I didn't see it. But the motorcycle and the man bounced off the car, flew across the street and fell on the pavement. There is nothing left of the motorcycle, it's destroyed. The car's engine ended up in the front seat, crushing the man driving. And the stalled car in half.*

The sirens of police cars, ambulances and or fire trucks cry in the distance, getting louder, as they arrive at the site; or converge at the point of the accident. It's as if they feel the pain those souls feel when they separate from their bodies. Paramedics arrived at the site; and parked their vehicles off the road.

The Man.–*What the fuck! Life is just a moment, isn't it? Now you're here, and the next second you're not. I ask, where do we go when we die. I'm glad I was not in the driver's seat of that car; did you see how it looked?*

The boy.–*No man, life is stupid. People don't care about life and destroy it for nothing. Did you get that guy on the motorcycle chasing the car because the man in the car was dating his teenage sister?*

The man.–*Hey, where did you get that, who told you?*

The boy.–*Yes, that's right. How do I know? I don't know... I only know now.*

A young teenage girl, about 18 years old, walks towards the man and the boy.

The girl.–*What happened? A car, a motorcycle, and five dead people.*

The boy stops, looking at the girl, and surprised says,

The boy.–*What an accident. What happened to you, your dress?*
Points to the overturned car.

–*Does that piece in the car look like the fabric of your dress?*

The girl.–*Yes, so it looks; and look at the two dead men; they dress as you two, the same color of pants and shirts. That one has one shoe, but it looks like yours. Wow, it must have been scary. Hey, you're also missing a shoe and on the same foot as the dead man.*

The Policemen, the paramedics and the coroners walk, taking measurements and photos, and or writing notes in their notebooks. They even walk alongside the man, the boy and the girl, but they don't pay attention to them, or worse, they ignore them.

The boy.—*Hey sir, we saw the accident; we are witnesses; aren't you going to question us? The police went through them several times as if they weren't there.*

The officers don't see them or hear them. Man looks, thinking and not believing what he sees; and then he says.

The man.—*Hey, you get it, guys? We are the spirits of the dead in this accident;* [looking at the boy] *so you remembered that the man was dating the girl. I lost my right shoe,* [looks at the girl, he says] *and look; you have the torn dress. We're dead, guys, that's it. We're dead, can you see it? It's time for us to leave this world.*

The man walked away, and the girl walks with her head down following him; and then he turns to the boy and says.

The girl.—*Yes, that's right. That's why first responders don't notice us; we're spirits, did you get it?*

The boy.—*What do you say? Hey, are we dead? Listen, wait; Where are you going? We're not dead.*

The girl.—*Can't you understand? I noticed when the car exploded, and a metal part that flew into the air passed through me while I was standing here; and didn't even move me. We're dead, aren't we? Maybe we are free from the dead. Where are we going; you have asked. How in hell would we know if we'd never died before, right? Come on, we'll find a way out of here; Come on, what are you waiting for?*

The boy becomes frustrated and says.

The boy.—*Wait, what a… I can't believe it; Oh, my God. Wait, I get it. I was driving the motorcycle, and you were in the car. Oh yes, I understand. You are my sister; You were running away with this son of a bitch. Damn it, wait, can someone explain what the hell is going on? Where are we going, what will happen now?*

The boy turns, looking at the man.

—*What is this? I'm not mad at you anymore.*

The old lady, holding the child's hand, returns through the smoke, and asks the man something.

The old lady.–*Can you show me and my grandson the way out of here? We want to go home; I couldn't find my way out there on the other side.*

The old lady points toward the street ahead of the accident.

The child.–*I want to go home; I want to be with my mom.*

The child cries.

The man.–*Don't worry, madam, just follow us, we're going in the same direction. Come with us. We're waiting for the right time to get out.*

A spirit that observed the accident from the street; it floats or sits in space on the back of the stage, watching the five spirits in a state of confusion says in a sweet and soft voice.

Guide.–*I am your guide; I come to meet you and guide you back. Hey, they're not dead or alive, you fool; you are in a transitional trance (a confused mental state). you can't leave your bodies until your bodies reach their "rigor mortis." That is their point of no return: the time to leave the material dimension.*

The spirit leaps down to the pavement of the road, and walks elegantly, and continues.

–*Your souls must separate from your bodies; and convert into spirits after collecting the energy of those bodies. Souls must go through this process, which takes about thirty-six hours. Death is neither simple nor easy. When a soul goes through this process of separation it becomes spirit again, and then the spirit can go away.*[xi]

What is this? The spirit-guide says that the soul is not spirit, that the soul must gather all the energy from the body to be spirit again. The soul waits thirty-six hours to become a spirit. Amazing! The girl turns to the spiritual guide and asks.

The girl.–*Who are you? When can we leave earth, can you say?*

Guide.–*Your minds continue to manage your bodies through their cycles of lives. You are souls outside your bodies and you must remain–hang out–for thirty-six hours until your souls (minds) lose their connections to the body. At the moment souls still respond to the sensations of their bodies; this is normal. At the end of this process, the bodies reach the posthumous stage, and at that moment the souls are no longer in the material dimension. Spirits can see the environment and listen to humans; after leaving the material dimension. Once here,* *spirits are free and out of the life cycle and outside of material life. This is the end of a life cycle. Spirits return to the global spirit; human bodies disintegrate and become land again. They completed their life cycle. Do you understand?*

The first responders left. Ambulances and paramedics take the bodies to a morgue. The five spirits follow their bodies to the place they take them. So, the boy goes to the guide and says.

The boy.–*You're full of shit; How do you know all that? I don't understand that circle of life, miss, ghost, or whoever you are.*

The boy, in his confused and does not associate the status of the recovered spirit.[14] The boy's soul still shows the manners of humans with his rude way of speaking.

Sixth step of the life cycles.

Guide.–Did you mean, whatever? A life cycle is simple, look at it, you'll understand; the diagram on the windows is my mind.

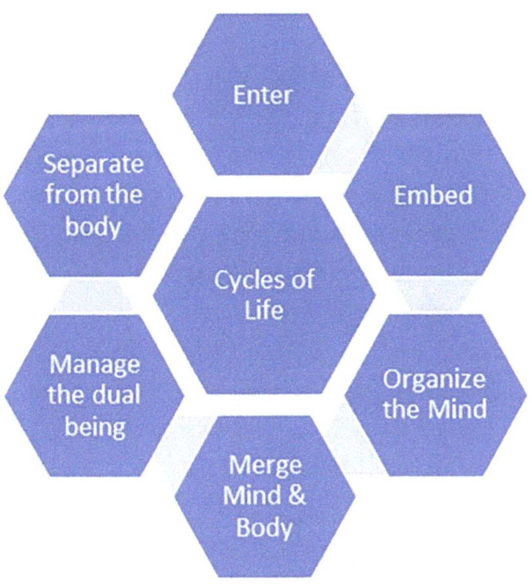

Figure 3: The Life Cycle

---

14 See endnote xi (on later pages of this book)

Two of the screens hanging above the stage floor allow the boy and the audience to look into the spirit dimension. They show a diagram of the model of the *"Life cycle"*. This cycle repeats for each spirit housed in a human body.

Guide.–*This info-graphic shows these six steps: (1) A spirit lodges in a human brain; (2) the spirit integrates with matter; (3) structures the mind; (4) synchronizes the mind and functions of the body; (5) administers human thoughts and actions; and (6) separates and returns to the spiritual dimension, at the end of the life of the body. After this accident, the five souls are in the sixth step: separation and return; and this takes at least thirty-six hours. The mind of each soul shuts down all mental procedures and memories stored in the brain is a–normal physical-mental process.*

The girl.–*When do we know we're dead for sure?*
–Are we dead now?

Guide.–*The brain has a few minutes only before it goes out, and the person reaches its brain death; however, the person is not dead yet. The mind releases organs and memory cells, a function that keep the body going. A soul must cut off the attachment to the material of the body before leaving.*

The four screens on stage show the minds of the spirits. They show places, ambulances pass through and a hospital where they autopsy the bodies. As the audience listens to the conversation of the spirits somewhere over the clouds, the dense fog on the stage floor.

The boy.–*Come on, what kind of shit is this. What is this functional dislocation? I mean separation or whatever.*

Guide.–*Listen, souls leave their bodies after the bodies reach rigor mortis; that is when the attachments of the spirits end. Souls become spirits and may return to the dimension of spirits. As you can see, death isn't just a boom-boom-bang and you're gone. No, it's not like that.*

The man seems a little impatient.

Man.–*Ok, that's fine, but what does it take to separate the spirit from the body, so we can leave?*

Guide.–*Mental functions hold souls with their bodies. They can cling to a close spirit at the time of their separation. You can see auras and or flashes of light, such as electric shocks, when that happens. So, you're* *in a process of functional separation and your soul waits for the final moment to go back. Some steps, which must occur before the separation.*

The old lady.—*What a mess, you know, living is difficult for us humans, why do spirits make it more complicated? But they made death ridiculously complex. I've had enough of this life and the cycle of death mentioned. I just want to know when we can leave this creepy world.*

The boy.—*Yes, when are we going to get out of here?* The five spirits still dress in their clothes, but an aura appears around them. Think about the subject of separation and see two problems. Humans know that they have a soul and a mind, invisible and intangible, that are not material. They have a conscience and an ego and observe them in their human; they have feelings, sorrows, remorse for their faults, they feel love, etc. Only the fact of recognizing good and evil they do is evidence they are not instinctive; they are not like the other living creatures that live to attend to their biological functions and perhaps some sensations, such as danger. Humans believe the soul goes somewhere when they die. They're not exactly sure, maybe they'll know ahead. The soul and mind join their bodies in their material life. But this union when the soul separates from the body. And it is acceptable for humans to think separation from the soul and body is necessary when it dies. How does it happen? It's a legitimate question. They also need an explanation of two other issues, the fusion of a spirit with a human and the separation at the end of life. The fusion and spiritual separation is real, just as is the existence of the human as a dual being.

Stages of basic separation.

Guide.—*It is what it is, madam; but I understand your frustration. But, in this causal process and each step depends on previous steps. Once the process begins, it cannot stop unless the spirit has enough energy to reactivate the body. Look, on the screen* [xii] *in Figure 4, you have five direct steps:*

1- *The brain shuts down;*
2- *The body becomes stiff and releases energy;*

3- *The body gets flaccid and releases more energy;*
4- *Rigor mortis comes, the body releases all of its energy;*
5- *The spirit collects all the energy and goes away.*

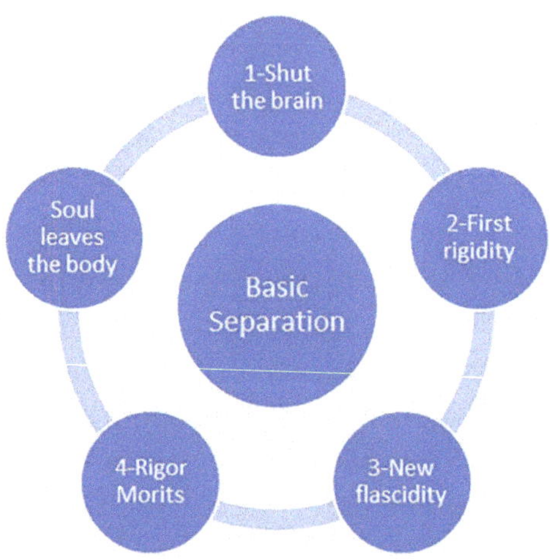

Figure 4: Soul Separation Process.

The above is the sequence of spiritual separation that souls performed when the bodies die. This is a natural process that humans go through at their crucial hours. The soul remains close to its body until it regains all its energy before leaving.

The old lady.—*Oh my God, this process is worse than having sex with an old fart who is losing abilities.*

Guide.—*Know that your minds continue to work as the separation of spirits continues. The mind is active until its body releases all energy. And it stays in place by managing the life process of cells, molecules, neurons, etc. The soul must shut down all components, ego, consciousness and mind, before leaving. Some bacteria remain in the body and produce in other living things in the dead body. Bacteria, which once helped humans live, now help the body with their conversion to dust. This is because life generates life, and death promotes death.*

The girl.—*Ah! I like it complicated; like a night of sex with a wild and violent tiger.*

The boy.—*Holy shit, that's a complicated thing; too much for a simple death. I thought people die, bingo, goes to heaven.*

The girl.—*Well, tell me what about my feelings, with my love, when I cross the border of the spiritual dimension?*

Guide.—*Yes, there is love in the spiritual dimension, pure love—but not sexual.*

The girl.—*I don't know if I would like it there: the sun would not come out in my mornings.*

Guide.—*It is the same love infused in the universe; which is energy, which we cannot create or destroy? The separation of the spirit of your body begins with the closure of the ego and consciousness. Human consciousness always knows what is right and what is wrong, but the ego does what it wants. The remorse of the ego and the repentance of sinful feelings come to light when consciousness forces the ego to accept its sins. These moments are not uncommon, but ego acceptance is. In the spirit dimension, all spirits are together because they are part of the global spirit; and their attributes hold them together at will. So, you will have the love for your boyfriend, but it is true love, total love; the same love that all spirits have for other spirits. Pure love is sentimental, it's not emotional or mental, it's not material. This is because you are part of the global spirit, which is absolute love. The absolute love of spirits has no imperfections; it is pure, eternal and without sex. You can love like this on earth, besides sexuality.*

The girl.—*But how am I going to find my boyfriend? He's the love of my life, and I don't want to lose him.*

Guide.—*Don't worry about it, you are a spirit; remember that the omnipresence of the global spirit is also yours and the spirit of your associate—you are parts. The omniscience of the global spirit is also yours and your associate. Therefore, they will find, therefore, easily. However, love for the human differs from the love of the spirit dimension. Spiritual love is pure, universal and eternal.*

The girl.—*How boring; that's boring.*

Guide.—*Life on earth could be different only if humans distinguish what is spiritual and material; then love would be pure and strong in their own character. Ego desires do not represent true love; desires on cultural beliefs, habits, and attitudes. These desires are paradigms of love that we must break to unlock the power of universal love. The thought love is sexual is a paradigm that is not true. Sex is a function of living beings; in humans, desires for sex arise from this biological motivator.*

Ego impulses or needs are often mistaken for love. Humans cannot live without sex; the psychological sex of lust. Living creatures receive the gender function so they can reproduce. But it is not love; pure love is how the mother feels for her children.

The stage darkens and five beams of light strike each of the five spirits, as seen in the glare. Stage lights return and spirits now wear a bright, white transparent dress. In front of the other four spirits, says the man.

The man.—*Guys stop that nonsense discussion; this observer has said it. It's what it is, end of story. Do you agree? We now know that we are spirits and that we are walking back to the spirit dimension. Therefore, let us promise we will be together and in communication there; not scolding like we did here. Let us commit ourselves to volunteering and to return to earth, together, soon. Let us promise we will act better on the side of divine justice during a new life on earth, seeking oneness. Experience always confirms the truth and passing knowledge.*

The boy.—*Wait, please, wait; let me ask you something. If this stage is the end of the life cycle, tell us where and how and when it begins?*

Humans think they're going to heaven, to purgatory, or to hell. And they see themselves in the human form, or image, they had on earth. But this is not true. Spirits have no specific shape, no volume or weight. In their plasma state, they take any figure or shape.

Guide.—*Well, the infinite space is full of finite energy and matter; which is the being of the creator: The soul and body of the creator live in the existence's dimension? For humans, it all starts with each new life cycle that begins and ends in the universe or earth… life cycles for all living beings; however, they continue forever. It's the same life cycle, but living creatures are as the stage allows.*

The boy.—*Hear people, we came to earth, and this accident made our stay short; perhaps, we must return immediately, and finish a full life cycle. We will stay together on the next trip. Hey, let's all sing the commitment: I honor the order and victory of oneness.*

Peace and calm come at last, and everyone agrees and walked together towards the darkness of the horizon [the bottom of the stage]. The voice of the observer came down to an inaudible level; and the man, girl and boy pass the portal of the dimension of the spirits. The old lady and the child at a slower pace follow those other three spirits. Thirty-eight hours passed and they're free. Meanwhile, a group of spirits enter the stage and perform the ballet *"Farewell."* Spirits dance in a circle, embrace each other several times; run to the back of the stage and disappear into the dark. It's a dance of pain, anguish, but full of love. It is a situation caused by the heartbreaking feeling of the detachment of the soul of his body. Perhaps this feeling is because the soul is–in synergy–accustomed to being with its body and remembers there was never any attachment to matter. [15] The soul is a limited spirit–a molecule of the global spirit.

The divine background music that accompanies also rests when the sound of that voice ends. The stage is dark. Five silhouettes cross the stage in bright shadows from left to right (near the curtains), stopping twice to look back, longing to stay; or reluctantly saying, see you soon. Soft and strange celestial music (of the mind) now sounds in the background; without following a melody or progression of definitive chords, such as earthly music, but it makes significant sense. Forced separation of the soul is not the intention of the universe, but the result of the actions of human "egos" -of brotherly jealousy and violence. But in the vastness of the possibilities of existence, the universe accommodates abrupt events. The purpose of existence is that its performance should never alter; although opportunities, forever, in disturbances.

In the center of the stage, standing humbly, a spirit with a sweet voice that resembles that of a human girl recites or sings a short poem.

The pigeons fly.

Five pigeons leave their earthly nest,
hastily flew to their initial abode
to prepare for another flight, no rest,
In sweet longing, that rode

---

[15] Attachment is a psychological and philosophical concept according to these two articles: (1) https://es.wikipedia.org/wiki/Apego and (2) https://definicion.de/apego/

behind endeavors of firm steps
on tireless trip, without deadline,
they travel the universe wide,
pursuing a purpose divine:
the purpose of Love.
For all of us in this globe,
they come and go to mitigate pains
of humans seeking to cure their souls,
looking for glory, peace in unity
with the universe. It is in your hands,
the order of harmony, to reach the goals,
to embrace the oneness of infinity
across the universe on all lands:
The Life cycles - in this infinite cove -
for all souls to live for Love.

Consequences of the separations of souls.

The existence does not isolate; for any system, especially a closed system, the behavior or performance of an element affects the behavior or performance of other elements, and that of the entire system. This is a law of existence that the universe obeys. Meanwhile, humans find another victim of the violence; this is another victim, an innocent person next to the overpass of that street, Arroyo Seco Parkway.

The curtains open; it's a cold foggy morning in this episode of the accident. A young man, Ivan, walks along the sidewalk of the overpass. He's on his way to work. Ivan hears someone moaning and stops, scared. On the embankment of the overpass bridge, trapped in the bushes, there is a person. Ivan climbs down the mound on the side that overlooks the accident area, careful not to slide down the side to the road below. The man surprised quietly says.

Ivan.–*Oh my God, that's a girl; she's alive, and badly hurt.*

Ivan calls 911 on his cell phone and reports the find. Paramedics and a fire truck arrive at the overpass, only about seven minutes later.

An intercom radio was on, saying, *"The victim is alive, unconscious; the victim may die; she has lost a lot of blood; the blood pressure is low."*

A small crowd had gathered on the bridge, by then, watching what was going on. The police arrive at the site and do their usual work. The crew of the fire truck secures the body on a stretcher and pull her up the overpass street. They quickly load the young woman in an ambulance and go to the nearest hospital. The police interrogate the young man who found the victim and then release him. Everyone leaves the place except me–no one saw me or they all ignored me; I'll stay a little longer. But after that, I found myself in the hospital where the ambulance carried the wounded body. The wounded girl was in a coma. The detectives found a piece of metal that may have hit her head. There were bloodstains on the sidewalk; she must have tried to get up; walked a few steps and fell at the end of the railing of the bridge to the place where Ivan found. It's funny, I'm in the emergency room, but no one notices my presence. I'm there as if was not there. Her clothes were on a hanger, and her shoes on the floor, carefully placed. I saw myself on the window glass, I was wearing the same clothes and shoes as her. Then I understood myself that I was her soul encircling her body. My body was alive, but in a deep coma. I am the soul of her body and free to move anywhere at will. I perceive what humans say and do; I have no pain or emotion. All this for me was interesting. So, I followed the five souls or spirits; and I will continue to comment on what happens in the adventure of those spirits, as long as it remains attached to the body.

The lights go out and the curtains close. The music continues in the background. It is music to meditate and improve the concentration of the mind. The curtains open; the stage is dark. An ultraviolet speck of light shines on the middle wall of the back, almost invisible, gradually growing in intensity to an almost blinding spark of radiant white light; the rest is dark. The volume of the music increases because of the intensity of that spark of light; and the music in crescendo elevated, culminating with a stroke of a Chinese gong. The bright lights disappear, and the music cuts off; silence reigns for a few seconds. The stage goes dark at that moment, but then it lights up, dimmed to twilight. The music begins once again, varying its volume from soft to strong and to stronger; as musicians say from *piano to mezzo-forte a forte*. The mood is mild; awake minds capture glimpses of the reality of these breathtaking moments. The stage is crystal clear when there is light and dark everywhere. There is an impressive silence of peace and joy filling the space; as of an absolute spirit that extends into infinite space. The scenario is creepy or scary; and the silhouettes appear and disappear in the shadows of strange lights on the stage. Black lights, ultraviolet lights or infrared lights; or maybe an overlay of these lights illuminate and darken the stage, making it seem surreal. The stage is like earth; it has plants and flowers as a tropical garden. The dimension of spirits shares total universal space; and includes planet earth, plants and animals. A slight aroma of incense fills the theater space. A strange white fabric covers the surfaces of the stage; and shines intermittently. Music reproduces the harmony of the universe in the background; and a chorus of soft voices of angels, bounce off the echo of this infinite space, coming from right and left. It is a music that humans normally do not hear, a music never repeated, is always a new and satisfying music that numbs the spirits. Flashes of lightning on stage show a sense of universal intent, occasionally. Light is the spectrum of the rainbow (ultraviolet, bluish, white and reddish dim), as in a twilight area where there are no shadows; and yet the clear space, magnificently clear. The shadows float from side to side in that twilight, on the ground, like they're behind veils. There's a grayish mist moving on the ground. Sources of fire cast flames that join in the middle of the center of the stage from the back center of the stage. In the center of the stage, a small flame rises and stays floating nearly six feet above the ground, then lowers twelve inches. The little flame lights brightly, and a column of smoke rises on the stage. A woman-shaped spirit appears behind the smoke when it clears, and in a sweet, soft voice with a little echo, standing in front of the audience, she whispers.

Moderator.—*I have seen the sequence of this accident; and I have seen how five humans died and lost their souls, ending their life cycles. I have gone through many life cycles and in several creatures, including snakes, frogs and spiders on earth. I am assigned to moderate and*

*coordinate the thoughts and actions of the spirits on this journey, so I will
be the moderator from now on.*

The moderator's voice changes from back to front and side to
side as if it were floating around theater space. The echo sends a
feeling as if it came from everywhere.

*—I understand your apprehensions of what you have witnessed. I
am here to explain existence in spiritual and material dimensions, terms
and meanings; I'll help you understand. The space of this theater is part
of our vast existence; matter exists in our intangible dimension, and
human bodies cannot enter.*

*—What we are about to present is normal in our spirit dimension;
although it may seem creepy or ghostly, creepy or scary. You may suffer
unwanted apprehensions, and you may feel fear. Those with mild to
severe heart conditions may watch this presentation live at their own
risk or leave the theater right now. The soul within you can suddenly
return to our dimension, and we don't want that yet. You may feel strange
events, strange sounds, and light flickering during this presentation. I
warn you; such experiences are not normal on earth. Perhaps the fusion
of these two dimensions will cause these strange events. Humans and free
spirits intermingle in the same space. But spirits exist in their dimension
and humans in their physical world. Anyway, let's get started.*

Other spirits detach from the walls and surfaces of the stage
floor in the silhouettes of humans, but they are not human. More
silhouettes come out from under the fog on the ground, in plants,
animals. They are visible as the fog rises from the ground, wandering
in transparent garments in all directions. Spirits ignore what the
bodies of other spirits look like. There is no malice in their minds;
everything is natural to them in the spirit dimension. The silhouettes
dance the waltz "rise of the spirits." The dance is perfect, following a
rhythmic music. The spirits gather to speak and stop to narrate the
situation. The stage gives a spooky, strange feeling of a spirit that
expands to fill the universe. The moderator (with her hand) calls a
spirit in the group to come to the front-center of the stage. A spirit
shows acceptance to volunteer.

Moderator.—*OK, Trues, come to the front, and explain the nature
of the separation of souls.*

Trues.—*Several independent pieces or small spiritual molecules, composed with the same substance of the global spirit, fill the stage. These spirit molecules have the attributes of the global spirit, just as a drop of ocean water have the qualities of the water in the ocean.*

Moderator.—*Five spirits returned to the spirit dimension. They will be on their own, hoping to start a new task in another life cycle. Spirits interact with humans without crossing their dimensional boundaries; just as looking through a glass wall where you can perceive, but you can't touch the individuals on the other side. Everything is possible along the line of the spectrum of reality; what seems ideological to humans, it's logical for spirits. Thoughts and actions are expressions of energy for both spirits and humans. Spirits may do what they want; they even have reflections of earthly events. Earthly events remain in the mind of a spirit such as waves or frequencies (brain waves).*

The four screens, like windows, hanging in space show the spirits' mind, or their mental images captured in space and time.

Moderator.—*Humans live in a physical dimension with four components. These components are (a) soul or energy, (b) matter, (c) space, and (d) time. Spirits are energy, omnipresent, omnipotent and omniscient, without limitations of space or time. And spirits are absolute love and have absolute knowledge; and within this love, we spread freedom and justice. We (spirits) capture the human thought, ideas or questions in their minds.*[xiii]

The screens show mental images and words of spirits; therefore, you can see and read.

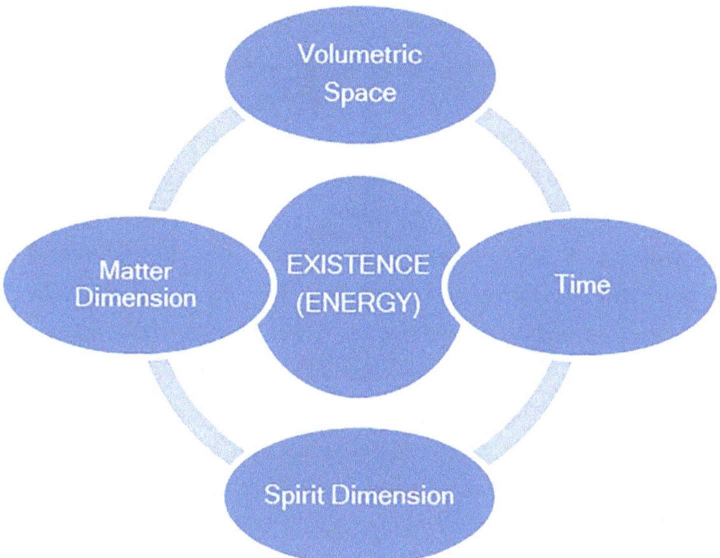

Figure 5: Existence

—However, they are now able of seeing what is in a spirit mind, present or future. You can read the thought of the spirits and what they see around them, on the screens of the stage windows.

At that moment, as the moderator speaks, the four screens or the hanging windows on stage come down in the dark; a beam of light. Two shadows enter the stage on the left front side, pushing a podium; they put it at a small angle (toward the center of the audience) to the left of the stage. A little shiny flame, like a candle, descends and stays behind, but above that podium. It's the spirit of the moderator. The atmosphere is still full of incense smell. Other floating lights illuminate the stage; Shadow silhouettes intersect from left to right, and from right to left, back to front, turning right or left create spooky patterns. Meanwhile, the music plays that strange music. That little flame on the podium emits a bright spark, and a plume of smoke comes out of the ground. A woman-shaped spirit appears behind the smoke, tall thin, with a beautiful figure. Then the shadow strolls, and stops behind the podium, and continues, in a sweet voice says.

Moderator.–*Trues, please continue.*

Trues.–*Humans think of a paradise above in the sky. There is no sky here in the firmament; but there is a dimension harboring spirits in the same space where the material dimension is. Both dimensions occupy the space of the universe, and living beings and spirits roam in it. There is no other space in the infinite universe. This space houses inorganic objects and living, organic beings in the universe; and the land as we know it. Although humans share the space of the universe with spirits, they both inhabit different dimensions. One is for spirits, and the other is for inert matter and living beings. Souls or spirits and the bodies of living beings live in two distinct dimensions and occupy the same space. But the universe is infinite, and there is nothing else outside of its space. The space of the universe houses all dimensions; and spirits intermingle with living beings in this space. There is life on earth, but there can be life anywhere else in the universe, perhaps in different forms, figure and nature.*

Wow! They say there is no paradise in heaven. The spirits are in the same space where I see the humans, and we neither see them, nor we touch them. They live here on earth, in our world, in the same countries, in the same cities and perhaps in the same houses.

Trues.–*The universe is a world of spirits, not of living beings and or organic species. Hey, guys, think about human mental limitations. Humans cannot perceive or conceive. Humans with a confused mind cannot perceive or conceive non-physical concepts. The concepts of spirits are difficult for human minds to understand. Most human minds do not understand issues related to spirits or souls; therefore, they resort to faith and beliefs. Souls, or spirits, such as radio frequencies, can pass through material things; spirits are energy, and it can pass through matter and our bodies, unnoticed. Humans cannot perceive spirits in normal physical circumstances, but spirits can, although they cannot touch or hold our material body. Some people can feel spirits that come into close contact with our souls. If you know there is a soul within each of us, you can understand that it attracts other spirits around us. So, you can feel strange feelings and feelings.*

This forum is getting hot. This is a night of spirits and spiritual affairs. Two spirits on stage push a bench to the center of the stage.

Moderator.–*The signs of limited minds are many; some of these are premonitions, apprehensions and fears. Spirits have minds without limit. This is true; humans are not aware of the complete reality of this material world (or dimension); for them, this is the only reality. The audience should know that the theater can cool down, but it is because of the concentration of spirits working around. They can absorb the heat of material objects and beings around them. Do not[xiv] be afraid and do not turn on lights; the consequences can be harmful.*

Trues leaves the stage raising his hand showing a victory V. There is a small pause, but then the moderator continues; the wind howls in the cold theater, and flashes of light of various colors adorn the dimension of spirits–this is strange. But the creepy music and the dancing of the spirits continue, while the moderator speaks.

Moderator.–*I invited two other spirits to join us in our conversation. I'll call you Robert and Sexis for the simplicity and convenience of the public. Their code names are (a) RBRT32121 and (b) SXZST68514. They are at an exit station waiting for their time to leave for the earth. They know what I think and can respond to my thoughts; so, I need not talk to them. But you can listen, and you can take part in the conversation with questions. Robert and Sexis, can you come in and introduce yourself? Ah, anyone in the audience can ask questions; I'll coordinate your presentation, understand?*

Two spirits roll two armchairs to the center of the front stage and place them in front of the audience at a slightly inclined angle to each other (always aligned with the center of the audience). Two lights, like flames of small candles, enter the stage, floating one from the right and one from the left and stop behind the chairs. Stage lighting changes with darkness and shadows, while music continues. The stage lighting only allows the audience to see candle-like flames. When the lights float to the center of the front stage, the audience hears the noise of the wind howling and a strong cold air blow over them. The two flames turn to smoke and the spirits appear behind the smoke. A sturdy, athletic man, and a woman with a figure of a model wait to enter the dialogue.

Other flames appear on stage; become plumes of smoke, and the spirits appear light-colored, semi transparent. And other spirits dance on stage, simulating the meaning of the story. The audience can see and hear the moderator behind the podium, and the two spirits move to sit down. The rest of the stage remains densely gloomy.

Dialogue of humans and spirits.

Moderator.—*Robert, please explain, what is the purpose of your journey to earth?*

The Spirit sitting near the podium he stands, and with a tenor, metallic, slow voice he says.

Robert.—*There could be no living beings if they did not have a soul in them; and the human body does not handle the mind. The mind handles the human body, thoughts, decisions and actions. We said that the spirit in a human body has an ego and a consciousness, but the ego has the power of free choice (free will). This is a problem; because the human ego may choose and pays no attention to the universal order of oneness. Most humans are selfish and greedy, envious and hateful. They think, decide, and act according to their selfishness.*

How can that be? The spirit says that, without a mind, humans are plants; creatures without thoughts. They say ego is our main problem, because of its free will. Then why do we have an ego? Well, if you had no soul within you, you would be an inert matter; without being aware of the surrounding reality. You know, living objects and creatures react to the forces and or factors of the environment. For example, most humans react to their environmental forces when they don't have what they need. There is a law that states that for each action there is a reaction.

Is that why spirits come and become souls within us? The spirits might explain why they come to planet Earth.

Robert.—*We make trips to earth to guide humans on their return to oneness. But the egos of humans confuse and or ignore this purpose. Existence is to preserve life in the universe. Your mission is to build, not destroy; though, the universe recycles those objects and creatures that do not contribute to the progress of existence. Material themes and things, such as wealth, fame and power, absorb the human ego most of the time. Maybe you're wondering what humans can do to achieve that* *purpose? I tell you that life is simple; is both knowledge and awareness of reality. Knowledge is in all objects and themes, and for free. All human knowledge is a small part of the information stored in omniscience. And humans can get what they need to describe everything in the universe, but only if they're willing to look for it.*[xv]

Yes, that's true. They're right! We only know what we learn and what we conceived using what we know. There's nothing more than this. We do not create new knowledge; we only apply what we learn. Our level of knowledge limits our minds, and we reason and judge with what we know. Listen!

—A human in balance or in harmony with the universe is in "unity" with it. Human beings who abide by the laws of the universe are with it in full harmony; this is a condition of oneness. Thus, they gain a stable state of satisfaction, conformity, and gratitude with life; while striving for higher and better conditions. Life is a long chain of moments that change according to current conditions and circumstances. However, a stable state condition must satisfy the laws of the universe; to be in harmony with the order of uniqueness. Humans need to understand the order of oneness, and this order is the main purpose of life. We (spirits) come to help humans. His mental state is the foundation of unity. Humans need to gain more knowledge to understand what oneness means. Just guess what it is. The universe with precise knowledge; knowledge that existed before the "big explosion" occurred. And we cannot create or destroyed it; it has an infinite existence, longer than the universe's life. Humans gain knowledge of the universe and apply it as their intelligences allow them. Knowledge belongs to existence and the spirit that leaves, while your human body remains a matter in the universe. All human knowledge gained so far remains in omniscience. Disastrous events in life join humans, showing one principle of oneness.

But how can we abide by these laws when we don't know them? I mean, we can't achieve oneness. I realize that conformity, satisfaction, and gratitude together is our steady state. And I ask, would we become conformist beings? Maybe not…

Moderator.—*SXZST (or Sexis), please come in and explain to the audience what happened in that accident; they want to know.*

I was there the day of the accident; I saw what happened, but I didn't know the causes. A man on a motorcycle was chasing a car; shooting at the car with his automatic pistol. The driver lost control by spinning before colliding with the concrete structure. In the chaos, the motorcycle collided with the car and then crashed into the other side of the structure. Then I saw the darkness in my mind and saw the rest much more clearly. I will fight this subject, but let's listen.

Sexist.—*When that accident happened, it scared them. Their souls, or spirits, surprised and confused them for a while; faced with death or the functional separation of their souls. Separation is the sixth step in the Life Cycle.*

I see a diagram that appears on the four window screens. Fundamental separation is, as they say, the sixth step.

—Humans do not understand the process and or the other five steps, as the graph in Figure 4 shows. They do not know how the laws of the universe manage the functional separation of their soul. Is it a mystery? No, it's not. The caveat is that humans are afraid to think about death. For the universe, the sixth step of a life cycle is a standard operation process. The laws that manage life cycles have clear specifications for each step. Those who wrote these laws also structured the cycles of life, long before the universe, and before living beings appeared. We have articles of the laws of the universe we could read. We still have time before our departure.[xvii]

Stage lights turn off and on to show the relocation of spirits to that beginning.

Robert.—*Omniscience is the knowledge of the global spirit. Because of the law of cause and effect, humans may know that the universe keeps records of all activities and events that occur in their space and time. Omniscience records everything humans know, discover. Humans can neither add nor subtract omniscience's knowledge; because no knowledge is out there, and your knowledge can only come from omniscience. Besides the laws controlling the behavior of the universe control the lives of all its contents. The content includes all inorganic matter; and all living beings in the universe. These are all parts of the material dimension; and there are scenarios where they are, allow their stock.*

Omniscience contains all the knowledge of existence and what the universe encloses in that knowledge–we see that knowledge. What's left for us to create? Spirits say humans cannot create or destroyed knowledge. It belongs to existence. What is the purpose of learning if we cannot add our knowledge? They say the laws control the universe and all the lives within it. What is the purpose of living? As Frank Sinatra sings, *what a world, what a life I am in love;* what are we in love with? We may not add knowledge to omniscience; but we gain knowledge through our inductive-deductive thinking.

-The dimension of the spirits does not allow matter within it. We know that souls occupy human bodies as energy that humans cannot see or touch in the physical world. However, if spirits lodge in human bodies, they can live in the material world.

Well, this really happens in the physical world. There is a spirit in every human structured in various components; this structure is the soul of the human, like the operating system of the mind. I accept that we have a soul and a mind in our bodies, but I do not understand the relationship or connection of the soul and mind. Maybe an infographic can help me clear my mind. [16]

–Humans; their minds, and bodies can only live if the conditions of the scenarios meet their needs. But the scenario may not provide the conditions; and humans must adapt to these, leave or die in the conditions of the stage. It's not the same for other living beings. They only know what they perceive and instinctively conceive and conform.

Sexis.–*But the limitations are not so severe for the world's less intelligent creatures. They adjust to the order of harmony of the universe automatically at birth–their free will is instinctive. The laws of existence and the universe are clear. Ensure that new humans learn and abide by these laws. Let me read you some of these mandates! (1) Existence will have only two states; they are the two infinite scenarios, the actual and unreal dimensions; (2) humans, and other living creatures, will only live in real scenarios; (3) Spirits cannot live on their own in the dimension of matter, they can live within a living being in that dimension. But independent of matter.*

---

[16] see Figure 15 on page 340 for further explanations

Robert.–*(4) Spirits can live in both dimensions. Free spirits will only live in the unreal dimension. They will live in the real dimension as souls housed in the bodies of living creatures. (5) humans and living creatures can live in the universe; but only in scenarios where conditions support life. Its shapes, figures and sizes; the place where living things are.*

Sexy.–*(6) The evolution of humans is a mental, intellectual, and not biological process. It is not the condition of walking erect that makes man, but the function of his soul. But being mental and conscientious functions, there is only the ego. So, the evolution of humans adapts the human ego to the order of universal harmony.*

What, did I hear correctly? There is no such thing as evolution; there are only conditions and circumstances of a scenario which objects and creatures must abide by. But human evolution is only for developing ego. The bodies of living beings are content with, and adapt to, the conditions of the environment in which they live.

A screen shows one of someone in the audience.

Person A.–*Are you saying there is no evolution?*

Sexis.–*Well, let's see.*

The screens show the thoughts of the spirit.

Robert.–*Darwin, presumably established in his mind, that all the species of life have descended over time from common ancestors; and in a joint publication with Alfred Russel Wallace, he introduced his scientific theory this branched pattern of evolution resulted from a process he called[17],[18] natural selection, in which the struggle for existence has a similar effect to the artificial selection involved in selective breeding.*

The key word is natural selection. Scenarios have their set of conditions that can change over time, and only allow entities that can adapt to them. Scenarios do not choose their occupants; occupants choose them. Living beings stay and adapt, die in adaptation, or leave the stage. A critical law for creatures is to find, as a river does, a path of least resistance–the riverbed of life–or a natural comfort zone; this is a steady state of satisfaction, conformity and gratitude–the conformity with the order of universal harmony. The theory that

---

[17] https://en.wikipedia.org/wiki/Darwinism

[18] https://en.wikipedia.org/wiki/Alfred Russel Wallace

all species of life have descended over time from common ancestors *excludes* the possibility that other uncommon ancestors would join in the mix.

Sexis.—*What Darwin said is fine; yet there is a warning. Each scenario in the universe has its own set of rules and conditions, and its resources are finite, and it cannot provide what it does not have. These conditions might restrict the life of the creatures within the stage. It's possible that a scenario does not satisfy the needs of living or inert creatures. So, a scenario can be hospitable, neutral, or hostile to one kind of creature; but it may not be for another. Living creatures have three options; they can leave if they can't live with the conditions; they can stay if they can adapt; and or they stay and die waiting for what they need. Scenario conditions are transient and may change. There are two types of changes, local and global; changes in the environment complies with the laws of the universe. Environment conditions can return to a previous state. If so, living beings may change to adapt to the scenario conditions— and they live. If the scenario imposes previous conditions, there is no evolution because conditions can be reversed; and the inhabitants, may all, lose the adaptation they had gained.*

Conditions are tough, aren't they? It is a typical case of accepting, or rejecting change conditions. Spirits say conditions can return to the previous status. Living beings, in such a case, face the consequences of changes in reverse. It is good if they can adapt; is this evolution? It might be, but let's think again, carefully. All living beings try to adapt to the conditions of their scenario as best they can. No matter if they go forward or backward, they follow changes in their environment. In such a case, there is no evolution, only the continuous process of adapting to the conditions of the scenario. Perhaps someone can say what about the learning process and the accumulation of knowledge? All is that after man, when all go and the survivors are alone, human knowledge, skills and experiences will fade out over time—in a few generations later.

Robert.—*Humans have no powers like spirits. There must be a reason, as there is for all things. Souls in humans represent the global spirit—they are different. An ego represents the inner self in the structure; but spirits have no egos. Your ego is a component of the soul; it manages* *your conscience, it composes your character and your personal identity. The ego receives the attribute of free choice, without restrictions; and this attribute is a source of ego errors.*[19],[20],[21]

Sexis.—*The purpose of existence is simple; as we summarize it in a sentence right away. Living beings live only once; their destiny is death; and they must work together to achieve harmony with themselves and with the universe. Well, existence gives hope to humans, at least.*

—Someday they can understand and respect the purpose of life. Then, and only then, the dual human—rather the ego—can synchronize with the order of harmony of the universe. Therefore, the dual being, the soul and the body, can live in both dimensions; that of matter and that of spirits, simultaneously. However, humans must train their ego to attain that combined spiritual and material state.

That seems logical! Humans must work together! And they know it and say *the union makes the force*. But the concept of *achieving harmony with themselves and with the universe* is not entirely clear. Spirits say that when we understand the purpose of our lives, we conform our souls to our bodies, and we can live in both dimensions. I'd live to see that situation.

Robert.—*All of that is not clear to humans; however, they must have discipline and patience. I will read a rule that says, creatures must cleanse themselves; their minds and souls to sublimate their material beings. Th souls must cleanse so that humans can move to the dimension of spirits. This condition is for creatures of a higher level of consciousness; like humans. So, the day when humans can exist as a body with souls without attachment to materialism or the material world will be the day when humans will reach oneness—they exist in the spiritual and material dimension, simultaneously. The key to open the mystery of existence is the condition of oneness; the spirit and body both in one being, in both dimensions.*[xvii]

Sexis.—*Robert, we have read a lot of data and information. Perhaps humans can now see, at some point, living beings live in the*

---

[19] https://www.dictionary.com/browse/ego

[20] https://www.merriam-webster.com/dictionary/ego

[21] https://www.vocabulary.com/dictionary/ego

spirit dimension even when they are in the material dimension—as material beings. But humans not will transcend the dimension of the spirit as matter; it is a misconception. In oneness matter (the body) and energy (the spirit) can freely interact with each other in both dimensions.

Robert.—*Yes, that's what we imagined. That's why we travel to earth so often; spirits do not need to cleanse themselves; they are pure beings. Humans need to control and purify their ego; their thoughts and decisions; and actions outside of their adverse attributes.*

Sexis: *That's it! Here, the writings say, and human bodies will be blind; They will have no mind of their own; they will live as corpses, and without brains they can only feel pain from their material wounds.[xviii]*

Well, that's nothing new for people to know, even though they say, 'I love you with all my heart.'

Look here we read, zombies—living beings walking dead or lifeless beings pretending to walk alive. Without a spirit lodged in the human body, people have no mind.

Do you understand that without a mind a human has no conscience? Therefore, you can think of this; without conscience, humans are spirits or zombies, with no connection to the material world.

Moderator: *Let me pause here. We must return now; our time to penetrate the material dimension is coming. The public hopes to learn how a spirit merges with a human body.*

Sexis: *Wait, please, let the audience hear this!*

Moderator: *Ok, you can read just one more topic.*

Sexis: *All creatures with high brain development like humans will have a mind; and their minds will be invisible and intangible. The mind is part of the spirit dimension, and a randomly assigned soul will handle it. Human minds are on many levels over the minds of all other living beings. The spirit carries all its powers before entering human bodies; but they lose a large part of their attributes upon entering a human egg. They keep a limited connection to the global spirit; and certain powers to protect the life of the human body they manage.*

This is funny! We care a lot about how we look, how we dress, how much we have; but they say that our bodies are just vehicles for the soul they carry. We are more about vehicles than about who drives it.

—*People recognize or assume that they have a spirit within them; they also recognize that they have a mind, a soul, and a conscience. Humans know they have an ego, wisdom, and a power of will, but they do not know how they integrate into their bodies and where they come from. They should train them on how to manage their willpower and how to ponder their situations.*[xix]

Robert.—*Let's go back, Sexis, let's go back.*

Sexis.—*Wait, Robert, please let humans hear this: Life on earth will have truth and not truth; but a mixture of truth and not truth will always be false, and only the mixture of truth with truth will be true.*

Pick it up! We have no choice but to tell the truth. Perhaps the founding fathers of the United States constitution knew that when they said, "Swear to tell the truth, and nothing but the truth, so help you God."

Sexis.—*Damn those who by choice are deceptive beings. Truth, not lies. Humans have a lot to correct. Hey, let's go back; let's go back.*

Their research has taken a lot of their waiting time, and they fly through time to their departure station. But they're still talking on the flight back to the station. And they continue when they come back. For me, this theme is fascinating, and I could read or hear if they narrate the truth of existence.

Robert.—*Oh, yes, our spiritual dimension is infinite; and we, spirits, move at will to whatever place we desire; we disappear from here and appear there when we want. There's no time, and we can move from one instance to another.*

Moderator.—*An instance is one year in human life. Robert means, to any other year of existence; Humans can't do that. We can see humans going through their clumsy daily activities; that's our entertainment. Humans are funny.*

But how can they perceive if they have no senses like humans? Maybe their minds capture the waves of thought and frequencies of physical activities; other than omniscience. The two screens at the back of the stage light up, showing humans in the streets, dressed as in the early nineties. Both screens turn off after one or two minutes.

Sexis.—*It's a comedy of trial and error but fun; like the daily series of a learning program in the late 21st century on earth—the apprentice.*

The left front screen lights up, showing a passage from President Trump talking about his plan. It obsesses him to legitimizing the 2016 election, and that Russia did not win the election for him; but still trying to get a foreign country to help it win in 2020.

—The president tries to rule the greatest democracy on earth as a dictator. Although we know all the future results, we do not intervene in the decisions of humans. We, spirits, know what each of you think. But this president doesn't get away with it, and he encounters big legal problems.

Robert.—*That's right, look! Republicans get angry, and democrats are laughing in the audience. Humans accorded to their taste, tastes and preferences. For us spirits, absolute knowledge is available to all; our minds and all the issues are transparent. We cannot hide our thoughts because we only think and communicate the truth.*

Sexis.—*Think, if humans could work truthfully, or if humans could read the minds of others, then no one could think or harm others.*

Robert and the audience laugh.

—Continue, Robert...

Robert.—*I rejoice in thinking about what a human would learn if they could read other people's minds. Sexis, you are a spirit; have you become a human soul yet?*

Sexis.—*I will continue to say that in our dimension of spirits there are no directions, no difficulties, forward or backward, to the left or on the right side. This is obvious; because spirits are ubiquitous; we all have the same powers in our dimension; in addition, we know where to go, using our attributes. We are part of and belong to the global spirit; and we have access to omniscience, omnipotence, omnipresence of existence. We hear what humans think or talk and see what they do across interdimensional boundaries.*

Robert keeps laughing, unrestricted.

—Robert... Robert, do you have anything to say? Go ahead!

Robert.—*We move faster than the speed of light and can travel in space and time at will. For example, do you see that pretty lady in the* audience? I'm sitting on her laps hugging her, and kissing her cheek, and I didn't move from my chair on stage, apparently.

Sexis.—*Now, Robert, who has already become human?*

Moderator.—*Robert, compose.*

Hey, let's not blame Robert; we humans are foolish and funny; and we have our wonderful human humor. Well, well, sometimes silly and in bad taste.

Robert.—*Please forgive me and don't worry; we, spirits, we can't grasp matter. We pass through material objects and creatures.*

Robert says, whispering...

We're not like a USA president or some other politicians. Our hands pass through matter. However, we have energy, because we are nuclear or electromagnetic energy; so, if we focus our minds to matter, we can bring about change and movement.

Robert keeps laughing, albeit gently this time.

Sexis.—*Hey Robert, what do you mean? It doesn't matter; you can think of anything else. Anyway, humans have a mental power they haven't learned to use yet. They may have experienced telepathy. And they may have communicated with other humans through their minds. That's like remembering or saying the same thoughts and words at the same time.*

Finally, Robert stops laughing and becomes serious.

Robert.—*That is true, but it is a phenomenon controlled by souls within humans. The existence makes our bodies of atoms loaded with nuclei always in balance. Their brains transmit low waves, and or frequencies; their thoughts are electromagnetic energy; that spirits can tune in or receive and read. It is the same energy of the universe that cannot create or destroy.*

Moderator.—*Please narrate what spirits do in your dimension, so that the public can understand.*

Robert stands up.

Moderator.—*No, Robert, this time you don't. Sexis, go ahead.*

Sexy stands up, looks at Robert, smiles and says.

Sexis.—*Nothing, we do nothing... we don't work; we don't study, there's no need for schools, we already know everything.*

Moderator.—*Sexis?*

Sexis.—*It's OK...*

She pauses for a moment.

-You call me Sexis… but I say there are no genders in this dimension. We play and have fun with the thoughts and actions of humans. For example, when they have problems and think about finding a solution, we help them rummage through omniscience. And the most important thing is that we help them think, meditate and create.

Now pause for a longer moment, as if waiting for the audience, and for Robert, to respond. Then she says.

—Oh gee, there are dirty minds in the audience. Hey, stop thinking about it.

She pauses again.

—But it is true; we don't have sex in the spirit dimension. Audience, could you live without that on earth? On earth, the rich and famous think they can feel women, and get away with it because they are rich and famous; Audience, have you heard of anyone like that?

She awaits the audience's response.

Moderator.-*Sexis, you've said enough.*

Sexis.—*Let me clarify and or disambiguate. Spirits are spirits, not like humans, we are neither men nor women; we are just spirits, genderless. We love, but not with sexual love. Our love is not lust. Our love is the love of the soul; it's not emotional, it's not selfish, it's not material. It's pure love, endless love.*

He pauses briefly.

—There's no fun, ah, as there is on earth.

She pauses longer.

—No, we don't have sex. She pauses again. We don't have Dodger hot sausages, double burgers, and things like that, do we?

She waits for someone in the audience response, and then she continues.

—In this dimension of spirits, we do not even have food; our food is spiritual consciousness. We don't have hot dogs, double burgers, and things like that, do we? We don't eat sushi; we don't have chipotles, pizzas or burritos.

Robert intercedes, abruptly.

Robert.–*We don't have drinks, even less, Bacardi, Jose Cuervo, Vodka; is it fun? We don't have drinks: Margaritas, mojitos or "Bloody Mary"; not even beer or water; we don't need drinks. Would you like your world to be like this?*

Robert waits for the response from the audience and then sits down.

Sexis.–*Well, there it is, you know. I'm not kidding, as they say on earth. Here, there is no fun, no politics, no free companies, the concept of ownership; as in, I have something. We don't have movies, no credit cards, not even HD Tv. Our entertainment is in watching the comedy of mistakes of humans carrying on earth 24/7; and this is more than enough, really.*

Robert.–*The comedies of everyday life of humans are fun. Man's uncertainty creates his ridiculousness.*

Sexis.–*In our dimension, we don't have department stores, supermarkets, as humans call them; we don't have Fifth Avenue in New York, or a city like Las Vegas. Therefore, women could not buy beauty products, shoes, jewelry or handbags, and men could not buy cars, toys or weapons.*

Robert.–*The spirit world does not allow humans in a state of matter, and humans are not yet ready to enter. The kingdom of spirits doesn't have a constitution or a second amendment like in the U.S., and we don't need militias. We don't have cars, like a Dodge Challenger; a Ford Mustang; Maserati; Ferrari; Lamborghini; Etc. We don't need one.*

What? There is no formula one races; and there's no Indianapolis 500. No baseball, football, football, etc. What is that?

–No, no. Here we fly, or we disappear from here and show up somewhere else. We travel back in time and see what's happening ten thousand cases ago, or what happens now, or it will happen any time. We know all this because the library of omniscience is open to all spirits, not just a select few. There's no fun, is there? We are part of eternal existence; we never die.

-You have a good time on earth; you have done it; but we have an endless living TV series of thieves, gangsters and cops, or the comedy of politics, righteousness and morality. Yes, that's right; humans live pretending to be holy. It's a long novel titled, "Clever Hypocrites." We tell

them that no president could harass women in this dimension. We don't have a corrupt government; we don't have a government. We all know what we have and must do. Here, there are no rich and famous spirits, no TV presenters with virtual reality shows. Here, in the spirit dimension, everything is real; a fraudulent person has no place in this dimension. Everything is as it should be.

Sexis.—*That's funny. I wonder, why do humans want to come to heaven? Is there a sky really? I say that humans do not understand what eternal peace is. What's the emotion? Eternal peace is not action and it is all actions simultaneously.*

Moderator.—*Robert, you've said more than enough about that. We need to focus on life cycles. Robert, explain what and how we begin the human life cycle.*

Sexis makes a nice body expression as if to say, see? Robert responds in his tenor metallic voice.

Robert.—*Oh yes, but first we must tell you it is not a simple task. Humans, and other living beings, can enter any scenario; but they can only stay in the scenarios that allow them and or welcome their lives. They can live in scenarios that meet the needs of their lives. There may be life anywhere in the universe, especially where conditions and circumstances embrace life.*

Sexis, raise your hand, as if you wanted to intervene.

Moderator.—*Sexis, do you have anything to add?*

Sexis.—*Yes, thank you; for example, humans appeared on earth when conditions allowed them to exist, as humans. The laws matter; a living human cannot exist by itself; a spirit must enter a human body to manage its actions. Only the soul has a mind, the intellectual consciousness; humans without souls will die. The rest of the world's creatures exist only with their instinctive behavior. Therefore, humans exist on earth as a composition of a spirit and a body; the energy and body of a human. But there are routines embedded in the brain neurons that affect the pure spiritual mind.*

Trues enters the stage on the right and intervenes in the dialog. He claps his hands twice and one of the back screens of the stage shows images of what he describes in words; they are images of what he visualizes in his mind. Trues walk through the front of the stage and disappear into darkness on the left of the stage.

—*The laws of the universe specify rules for spirits who come to the spirits in quests. Spirits cross into the material dimension; where, each spirit lodges in a human body, or in a body of a living creature; download and install your operating system, called mind, on the human. Humans cannot change or alter the laws of existence. Human beings cannot function well without their spirits. You may ask, Is this program big or small? Well, on earth there are now about seven and a half billion humans. Humans breed at three hundred and sixty thousand eggs per day. Spirits inflect into these many eggs every day. But there are other living creatures that multiply. There are four accommodations per second; in addition, the lodgings in the other living creatures. Can you imagine the size of this program?*

Moderator.—*We see about eight billion people walking on planet earth by the year twenty thousand twenty-three. Eight billion spirits will exist in these many humans. This is an important project for us; humans add up to about one hundred and thirty-five million per year. Humans, they only think of themselves, and they don't think about the souls of other humans.*

I am not surprised to know that earth is overcrowding; what should scare people the most is the speed at which the world is populating. This rate exceeds the rate of supply of products, and services. I see that before humans reach this point, violence will explode everywhere on earth in a struggle to survive.

Robert.—*In this sense, humans are blind. Irresponsible human egos produce more humans, without thinking about how the world will sustain or feed themselves. They don't measure the consequences. Some humans believe that God has commanded them to populate the world unrestricted. The food cycles of this world take a specific time and may not meet the future needs of humanity. The Earth is approaching the point of resource's scarcity; humans are close to the equilibrium of production and consumption. On the days when resources are not available, humans will disappear from this world. This is sad for humans, but it is the truth of existence; humans must learn to live in harmony with the universe to delay the end of days for human life. The project of the universe of dual* *humans may perish; If humans do not learn to live in peace with the order of universal harmony. This is the goal of existence: total uniqueness.*

Some audience scream from behind.

-What do the spirits bring with them?

The spirits light on the chairs flash and almost disappear.

Moderator.—*Please do not shout, high frequencies repel spirits. Raise your hand, and I'll read the question in your minds. Spirits bring order, intelligence and logic; bring love, knowledge, life, art and joy. Robert, please, you can go on.*

Robert.—*Existence pre-plans the life cycles. Spirits don't need to do anything but come to a departure station. We go through a process of inflection; we carry nothing more than our (energy) and the attributes of spirits. Sexis, you're right to say that spirits don't have sex. Existence defines the genre of living objects and creatures that can exist in the universe. The universe specified that a human body needs a soul and a body to live; and that soul drives a human. Existence divides the human into two elements; soul (energy) and body (matter).*

Robert invites Sexis with his hand to move forward with the speech.

Sexis.—*fortunately, humans work in two dimensions; well, at least partially, for now. Their souls live and feel in the dimension of spirits; but their bodies act and move in the physical dimension. The human ego is the element of the soul that coordinates interaction with the physical world. Their souls speak with free spirits outside through meditation, using the function of the mind.*

Someone in the audience has a question and raises a hand.

Person B: *Can you tell us what the mind is and where it is?*

Trues jumps in conversation; and Robert getting up returns to his chair.

Trues: *Yes, when the spirit lodges in a fertilized egg, it establishes the roots of the mind in the nascent zygote's brain. The mind represents the spirit within you. It is the superior function installed in the brain of material human bodies. The mind shapes and maintains a connection between the imbued spirit and the brain and the global spirit. It is a channel that the spirit in a human body uses to speak to other spirits around. The mind sends frequencies that excite and or activate neurons* *in the brains of humans. It sets in the brain ways to process the gnosis data that minds use to create concepts and ideas.*

Robert: Well said, Trues, well said!

Sexy.–*Let us return to the beginning; the first step is the inflection or accommodation of the spirit in a human egg. In this step, the spirit structures the human mind in the zygote; and synchronizes it with the emerging human brain. The mind implants its main mental-logical processes; establishes circuits in the brain to carry on its functions. The spirit installs and activates these mental functions in the areas of the human brain. This process follows the development phases and steps of the brain in the human embryo. The mind creates the conscience; installs the wisdom, will and morality, but these are not active yet. The mind creates the ego of the person; below it installs character, awareness of the environment, and identity of the human. The mind implants the ability to think about the human. This capacity grows with the growth of the human embryo; and within a few weeks the embryo compares its sensations.*

Robert.–*The logic of the installation follows a sequence of use; first the functions of the users. Therefore, the function of thought comes first, mental functions, psychological functions, moral, etc. Second, the mind installs wisdom, willpower. So, integrates these three into the human consciousness. The mind then sets the will (do) and the ego. The mind gives the ego the power to define identity, the character of the human, and gives it freedom of choice along with the link with reality, internal and external. At this moment, the embryo reaches glimpses of consciousness.*

Robert invites Sexis with his hand to move forward with the speech.

Sexis.–*the embryo has no reality awareness; However, in a few months, and before birth, the embryo may feel emotions. At first the mind is a tabula rasa, an empty whiteboard. The mind is not functional until a few years after birth, but the reasoning begins a few months after birth. The natural thought process of the mind works to find truth in thoughts and actions; free choice; emotions; feelings; moral behavior. Embryos are not self-aware until later in their developmental processes; or even after birth. But the mind collects images of the growth and sensations of the embryo during its growth. The mind continues its* *development throughout the life of humans. The imbued wisdom grows with experience and age until the day when the mind no longer functions properly.*

Moderator.—*Trues, come join us in this dialogue.*

Trues had been in the back, sitting at a small table and listening to Robert and Sexis' conversation. Trues brings his chair and joins the group.

Trues.—*The second step of mental configuration in humans is to seek knowledge. The search finds and takes information from omniscience stored in the spirit dimension; all this happens during thought creation processes. This stage processes gnosis (knowledge bits) and integrates them into ideas or concepts of the mind. The mind structures the function of consciousness as the brain's development continues. Consciousness deals with questions, thoughts, and actions related to [22] what is right or wrong; just and unjust; good or bad; and even the pleasant and unpleasant. Consciousness shows the ego how to achieve oneness with the universe. The above is the morality of the human. Willpower functions as the executing function of consciousness (the morality element of the soul); So, willpower works by enforcing the standards that conscience sets. [23]*

Robert.—*In the third step, the spirit implements the functions of the ego. The spirit works in creating the structure of one's identity and the character that the human gets. Self-awareness and awareness of the environment reach the minds of human; in this gradual process. The free will function activates. The willpower function links consciousness and ego, and willpower strives to guide the ego, showing it the right path in its choices, decisions, and actions.*

---

[22] https://www.merriam-webster.com/diccionario/conciencia. The definition of conscience is the sense or awareness of the moral goodness or guilt of one's own conduct, intentions or character along with a feeling of obligation to do the right thing or be good.

[23] https://www.biblestudytools.com/diccionario/conciencia
Consciousness-Consciousness is a term that describes an aspect of a human being's self-awareness. It is part of a person's internal rational capacity and is not, as popular tradition sometimes suggests, a hearing room for the voice of God or the devil.

Trues.–*The mind configuration continues with the second phase. This phase covers the installation and configuration of all terms and conditions for human behavior; current and future. Terms and conditions include the attributes that spirit inherits and can use in your work. Spirits gain all knowledge, they can be anywhere, and they are all powerful; but that's in the spirit dimension. Souls do not store these attributes when they are in human bodies. Spirits that work in humans maintain parts of their attributes; as they use their ability to access the omniscience of the universe; meditation and or deep thinking. If they ever had a problem, for which they did not see a solution and become disillusioned and deeply worried, but suddenly, they wake up and jump jubilantly shouting; I have it; This is it; I have a solution. They connected with the omniscience from where they got the solution–the solution comes from omniscience.*

Sexis.–*The mind is not part of the material dimension; it is an intangible element. Nor is it a material part of the human body; Maybe. Can you understand this? The spirit lodged in your body can communicate with spirits in the dimension of spirits. When you ponder a problem, your mind searches the libraries of knowledge; that is in the spirit dimension. And perhaps their minds find that information in the omniscience. But when minds get that information, humans assume that it is a product of their intelligences; or it's an inspiration and or their imagination. The creation of thought is a function built in the human mind to touch, navigate the infinite knowledge set of the universe. The knowledge group is the omniscience of the universal spirit. But omniscience is the main attribute of that spirit; so, thought is a product of a dialogue between minds with the global spirit.*

Oh! Is this what happens when we meditate or deliberate on a topic: I mean, do we talk to the global spirit? Spirits have just said that we humans enter absolute knowledge, seeking solutions to our problems. This is what some humans do when they pray to their deities. Some scientists claim that extraterrestrial forces inspired them to write their theories, inventions and or their work art. Could that be it? The forces of spirits may have inspired Einstein, and or Shakespeare.

On stage, on an old desk dressed with objects of his time, Shakespeare speaks what he writes *"be or not to be, that's the question,* *if..."*The image fades as his mind shows its thoughts on the screens. Two spirits play the Episode when Juliet commits suicide after discovering that Romeo had killed himself. The spirits disappear and Albert Einstein appears standing next to his old desk, covered with books and papers. He writes on an old black board, e-mc^2, and shouts, *"This is the relativity."*

Sexis.—*Inspirations can reach human minds in different ways; but in all cases it is knowledge we do not take before. Inspirations come in the same way for many areas of knowledge; as it is in poetry writing; or the creation of musical works, or making scientific discoveries, etc. Did you read Dante's Divine Comedy, or remember the Phantom of Andrew Lloyd Webber's Opera? You can consider this work of art as wonderful products of inspiration.*

A mist covers the ground and rises gently. A spirit dressed in a transparent veil dark blue enters and sings "Night Music," from The Phantom of the Opera, and comes out. A second spirit–male form–enters and sings Love is a splendid thing, from the "Sound of Music," and comes out.[24,25]

Trues.—*Imagination is a function that builds the real and or unreal; logical and or illogical, objects, problems and or creatures. It is a thought-free function of the mind that accesses omniscience. It works by building concepts and or ideas that might be feasible in your material world. Is it unreal? No, it's not, because existence has as much real as the unreal as possibilities. Some may say it is the work of a genius if it is workable; or the work of a delusion individual if it is not workable. Virgil's Divine Comedy is an epic poem written in three parts; it's an excellent job of imagination. And "Disneyland or Disney World" extends imaginary engineering.* [26]

Robert.—*Maybe you have seen a spirit or might have had an encounter with the spirits; but you never mentioned it to others because you would not have believed it.*

---

[24] Charles Hart lyrics. Richard Stilgoe and music by Andrew Lloyd Webber, Phantom of the Opera, musical

[25] George Hurdalek (with partial use of ideas by) (as Georg Hurdalek), Howard Lindsay (from the musical book), The Sound of Music, 1965.

[26] Devine Comedy by Publius Vergilius Maro (Virgil)

They wait for an audience response; The people raises their hands. While a little girl (a spirit), five years on stage, looks at the shadows walking near her window, slightly visible.

The girl.—*But we, the spirits, are harmless beings of light and parts of the universal spirit; Their mission is keeping, preserving and maintaining life in the universe, the earth included. They do that with love and only for love. There are no evil spirits, except that ego—a spiritual part—of the mind, the source of sins and diseases in the lives of men.*

In the dark stage, two beams of light shine and two spirits appear at half height; one to the right of the stage and the other on the left of the stage, at an angle to the other, under these beams. The rest of the stage is dark and dimmed. The music begins, with a tempo *"staccato,"* of seventy strokes per minute, more or less. The scenario is disturbing and creepy, as if something is about to happen. These are the things that humans perceive but rarely give them importance. There are those who call these sensations premonitions. Others say they're omens when they tell the public. The first spirit recites a poem, conversationally; and other spirits continue their dance. The lights go out; and the spirit of the left emulating a tender earthly female, in a trembling voice, says this.

> *I am a being of light*
> *perhaps seen or not seen;*
> *Love, pain and cross,*
> *the light of the universe, bright.*
> *the love of enlightened scene;*
> *the words of my verse across.*
> *I'm unique in enchanted concepts.*
> *I am cold light, warm light, of peace,*
> *the soul embedded in the precepts*
> *of the wondrous universal crease*
> *calling on your conscience*
> *from the depth of omniscience.*

The spirit of the right: imitating a male tenor, also with a trembling voice, he recites.

Blessed who surrender their soul
heart to altruistic life
and he keeps his sorrows on shelves,
those who fill with love and calm
others' souls without selfish intent;
and those who come to heal
your sensitive soul, at crucial time
come out of love, to love,
saving you from evil.

The spirit of the left:

Are they martyrs? No, not;
their altruistic work is full of kindness
stretching every hour, every minute
sharing generosity
as a scent of pink incarnate
for your tired soul.

the spirit of the right recites:

We are beings of light, ephemeral
spirits that come to you,
generous, sometimes shy,
at an atrocious event
that threatens your soul, your life
we are the love that forgets you not.

The girl at the window runs to the spirits and recites.

The little girl.-

I am love... I call you true;
You are love as me.
So, embrace me, I love you;
you can love me, you see?

The girl bows; and the three spirits disappear, the rays of light are extinguished, and the music changes to that heavenly light.

Moderator.—*Sexis, do you have anything else to add to the theme?*

Sexis.—*Yes, thanks! If you adults can be happy to know that in our spirit dimension we do not work for any employer, there are no employers. We need not repeal the Obama plan—the affordable health care bill.*

The fog still floods the stage floor, and many spirits dance, converse and gather flowers; they feel and meditate, as in a sneaky state of happiness. They represent the meaning of narratives in their dance. Sexis continues.

—There is no slavery in the spirit dimension. There are no clubs; there are no opposing groups, such as political parties, organized religions. There is love, and spirits are love; there is no prejudice, no discrimination, in this dimension. We do not pay taxes or receive back tax reimbursement. Nobody charges us for existing. Spirits have absolute freedom; and their thoughts and deeds never alter the harmony of other spirits. Spirits keep the greatest respect for the right to be part of each object and creature. Definitive laws and policies guide the peaceful existence, not coexistence, of the content of the universe; us, and you are active parts of all this. The only rule of law is love in the dimension of spirits. For this love is that there are no evil spirits.

She pauses and then says.

—In addition, the treasures and wealth of the universe belong to the universe, and have not assigned them, ceded, leased, or sold to specific humans. The richness of the universe is for all living beings within its space; and from the beginning, the universe equally exists for everyone— never for a selfish few. Human egos work, by any means, to appropriate and accumulate that wealth, contradictorily. Today, a few humans possess ninety-nine percent of the land's wealth. And that gives them power to control the rest. Absolute justice for all is in the spirit dimension—not within humanity.

Moderator.—*Robert, do you have anything else to add to the theme?*

Robert.—*Yes, thank you. Spirits do not depend on faith or belief; they do not need guidance from institutionalized religions to be good. Spirits maintain absolute honesty, omniscience, and truth; act out of everyone's kindness. Creatures in the universe need not pay tithing* *for insurance that guarantees saving their soul with a pass to the spirit dimension. Tithing accounts for ten percent of your wages or salaries. Here, all spirits receive equal attributes; the concept of "right" has no meaning for spirits. We do not encourage or avenge holy priests, nor the Pope, nor canonize new saints—we are all equal. We should not offend you; we are just explaining the dimension of spirits. It's your belief.*

Moderator.—*Trues, do you have anything else to add to the theme?*

Trues.—*Yes, thank you. Well, spirits don't run a government, they have only one rule, the Rule of Love and the mandate to share it. Thus, we love each other deeply and work to spread love on earth. This is a fact; just look at the universe, nature for all without preferences. The world has given humans everything they have; almost free. The mandate of the universe for living beings is to live with love, for love and to love one another. Humans do not follow this mandate; so, the life cycles will continue until they understand it. This world, or planet earth, is purgatory for the egos of humans, but not for their souls.*

Robert raises his hand. Trues gestures back to go ahead.

Robert.—*Ah, spirits only need a total and individual attribute; we are spirits governed by Truth and Love, unlike humans on earth, dominated by their ego. The light of knowledge shines forever in our dimension; and it is free-for-all spirits, and for those humans who seek in the library of omniscience. This is true equality for all, without distinction.*

Trues intervenes.

Trues.—*The dimension of the spirits does not have climate changes; we live in an eternal spring. And though we inhabit a tiny space of the universe—on earth, for example—climate changes affect us. But yes, climate change is conditions that affect the lives of the bodies of living beings. We, spirits, are all the same.*

Spirits direct that question to the audience.

—*We can't hear them.*

They're waiting for the answer.

—*Humans carry in their ego the AGHAPEE, a seven-headed monster. And humans must get that monster out of their egos soon—before humans destroy the earth. That day will be when the dimensions of spirits and matter come to life; and it will be the triumph of the spirit of existence—the dawn of the new human, material spirits and bodies under the same purpose. Humanity lags far behind the itinerary set for this day.*

Moderator.—*We warn the public we must suspend our conversation; the time to go has come.*

Soon the day will come, the spirits say, but it will take many generations and centuries before humans see the light of uniqueness. Humans must change to this state now. All spirits dance and come out on the stage, on the right and left; the lights on the stage off; the shadows move in the departing station fog. The moderator, Sexis, Robert and Trues also leave the stage. The lights go out and the stage goes dark. The silhouettes walk in the twilight of dying light.

Flights of spirits to the earth [xx]
Wednesday, December 20, 1989.

The lights come on. A spirit is alone on an exit platform. A group of spirits walks to a departing platform, as they happily talk about their journey to earth. That spirit walks towards the group of spirits. Transparent bluish-white garments reveal their human figures. They are beings of light. Other spirits walk in the opposite direction, from left to right and from right to left. The place looks like a well-occupied underground train, or a light rail train station in New York. The spirit that awaits the group is the guide or leader of the group. It's a happy place; the spirits show excitement and eagerness to embark on the journey to earth. This is a new experience of an uncertain reality.

Guide.—*The time to merge into a human egg has come for many spirits. They're ready at an exit station, ready to merge. Thousands of spirits inflect in human eggs every second to become souls. Spirits who know everything know that when they are souls, they will know nothing and will learn from the real universe. The soul can connect with omniscience to conceive of another knowledge.*

That's despairing, knowing that you don't know when everything; it's like finishing every course in the world and getting a PhD and then losing your memory. Perhaps this is the other goal of human life—to learn everything *again*—by studying against the time of a short life. A spirit enters from the right of the stage, floating quickly, stopping in front of a group of spirits waiting their turn to travel to earth. Start reader, you don't have time to waste. Five spirits came with the messenger who announces the following.

Messenger.—*These five spirits volunteered to return to earth; they will travel from this departure station to complete a mission. They came back due to a car accident. They are spirits and they are no longer the old woman, the boy, the man, the boy or the girl they were during their accident. However, they still show human silhouettes, but they are free spirits. Spirits are ageless or do not age; so, the old lady is just another spirit. Remember, only matter ages and decays. Another issue, gender is living creatures and determined during fertilization. Please allow them to take a forward position on the line.*

Guide.—*Spirits need not speak; the minds of spirits convey their ideas on various frequencies or waves. All minds belong to the mind of the global spirit. Spirits communicate with their thoughts, not words. We, spirits, do not carry names, we do not baptize; we do not need names; we know each other because of our omniscience. We can use a code to identify each spirit, sometimes as for this dialogue. So, let's start our life cycles and pay attention.*

Oldie.—*Here we go again; we have just returned and we are going back to earth. This is like being in an amusement park on earth; you hop on the games as often as you want. Who wouldn't like to take a trip to Orlando, "Knott's berry farm or Disneyland"? However, anyway, don't bother me just because I was an old lady on my last trip.*

Tzzs.—*There are other spirits part of this group. Three spirits from this group have left this departure station. The first spirit came out in the nineteen eighty year; the second departed in nineteen eighty-two; and the third traveled in nineteen eighty-four. These three spirits are already working on the earth and waiting for the rest of the spirits of the group. We tell them that many thousands of spirits are going out too many parts of the world today. Guess how many spirits go?*

Bochar.—*We all know, but I'm glad you asked. So, let me say it again, for the public's knowledge. Three hundred and sixty thousand spirits penetrate the eggs of human women every day, at the time of fertilization.*

Tzzs.-*There are three hundred and sixty thousand human births per day, or four births per second, not counting non-human creatures. The spirits wait at this departure station, but they won't go together, or all simultaneously.*

Bochar.—*Yes, I know, but it's good to say it again, so the humans in the audience can hear it. The population of the world rises by three hundred and sixty thousand people a day. This means that the population can reach up to eight billion people in the world by the year twenty thousand twenty-three. They will soon face major problems with the supply of food and water, diseases, famines and deaths. Many spirits could return to our dimension before they complete their journey, but it is not the fault of the spirits. All humans have the right, the freedom of choice, what they say and do in the material dimension; it is their responsibility. The component of the soul, called ego, is to blame. The ego has innate freedom of choice. The ego is a figure with individual preferences, tastes and dislikes, and other psychological attitudes; but does not think what it says and does. The ego is the animal part of a human; is impulsive and instinctive.*

Tzzs.—*I see your transition order; it's not up to you to implant yourself in a human; but you must implant yourself in a pig on an experimental farm at Iowa State University.*

Bochar doesn't bother; it does not have to. The spirits know everything, so there are no offenses and it says.

Bochar.—*Yes, I know. I just wanted to talk to you while I wait for my time to inflect in a pig's egg. I go much later, and anyway, thank you.*

Bochar gets up and disappears into the crowd.

Tzzs.—*Understand Bochar; I know it does not want to be in a pig; there are thousands of spirits that will enter various animals, insects, birds in a few seconds. Bochar knows that and knows his mission is important. I wonder if the humans in the audience wants to inflect in a pig, or any lower living being who is not human, in their next life cycle. I'm bothering the audience. Once a spirit lodges into a human, this spirit is not inflecting into any inferior living creature; it's only implants in human eggs, from there on.*

Other spirits standing around exclaim, in unison:

—Don't blame Bochar; for humans it is difficult to know that your mission is to be a pig, in a life cycle; even though it's a short cycle. People grow pigs for their food; people make carnitas or burritos, bacon, etc., with their body. Pork is a product for the food industry; especially for Mexican restaurants; and chains like McDonald's; Carl Junior, and many others. For spirits, a mission is just that and fulfills it with the same love. Blaming someone is one is a flaw in the human ego and their pride would kill them.

Guide.—*Spirits first enter living beings at the lowest point on the scale of consciousness; until they advance towards humans. The spirits know their order of transition; might be that some spirits inflect in a hen, a goat or a cow. It's a way of understanding how humans behave—learning from the outside.*

The audience laughs and the spirits wait for the audience to finish laughing.

Keta.—*Bah! There is no need to check, we all know it from our omniscient attribute.*

Cenia approaching Oldie curiously.

Cenia.—*Hey, how often have you stayed in a human, how has your life been within those people?*

I understand, spirits lose their knowledge when they enter a zygote, and souls lose what they learned on earth when their bodies disappear. Why? True, not everything; the soul takes something away.

Oldie.—*Yes, we do it to a certain extent. We maintain some awareness and ripples we receive and preserve from our previous travels or assignments on earth. We keep them as waves and frequencies. We lose the knowledge we gained when we went through our process of separation in the material dimension; when we return to our spiritual dimension. We can bring images of things, problems, objects and or topics that would have excited us the most; and we can show these trends as human when we return to earth. The frequencies of some things, thoughts or emotions, can stick to us; and we can see them, in space, past, present or future, even simultaneously.*

Keta.—*True, I recite the poems I heard in Europe during the Renaissance period. I remember the poems I inspired the humans I lodged in. I keep the music that excited me; and I get excited again when* *someone plays it while I'm on a new mission. We carry these travel-on-the-go frequencies in our minds; and could appear as human attitudes or tendencies later.* [27]

Cenia.—*That is correct; now it is part of the sublime love we carry. We use this power to exist and space.*

Guide.—*We still have time to entertain the audience with a brief drama of the ogre living in the human ego; we called AGHAPEE.*

AGHAPEE temptation (the ogre in the ego)

Seven elegant and thin spirits (four females and three males) arrive on stage and dance to the walking rhythm of time music. The four female spirits dance clockwise around a triangle of three male spirits. The men escape the circle and the females chase them to lock them up again. The dance repeats this pattern. Four other spirits, two females and two males, walk in pairs on stage to the left front of the stage and to the right front, carrying a book in their Hands. The male wears light blue and female, transparent light pink garments. Once established, they recite a poem, taking turns, but they start with a musical track. The speed of the spirits' voices reciting the verses coincide with the tempo of the music. The dancers stop when spirits change to recite, spinning and intersecting to form a line. At that moment, the seven spirits dance around a spirit sitting on a chair, each carrying a letter. The spirit in the chair has on its chest a label that says 'EGO'. The man thinks, cares or cries, with his head down. At the end of their run, the spirits line up in front of the audience to display the letters by spelling the word AGHAPEE, for a few seconds. The drums mark the rhythm of the dance and the sounds of the gong when the spirits align by showing the whole word. The next spirit immediately recites parts of the poem, and the cycle repeats itself.

They recite the poem in alternating dialogue in shifts; is the dialogue of oneness. The music plays softly in the background—Spirit 1 on the front side- left of the stage; Spirit 2 to the front-right side, Spirit 3 to the front-left side, and Spirit 4 to the front-right side.

---

[27] Ver nota al final, xxx—Ondas cerebrales humanas

The dancing and declamations of the spirits continue in perfect tempo with the music. Perfection is one of the standard qualities of the dimension of spirits.

Oneness dialogue: The death of AGHAPEE.

Spirit 1.–[Man] *They made for me! I see the way I exist in scattered structures. I don't care about justice, equality, which I can't see. I don't care about oneness; we cease; Who gives a fork for a divine plan? The intention of caring and sharing is nobody's, not yours, not mine. This world enslaves, frightens and dares; it's for the intelligent, far from the sublime.*

Spirit 4.–*You left Eden, the promised place, the horn of abundance, the garden of love, tranquility and peace. Everything was wide open... nothing hidden. Everything in order, never empty; perennial flowers... under the gentle breeze.*

What are they saying there was Eden? Is Eden a symbol of a conditional state of life?

Spirit 3.–[The global spirit] *You came out of your role, giving up your life in Paradise; you chose a mind of your own. What a pity you ruined everything, you took a chance and threw your dice, preferring fate, good and evil.*

Spirit 2.–*The awareness of your future is out of your sight, for a blind man cannot see beyond his nose. Your thoughts, once clear, have doubts, and your darkened reasoning is flawed and slight. A blind man can only see what is nearby; through the fog, your wisdom has no influence.*

Spirit 4.–*Circumstances, jungle of conditions, tall treetops, cognitions, countless choices and then some riddles of reality numbs your mind. The Attributes that made man before, now leave him cold; Ran. Yes, blind man, you chose reality, it seems; materialism is the reality of your dreams.*

Spirit 1.–*Look, a blind man lost in this world cannot find his way back to paradise; for he faces countless options. He spins in puzzle mazes; he swirls in permutations of choice, its prizes and passages. He's lost without a trace.*

Spirit 3.–*Humans have a myriad of thoughts and beliefs, pieces scattered in their minds. Deities with equal potency fly over your brief reasoning and abundant beliefs of all kinds. How can you repair the cracks? The dichotomy of existence, the obvious gap that never fits between matter and spirit, lives from that day on.*

Spirit 2.–*Although people are different, the origin is one; the common attributes of individuals, selfishness, envy and hatred, today. A weak plan for each of us is always in dispute, like a distorted plot in the daily debate.*

Spirit 4.–*How sad is the history of man? He traded security for nothing true. It was by knowledge, by a kiss, in ignorance, and sank with you. How sad this story is, a dark long night? The man thinks he knows it, but he doesn't want to see. His mind wonders, he is no longer bright, blind in a forest, crashing into trees. Sad story for everyone and for you.*

Spirit 1.–*Isolated individuals gain attributes in the game of life: Greed, Hate, Greed, Ambition beyond; but they do not respect brotherhood. Every man is a number, a distant face, no longer a soul, he is a resource, a bond, a client to exploit without remorse.*

Spirit 3.–*Deception, the deceiver deceives, is the game. It is leaning his goal? The powerful perception that ends justify their means. Priority over your health, a plot to get more wealth.*

Spirit 2.–*The blind, confused, a lone wolf looks for prey; hypocrisy by hand, sadly profuse having is better than being an honest person of loving ritual: A man of thoughts, kind, spiritual.*

Spirit 1.–*The fallacy is to gather richness beyond your need to live well, if you know that matter stays on this side. Even your body does not stoke the secret of the blessing of death; because it also leaves, as the years go by, day by day.*

Spirit 4.–*The way is from the material to the spiritual: Two dimensions live in one space. And in this space lies all the visible and tangible and all the invisible and intangible–without interference. And at the level of your consciousness, each has a point where your mind connects your soul with the global spirit. And distance and closeness, such as perception and conception, are the same. Two dimensions and you live in both.*

Spirit 2.–[The global spirit] *The ego falls in love with greed, a beautiful goddess; and seductive Venus traps his mind with material desires. He loves lewdly needed because he lost his mind, his deductive logic, in the lust of wealth, fame and power he aspires to have.*

Spirit 4.–[the global spirit]. *Flames of ambition and greed burn your being from the inside out. The passion of having everything you can, irresistible forces embrace you, feed you; and then envy and selfishness come to caress your ego wherever you are.*

Spirit 3.–[The Man] *And so, the oneness of where I came from has long since gone; I have no way back. The way to Eden, Paradise covered in greed, clothed in shame; it hides beneath our solitary track. How sad is the story; is sad!*

Spirit 1.–*How sad it is, how sad: My selfishness leads me to drift; it makes me think it is all about me. Power and wealth are my only work dependent on what I do every day. No one can have anything; it's all for me. How sad a man is as you read in history! He doesn't care for the others' needs.*

Spirit 4.–[The global spirit] *Greed, your lover, charming and sweet, a passionate lover burning your soul, kissing your ambitions with lust. And murmuring comes to fulfill thy destiny; and you take everything without thinking, without inhibitions.*

Spirit 2.–[The man] *The door I entered is still here, I touch it; I see it there. I locked it myself on the way out. I can't come in now.*

The global spirit.–*There is a door is inside of you, your feelings rusty and enclosed, but waiting to open it.*

The man.–*But, I have no courage to open it with the code, the old key? It doesn't fit; it's for all of us at once, not just for me. You, them?*

Spirit 1.–[The global spirit] *The key? It's a simple act–a decision of your conscience. Yes, it is, and you'll know when you open the benign gate of Eden and see its interior. You will see its goodness, its freshness, the garden of power, its clarity. But that garden is here on earth, where humans live.*

Spirit 3.–[The Man] *O my God! It's all hard now, yes, isn't it? A simple commitment to change; I'm at the door, but I can't get through. Material possessions won't let me in; I keep fighting with my envy and revenge. Oh, my God! Please have* one class of us.

Spirit 2.–*You, man, your ego is not yet clean. You have greater sins to cleanse; therefore, you cannot enter my dominion: The sphere of peace you have never seen, the glory of Love you need.*

Spirit 1.–*Ignorant man What part you do not understand? Cleanse your ego and mind from prejudices you've twisted since early days, those you exchange for power and wealth when you find them.*

Spirit 4.–[The Man] *And what should I give up?*

[And the global spirit]

Spirit global.–*It is your AGHAPEE: The attributes of the inner self that come to numb us all, yes, you and me.*

Spirit 3.–*AGHAPEE: Ambition does not let you be; greed makes you want more and more. Greed urges the wealth you worship. The hate that eats your soul; the ugly attitude that kills Love. Avarice is your insatiable desires to have more. Prejudice is the irrationality that creeps in you. Envy makes you want the well-being of others. And egotism, the selfishness that fuels your self-importance. This kills your chance and don't dare take care of and share.*

Spirit 1.–[The choir sings]: *AGHAPEE, AGHAPEE: The snake that enchants you with its singing, its spell, fatal elixir; it is already in you. You're lost; change and let it go.*

Spirit 2.–*Give up your AGHAPEE; it's your chance. Now you know the code; kill the AGHAPEE, it's your way back; your choice is a righteous path, but it can be a promise you might not make.*

Spirit 4.–[The man]: *Will I save myself the day I kill my AGHAPEE?*

The global spirit.–*I will be you and you will be me. Your being will vibrate with the frequency of love. Your thoughts will be innate, and there will be no crime. We will meet at synergy the plane of wisdom and I'll see your soul through your thoughts. You'll not be crazy anymore, and you'll see what you didn't get.*

Spirit 3.–*You saw when you were blind. Now you will see your horizons and beyond; there will be no worries to found. Happiness will be your greatest bond, sharing your love with a synergy of trust. And you'll be a new individual. And when humans do that, they will live happily with each other, relatives, father and mother; and everyone attending to each other and sharing each other's love; in oneness with Universal Love.*

Spirit 1.—*So even if you use material things, you will be the essence of a pure being. Your soul will have no anchors or bindings to earthly material objects, or materialism. You will have no more materialistic themes, or the attributes and lies of AGHAPEE. Then you are with me, and I am within you for your sake; without distinctions or sadness. But your mood changes and you will finally enter oneness—the state of the order of harmony of existence; stable state of satisfaction, conformity and gratitude.*

Ego-Spirit.—*I am your ego, and AGHAPEE are my seven protective attributes that guide me to sin, but I have free will and I can do what I chose.*

The ego-spirit throws the letters to the ground. Bright sparks come out of the letters when they hit the ground, and the stage darkens for a few seconds, and then the lights come back. The spirit sitting in the chair vibrates and bursts into flames; and a cloud of smoke envelops him; and when the smoke rises, the spirit is gone. The seven dancing spirits kneel and lift the chair offstage. And on all four hanging screens, the ego-spirit appears and says.

The ego-spirit.—*The seven letters of AGHAPEE broke on the floor. I broke my attachment to material things, issues, and materialism; I am free at last.*

Wow, it was a fantastic job, wasn't it? Humans may choose the best. What I take from all this is that, yes, we are beings of light, spirits; our souls send everything we do. The body, and its actions, is the part that places the human in the material dimension. The rest is spiritual; so, humans are not materials. And our ego is the bond with materialism, making human materialistic. In addition, the seven attitudes of the ego prevent us from achieving the harmony of the universe—uniqueness. The Guide awaits the response from the public.

Keta.—*We will look for each other while we are on our missions on earth as soon as we enter a human body. We know that our spiritual attributes while we are within a human body. The power of our minds will alter conditions and circumstances and unite us on earth.*

Everyone agrees on his thoughts, saying:
Yes, that's right.

Guide.–*The two spirits–Cenia and Keta–highlight that spirits are part of a supreme spirit; and this spirit fills the universe. They also show the audience what spirits do.*

The stage darkens; a bright lightning illuminates the stage and a loud explosion shakes the theater. The lights come back on a few seconds later; three spirits remain on the platform of the exit station. The date is Tuesday, February 13, 1990. We have a lot of fireworks on this platform. Cenia gets up and says.

Cenia.–Two spirits remain; Keta and Tzzs left, passed their turning points. establish Everyone answered.

Oh, yes, those spirits left, now; they may be now establishing functions for material performance on their receiver.

Oldie.–*For the next period, we will all go through our turning points. It's funny that we maintain omniscience, but it's not clear which recipient we're entering. Human DNA is a material biological factor; and the spirits work with it. We, not you, know, but you don't guess what spirit you get. That is one mystery of mortality. But it's good you think we'll be together after that instance.*

The stage darkens; I hear a loud explosion, and I see bright glows one after the other. The lights come on. There's only one spirit left at the exit station, Cenia.

Thursday, February 22, 1990.

Cenia.–*Oldie left. Well, dear audience, this is it, I'll soon see you on the other side, on your side, earth.*

I hear another loud explosion; I see a bright glow, again. The lights come on. The last spirit of this group has left the station.

Saturday, March 3, 1990.

I wonder where Bochar is. I know he's still somewhere at an exit station. Bochar is part of this group even though it is not to work with in a human embryo. Maybe we'll discover later.

Elucidation of concepts.

I don't understand what happens when spirits leave the station. I realize the public didn't either. We need to concepts.; we deserve an explanation of what's going on. Lets hope the spirits tell us. Here comes the guide. The guide arrives at the podium and speaks to the public.

Guide.—*The audience can see and listen to the spirits in this theater tonight. But also, people, perhaps, didn't understand the details and or the meaning of what just happened. We've completed the five exits you saw, but you may wonder what's going on at that instant.*

Sexy.—*You read doubts in your minds. I know it's hard to eradicate the beliefs that live in their minds for years. Spirits and humans live in different worlds, or separate dimensions. But the journeys of spirits to human bodies are a reality that no one has told humans. Perhaps now is the time to expose human minds to the intention of creation and the purpose of the life cycles. But for this time, spirits and souls in four bodies coexist in the same dimension in this theater. Perhaps a public forum on this matter will help clarify the theory; and you, the reader and the audience in your mind, take part with questions.*

The guide didn't have to wait long, maybe a part of a second. Auras shine on people's heads and illuminate the audience's side in the theater. The energy field in the theater rises to a level that humans have never had; but spirits capture him instantly. Who wouldn't have an interest in learning the true story of their inner self? The excitement of the audience was obvious; and the energy of the field slides to fill the theater. The glare overflows the theater. I can see it from the space above the ceiling. The screens show a spectacular view.

Person C.—*How does a spiritual inflection work in matter?*

The Guide points to the scenario where the beams of light shine on the front screens right and left; screens instantly display images or graphic diagrams of fertilization.

Guide.—*Any event that occurs now depends on the events that occurred; otherwise the new event does not occur. Energy is the spirit of existence; and fills the space of the universe and all the dimensions within it. Robert and Sexis are back to talk to you. Robert, could you answer the first question? Sexis, please help and complement the answer.*

Robert.—*The moment a sperm fertilizes an egg, the dimensions of spirits and matter merge into the zygote; and inflection happens. A molecule of the global spirit enters. Fusion begins at the subatomic–quantum–level of sperm and egg. The interaction changes in a force field in the zygote. The force field grows in and out of the zygote; produces electric shocks; and either generates electrical and or electromagnetic work, inside* *and outside the egg. The electromagnetic force field drags the spirit into the zygote. In simple words, a molecule of the global spirit inflects in the human zygote. You know that a molecule is the smallest part that keeps the properties of the substance from which it comes. Therefore, a spirit molecule has all the attributes of the global spirit. After fertilization, the female body changes amid the heat of the body's reaction; symptoms such as dizziness, cravings, vomiting and more. Electric currents flow into the cells that deploy from the zygote, and even in the brain cell of the emerging embryo, this action disturbs the mother's body.*

Robert gestures Sexis with his hand to contribute to the speech.

Sexy.—*The spirit enters matter when a sperm pierces the vitellin membrane and plasma membrane that covers the female egg. This is when the spirit merges with the sperm and egg that forms the zygote. Now the spirit is in the body, and it becomes the soul of the zygote. Electric shocks spread through the membrane of the egg; and the microvilli extends to hug the sperm that penetrates the egg at that instant. And then the spirit animates the zygote. Now the human zygote has a soul, and the soul manages the life of a being in progress. This moment is the point of no return—for the mystery of life or the composition of a dual being, spirit and matter—and they achieve an inflection. The embryo germinates just after, with its common reactions. Electrical signals flow through all neurons in the embryo in a quantum state.*

Robert.—*The soul begins functions by organizing the sections of the brain. There is still no human; and it's all in a relative sub-atomic stage. There is no way to be human yet; there are only chemical reactions and the exchange of electrical energy. The soul installs all human functions in the brain. But it takes days, or weeks, to organize the structure of the soul in the zygote, and to define the dual human.*

Sexy.—*The spirit suffers a reduction of its attributes by transforming into a soul. It loses omnipresence and omnipotence; and loses most omniscience; when it stays in the zygote. Souls keep experiences they gained in previous missions, such as waves; vibrations that excite them. They keep waves in their minds; and when these vibrations or waves appear, they can stimulate the mind. The mind assigns the functions, upper and lower, to the brain and the objectives of the driving soul. It is also likely they setup paranormal functions of the spirit in the neurons;*

but that depends on the number of neurons activated in the human brain. For now, we must wait.

Someone in the public.–*Zygotes become human, when?*

Whoever asked this question must be a lawyer or politician looking for a definition.

Robert.–*Great question!*

He pauses and then says.

Robert.–*Your question concern issues regarding abortion, and criminal action, a moral issue for humans; but we do not want to make this dialogue a court of human laws. The love of spirits is life, and life is love for humans; so, what destroys life destroys love, and that can be criminal in the sense of human laws. Besides, humans' souls have conscience and ego, and the ego has freedom of choice–the right to choose. So, spirits do not interfere your volition, it's your sacred right–free will.*

Thus, according to the laws of existence, which grant humans the freedom of choice, to choose their thoughts, decisions and actions, just remember that we cannot create or destroyed.

Robert stops again and adds.

–ego and conscience. The soul has an important function called mind, which both components use. These two components and the mind embed in the body making up a dual human. But the soul and the body do not fuse into one being, they only work together. A spirit is the essence of the existence; the soul is the core, the essence of something or someone. The soul maintains the life force of the spirit and animates the inner self of the human. Spirit and soul are the same, and the soul, or the spirit, and the human body work together in the same mission, life. The distinction between spirit and soul is in freedom of action. All spirits are free in the spirit dimension. They have all three attributes–when they are there; omniscience–omnipotence; and omnipresence. Besides, they have absolute love when they are in their world. The soul is a spirit with reduced attributes. The soul is not omnipresent; it is not omnipotent; and it's not omniscient. Therefore, a spirit that enters a human zygote loses its omniscience; but receives the ability to gain knowledge through learning; loses its ability to be in multiple places simultaneously; and loses its power to do everything possible when lodged in a human body. But souls can learn from omniscience through their thinking, reasoning, and

meditating skills. The mind connects the soul with the global spirit and with any free spirit in its dimension. Similarly, spirit and any spirit, part of the global spirit, can connect with a soul through the mind on certain occasions.

Sexis.—*Thus, a soul and a body merge to work as a unit; but souls maintain the nature of spirits, identity and integrity. The soul and the body belong to different dimensions and do not become one, for now. Then the spirit becomes a soul, a limited spirit, when it is in a body of a living creature. The human body is a living matter, just like that of any other inferior species. Without a mind, the body is not of a human; but when the functions of the mind become operational, the body and mind become a dual human.*

Robert.—*The chronology of human embryo development shows that the mind sets the brain between the ninth and sixteenth week; after the heart, vision and auditory functions develop. Therefore, the mind sets the five senses first before the reasoning role of the mind. While the soul is busy establishing functions in the neurons of the body, the mind works on the neurons of the brain simultaneously. The mind's ability to think comes after brain neurons are functional and active; that is around the 16th week of embryonic development. The spirit establishes the mind, the components and the functions during this period. When the embryo first learns of its surroundings, its conscious life begins as a living creature; but when it learns of presence and functions, human life begins as a dual human. [28] You can find in the "Internet" world opinions, and or views about when an embryo becomes a human; the consciousness of humans.*

Gee! I can't believe what I'm hearing. This is impossible! They fuse the concept of inflection with knowledge of human biology on earth. They debunk certain beliefs of the human genesis. Experts in human biology should study this theory and offer their feedback. The guide plays on the podium and looking at the audience; she says.

Guide.—*This is a complicated mess! Well, you've heard a colossal discourse of spiritual inflection. I will now make observations. We cannot create or destroy the spirit (energy) or the body (matter); this implies that*

---

[28] Christof Koch, Scientific America, Road to Awareness, https://www.scientific american.com/article/when-does-consciousness-arise, September 1, 2009/

humans do not destroy other humans, they cannot. They mean that living creatures never die, and no one kills them. When a creature dies, it loses its physical presence in the material world; And nothing else. Here, it no longer has life, nor does it share or care for others. This is a tragedy for the whole universe. The abrupt death of a living creature speeds up the separation of its spirit from the body; that ends its tenure. An abrupt end to life puts an end to the opportunities that appear in life; these actions deny the concept of the preservation of life in the universe. Therefore, the destruction of a living creature puts an end to that living creature; and suppresses its contributions to humanity.

For existence there is no destruction; its balance. Is this true? For example, when the world overcrowds and cannot maintain overpopulation, the environment triggers conditions to clean up the situation. A famine can exterminate excess, and the environment sets a new balance. Any environment only takes creatures satisfied with, or adapting to, their conditions. This is a way to purge the weak, the least capable. It is a natural way to deprive creatures. The strongest should not exploit or take advantage of the least capable, but help them remedy their situation. This is how existence protects life-an environment keeps the living creatures it can support.

The curtains close, the stage darkens; but in the background the music continues, while the spirits change the stage, quickly.

People say *what goes up comes down or what goes around comes back around,* and these intuitive thoughts are, perhaps, true. In the dimension of spirits, both the logical and the logical are possible. Why not? The evidence of the last statement lives on in the human imagination, especially of children and the minds of the elderly who delve into illusions, delusions and or fantasies. Humans call children visions products of creative imagination, but they call the stories greater products of senility, dementia, etc. But is this trial right or wrong? Maybe in the cases of children and the elderly their imaginations take advantage of the omniscience only of existence. So, every thought or concept is possible and true. It seems true, like strange dreams we have during our sleep. The logical explanation is that our minds, or souls, wind out of the body into the dimension of spirits, where all concepts are possible. Our minds conceive nothing beyond the omniscience of existence. No knowledge is outside of existence; therefore, all gnosis and or concepts must come from existence. Let's think about it. There is consensus, and evidence, that humans carry a soul, and a mind within to manage their thoughts, decisions, and actions. But neither the soul, nor the mind, its thoughts or decisions, are material. No, they're not; they are invisible and intangible; they are spiritual. Regarding spirits, they are a concern, and they must explain how spirits enter living creatures and become their souls with an independent controlling mind.

In the physical world of humans, we hope that–if something is observable–it must have a history a life and an end. This concept is further supported by the law of cause and effect. It is a fundamental premise for any hypothesis or theory about spirits. Humans observe their minds in action, the feelings and emotions of consciences, and the actions of the ego. But all this happens at a stage of spiritual functions, which humans cannot see or touch. This, by itself, is a strong proof that humans are not material beings, but spiritual innate beings. If humans have a soul, a mind, a consciousness and an ego, a human experience, then they must find out where these elements come from. We must answer the question; how these elements enter a human egg?

But spirits move on to the world of humans at the time of egg fertilization, neither before nor after fertilization. Why so much precision? Well, no, not so much for accuracy as the causal sequence of the process that we can't alter or delay. The inflection cannot take place before fertilization because there is no room available for the spirit to stay. On the one hand, the omnipresence of the spirit of existence commands it be present in all that exists and what that exists, mainly matter with volume and takes up space. So being matter the sperm and the egg by the omnipresence of the global spirit actually already fills these two elements. Spirits cannot enter later because the zygote cell–the fertilized egg–slashes to start sperm preparation for several hours; the fusion of the sperm nucleus and egg begins. Therefore, the spirit enters a moment before the zygote seals itself, or before beginning sperm preparation.[29]

If humans understand the above, then they can understand why and what spirits expect at the exit station. The spirit's energy that enters the egg expects this moment to incorporate into the oocytes. Electric currents and discharges that occur during the fertilization process show the action of the incoming spirit. The spirit is part of the fertilization process. When the oocyte establishes, the spirit begins the installation of the mind and the configuration of the brain. The final steps of human sperm and egg fusion and prenatal embryo development could not work if they exclude the mind, conscience and ego; the three main elements of his soul.

Greek mythology created a half-human and half-horse creature, the *centaurs;* centaurs have the torso, head and arms of a man and the body of a horse with its four legs. Centaurs represent animal strength and human abilities. Greek fantasies were not crazy. Well, humans are half spirit and half matter, a soul (mind) and an animal body. One half is invisible and intangible, and the other half is visible and tangible. Human thoughts, emotions, feelings, come from the dimensions of spirits, and physical actions belong to the material dimension. So, humans are "mentaurs." This duality proves the coexistence of the two dimensions of spirits and matter.

---

[29] https://en.wikipedia.org/wiki/Human_fertilization

CHAPTER 4

The birth of Souls

Abstract

6: Dawn

Light always comes with every sunrise; and every birth and death bring tears. Life begins with tears and joy and the glory of birth obscures the mother's agony and pain. Life ends with pain and sadness, but its departure truly restores the satisfaction and joy of eternal peace. The baby attracts a new soul to this material world, as well as a new body and new intelligence will interact with the real world. Let us not fail to see the baby's soul and all the attributes of the spirit that is lodged in his body. Because that spirit manages the life of the new human being from birth to death. Mind, Ego and Conscience are the components of the new soul—intangible and invisible. But humans only see the actions of the material body of the new beings and not the reality of their inner self—their real beings. True, all humans are born the same way, but they are not the same. The whole humanity makes equality or inequality at the will of their egos' tastes, preferences and whims.

Dual beings are born.

Saturday, February 3, 1990. We're eleven days away from Valentine's Day, the feast of love. People change their moods and attitude. People talk about love, as if they felt it for someone, parents, relatives, friends, and human companions. They send flowers to each other; email cards written with sentimental, precious words. The world would change if people were like this all the time. Either way, we're back in the old theater, that creepy theater. The curtains open. I see four window screens in space, two behind the stage; one front and left of the stage and one forward and right of the stage; placed them for the convenience of the public. The stage is dark; and the back screens on the stage light up, showing galaxies in space.

Spirits don't count hours, minutes, or seconds in their world. They don't care about time; it's infinite. Spirits do not have a waiting time; they have only existence, and that is also infinite. Therefore, they may delay their departure by days, weeks, months, or years in mortality; Never mind.

Wait, the guiding spirit returns.

Guide.—*I have good news for you. The global spirit has granted 'contact attributes' besides the ability to see and hear from this pace forward. So now humans and spirits can interact at will, but in this theater, on stage and in the audience, just for tonight.*

Let us think. What would it be like if we could see, touch, converse with the spirits, what benefit would humans have? Let's see; the stage illuminates with flesh color and on the ground small points of light move in a random pattern. A group of spirits flows from the front, left and right of the stage, simulating a current and mixing into a whirlpool. Spirits and dots of light suggest chaotic and desperate competition. A spirit playing the role of a human egg dances inside a crystal bubble in the center. The dancers play the role of sperm, chasing the egg and trying to penetrate the crystal bubble. After so many attempts, a sperm finds a port, penetrates the bubble and hugs the egg. This is ballet, Spring of Life, which is when a spirit merges with an egg. It is the mystery of inflection, when the soul, sperm and egg are mixed to form a zygote. The lights go out and the stage darkens, but repeated flashes of bright lights and black lights emphasize jubilation. When a spirit exhausted on the ground, its dancing ends. The egg still dances in the bubble, but now under the power of the soul in the zygote. Lights flash on stage. Bright lights flashing quickly illuminate several parts of the audience. The stage and the audience darkened. The four screens light up at once and as this happens the egg walks to the front center of the stage, radiating its light. The wind howls as if it came from deep canyons; meanwhile, the egg recites in a sweet, tender voice.

The ovum–the soul.

The light breaks at dawn,
illuminating with splendor,
and in the reality shown
of a being's life in its candor,
the innocence of love,
begins a life cycle and flows
with death:
Matter or spirit, a lighted candle,
travel alone in a dark depth
of a current they must handle.

In the dark scenario the spirits rise like lit candles; half slowly enter the stage from the left and half come from the right.

Guide.–*You have attributes of the global spirit; so, you can touch, hear and see the spirits in their spiritual dimension. But you won't see your soul in your material being, not for now, unfortunately. I advise you not to use these powers on another person or people sitting around you; there are earthly policemen and lawyers waiting in the lobby.*

The guide returns, but now, the audience can see the spirit of the guide; dressed in white with a bright halo over his head. Says.

Guide.–*They are now in spiritual and material dimensions, and we communicate with you in their normal earthly form.*

She pauses.

—The dimensions of spirits and matter are relative, opposite and separate, although they occupy the same space. One is pure energy and the other is pure matter. Existence tries to merge them, as we are doing now. The silhouettes you see on stage and walk in the audience are spirits that carry out the tasks of their mission. They are always happy to take part and share—they do not resent, deny, or rebel against their duties. Please do not grope, caress or pinch the spirits; the discharge of energy into your body can damage your brains. Male and female ushers are spirits that serve while the show is taking place. If you need to go out into the lobby, raise a hand; and think because you want to go to the lobby, but don't say what you will do there. If they leave, a spirit will cancel its power and reset it when they return to these built-in dimensions. So, let's move on.

Victor is born in Manhattan, New York.

The theater lights are off, but the four window screens light up, showing the planet earth as seen from a satellite. They focus on the city and then the streets, it's New York City, on Manhattan Island. In the dark background of the stage, many human figures eagerly move through the streets, walking along the sidewalks on either side, dressed in transparent white, looking around. They're spirits wandering the city.

Monday, October 29, 1990.

Guide.—*We all travel backward in space and time to New York City. It was at the end of 1990; approximately nine months after that day of inflection of those spirits.*

The guide walks to the front center of the stage and says.

Guide.—*Remember that spirits and humans share the same space, even though they are in two dimensions. There, humans and spirits coexist and interact. Spirits appear and disappear at will and walk, or move through material objects and human bodies. Spirits are like radio frequencies; and so, they can pass through material things. It is the way both entities coexist in the same space.*

The music continues; and the spirits are jovial and happy, performing a ballet or jazz dance in perfect choreographic performance on stage. Their silhouettes are clear through their garments. They finish the dance, and the theater darkens; the screen on stage left turns off. I hear a roar, like a thunderstorm.

The curtains close. The lights come out on stage. Carol Richland, a wealthy woman, is about to have a baby in a private delivery room at an expensive hospital on First Avenue, New York. The obstetrician, Dr. Francis Gentile, enters the room dressed and ready to attend the delivery. Carol's husband followed the doctor a few steps back; wears a surgical green suit. Two nurses, Martha and Janet, in the room are ready to help Dr. Gentile. Relatives try to look through a large window on the wall of the room. The back screens of the stage show views of what is happening inside the surgery room simultaneously.

Carol screams in pain, and cries in a trembling voice.

Carol.—*Is my baby coming, doctor, is it coming out, doctor, doctor?*

Janet.—*Breathe, Mrs. Richland, please breathe... push, push hard, breathe, push; breathe, push.*

She wipes Carol's forehead.

Martha whispers Dr. Gentile.

Martha.—*The scanner shows that the baby is sideways; it is a large child.*

Mr. Richland.—*Dr. Can you do anything? Carol's in pain... do you want me to call another doctor, who may know what to do?*

The arrogance of the rich appears; they think they can buy anything with their money. They are unaware that in the processes of birth, life and death, everyone is the same. Dr. Gentile does not respond and ignores Mr. Richland. Despair is increasing with every second, and Mr. Richland can't stand the situation and goes to the waiting room.

Ariel, the spirit lodged in the body that once had all its powers in its dimension, now only has powers reduced to virtually nothing—there is nothing it can do, and shouts in his mind.

Ariel.—*I will get out of here; this baby will fail and my mission will perish; and I will have to go back to my dimension—I need not let this happen.*

The mission of the spirits is to protect and promote life in the universe, it is their automatic reaction. Nurses run from the birth bed to the cabinets, Dr. Gentile sweats, and Carol cries; the nurses run back from the cabinets to the delivery bed. There are problems, you feel it in the space.

Carol.–*It doesn't matter if I die Dr. save my baby, please... save my baby.*

I'm sure Carol has a sincere desire. That desire is a sign that Carol sends to the dimension of spirits; as spirits say, it passes. Answers come back as miracles, unexpected help.

Ariel.–*I have to get out of here immediately; I have to force my situation right now. I must save the baby and my mission on earth.*

Martha.–*Doctor, do I push the baby–his shoulder–to align him?*

Time is running out, baby's not moving, still sideways.

Dr. Gentile.–*Yes, please, quick–Martha, do it to the account 1, 2, 3; I will push its knees to the right; push your shoulder to the left, now, 1, 2, 3.*

The situation is dire, life and death. They push, they wait.

–Martha, let's do it again, 1, 2, 3.

They push and wait. The baby turns, aligns head down.

–I see the crown, well. Let's do it one more time, let's push, 1, 2, 3.

They wait.

Janet.–*Mrs. Richland, please breathe, please follow me and push down when I tell you.*

Carol watches the efforts of Dr. and Martha.

–Carol, push, push, push.

Mr. Richland.–*Dr., is it coming out, is it going to come out? Do something, for God's sake, do something.*

Carol.–*Is my baby coming out, is it coming out? O my God, let him live; let me die.*

Silence is deep in the delivery rooms and waits. Carol is in severe pain. A cloak of uncertainties covers frightened minds.

Ariel.–*There is nothing more this Dr. can do. I'll get the baby's body out by pulling his legs.*

Ariel can't leave the baby's body. But will it be too late? The baby doesn't move.

Janet.–*Dr., Dr., Mrs. Richland is turning blue.*

Martha looks at the ultrasound scanner, she screams.

Martha.–*Dr. the baby does not move; we are losing it; we are losing it.*

Dr. Gentile. *Let's keep pushing Martha; let's keep pushing.*

Ariel.–*What's going on? I can't get out; I can't get out.*

Dr. Gentile leaves the room, walks outside, and tells Mr. Richland and other relatives.

Dr. Gentile.–*We have to operate as an emergency to save the baby. Mr. Richland, I need your consent to operate. The head nurse will bring the authorization form.*

Mr. Richland shakes his head in acceptance; the doctor returns quickly. Meanwhile, another spirit watching the episode jumps into Carol's mind, causing her to contract her muscles by pulling back the baby as Ariel intended. Ariel blows air into Carol's uterus and presses her belly to push the baby's feet; The other spirit says.

–Ariel, I will induce several strong contractions of Carol's mid section muscles.

As washed away by a strong current, the baby slid out. This happens in a millisecond (in earthly time). As she prepares operating tools in a hurry, Martha sees the baby's head coming out, and screams.

Martha.–*The baby is coming out; Dr. Gentile, the baby's coming out.*

The Dr. rushes in and approaches the bed, sees the baby coming out by himself; the baby trembles a little, and once out, cries, but still attached to the mother's womb. Martha takes the baby out and faints. Ariel, in light, shines on the baby. Ariel's energy alters the force field of gravity and the baby floats to the edge and the spirit holds him in the birth bed. Janet returns to the room to help, screams at full throttle.

Janet.–*MIRACLE!*

Janet faints; The two nurses passed out. No one pays attention to Carol; she doesn't move: she seems to have fainted after breathing and pushing so hard so often before. Dr. Gentile quickly takes and lifts the baby and continues her work. But she doesn't pay attention to the nurses on the floor.

Dr. Gentile.–*Janet, bring the sheets and the warm blanket, quickly.*

As he looks at the other spirit, Ariel thinks.

Ariel.–Thank you, Lucius.

The other spirit, Lucius, disappears at that moment. Outside the room, relatives, and Mr. Richland screams, looking through the glass window.

Yes, yes... THANK YOU, GOD... The baby's alive.

Relatives were thinking about the baby; maybe, that's because they don't know about Carol's situation. The situation is difficult for Dr. Gentile; now knows of Carol's situation and must inform Mr. Richland. After a few minutes, she leaves the room, serenely but sadly, says.

Dr. Gentile.–*The baby is fine; but we lost his mother, I'm sorry. The baby is a child; he's the son of a miracle.*

Dr. Gentile walks down the long aisle with her head down. Maybe she's studying the case, but the baby's situation in Carol's uterus caused the outcome. Mr. Richland and the relatives break down in tears, hugging each other. A few minutes later, Mr. Richland regains his composure, cleans his eyes and says.

Mr. Richland.–*I am deeply hurt and sad about losing my wife, Carol, and I thank her for the son she gave me. This baby is the product of her courage, and it is worth the price of her love and life. She didn't leave us in vain. That's why I will be indebted to her all my life. The baby was her victory, so I'll call him, Victor Richland.*

The curtains close; the audience hears the crying in the waiting room. The lights go out; the theater is dark. And from the dark, the guide explains.

Guide.–*We understand the feelings of sadness. But humans conform to the conditions and circumstances of this world. Today, we have witnessed a miracle on earth; but in our spirit dimension, we have no miracles. What is a miracle? It is an event that occurs when the expectation of its success is almost zero. It is a law of existence that "death happens for a new life to begin."*

Two spirits float through the delivery room, speaking.

Spirit 1.–*Did you see all that? Here they converged past, present and future actions. These two spirits came to rescue the baby just in time, while existence decided: the mother or the baby.*

Spirit 2.–*Yes! The result was the mother's last wish for help; and they heard it in the spiritual dimension. The second spirit that came to help is the spirit of Mrs. Richland leaving her body. For the Richland family, their pain and happiness fused simultaneously. The path of life changed for the baby because of the death of his mother. Now, everyone's hopes depend on the future of the newborn baby she left behind.*

Spirit 1.–*For us, the spirits, what happened is a normal fact of existence: someone dies so others can live. The mother's liberated spirit returns to our dimension when Mrs. Richland reaches her rigor mortis. And the soul embedded in the baby begins his journey; now he is ready to freely act.*

Spirit 2.–*That is the life cycle, a ring that never closes; the relationship resolves its difference in infinity. How can humans understand exact measurements, the circumference (the longing) and the diameter (the efforts) of a (animated) circle, generate the singularity called infinite? Here we are in only half the circle of life. Because if we try to unite birth and death in a circle, we can't make them match at one point. Maybe it's because the difference is always infinite. And infinity is the global spirit and infinite existence,*

Truly, the infinite existence has a spirit (its energy) that is infinite. Existence and its spirit are omnipresent, omnipotent, and omniscient. The cycles of life are infinite, although the life of *mentaurs*, about one hundred years, can only close their effort and longing in the infinity of existence. At that point the relationship is one, and only one, for the life cycles of all living beings.

The half circle of life.

Just like before, two spirits, A&B, dance; but this time, they pass each other, back and forth, a ball; five or more spirits dance alone, trying to intercept the ball. It's a strange dance; and what this dance represents.

Spirit A appears on the left front window screen.

Spirit A. –

> *If you are not, perhaps you will,*
> *and if you are perhaps, you will not.*
> *Go on, live your life until you stay still*
> *in the cycle in which you are caught.*

Spirit A appears on the screen hanging over the stage on the right. Other spirits dance on the floor and stop when each spirit passes the ball.

Spirit B. –

> *Of what you see there is more unseen:*
> *Your life is only in between.*
> *What will begin will end,*
> *but what will end, may not begin:*
> *This is a law you cannot bend,*
> *the prize of eternity you cannot win:*
> *for living beings… for instance,*
> *it is half of a circle of existence.*

Spirit A. –

> *So, live your life to full extent;*
> *do not leave actions undone.*
> *Give until your heart is content;*
> *Share and care until you are gone.*

Spirit B. –

> *But, just remember this,*
> *when gone, you may not be back.*
> *And if you do, you will not be the same.*
> *Though life may be for you a bliss,*
> *meditate and keep your thoughts on track,*
> *but this half a cycle you cannot blame.*

Spirit A. –

> *Thoughts in actions near impossibility,*
> *a hope realized above its common thread;*
> *the effort done beyond one's own ability*
> *may return to life after one is dead.*

Spirit B receives the ball and throws it into the air for any spirit to take. One picks it up and leaves the stage, while the others chase him. While the spirit is eternal, the human body lives only once; spirits lodges in the zygote, but one at a time. They travel to the material dimension often; because its time is infinite.

Guide.—*People in the delivery room or waiting room cannot see the spirits. But the public in your mind can; they received the power to see and listen to the spirits.*

As the guide speaks, the silhouettes empty the stage, and the spirits perform a dance in the twilight of life and death, a few minutes long. The curtains close and the stage changes.

Moses is born in Santa Tecla, El Salvador.

Wednesday, November 7, 1990.

The curtains open. All four screens show calendars passing pages to one day in November. The lights go out on stage, followed by another rumble. Lightning lights up the stage. The screen on the right front of the stage comes on. Spirits dressed in transparent pastel garments dance as they change the stage. Two screens show planet Earth, as seen from a satellite; then they focus on the city of Santa Tecla, El Salvador, Central America. The screens show images of the neighborhood and focus on the streets. The screens go off, and you hear a loud sound like a thunderstorm. The lights return to the stage, and the screens show the corrugated zinc leaf roof of a debris house on the outskirts of the city. The screens then show the inside of that house full of scarcity, poverty and anguish, which its occupants call home. That debris house is typical of third world countries. In the background, an old radio plays music. Typical Salvadoran music comes from a local radio station, mixed with news. People dress and look like typical low-income farmworkers in poverty.

Juana (thirty-one years old) is lying on a homemade canvas stretcher covered with an old white sheet. Juana expects a baby. People are in a state of panic and despair in the house. Celia is not an old woman; she's only fifty, but she looks old and tired. That's probably because of the hard life she spends in poverty. Celia runs to find items that the midwife asked for, or needs. Esperanza (sixty-five) is one of the few native Salvadoran midwives in the city. Esperanza has given birth to hundreds of babies from rich and poor families in the area; she's well known. She says her mission is to bring new souls to this world, even if they do not pay her. She adds that when a spirit wandering around gets into a baby, it becomes the baby's soul. Esperanza says there is a great spirit from which all spirits come to earth. This global spirit told her, she says, that the equality of humans is not in the way they are born; not in the way of life, but in the right to receive equally the generosity of the universe. The universe equally shares everything it contains inside with all living creatures. She says that goodness will come when all selfish humans disappear from the earth, in time given; only those who recognize the great purpose and abide by it will remain with the global spirit, forever. This is a revelation, not a whimsical thought. It's the great truth that people don't understand; at least not yet.

Esperanza continues to work on Juana, giving orders to the rest. Two young girls, Maria (seven) and Isabel (fourteen), are waiting to help the midwife. All the people who care about Juana's welfare are here. Julio (thirty-two), Juana's husband, Emilio (fifty-two), José, Juana's father, two friends, and several neighbors are also here. Everyone waits outside the house, ready to help as they can. In the backyard, two elders are sitting in straight rocking chairs to back up high; they are Juana's grandfather, JesÃºs, (tata Chu, sixty-four), and Ma' Lina (sixty-two), the grandmother. Ma' Lina prays by following a rosary in her hands. Inside the room, the effigy of the Virgin Mary adorned with flowers is on a small table against the wall on the right, near the corner. Two tall, thick candles placed on both sides illuminate the effigy on the table. The place, although rustic, is humble.

People merged with nature, living with what nature generously provides them every day. Tears come out of my eyes; I feel like I'm still a human. That's the life of the poor, too far from the Richland's opulence in New York City. And I wonder, why is there so much difference in this world? I find no answers, except for the unheard-of selfishness of other humans. I note, however, that selfishness deeply engraved by levels on all social scales of the world (earth). Haunted humans are slaves to the ogre AGHAPEE who dominates their egos. People here in this house speak Spanish, but with the power of the universal spirit, we also listen in English. The screens at the front of the stage. Juana moans, sweats and screams.

Juana.—*ay, ay, ay, ay, ay, ay, ay. What the fuck, why did I get pregnant?*

Juana breathes and exhales, groaning like a marathon runner who has run many miles. Outside, at the front of the small house, a group of neighbors wait seating on folding chairs lined up along the wall, or standing to the right and left of that scrap-material house. This meeting is typical in slums in third countries. They're worried, curiously waiting for the baby. Life is the same for the poor and rich: we are born, we live, and we die.

Esperanza.—*Run, lazy, bring clean clothes to clean this woman. Bring some hot water.*

She referred to Juana, who just broke the fountain. On window screens, the translation of expressions in Spanish passes as they speak. A skinny dog, sitting by the door, looks surprised at the commotion, as flies fly over and around Juana's bed. Esperanza, she doesn't even wear gloves, and she coughs up the air–the situation is chaotic and unhealthy. Simultaneous executions flow in time on screens. Juana continues to moan and cry, sweating and cursing.

Esperanza.—*Run, come, get rid of these flies. Damn it, hurry. Bring a pan, put a towel on its bottom and pour some warm water. Damn it, hurry, lazy turtles.*

Juana.—*Oh, oh, oh, ay, ay, oh ay. I can't take it anymore.*

Esperanza.—*Breathe, Juana, push, breathe, push, stronger, damn it. The baby is coming out, pushing; pushes; Pushes. He's almost out.*

The baby comes out smoothly. Esperanza grabs the baby by the ankles, hangs his head down, and hits him on the buttocks with the palm of his hand, and the baby cries. The midwife says.

Hope.–*Son of a bitch! This baby is handsome; and he's got big balls, the son of a gang.*

People outside the house; relatives and neighbors hear the baby crying and say.

The people.–*The baby came out, just came out; God bless, the baby was born.*

Some murmur that the father is Vicente, the tailor of the "People's Tailoring"; others claim it is Camilo's owner of the "Nile dining room". Well, really, only Juana knows who. The spirit in the baby: Maybe the existence should shorten the pregnancy time to less than nine months. Maybe we can reconfigure the mind and establish its functions to require less time.[xxi]

Juana.–*Thank God this damn pain is over.*

Esperanza.–*He's a handsome boy, Juana; look, Ma' Lina.*

Grandpa.–*Ma' Lina, I saw him alive before he was born; I saw a little man... his name is Moses, like the one who freed the Israelites from slavery in Egypt...*

Esperanza cleans the baby, dries him with a piece of an old but clean dress; she dresses him in a hand-embroidered white dress, and delivers it to her grandfather, waiting in the backyard. Joseph, the grandpa, lifts the child to heaven, and aloud makes an offering.

Grandpa.–*Oh heavenly Father, here is Moses, who will make a pilgrimage to save his people. Tonight, we will celebrate your birth, Moses.*

Juana is still in bed, but from the room she screams at the top of her lungs.

Juana.–*You'll see this shitty, nagging brat, the spank I'll give him when he grows a little.*

Juana means she'll get even when the baby's a little older. Either way, everyone's happy getting ready for the party. Mary runs into the neighborhood announcing the birth of Moses. While Isabel carries the child and sings to him. In the late afternoon, the celebration began. Neighbors contribute food, help clean an area in the backyard for the dancing. Two guitarists and a marimba player tune their instruments and play. The party lasted until after midnight. The curtains of the theater close while the party is still going on. The stage lights go out.

Rex is born in Henderson, Nevada.

Friday, November 8, 1990.

The stage is dark, and we hear a rumble sound. Lightning illuminates the stage and audience for a few seconds. The theater continues dark, but the right screen at the front of the stage lights up, showing planet earth as seen from a satellite; then the image approaches the city of Las Vegas, Nevada. The screen focuses on the streets, the storefronts, the magnificent buildings, and the crowd rushes from one casino to another. Some spiritual silhouettes also walk on the sidewalks, but in the dimension of the spirits. The views of this booming, rich, and exciting city are splendid. The city doesn't look like Santa Tecla. The lighting is dazzling; there the money runs like water of a flowing river, and the enchanted people get there to spend it. That contrast with those streets of Santa Tecla, where poverty obscures its dirt streets. The scenery is different, a city full of light, people and life, a city of sin and play, a city for drinking and sexual relations. Maybe the streets have too much light for spirits. The view moves southeast and the Casinos-Hotel station appears on the screen.

The stage darkens again, and the front screens, left and right, of the stage light up. An intense energy field covers the theater; perhaps because of the large number of energetic spirits concentrate on stage, and in this building. In the stage background many spirits, in human figures, busily move, men and women, dressed as gambling people. Spirits dressed in transparent white garments make a choreographic ballet or a soft rock dance, while working the stage - silhouettes are transparent figures. The music is typical of the late nineties.

The stage opens its curtains, and the public sees a maternity ward at Henderson Hospital at 1050 W. Galleria Drive. Jim and Ryan brought Vicky into the emergency room and they're in the waiting room, talking about the lady in labor. They wait for the head nurse to return with the proper form to take their information. While they're talking in English.

You, the reader and the public can hear what they say in Spanish, because of the power they received from the global spirit.

Jim.—*You know? I almost left that lady alone in the lobby-hotel. I'm glad we brought her to the hospital. What's her name?*

Ryan.—*I don't know. She never said a word there, being alone, you know... she was about to give birth. What made you bring her to the hospital?*

Jim.—*I don't know. I saw her on the couch in the lobby, crying in pain, and when I saw her belly, I knew she was in labor. I checked my watch; it was 2:30 in the morning. I felt a strange shiver; my hands froze and then a heat, abnormal. At that moment, I felt the need to pick up that lady, take her in the car to the nearest hospital, to an emergency room. I'm glad you came back at that moment. I couldn't take her to any hospital. You had the car keys.*

Ryan.—*Yes, everything happens for something, those guys in the exchange box, they didn't want to cash my ticket, and I said, screw this crap I'll be back tomorrow.*

Jim.—*Well, we did what we had to do; let's get out of here.*

Yes, random events cause everything, but by the chains of activities and events that bring each current events. The baby's spirit in the mother's womb or the mother's spirit asked for help, and Jim's spirit answered the call. Ryan was late in the exchange box, and Jim had to wait long enough in the lobby.

When the head nurse returned with the hospital admission form, the two guys had left. In the delivery room, the doctor on duty, Jeff Spencer, asks the lady (Vicky). Everyone here speaks English, but you listen in Spanish.

Dr. Spencer.—*Excuse me madam, what is your name, who brought you to this emergency, do you have any relatives here with you?*

She is suffering, but slowly and in a weak voice, she says.

Vicky.—*My name is Vicky Martin from Los Angeles, California. I don't know who brought me here; a young man picked me up from the couch in the lobby-Hotel Station, Henderson, before passing out; I think he brought me.*

The nurse, Stephanie, went to the waiting room and came back, saying. There's no one, just the nurse on duty, on duty at night. She said the two young men who brought her in already left. While working in a hurry, assisted by a single night service nurse, the doctor says.

Dr. Spencer.—*It's okay. Vicky, relax.*
The doctor turns to Stephanie and says.
—*I wanted to ask them if they noticed blood on the couch where they picked it up at the casino. She's having trouble; I see in the scanner twin babies, but one is inactive, does not move. Stephanie, call Dr. Carson, tell Barbara, the head nurse, to prepare the surgery room for a sectional operation, C-section. We don't have time to waste.*

Meanwhile, in the lobby-Hotel Station, a man desperately searches for his wife; is asking the people still in the lobby, showing the picture of her. After more than an hour a woman cleaning the hotel passed through, with an obvious Latin accent speaking English, she told him.

The cleaning lady.—*Mr., Mr., I saw two young men, one took the woman and carried her in his arms outside the hotel, about an hour ago; they went out into the parking area.*

The man, Jeff, runs in the direction pointed out by the maid, and goes out into the parking lot. He runs to the exit booth and asks the assistant in service. Desperately showing in his voice almost nearly at crying, speaking English, he asks.

Jeff.—*Did you see two young men who came here carrying a woman an hour and a half ago?*

The parking attendant with a strong Spanish accent speaking English, as does the cleaning woman, says.

—*I saw two guys take pregnant woman. They said she's having baby; asked for a hospital, I know of the emergency; I told men about Henderson Hospital. Is that the woman?*

Jeff turns and runs to the parking lot, to his car and drives to the exit door where the attendant, understanding the situation, had lifted the bar from the exit stop, and shouted.

—Who pays me for the parking fee?
Jeff answered.

Jeff.–*Your mother.*

Jeff points to the sky with the middle finger of his left hand through the window. At Henderson Hospital, two doctors, three nurses work on Vicky Martin–the situation is difficult–it has been more than an hour since they started surgery. It is around 4:00 am. At about 4:20 in the morning, Jeff rushes to the emergency desk; no one was there. A nurse, the chief nurse, walks out of a room and walks to the emergency desk, saying.

Barbara.–*Can I help you?*

Jeff.–*Madam, I'm looking for my wife.*

Barbara.–*I'm sorry, I'm already married.*

She makes insinuating, sexy body movements.

Jeff.–*I'm not kidding, I'm looking for my wife, she's having a baby and she's been brought into the emergency of this hospital, is she here?*

Barbara.–*What's your wife's name?*

Jeff.–*Vicky Martin*

Barbara.–*And what's your name, can I see your ID?*

Jeff.–*Jeff Anderson; this is my driver's license.*

Barbara.-*But you just said, Vicky Martin is your wife, are you married to her?*

Jeff.–*Ah, well, ah, we, we, we're not married yet. We...*

Barbara.–*She's not your wife, is she?*

Jeff.–*Well, no, but she's carrying my baby, and we're getting married.*

Barbara.–*Wait a minute; you are not married, but she is expecting a child of yours, how is that?*

Jeff.–*Well, we'll get married when she divorces her husband.*

Barbara.–*Please wait, I'll be back in a minute.*

Barbara gets out and walks to the surgery room. Jeff leans over the counter and collects his license. Barbara comes back thinking out loud.

Barbara.–*I can't wait for my retirement. Here I am running back and forth for nothing.*

Vicky was under anesthesia and the doctors were in the operation. The head nurse returns to the emergency reception, but Jeff was no longer there. Meanwhile, at the Casino-Hotel Station: At the casino-hotel's underground parking entrance, a man dressed in full coat and tie was standing by the door. Jeff arrives, but he doesn't see that man. He parks his car near the entrance of the casino exit and walks to the glass front door.

The man.—*Hey, motherfucker, let's see if you can take this off me.*

Three shots rang out in the underground garage. No one was around that time in the morning. In the silence, I heard the squealing sound of wheels of a vehicle spinning on the pavement. Hotel security guards come out to check the sounds of gunfire. They find a dead man. There's a commotion at the back of the station's casino. Paramedics arrive: two ambulances, two fire trucks, a dozen police cars from the city of Henderson, a coroner. Two detectives from the criminal division inspect the site at the entrance to the Casino parking lot. Several police officers place barriers on the street and yellow ribbons to remove access (Stay out-crime scene-) and secure the area. Hotel guests, Ryan and Jim, woke up to the siren sounds of police cars, fire trucks and ambulances, Ryan still in pajamas goes down to discover what's going on. Jeff's spirit in agony tries to tell the police who shot him, but the police ignore him. Jeff dies. The spirit runs towards the dead man's body, in despair, and tries to bring Jeff's body back to life in process to his rigor mortis. The ambulance leaves taking the body, and his spirit follows the ambulance. Going down to the underground entrance a few minutes after Ryan.

Jim.—*What's the matter?*

Ryan.—*There was a shooting at this parking lot entrance to the Casino-hotel. They shot a man dead about 10 minutes ago. Nobody knows who shot him.*

Ryan and Jim return to their room 20 minutes later. They order breakfast through the hotel's room service. Turn on the TV while they're waiting for your order. Meanwhile, at Henderson Hospital, doctors had completed the C-section operation on Vicky Martin. Dr. Spencer talks to the chief nurse at the front desk.

Dr. Spencer.—*Please transfer the woman to intensive care, the baby to day care, and call the coroner, clean and disinfect the surgery room. I'll be in my office if you need me.*

Barbara.—*Yes, sir, and turning to Stephanie, she asked. Why should I call the coroner?*

Stephanie.—*A baby girl did not make it. They were twins. We have to call the father, somehow. Vicky said she doesn't know where he might be.*

Barbara.—*That will be very, very difficult, but we'll try. The man who came looking for his wife seemed to have an affair with her, but he wasn't her husband.*

About 15 minutes later, a man well or elegantly dressed in a dark suit and tie arrives at the emergency office, asking about Vicky Martin.

Mr. Martin.—*Ms. my wife is here having a baby, may I see her; I'm Rocky Martin, her husband.*

Barbara.—*For God's sake, how many husbands does this woman have? Poor me, I'm still looking for the first one.*

She gets up and moves provocatively.

Mr. Martin.—*[Surprised.] What did he say?*

Barbara.—*Oh, nothing sir, I was talking to myself. Sir, did you say Ricky Martin, ah, could I have an autograph?*

Mr. Martin.—*Miss. I'm not kidding; I'm Rocky, Rocky Martin, do you understand? Here's my ID.*

Martin hands his driver's license to the head nurse.

Barbara.—*Yes, sir. They took her into intensive care after her C-section operation; it's probably still under the effects of anesthesia. Can you fill out these forms for me?*

Martin politely asks.

Mr. Martin.—*I fill out the papers later. May I see my wife, now?*

Barbara.—*Yes, you can go through that double door to the third door on the left. You can bring back the insurance and hospital forms later, but before you leave.*

Rocky Martin.—*Thank you much.*

Rocky turned, walked and walked through the double-glazed door.

Barbara.—*Wow! I need a husband like that.*

Barbara returns to work at her desk, when only five or ten seconds later, three gunshots (bang, bang... pause bang) sound in the

ICU–. The hospital staff were arriving for the morning shift; Barbara and three nurses run to the third room on the left. Stephanie had finished her night shift and was on her way home, she said.

Stephanie.–*Barbara, did you hear the gunshots?*

They run to Vicky's room.

Stephanie.–*Barbara, Mrs. Martin in her bed, someone shot in the front of her head and in her chest, in the heart area. Jesus Christ, she's dead.*

Barbara.–*look. By the bed, on the floor; is Ricky Martin dead, it looks like he shot himself on the right side of his head. He's got a gun in his hand. I'll call the police.*

Barbara runs out of the room to the emergency desk. She's scared but aware; she will call the police. He forgets she'd called the police before.

The coroner, three police officers and two detectives from The Henderson Criminal Division arrived to assess the dead girl's case. The nurse told them about the fatal shooting. Nurses, coroners, police and detectives run to Mrs. Martin's room.

Chief Detective.–*Secure the site immediately put the entire wing out of bounds to investigate. Secure the security camera tapes. Tell the staff on this floor not to leave and question them.*

Looking at Stephanie and Barbara, he says,

–*touch nothing, please leave this room.*

The chief detective interrogates Barbara, the chief nurse, in an unoccupied ward room.

Chief.–*Madam, did you see the suspect? Mr. Ricky Martin, where is he?*

Barbara, think for a moment.

–*he calls me madam, I am a girl, looking for a husband.*

Then answer, quickly.

Barbara.–*It's Rocky Martin, sir. Yes, he showed me his ID photo... he is dead, he shot his wife and killed himself; he is dead in the intensive care wing, third bedroom on the left, through that double glass door.*

The detectives had picked up the wallet from Rocky Martin's pocket and showed a driver's license to the main nurse question.

Chief Detective.—*Is this Mr. Ricky Martin; I mean, Rocky Martin?*

She said yes, and the interrogation continued for two hours with all the staff in the ward during the crime. When Barbara finishes her statement, she returns to her desk. Barbara stays at the front desk. Dr. Spencer comes to see the chief nurse to ask about the crime situation. And after informing you, he suggests.

Barbara.—*We must record the birth of the baby, but we do not have a name. Both, supposedly, mother and father are dead. Until we find his relatives, the baby is alone. I'm asking for permission to call him Rex, because we rescued him.*

Dr. Spencer.—*Yes, okay, I'll sign the birth affidavit with that name, Rex Martin.*

Meanwhile, at the Casino-Hotel Station, detectives questioned the parking attendant, Carlos Madeira, who declares the following, in rough English with a strong Central American Spanish accent.

Carlos.—*I told you, I saw two men. They're guests at the hotel. One's name is Jim, the other Ryan-they took a woman in their car. A man asked for an emergency hospital. I said Henderson Hospital. One was rude. He gave me the middle finger. He didn't pay for the parking ticket.*

In less than 10 minutes, police arrested Jim and Ryan; but after interrogating them in their hotel room the detectives released them, but ordered not to leave the city. The lights went out; the curtains close.

Sergio was born in Arriaga, Chiapas, Mexico.

Tuesday, December 18, 1990.

Figure 7: Poverty house

The curtains open. The lights are coming back; I hear a roar. Lightning illuminates the stage and the audience. The theater looks dark, but the front-right window screen lights up, showing planet earth, focusing the map of Mexico, then approaches the city of Arriaga, in the state of Chiapas, Mexico. The screens show the streets and focus on a small house at the end of a cul-de-sac. Inside the house, a woman, Teresa, was undergoing a premature birth, a little over eight months pregnant. A poor family of seven lives in that little house, fighting one day at a time: Grandpa Julian, and Grandma Ophelia, Teresa, three children, Alfonso, nine, Jorge, seven, and Clarita, four years old.

Ophelia.—*Hurry, Alfonso, run to call Mrs. Ramona (Ramona), the midwife; ask her to come, tell her that Teresa is giving birth, but go, boy, go flying. Julian put a pot of water to boil, hurry Julian. Clarita, bring me the washed clothes that's in that chair, run girl, but now.*

Alfonso.—*I'm going.*

Alfonso leaves the house, running; in the corner, he meets a friend.

The friend.–*Where are you going so fast? Look, I brought you the baseball cards you asked me to look for.*

Alfonso.–*I can't, I am running to call Mrs. Ramona, wait for me when I get back.*

The friend.–*What a heck; I can't; look at them now, and if you like them you pay me later. Come on.*

Alfonso stops and looks at the baseball cards and says.

Alfonso.–*I like these; I take them, and I pay you later, then.*

The friend.–*No stupid, you pay me now; I have to go. Look at these others, look, look.*

Look, I got better ones, look.

Alfonso.–*You told me I could pay you later. I told you I don't bring money with me; wait until I get back, stupid.*

The two boys argue this issue at the corner. Meanwhile, in the little house. Grandpa screams from the other end of the house where they have a makeshift kitchen.

Julian.–*Ophelia, the water is already boiling.*

Ophelia.–*Well, bring her in a bucket and bring the pan - the one we use to put the oranges - over here, did you hear me, Julian?*

Teresa.–*Oh, oh, Grandma hurts me a lot.*

Ophelia.-*It's your fault you looked for it. Who commands you to be cheerful having children you can't support? And the dirty men you pick, they don't give you a cent for the kids like those drug-cartel men who abuse women. Hold on. Breathe and push, push, push.*

Clarita comes back sweating and panting; maybe she ran forth and back.

Clarita.–*Grandma here is the washed clothes, which you asked me to bring.*

Ophelia.–*Well, put it by the bed, where Ramona can see them and take it.*

Clarita placed the clothes on a folding chair on the right side of the bed.

Clarita.–*There it is, Grandma.*

Ophelia.–Gee, don't understand, Clarita, I told you to put it where Ramona can grab it, don't you understand? Here, on this side, stubborn.

Ophelia says, screaming.

—*Where's that dumb boy, Alfonso, Alfonso, Alfonso? Damn, that worthless boy is not back yet, and Ramona doesn't come.*

Clarita.—*Yes, Grandma, here it is. I'm running for it.*

Ophelia.—*Pray, you'll see, if I do not give that boy his due... the baby is coming, and Ramona?*

After a long while, Clarita returns with Alfonso.

Alfonso. Grandmother *Ms. Ramona says she is coming immediately.*

Ophelia.—*Where you stayed, scoundrel boy, those little cards make you useless; pray, I will burn them, and with a beating I'll take you out of that lazy stage. What a problem. The fountain broke, the water is pouring out. Where is the Ramona; Run, Alfonso, go get Ramona.*

Worried, Ophelia prays.

Ophelia.—*Let us pray.*

Mother Guadalupe,
queen of the forgotten,
merciful mother, help me with this problem.
Let my messes come untied;
Mother Guadalupe ...

Ramona finally arrives.

Ramona.—*Ophelia, Ophelia, I'm here, he told me, Alfonso, a little while ago that Teresa will have her baby.*

Ophelia.—*What, Alfonso saw you a little while ago? Fuck... I sent that worthless over an hour ago. Come Ramona, come, Teresa has already spilled the water and the cervix is opening up fast, come, walk. May the generous hand of God help us.*

Poverty leaves no room for action, or is not how the conditions of the moment. I mean, nature commands it might have it. There are no doctors there, no medicines, only home remedies. Ophelia interrupts Ramona's work with her strong prayer.

Ramona.—*Oh, shut up Ophelia saves the prayer for later... Breathe and push, Teresa, breathe Teresa, push, breathe and push.*

The situation is getting out of control. The Spirit in the baby reacts: The baby's spirit concentrates on inducing an action on them. Ophelia says.

Ophelia.–*Ramona, hurry, hurry, the baby is crowning, HURRY, HURRY.*

Ramona.–*Holy God, merciful, give life to this child who died at birth, save him.*

They can't hear the baby's spirit. The baby came out cold and stiff; doesn't move. There is no more time to waste; the baby is getting blue and cold.

Teresa.–*Oh no, Holy Virgin, no, not my baby, please don't... ay, my son, save him oh, Queen, Virgin Guadalupe... ay, ay, ay.*

The end always comes when there's nothing else we can do. That's when nature takes control and takes its course. Teresa, as exhausted as she is, still listens what Ramona says and screams loudly. Ophelia says, crying.

Ophelia.–*No, no, not for God's sake, no.*

The pain is intense. Everyone mourns, sadly in that house of rubble, the death of an unborn human. Ophelia pulls a rosary out of her apron's pocket and prays, whispering.

Ophelia.–*Mother Guadalupe, queen of the homeless, merciful mother. Please help me with this situation. Let a solution to my problems come now...*

She repeatedly goes over her litany. The dim light of a single bulb flashes quickly twice; there are no other lights in the room. However, a bright flash illuminates the entire room, and then a striking sound, the light bulb explodes. The spirit in the baby sends signs of anguish and another spirit comes to help.

A close spirit.–(Thinking) *I will start his heart.*

The soul embedded in the dying baby leaves his body; when the process of spiritual separation begins. But think.

Embedded spirit.–*I will excite his brain.*

The two spirits work on the baby's mind and body, reversing the script of death. The baby goes from blue to brown, to red and back to blue. The baby's spirit transmits its energy on the baby's brain with double doses of energy, and the other spirit induces strong contractions in the heart to make it pulse. Meanwhile, Ophelia and Ramona don't know what to do; they kneel to pray outside.

Ophelia.–*Let us pray, Ophelia, let us all pray together: Our Father, you are in heaven, hallowed be thy name, thy will be done.*

The echo of the deep silence in the small house of scraps repeats aloud the perfect chorus of people reciting the Most Holy Father. Meanwhile, the two spirits continue their work on the baby's mind and body. And after a few seconds, the baby goes from cold blue to brown, to pink. Finally, the baby cries loudly, for the first time. Ophelia and Ramona, surprised, get up and run next to Teresa; she was exhausted by her intense efforts. The baby moves and cries louder. People think it's a miracle, the answer to their prayers.

Ophelia.–*Miracle, a miracle. Blessed be the Lord. He listened to my prayers. Is this a miracle, or is it he conditions of causal and random events are so close to the borderline of impossibility? This is something humans don't understand. And…*

Ramona protests, for she also prayed.

Ramona.–*And mine? I pray too. Let me do it, Ophelia, give me the child, I will clean it up and dress him.*

Ophelia hands the baby to Ramona.

Ophelia.–*Clarita, search the closet, and take three candlesticks.*

Clarita runs and comes back with the candles.

Clarita.–*I have them, grandma, what shall I do with them.*

Ophelia says while she collects the clothes.

–Is it a human delusion or a miracle?

Maybe they're both true, simultaneously. Humans tell and hear stories like this in the world and wonder. The event needs an explanation. But how can they explain it to humans? Existence has the law of cause and effect that humans can use to reconstruct everything that makes an event possible. That is the point that miracles can be results of the work of the spirits do and that we do not see, do not realize or do not want to accept as real facts of the spirits. For this event, the help the spirits give us is a clear truth. In addition, existence records everything that creates an event. Therefore, the universe stores all the problems, activities, and conditions (the string or the network) that the event creates. Humans often forget all that, but they could paint the truth with brushes of requirements and restrictions for each event as they return to the past. Sergio's birth is visible and tangible evidence of a stillborn baby coming back to life. Several signs may show evidence of death. Here, the time elapsed, the body does not respond to stimuli, lack of movement of the body, and absence of breathing; this is evidence of death. Why is this? If we think something happens because something else happened earlier in support the first thing, then there's a reason. Perhaps paranormal forces interact to reverse the process of death, and these forces may be the spirits that work on the baby. Other efforts to save the baby were in the process and fail.

The guide.—*Two matters are a miracle and the actions of the spirits. Divine justice forgets nobody. The poor always have something to look forward to in life. They live like birds that always find food every day.*

Ophelia says, while she's picks up the clothes.

Ophelia.—*Quickly, Clarita, place the candles at the Virgin of Guadalupe, and light them. Then go quickly to buy flowers to adorn the altar. Take this money and buy them from Hortencia's market at the corner.*

Standing at the door, Julian announces this.

Julian.—*Tonight, we will have a thanksgiving party, Alfonso, go call Vicente, ask him to come and bring his musicians to celebrate this miracle: the birth of Sergio Maltes, the newborn baby. Hey, kid, don't stay in the corner exchanging baseball cards. Go, quickly.*

Alfonso.—*Yes, grandpa, for my new brother, Sergio, I'll go in a hurry.*

The public can say a party, arent they in poverty? But in the places and hearts of poor people the neighbors come together, caring and sharing what little they have. That's one way to have a time of pleasure and gratitude. It's different here in America; people don't even know their neighbors, let alone share and take care of them. The mission of existence is for all living creatures to live satisfied, conformed, and with gratitude. The whole universe and everything inside it are for everyone. In the true meaning of the phrase *"Love thy neighbor"* exists only for people in poverty, and for people suffering a major disaster like an earthquake. Their beliefs keep their souls and minds going, knowing that their chances of surviving one day are in the hands of the conditions and circumstances of their environments. God bless their souls!

Guide.—*If you like to call it a miracle, so be it. But another guardian spirit came to help, to save the baby's life, Sergio, and the mission of the baby's spirit.*

Ophelia, Ramona, Julian, Clarita, they all there saw a dead baby, and then they saw the baby alive. For them, this is nothing less than a miracle; they did not see the spirits working diligently and using their powers. However, you saw the spirits as they worked hastily to save the baby. Now the baby's spirit can carry out its mission. This is how spirits work to preserve the lives of creatures and can carry their mission. A thin curtain runs in front to block the view of the house room where activities continue beyond the darkness of the night. There is a deep silence for a moment, as if everyone fell into a deep retrospective, but then someone in the audience raises a question.

Persona D.—*Why do spirits come to help, are they guardian angels?*

Guide.—*Good question! The concept of "guardian angels" is not a concept of spirits, but of humans. In the dimension of spirits, only spirits live as molecules of the global spirit. [xxii] The primary mission of spirits is to generate, protect or safeguard, and to maintain life in all its forms. We said that the two dimensions of spirits and matter occupy the same space in the universe; this space is one, and only one, a unique scenario. The mission of spirits is to protect and lead people if they live in their bodies. Its purpose is to promote and support lives. Sometimes, when someone else shows up or comes to help you in situations of threat or fear, that person's spirit comes to protect you. That protecting spirit could be an animal, a person, or a spirit wandering around you, but in the spirit dimension. You can call this living creature a guardian spirit or a protective angel. So, another way you can call him if the result of his action is to help you get out of the mess or difficult situation you find yourself in. This is more not what they care about if they are doing wrong or well—they only prevent the harm and consequences of life. Free will is yours alone. The* party takes some time after sunset. Neighbors had brought often, tamales, and "carnitas" and handmade tortillas, ah, and mescal, a homemade alcohol, something like moonlight ("moonshine"). The musicians fine-tune their instruments, marimba, accordion, guitars and bass guitars (guitarrones), was a little mariachi; and the 'party' started.' High in the early hours of the morning, maybe two hours before sunrise, the party was still alive. They were happy people having a great time. The stage slowly dimmed as our minds move away from the event until the stage darkens again. The music goes on playing after the lights go off. We live another day, we fight another fight, and we sleep a night to wake up to go continue fighting. Trues, going back from the left-side stage, says with humor,

Trues.—*To have him, what a feast; we have nothing like that in the dimension of our spirits. Eat, drink, dance, laugh with joy. Do you want to leave this land?*

Trues walks to the right side of the back of the stage. Standing in the backstage, cups his hand over his right ear, wait a few seconds. And then he says.

—*We can't hear you.*

Someone in the audience raises a hand. The Guide nods her head, consenting.

Person E.—*If the spirits see the past, the present, and the future, they could have seen what would happen to the baby. But if they didn't, why didn't they?*

Guide.—*That's a big question! Let me summon Robert, Sexis and Trues to address your question.*

Trues.—*Free spirits see future events, but spirits in humans cannot see the future, although they can guess it. Free spirits must allow free will and the decisions of humans. We have said that when a spirit inflects in human matter; it loses most attributes of its spirit and its powers. But spirits roaming in the vicinity can see, and hear, what is happening near them and can transport their energy across the dimensional boundary.*

Robert.—*Their minds send requests for help to exist, hoping to get the answers from the spirits. Spirits bind and unite their external and internal energies to influence matter. But the baby's spirit conveyed the stress signal. Is that all right?*

Sexy.—*Besides the above, notice that the baby was brain dead in the brain and the process of separation of the soul had begun. The baby's*

spirit was outside the baby's body, and he connected with another spirit easier. Fortunately, two spirits connected and did what was necessary to stop or reverse the process of soul separation.

Guide.—*Let's continue our presentation. Now they have seen that human life is different in different parts of the Earth, as it is different for rich and poor. The process of human creation is one unique life cycle. Perhaps, therefore, this is why the America's founding fathers thought of their famous phrase.*

A stage window screen shows the phrase, and a spirit dressed as the clothes of the founding fathers recites that phrase.

A spirit recites.—*We consider that these truths are evident, that all men are created equal... endowed by their Creator with certain inalienable rights, including Life, Freedom and the pursuit of Happiness.*

Sexy.—*The human world is fraught with injustice and inequalities. You have just seen life on earth; is full of violence. The behavior of humans causes a heavy spirit, emergency terminal separations and traffic to and from and across interdimensional boundaries.*

Robert.—*The laws of the universe on man's behavior are strict and specific. Spirits shall not intervene in human actions; the spirits cannot do that. One reason is that spirits cannot transcend the limits of our spiritual dimension; another reason is that human egos have freedom of choice and volition.*

Trues.—*Yet another reason is that the brain structure includes a process of perceptions that generate delusions, chasing fame, wealth, and power because humans use their egos' freedom of choice in selfish ways. They express selfishness with their preferences, tastes, ambition, envy, hatred, etc. They're ego seekers.*

Sexy.—*Spirits cannot control that; and humans must create their own changes to satisfy the universal order of oneness. In addition, humans are responsible for their dual life, spiritual matter; it is their duty to control their egos or pay the consequences of their decisions and actions. Dual humans must understand and undertake for themselves a balanced-harmonious behavior to achieve oneness.*

Person F.—*How do spirits interact with the spirits of other humans?*
Guide.—*That's an excellent and curious question.*

Robert.—*Free spirits are in the spirit dimension and interact with spirits housed in living beings, using electromagnetic waves directed at the mind at the quantum level. The brain is where human energy concentrates in animated beings. The communication of spirits is energetic. In humans, sensations are chemical and electrical signals needed to build gnosis in neurons. Neurons collect these gnoses or fragments of knowledge and integrate into images; just as electrical and chemical signals generate perceptions to build gnosis in neurons.*

Trues comes in a hurry from the back and right of the stage, waving his arms in the air, he says.

Trues.—*when a human is in danger, the mind sends distress signals, a vehement desire, and spirits react to help and respond immediately. Even evil desires and cravings generate waves of energy that travel in a certain order, or code, through space—and remain there. Spirits excite the structure of matter in objects or neurons in a human or animal brain, causing impulses that create thoughts, which translate into action. For example, when Carol said, "I don't care if I die... Save my baby, please... save my baby" her thoughts sent a distress signal. A close spirit captured the wave, responded, and came to help Ariel. In physical reality Carol did all the work induced by spirits, this other spirit and Ariel played the role of protector spirits.*

Trues, walk to the left of the back of the stage and disappear into darkness.

Sexy.—*We advise you to ask mentally and humbly when you need something, longing to have it vehemently; however, you must commit to resign and be happy, knowing there is a possibility you cannot get it. You can always try again.*

Trues returns, taking only a few steps towards the center of the stage.

Trues.—*One more note, please.*

Guide moves his head by consenting.

Trues.—*Humans pray, pleading for mercy or asking for help from their supreme being, according to their religious beliefs. As people pray or meditate, they open and connect with the global spirit in the spirit dimension; this communication is between a soul and a spirit and or the global spirit. All spirits pick up those waves.*

Sexy.—*Praying is an intense focused yearning of human minds, and meditating, to solve a situation, problem, tribulation and or suffering, believing that a supreme being will listen and mercifully solve their problem. The mind transmits one or the low-frequency mental waves by which spirits communicate with each other.* [30]

I'm back in the hospital where paramedics took my body the day after that horrible accident. Well, the date is now Sunday, May 9, 1993. People in America are celebrating Mother's Day. I'm in the waiting room along with seven other people, who seem to be the parents and relatives of that less fortunate girl. As you may recall, a flying object hit her head, and she's been in a coma ever since. This is the day her parents will disconnect all instruments and life support equipment from her body. All seven people cry in the waiting room. It's eleven o'clock in the morning; and they had been waiting since eight in the morning. There's a lot of commotion in the ward. Three nurses and two doctors run to the women's ICU ward. A few minutes later, the blue lights flash in the hallway; and the public system announces.

The PA system.—*Attention, Attention, Dr. Ceri Bello and Dr. Neurons, please report immediately to UCI Room 674.*

The PA system (again).—*Attention, Attention, Dr. Ceri Bello and Dr. Neurons, please report immediately to UCI Room 674.*

A few moments after the announcement, two doctors and their respective staff walk hastily down the aisle, and go straight to the ICU room, where the girl is. Dr. Ceri Bello is a well-known specialist in brain surgery, Dr. Neurons is a famous neurosurgeon. Nobody knew what was going on. Hours passed; were about three o'clock that afternoon. The media had their equipment, cameras and people anchored, and reporters awaiting the outcome. The comatose girl witnesses the criminal case where another man, the driver of the car, shot twice in the head. Outside in the waiting room, curious people came after the news preview broadcast this event in evolution. The hallway in the ICU room was full. The two doctors and the nurse

---

[30] Read about brain operating frequencies in the end notes.

chief in the ward leave the room and stop at the door in front of the mountain of microphones, and Dr. Ceri Bello says.

Dr. Ceri Bello.—*Today, we experienced a physical phenomenon. The patient in a deep coma for over two years showed signs of change in her conditions. This morning the nurse on duty saw the patient opening her eyes and shaking her head, as if wanting to say something. Technologists installed equipment and encouraged the patient to do what she wanted. The patient made certain vocal sounds that they will pass on to phonetic experts to decipher them here in the hospital. Dr. Neurons expects the patient may get out of the coma, aided by careful treatment. We notified the respective authorities with legal jurisdiction. A detective on the case has taken possession of the recordings and work with forensic experts in this hospital. This is all we have for now. Thank you all for coming.*

The doctors left amid a deluge of questions from reporters. The people walk out of the waiting room and the hallway. Amazing! What happened is incredible and extraordinary. Parents and relatives built high hopes of the girl recovery. The evening passed. It was a normal night at the intensive care unit ward; but in the morning, when the head nurse entered the room, found the patient had died at about 4:30 a.m. The patient's weak heart, perhaps, could not withstand the emotions and failed. Nurses found the life supporting device disconnected from the patient and wall outlet. I see the tattoo on her arm and a scar on her left eyebrow; I have the same tattoo on the same arm and a scar on the same eyebrow. I am the soul of this girl; I'm Diana Van Sander. Now she's dead and in thirty-six hours, I'll be free. But I pledge to continue commenting and giving opinions on this Life Cycles presentation–I am the producer. The head nurse found in Diana's backpack a copy of Miguel Soto's book "Misterios: Amor, Luz y Vida," a 410-page Life Cycles manuscript, and a handwritten note on the cover that says, *this book is the glory of my dreams*. The curtains close.

Guide.—*Now, we are ready to take a break, remain seated while I restore your human conditions. When you cross the gate portal, you will no longer have the powers you received from the spirits. Please close your eyes, 1, 2, 3.*

Three flashes of bright light come one after the other. The theater lights come on.

Guide.—*You now are clean and safe to go out into the lobby.*

INTERMEZZO

CHAPTER 5

The human situation.

Abstract

The dawn comes with light and glory, without agony, without pain; more life with tears, joy, delight with hopes, repeatedly. But death brings tears; and life ends in sorrow, anguish, loss, regret. Endless testing efforts are sad nights without tomorrow or like an unscented flower. Birth is beauty and perfume, full of plans, efforts, and dreams. It's a sweet love, or so it seems. The body and soul, divine pair, are two sides of a coin with its bright future, we assume. Eternal couple who travel in the air, through space and time, bringing together two worlds, two dimensions. Reality and unreality to love, not to casual intent: This is the dual human. The soul and body are always and will be two distinct and separate elements. The body of living beings are only the device and tool for the soul to express itself. And the life of dual beings, like that of humans, is only the sequence of soul actions in the body. We are the soul but not the body, but it is us because the body is not. This is the human situation: a repertoire of uncertainties created by a scarcity of knowledge of the reality of existence or the world in which we live.

The human situation is dark. Humans are toys of the ego we bring in our souls. And we suffer sorrows, tribulations for the inconsequential acts of our egos. Perhaps it is the mistake of creation to have endowed the ego with free will and with the representation and bond of us, souls, with material reality–the great discrepancy–, free choice with the availability of the resources of the universe. As long as this situation endures, humans cannot attain oneness with the existence. And corruption, abuse, criminality, wars, destruction will continue. It all depends on human performance.

Human performance.–Spirit, and body.[xxiii]

In the background the music plays the composition of Our Day will come. [31] A chorus of spirits sings the lyrics that says.

Our day will come;
(our day will come)
And we'll have everything.
We'll share the joy,
(we'll share the joy)
Falling in love can bring.
No one can tell us we're too young to know;
(young to know)
I love you so (love you so)
And you love me...

The curtains open. All four screens are off. The stage is dark; the screens at the bottom of the stage light up, showing galaxies in space. Until this moment, we have witnessed two phases of what spirits call Life Cycles: (1) the separation of the soul and (2) the inflection of spirits in human eggs. Spirits present a fascinating theme in common language; that humans can understand. The universe itself speaks to us to expect an event to happen. It's a silent language we can't hear,

---

[31] A song composed by Mort Garson, and English words written by Bob Hilliard, released in 1963.

but we can understand. However, I would like to know how souls act by guiding human bodies, and how souls communicate with other souls and free spirits. The situation of the life of dual beings–human *mentaurs*–is violent. There are wars of all kinds for power, fame and wealth. We have seen two world wars and a third world war can break out at any moment. We see social, political, economic and religious systems exploiting the people of the world. In the soul we carry a monster, AGHAPEE, which induces the ego to act on a path contrary to the purpose of existence–oneness. The ego with its AGHAPEE is the real cause of the adverse human situation. We, the spirits, have seen this situation since man appeared in the universe and our mission is to modify those conditions. Thus, man can return to the path that leads him to oneness consistent with the order of harmony, of existence and the universe.

The spiritual situation is different. See? Remember the date of that fatal accident? It's a Friday, December 15, 1989, around 5:00 p.m. We were in that old theater when the accident happened, about twenty-eight years ago. We've come a long way since we travel back and forward in time. Today is Thursday, December 20, 2018, and we will return to that old theater to discover what happens to Victor, Rex, Moses and Sergio, and other spirits.

Diana's appearance.

A woman appears dressed in transparent white loose clothing. She's the guide, she walks to the podium and says.

Guide.–*And so, now they see me in human form next to the podium, on stage and perhaps in the audience. You can also see me on the four screens of our minds, hanging in space. But I continue to coordinate the life cycle of the spirit as souls advance through the material dimension. A spirit has been commenting on this work while her body was in a coma for over two years. Today, Diana's soul separates from her human body and becomes a free spirit. I mention this work "Life Cycles" is a Diana's production inspired by her book. As an independent commentator for humans, Diana will continue to give her views and opinions, but not as part of the cast.*

True, I'm Diana. I am not part of the eight spirits in the cast of the main spirits. I am the author of the manuscript that caused this book, "Life Cycles", a theory of the role that spirits play in the lives of humans. The reality of the script is in the quality, in interpreting the spirits; and in the trials that relate spirits to the material world.

Dialogue base.

Guide.—*Welcome back to the travels of our spirits. We travel back in time to that instance. Our logistics show that our four typical inflections succeeded in addition. The results show the following.*

The two front screens turn on, showing the current instance. A group of spirits dance the ballet "Death of the Swan" following the soft music played in the background and lasts only a few minutes. The two rear screens of the stage light up, showing the names in the cast, giving time for the audience to read. The ballet dance continues.

Guide.—*We travel to our current time 2018. The situation is chaotic politically and socially, but somewhat economically stable. Trump inherited a growing economy and he is riding on that success; that's the basis of his administration.*

Trues enters the stage ambling and intercedes.

True.—*Please wait a minute. The new government elected in 2016 promised to make America great again. However, its president shows attitudes, behavior and intentions to institute an autocratic government, following the playbooks of strong men or dictators such as Putin, Ortega or Maduro. The social situation shows certain characteristics of white supremacists—ultra right—with a racist touch of persecution of minorities. The Republican Party controls the legislative branch of government; however, because of current performance and behavior, political winds suggest a radical shift in power towards Democrats. That's how the weather of the situation is.*

Trues walks backwards, right off the stage and sits on the ground. A question appears on the window screens.

Person A.—*What is the 'duality' you just mentioned?*

Guide.—*Who posed this question? Not bad. Their spiritual and material composition. You may ask about the duality of the human. Conscious life is of the spirit, it is not of the material human. Spirits work with and within their material bodies. The mind and consciousness* *of spirits belong to an intangible dimension, while the human body and its brain are a matter of the material dimension. If you understand this duality, your performance in mortality is easier and easier.*

STAZE (or Stacey) enters the scene.

Stacey.–*Trues, you know; it is difficult for humans to lead a life without knowing what or who they are. They cannot see their future, nor can they go back to the past, they can only be in the present space that it is so thin that every next second is. And this is your biggest confusion and constriction. Human life is like walking blindfolded through a dense forest, bumping and bouncing against trees–the conditions and circumstances of life–of this forest.*

Trues says, speaking from where he's sitting.

–Yes, Stacey, worse, they do not know where they come from or where they go after death. Some believe that God created them. What if they knew their lives were continuous cycles, the Life Cycles, what would they say?

Stacey.–*That notion is fine for them.*

But what if they knew the truth?

–Perhaps they must realize that human life, or other lives, can only exist if the conditions and circumstances of the scenario permit; this situation is true for all lives anywhere in the Universe.

What if they discover that creation tries to cleanse egos from attachment to the material world?

–Then the global spirit will receive them in the dimension of the spirits, the material body with the hosted spirit?

Trues gets up and walks towards Stacey, slowly and cockily says.

-Maybe they don't understand that; maybe they're not sure about that. Maybe they knew, but they forgot.

Stacey.–*Yes, for example, many humans believe that the universe in six days. Absolute intelligence may have done everything, but not in six twenty-four-hour days that humans know. The days of existence are not earth days, or days equal to a rotation of the earth around the sun. The universe allows and provides conditions and support for life with love, for love and to love.*

Wow, Stacey is right, humans are slaves to their stage; they do not understand their ego, and they ignore that they could have a better life if they understood that life is not material, but spirit love.

Trues.—*That's right. What if humans discover that the Great Explosion was the beginning of the universe, but not in the way some humans, the scientists, reason? It was rather the spirit of existence that transformed its energy into the matter of this universe, space and time, by its own power. The humans would know the mysteries of the universe. They would know that the spirit of existence is tangible energy and the matter that fills the universe. [32] The human being perceives and works with a spirit housed in its body. They would know the truth that would make them free at last. They would know that what they must take care of first is the life of their soul, not the material life they know.*

Stacey.—*Regarding life, Trues, humans ignore that existence defines and specifies there can be many life forms and categories; categories and forms shaped by the conditions of each scenario, anywhere in the universe—the universal scenario. Scientists are right to assume there may be life elsewhere in the universe. They suspect they may not be of human form and substance. But the problem is that aliens' mental states may not be compatible.*

Trues.—*I hear the thoughts of a person in the audience asking, what is the mind?*

Stacey.—*Note that the body, or any part of it, has no skills to think, neither the brain nor the heart. Both are biomechanical parts of a material machine. Only the mind thinks. The mind is a superior function of the soul, a cybernetic program designed to handle human thoughts and actions. The brain collects and processes the information that the mind needs for thinking.*

All four screens show another question.

Person G.—*Can you explain that further?*

Stacey.—*Oh sure, I will gladly explain the matter of your question. The brain is a tangible living matter that has between 15 to 33 billion neurons, interacting to process life-specific programs: heart rate, body temperature, digestion, waking and sleep states, breathing, muscles, etc. [xxiv] The heart only pumps blood to the body material, including the brain, distributing oxygen and nutrients to the body. Five senses collect and send sensations to specific parts or neurons in the brain for image conversion. The brain uses these senses to capture material reality. The mind needs*

---

[32] Misterios: Amor, Luz y Vida, de Miguel Soto, 2018.

the brain to process images into thoughts, which can become actions. It acts as a relay center, controlling bodily functions. The brain is just a functional mechanical component that does not think or reason by itself.

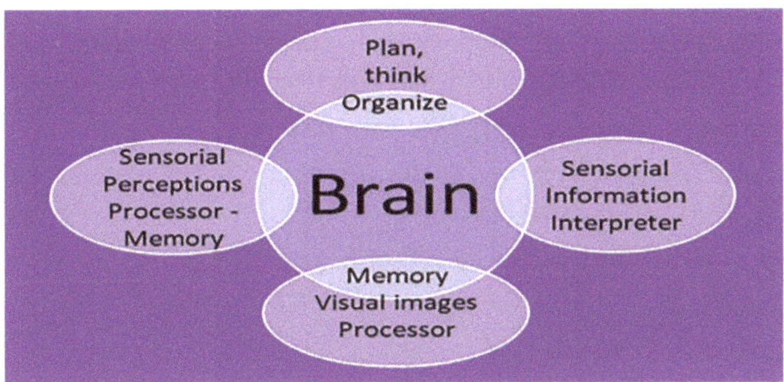

Figure 8: Brain Functions.

Thinking is a superior function of the mind. The screens present a diagram of four major relative functions of the brain.– Inside the brain (according to "Mayo Clinic"[xxiv]) there is an area called Cerebellum. The Cerebellum controls the vital functions of the body. Emotions and memories in two twin areas reflected and in the center of the brain mass. Three subareas divide those twin areas, as shown in figure 9 below.

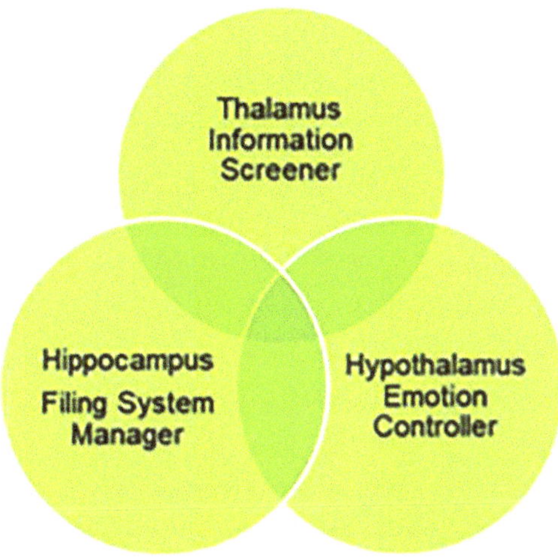

Figure 9: Cerebellum subareas

No part of the Cerebellum, and of these three areas of it, reveal the process of thought or meditation; but suggest that most brain activities are to control each process. They warn that neurons achieve their intercom with electrical impulses transmitted and captured by neurotransmitters. The mind thinks, conceives, selectively analyzes and or synthesizes realities or unrealities.

Apparently, the mind is a superior process of the soul that depends on the functions of the brain, but the brain does not produce thought. Interesting, isn't it?

Another question flashes on all four screens.

Person H.–*So, can you tell us what it's the mind?* [33]

Trues.–*Yes, the mind is the superior function of the spirit housed in a human body. The human sees through it, studies and touches the surrounding material reality. The mind structures and manages the operational physical-perceptive program of the soul, but it is a superior mental-conceptual function: It is a cyber program that manages thought, controls, monitors, thought processes, reasoning, meditation, integration of gnosis into ideas, concepts and understandable knowledge.[34, 35] This process integrates the unverifiable intangible reality of the spiritual dimension and the predictable, tangible reality of the material dimension. The mind thinks, meditates and conceptualizes knowledge. The brain cannot think for itself, and the body is the robot that performs the actions that the mind commands the brain to execute. Senses are active sensors that collect information from the surrounding reality in sensory perceptions. This is how we realize reality–substance and form–in the material dimension. The senses pass perceptions (chemical or electrical signals) to the brain, which stores them in its memory. The brain processes or converts sensory gnosis into mental images, which can call mental perceptions, such as photos of external realities. However, the brain makes no decisions; because it is an operational body, except predetermined routine as in the sense of preservation.*

---

[33] See note xv in the later pages of the book.

[34] Wikipedia, cibernética, https://www.merriam-webster.com/dictionary/cybernetics.

[35] https://en.wikipedia.org/wiki/Cybernetics

Ok; we know that the brain is an operational organ; and we know that the heart is a driven physical organ. These organs have no attributes of making thoughts. True, we ignore the location and function of the mind. That's all right; but we can only analyze the soul and mind for the physical results of their actions. How can we connect the soul and the spirits?

Guide.—*Note that spirits have a logical and non-logical reality in their dimension, and both as facts of existence.* [36] *Humans have only the real dimension.*

Stacey.—*That is correct, and humans must establish a channel of communication to see both realities. Humans can shape a connection between spirits in human bodies and the global spirit of the universe. To open and activate a channel of communication, each person's mind must reach a high state of calm and tranquility—and separate from the material.*

Yes, we realize there are logical and ideological aspects of reality, and we refuse to accept what seems illogical, it is because we think and judge situations with our physical knowledge of the moment. How do we establish lines of communication with spirits? Robert and Sexis return to the dialogue.

Sexis.—*Humans should detach from material thoughts and the dependency on them. Sometimes, if you take your mind into a deep state of concentration, you can get to a point where you are no longer aware of your material environment, including your body. You can almost think you've reached an out-of-body state. The deeper you enter your mind, the further away you will be from your material being. Humans don't leave the material dimension.* [37] *The soul (and mind) always remain united to its body; you have no active concern about, or do not think about, material perceptions or conceptions. This is the state of suppression of consciousness we mentioned.*

Guide.—*Robert, a person in the audience, has a question. The question appears on the screens.*

Person I.—*Are feelings generated and stored in the heart?*

---

[36] See final note XV – Dimension spectrum.
[37] Read final note xxxiii – Introspección.

Robert.–*What do you think? Oh no, I'm kidding. Your question is very important. I'll tell you this. Humans have deep feelings and do not know how they create them or where they formed. When a soul structures the human mind, it also integrates its functions and sub-functions. The heart is only a vital organ for a biological function of the body; it doesn't process thoughts, ideas and feelings.*

The rear-left screen of the stage shows an image of human work in its biological process.

Sexis.–*A heart has no skills to detect feelings, emotions, such as love, let alone the fitness to store feelings. However, feelings influence the functional behavior of the heart. The screen shows a view interior of a heart. It's a diaphragmatic pump that sucks and thrust blood. It's a vital organ. It performs no psychological function other than a sped-up pulse when the mind excites it under certain emotional situations. Feelings are attitudes of the soul, and part of the mind. There we feel love, remorse, hatred and other emotions. The mind works by following established functional processes. After human senses capture physical reality through sensory stimuli, and chemical reactions take place in various organs of the body, the brain produces images and stores them.*

Trues.–*The mind uses these images and with predictable routine algorithms validates the veracity of each sensation and encodes them as true or false, possible or impossible. Imagination, which preserves the freedom of thoughts of the spirit dimension, rational or irrational, uses logical and ideological images to create anything.*

Robert.–*Imagination can create a horse with the head of a bull and a lion's tail; an image acceptable in the dimension of spirits. People would consider crazy a human claiming that she, or he, has a pet like that, a person who lost touch with reality (physical), human reality. Inspiration also takes both types of images and plans new images that are fantasies in the material dimension. Poets, for example, write verses in the realm of transcendent pictorial thoughts, using a metaphorical description (something that might or may not be). Returning to the point, feelings in the heart; we keep feelings within a compartment of the soul, an element of the mind.*

Well, maybe we're wrong when we say *I love you with all my heart*. But I think we should put the issues and things in their proper places. Otherwise, we live in a fake reality. Did I hear that the function of imagination takes advantage of omniscience, where anything, subject, object or creature, can be real or unreal, logical or illogical? Is it possible that a person we call crazy, schizophrenic, delusion isn't that at all? Could it be that a vortex of illusions or imagination absorbs them? How can we control this situation and stay connected to physical reality while roaming in the realm of the unreal?

Manhattan–NY, 1992.

Guide.–*Wait a minute, I just found out that in a few minutes the New York Police Station in Manhattan, New York, will provide news on Richland. Let's open a channel through Stacey's mind to watch it live from New York.*

The show changes Stacey's mind; an image on the back screens (right and left) of the stage. Stacey's mind travels to the New York Police Department station number 120 82nd Street, New York, and focuses on the following. The head of the New York City Police Department reports: On the case of Ms. Carol Richland's death.

Chief of Police.–*We reported that after a detailed autopsy demanded by Mr. Richland, the coroner determined that the cause of death was not a natural death. The study shows a possible excessive time for Ms. Richland exposed to mitigating efforts and delay in medical care. We have no more details. Mr. Richland has filed a $100 million civil lawsuit against the hospital and the medical assistant. The coroner will take some of your questions.*

A question appears on the window screens.

Person J.–*Was that excessive time a medical negligence in Mrs. Richland's case?*

The coroner.–*Well, as for the records in the file and forensic analysis, yes, it was medical negligence.*

The main issue is nothing we can attribute to the spirits; everything results from ego. Humans need to correct this.

Dialogue with the audience–2018.

Guide.–*Trues, please continue.*

Trues.–*Listen to the thoughts of my mind. In an isolated state of mind, there are feelings, but not in the heart. A psychological or* *biological event can trigger emotions or feelings, but feelings are attitudes elsewhere in the mind: the soul. Pain, sorrow, and remorse are attitudes of consciousness in the soul. Its location is inaccurate; changes depending on conscious activity, but is within the soul.*

The right front screen of the stage appears, showing three moving elements in dark space.

—These elements of the soul are mind, consciousness and ego, floating on top of each other in the rare space of the mind. Suddenly, they freeze in one last visible arrangement, and that case is an image composed of attitudes.

Stacey.—*Let us clarify; feelings are attitudes—states of mind—excited by a situation, something that happens, such as an opinion. The mind is part of the soul, just as the consciousness and the ego are within the soul. They behave as sub-strata of the soul, free to move depending on the activities occupied by the other parties. But all this is spiritual, it's not physical or material.*

A question appears on the window screens.

Person K.—*Please, what are attitudes?*

Trues.—*Attitudes are reactions to the conditions and circumstances of the moment. The ego begets attitudes because of their tastes and dislikes, whims and preferences, their knowledge or ignorance, or their self-centered nature etc. Attitudes are personal forms towards issues, objects and/or topics, depending on the level of knowledge and/or understanding of the application. Ego is the source of tribulation.*

Guide.—*Wait a moment, please, we receive permission to take the audience a decade back in time, to the performances of dual beings. First, we will travel to Santa Tecla, El Salvador.*

Thursday, April 23, 1998, 5:30 p.m. Santa Tecla, 1998.

Moses is now eight years old; attends the last grade in school. Moses and his best friend, Carlos, are sitting on a tree trunk lying on the ground at the front of that house.

Moses.—*You know, Carlos, I would already like to be a grownup to work and help my family.*

Carlos.—*But if you're already working, you sell gums to the square in the afternoons after school.*

Moses.–*it is not enough and does not help.*

Poverty is sad, abandonment, when no one cares about the welfare of others. That is contrary to the purpose of life: to care and to share. But it is even sadder to think calamities scathe the innocent souls of children who still understand little about life. And adults know it.

Carlos.–*But we are children, we cannot be responsible for the whole family.*

There is no hope for people in poverty, and it is the situation we witness in homeless people in the United States. The difference is that, in third world countries, poor families live together in ghettos outside the city in small houses made of cardboard boxes, tree branches and debris–such as the favelas, in the hills–of Brazil. They're still looking for work, or working for food; don't beg; only in rare cases. Perhaps the dignity of the human is still in their souls. However, neither souls nor spirits intervene or interfere with what ego does; you have freedom of choice.

Moses.–*Yes, I'd like to do that. How I need my grandmother, Celia. She died almost two years ago, in 1996. You know, here in the house, just my mom, Juana, works and in two jobs, cleans the house of the Romero's, a family of a lot of money, and in the evenings and evenings, wash and iron clothes of the rich. My grandfather, always thinking of my aunt, Isabel. He dreams she's coming back.*

Carlos.–*Who is that aunt you talk about so much, where is she?*

Moses.–*I don't want to play with spinning tops anymore; I want to be alone, go.*

Carlos.–*What did I do?*

I've seen misery and poverty face to face, but I escaped. I understand the frustrations of these people; they live life for a long time with uncertain tomorrow. We see forgotten souls on the margins of societies; not even pretending to find a helping hand to take. They are in their own misery, waiting for the day of their death. Maybe death is the best chance they've got. This world has no equal opportunities for them, the rich, famous and powerful reserve all the better rights of life. Everything is dark for the poor, they have no hopes, no ambitions, no dreams; all this is dry in the desert of their misery. Who can help them? Religious people say that God can; but for the poor, help never comes. It is proof that in this mission our souls are or live on their own with their free will. But this could be the work of the soul creating conditions and circumstances to force an expected event. Perhaps we see the success of the purpose, later.

Moses.—*Nothing, Carlos, nothing. I'm sad. They say I'm a boy, but like a big guy. We live where insomnias devour our weak dreams. I can't see, I can't bear, the poverty we live in, one day we eat, another day we don't, and so we go.*

Carlos.—*But you're alive, you're studying, and you work… well, a little.*

Moses.—*just don't want to think about my mom dying, only she works. What would become of all of us?*

Carlos.—*Well, you didn't tell me who is that aunt, or where she is.*

Moses.—*No, I didn't tell you. She is my Aunt Isabel; she went to The United States, after I was born. I was less than a year old. That's what my grandmother told me shortly before she died. My aunt writes to my mom sometimes. She once told my mom she'd take me to where she is to study. My Aunt Isabel was about 14 when she left; really, I don't remember her. My mom got a little photo of her when she graduated from elementary school. I love her much for just what they tell me.*

Carlos.—*You're my best friend, now I have to go, I'll leave you alone, are you going to be okay?*

Moses.—*Yes, Carlos, go. I'm fine. But I keep thinking, I don't sleep, thinking about what I can do to grow faster, and help my family to the fullest.*

Carlos.—*See you later, take care, okay?*

Moses stays where Charles leaves him, immersed in thoughts, crying, growing with every tear that rolls down his brown cheek roasted by the tropical sun. The sun plunged below the distant horizon line; Moses rose and looked like an older boy, much older, very determined. It is difficult to live in a state of helplessness, impotent; it's as if we're in a thick glass bubble, at the mercy of others, with no resources to keep living. Death is there, at the end of a few more breaths. The sound of Moses' thoughts bounces back and forth in the echo of his empty soul. The ugly feeling or feeling that it is better to be dead than to suffer the endless agony of being alive. It is neither simple nor easy to feel helpless and hopeless. It's like being at the bottom of a dry well of water where no one can hear us outside and with no way out. But life always goes on like a river, drowning the tears of pure feeling, like love? We may never know as long as selfishness keeps us blind.

We arrived in mid-fall at the end of 1999. Moses is nine years old and finishing primary school, but he doesn't even think about Christmas. For him, there is no Christmas; there is no tree with lights and ornaments, no toys. You can only see reserved for the children of the rich. Juana is cooking "*Gallo pinto*" while placing several tortillas in a clay pot. The strong coffee aroma fills the space of that small house, and the roosters sing to the twilight of the morning that paints the reality of a new day for life cycles. The scent of love like that of coffee fills their souls.

Juana.—*Moses, son, get up, wash your face and come to eat. Remember that you have to go to school early for your graduation rehearsal.*

Moses.—*I'm coming, I'm coming, Mom. Yes, I remember. First, I go to the yard to collect firewood for your kitchen.*

That afternoon, after school, as usual, Moses goes to the park [plaza] to sell gum. Sitting at a wooden table with concrete benches, three men talk about how to get to the United States. The older man, Gregorio (El Coyote), in his forties, convinced the other two, about twenty years old, to venture north. Moses is listening to the conversation, standing behind the Coyote.

Gregorio wears new attire, trousers and shirt, (typical garments of people well-to-do in tropical cities); he wears gold rings on his fingers and a thick, heavy gold necklace hanging around his neck. He looks sideways at the coyote and sees Moses' shadow, spins quickly, and screams.

The Coyote.—*Grab that little boy, follow him and grab him.*

Gregory pulls out a 9-millimeter automatic pistol and fires five shots at Moses, but fails. Moses, surprised and frightened, fleeing, and after a few blocks, running through backyards, lost the men. He says out loud.

Moses.—*They almost grabbed me, almost killed me. Those two men already know me and they will look for me.*

That afternoon, like all the others, Carlos came to play with Moses. They were sitting on that old tree trunk, their favorite couch. Moses often looked over his shoulders, right and left.

Carlos.—*What's the matter, Moses, you look scared, did you see the devil?*

Another situation pressures Moses, the fear of the Coyote. It is not only the poverty in which he lives, the anguish of hunger knowing there is nothing to eat, but that now his life is in danger; next to his dream about him and Isabel. Moses breaks his silence and says.

Moses.—*The thing about me, Carlos, is that two men are looking for me. They were in the square; I went to sell my chewing gums; they talked about how to go to the United States, which only cost three thousand dollars, but they didn't have to pay anything because along the way they would work to deduct the payment. There was one old or older wearing rings and a gold chain around his neck, explaining to the other two, the ones looking for ways to leave.*

Carlos.—*Oh, Moses, what a mess you got yourself into. That one on the chain is a coyote. They say he's already killed several. What are you going to do?*

Moses.—*Well, I have to hide and stay away from the square, and I don't know what else. I'm lost. They will look for me at school.*

Carlos.—*Look, come live in my house, it's behind the school so you won't have to walk the streets. You can tell your mom we will get ready for the final graduation exams, which you think.*

Moses.—*I don't know, maybe I can't, I help my mom with housework. I will think straight and I'll tell you.*

Time passed; graduation day from school came and nothing happened; Moses forgot about that scary incident. It's the year 2000. Moses' graduation came and went without fanfare or celebration. Only the rich can celebrate. Moses could only see from the outside the expensive feasts they throw. That morning, Moses goes to school to collect his graduation certificate, and a successful completion statement. Moses graduated with high-grade points. The two men who had chased him once followed him to school and were waiting around the corner.

Ismael.—*Come, you son of a bitch, boy.*

One short man, Ishmael, holds Moses by the neck while the other, thin and tall, Chester, twists Moses' arm behind his back; they tie him up and push him onto the dirt street floor, face down.

Chester.—*Now you will see what happens to a nosy piece of shit.*

Chester went to pick up the black van and parked along that dirt street, yelling at Ishmael.

Chester.—*Hurry, Ismael, get the boy in the van, let's go asshole. The vehicle speeds up leaving behind a cloud of dust and drove fast straight to Gregory's house.*

Gregorio.—*Bring that brat and sit him in the room.*

Moses had his hands tied behind his back, a handkerchief in his mouth tied around his neck, and a thick bag of black cloth over his head.

Gregorio.—*From now on you will be with us until we sell your organs to the traffickers. This is your reward for listening to conversations that aren't for you.*

Gregory addresses his hitmen and says.

Gregorio.—*Lock him up in the box, and if he bothers you, beat him. We'll remove his organs when Dr. Raphael returns from Puebla in a few days... kill him if he gives you trouble and then refrigerate him.*

Chester threw Moses into a single-door room of steel and no windows—the box; they also threw in his backpack. The day passes, and the afternoon comes; Moses' mother, worried and desperate, looks for her son in the neighborhood.

Juana.—*I don't know why my Moses has not come. He should be back by now, and he just went to collect his diploma.*

The night passes slowly, and Juana is so desperate and immersed in her anguish she cannot sleep. She is tired and her mind overwhelmed, and her eyes rigidly open looking at the corrugated zinc, metal sheets, that cover the small roof of the house. In his captivity, frightened to death, Moses tries to suppress his fears and cries.

Moses.—*There was someone at that corner where they picked me up. Yes, someone saw everything. Oh, if that someone could go see my* *mom or the police. This dark room is damp and freezing. Ah, how good here is my backpack; they didn't take it away from me.*

That morning, Juana attends the police headquarters at eight. Besides a guard at the door, only the police chief, Commander Ruiz, is at the reception, arrogantly and rudely says.

The commander.–*How can I serve you, madam?*

Human life is so full of vicissitudes that the busy soul solving the tribulations, slobs and problems of the ego comes to think it is material, forgetting its origin. The ego itself thinks it belongs to the material dimension. He is a child with new material toys he did not have in the spirit dimension–to say something. Here you have your tantrums, your whims, your cravings, with the backing of AGHAPEE. Spirits have no ego, only their thinking mind.

Juana.–*I want to make a complaint; my son Moses has not returned to the house since yesterday afternoon. He doesn't do that not to go home.*

The commander.–*Madam, we can do nothing, wait seventy-two hours to report a missing person. But give me the boy's data. I'm opening an information file, but not filing your complaint.*

Juana.–*Moses, Moses Suarez, he is only eight years old; he has just finished his kindergarten studies.*

The commander gave a paper form on a tablet with a presser to Juana. And he says.

The commander.–*Madam, fill out this questionnaire.*

Juana fills out the questionnaire with Moses information and returns it to the officer. Juana waits, standing by the counter; and the commander rudely says.

The commander.–*What do you wait for, there's nothing more to do. Juana breaks in tears, leaves the office, crosses the street towards the church across the square.*

The officer waits for Juana to leave and with a tone of superiority screams.

The commander.–*Private Lopez. Find the Toad Ortiz and tell him I want to see him right away.*

An hour later, Toad enters Commander Ruiz's office.

Toad-Ortiz.–*At your command, my commander.*

The commander.–*Look, son of a bitch, I know you kidnapped Moses Suarez, that eight-year-old boy. I don't want you to get me in and trouble. Did you hear me?*

The commander and the toad know what's going on, but the commander wants to keep his hands clean. Toad's plan is to extract Moses' organs and sell them. Commander Ruiz will take his usual part.

Toad-Ortiz.–*Look, my sergeant,*

The commander.–*You look, son of a bitch, don't call me sergeant, I'm the commander-chief of police.*

Toad-Ortiz.–*My commander, that meddling boy, heard what I was saying to those two boys I told you, the ones who want to go north; and I catch him and I have him in my house well kept. I was coming this morning, but you're ahead of me again, as usual.*

The commander.–*Like I told you, son of a… I want no trouble. Get that boy out of the country now, or give him back to his mother, and you'll face the consequences. I'll say I know nothing about your business, and this business is over. But no matter what you decide, you always give me my share in cash or I send you to hell.*

Toad-Ortiz.–*So, I will my commander, so be it.*

The commander.–*Don't overdo it or try to do something without telling me, I know that Dr. Raphael is coming these days to collect organs. I've got you in my sight, you understand?*

Toad-Ortiz.–*Yes, my commander, I take all of that into account.*

The Toad Ortiz leaves, closes the door of the commander's office and runs to his black van parked in front of the police station.

It's been three days or seventy-two hours since Moses disappeared. Juana returns to the police station to file a report of a missing child. And after completing the paperwork, and the commander reviews the complaint, the clerk informs Juana that the investigation was officially underway. Juana returns home, hoping that Commander Ruiz could bring her son Moses back.

Corruption spreads everywhere, at all levels of power, business and society. They speak in codes so people don't understand. The mode of operation is to engage key people to control or manipulate their actions. The code of action is in famous phrases, as one favor with another favor; I scratch your back and you scratch mine later. Is this how the cartel controls entire villages, such as the Medellin and Sinaloa Cartels? The Early nineteen, the Italian Mafia, offered protection to small businesses against the vandalism of the same Mafia. Some spiritual organizations offer *"soul salvation"* by voluntary (fear-driven) donations. The exploitation of humans by humans is real; is a free enterprise, in the open free market. The people vote and choose mafias for their government? Maybe not, but humans should study this situation. People should analyze the truth of value added, or the genesis of wealth. We know that only physical human labor does all material items such as goods, products, and services. They use materials that come out of the physical world. But AGHAPEE, the ogre who lives in the egos of humans, stimulates corruption, and the tribulations of humans are direct consequences of their attitudes towards life. Reducing, eliminating and making sure AGHAPEE doesn't return is the main goal of spirits entering human bodies–tainting the ego. Moses' situation is transforming. Now the cartel forces want to send him away, dead or alive. The path of his life is narrow.

Dialogue with the public -2018.

The situation in Manhattan, NY - 2001.

Breaking news is coming to the television networks. The right and left screens of the stage background turn on. A female reporter breaks the news, showing a view of Mr. Richland's young son Victor. Victor has just graduated from elementary school at eleven with great honors. He will move to the intermediate school, Fairmont, one of the best and most expensive schools in New York City.

Presenter.–*This morning Victor Richland receive his school diploma.*

Young Richland said he will attend a campus. He wants to pursue his father's career in business and real estate. The boy left school and boarded a limousine armored by several armed bodyguards at the school entrance. The graduation event was still ongoing. A spokesman for the family stated that Mr. Richland asked his son to return to his mansion immediately. Mr. Richland planned a graduation party for his son, inviting the wealthiest billionaires in the United States and the world, and was waiting for his son at his mansion. This morning rush was only to give Victor a gift, an Andalusian horse, white, thoroughbred. Reporters may not take photos and/or videos of family members and or the mansion. The family invited a select group of renowned reporters to cover Victor's graduation party. A mile from the beachfront at the back of your mansion, a private property, and reserved for the Richland family. The horse jogs on the seashore, guided by special trainers. Our network sought current laws and found that the coast is state-owned and not exclusive to anyone. This may be a hole in the law, something the network's legal team will investigate.

Guide.—*We, the spirits, observe the growing social and economic gaps that divide humans. The phenomenon is this socio-economic imbalance can explode and change conditions soon. Several cases in human history have showed this phenomenon: in France, in Latin America and in the American colonies. Anyway, let's go back to the four typical trips in life cycles.*

The situation in Henderson, Nevada–1991.

We're going back in time to a year after the shooting at the station's casino parking lot in Henderson, Nevada; the massacre in the ICU of Henderson Hospital. The investigation by the City of Henderson criminal division into the deaths of Rocky and Vicky Martin, and Jeff Anderson, is neither closed nor closed. The Chief of Police talks to reporters in the criminal division of the police in Henderson.

Reporter 1.—*Sir, what is the status of the criminal case involving Mrs. and Mr. Martin and Jeff Anderson, Mrs. Martin's lover?*

The Chief of Police.—*This case remains on hold, pending additional evidence we may collect; however, the case has sufficient evidence to lead to a conclusive determination. The criminal division and the coroner's office concluded that Jeff was not a lover of Vicky Martin, legally married to Ricky Martin, I mean, Rocky Martin. Rocky and Vicky married ten years before their deaths. A family feud led Vicky to escape her abusive husband, who was jealous of Vicky. Jeff, his accountant, offered him a hiding place* *in Henderson, Nevada, believing he could make a life with Vicky. Jeff was in love with Vicky, but not the other way around. The Couple Martin left a son named by the hospital authorities as Rex Martin. The social work department assumed custody of the child immediately after the events and handed over to an orphanage. Through our research, we found legal evidence that the Martin family had a wealth of about $360 million in current assets and nearly $930 million in fixed assets in California. Rex Martin has no relatives, and as a minor he gains the right to dispose of his full inheritance at 21. Nevada declared Rex the sole heir to that estate, and appointed a legal guardian/administrator, California resident. The Nevada Attorney General has legally transferred all legal responsibilities to the California Attorney General. Nevada has also determined that it is legal and appropriate to allow the legal/administrative guardian to move Rex to his home in Beverly Hills, California, at the most convenient time for the child. Is there a question?*

There was a momentary silence, but then a MZNDC reporter asks.

MZNDC reporter.—*Did. you or the responsible coroner do a DNA test?*

Chief Detective.—*Yes, the forensic officer, Kurt Ima Ginette, and the coroner, Sam Corpse, ordered and supervised a DNA procedure, officially concluding that Rex Martin is by blood, biological, legitimate son of Mr. and Mrs. Martin. This evidence defines and establishes Rex Martin's right to inherit the Martins' estate. We discovered a written message from Vicky that says, "Jeff, I'm pregnant, can we do this?" Apparently, Vicky had an affair with Jeff, so Jeff thought he was the father. There is no evidence this matter has occurred; the message could also refer to his escape to Henderson.*

ZMN International Reporter.—*As for the bodies of Jeff, Mr. and Mrs. Martin, who claimed their bodies?*

The Chief of Police.—After the legal term, and noting that no one claimed Jeff Anderson's body, and, having heard no claim for the remains of Mr. and Mrs. Martin, and for humanity, Nevada allowed the legal administrator of Rex Martin taking full responsibility for the burials. No more questions, thank you much. The screens went out and the guide came back.

Back to year–2000.

Rex Martin grew up in a very protected environment, but perhaps not as sophisticated as Victor Richland's case. Rex needed nothing. Because and the way his parents died in Henderson, Nevada, and because of that mistake by the head nurse at Henderson Hospital, Rex's schoolmates call him Ricky Martin. Rex is by nature very charismatic and popular. A day after his grade-graduation, Rex's mood changed. However, he is now ten years old, and decides on his own actions. Later, one day at the beginning of school at Junior HS, Rex and his tutor (guardian) reviewed which high school to attend.

The Guardian (a middle-aged woman).–*Rex, I've been going over which HS you should attend. Here's a list of Los Angeles County higher education, plus Beverly Hill.*

Rex has been calling his executor 'mother' for a long time, almost after he talked. She's the mother he knows.

Rex.–*Mom, could I choose the school I can attend?*

Guardian.–*Well, tell me which one you want to choose.*

She pushes Rex her list of schools on the table.

Rex.–*Mom, I don't want to go to any stiff necks' school. I want to go to a public high school, may I?*

The guardian, with a London accent, says.

Guardian.–*God, why do you want to do that? Public schools aren't for you.*

Rex.–*Mom, why not? They are good schools; millions of children attend public schools. I want to go where the real kids are going. I don't want to be a fake kid.*

Rex needed to mingle or partner with normal children and people. What is the meaning of this impulse? Maybe Rex senses that people in her class base her feelings and behavior on the gain they can draw from a friendship. Maybe people of scants are more sincere. Maybe! In reality, the whole society is corrupt full of envy, ambition, selfishness, etc. Maybe at your level don't fight for anything, if you have everything just by asking for it–without challenges. Is the latter what Rex thinks like to be a real kid? We don't know, and maybe the spirits that know condition Rex's mind. See!

Guardian.—*Well, your personal safety for example, and then there's a private relationship with your schoolmates. They belong to a lower economic level, and that can be a difficult situation for any friendly relationship, you understand?*

Rex.—*Mom, all I want is to have a real child's life, not a child's life in a glass bubble.*

The guardian stops to think and consider what Rex just said. His thought was not simple. Rex's thoughts had a profound meaning, not normal for an eleven-year-old. All humans live in the bubble of their own ego; bubbles that separate their souls, preventing them from relating to pure honesty and love.

The guardian collects the school list and says.

Guardian.—*Rex, I think you might be right, I'll think about it for a few days, so we'll talk about this again.*

Guide.—*Maybe the guardian has overprotected Rex. She always had private tutors for her learning and a Spanish-speaking nanny, Celia (Chela) who took care of her needs, including playing with toys, and hiding in the garden and house, or when Rex enters the pool. Rex was very intelligent and was ahead of children his age.*

Two weeks later, the executor finds Rex in the house's library, lying on his belly, on the floor, reading a book about the history of the independences of Mexico and Central America.

Guardian.—*Rex, I've concluded that you can go to the high school of your choice. I've fixed your personal security and protection, especially from the press. I think for a while, you will go to that school, but you can't visit or spend the night at any friend's house you can develop. Is that a good deal?*

Rex.—*Mom, yes, I really love you. Yes, thank you.*

Rex got up and hurried to kiss her and says.

Rex.—*That's great!*

The guardian and Rex, both, are right. But the guardian has a duty and responsibility to protect and secure Rex. Anyone can try to take advantage of Rex's financial conditions when they realize his fortune. Rex goes out and goes to find his Nana Celia to tell her the good news. Celia was a young woman, relatively, perhaps in her early thirties. There are days when Celia brings her son, Jaime, a year younger than Rex, and they play together in the garden, though not in the mansion. Rex calls him Jim. Jim was a good-looking, quiet and very intelligent. He was very adept at putting things with the Lego pieces. Rex learned a lot from Jim. I see here again the social and economic gaps in human society that impede or block the evolution of humans to oneness. Humans have a long way to go before a synergy of the two dimensions, when spirit and matter harmonize to coexist in a single dimension.

Guide.—*Audience, let us open this problem in a forum so you can ask questions. Sexis, Robert and Trues will join us.*

Person L.—*Yes, please define what you mean by 'oneness'.*

Guide.—*This is an excellent question. The theme, however, is profound and very significant.*

Robert.—*...and the power of will work with the human ego.*

If you understand what is unique and implement it, you will speed up the evolution of your human towards the goal of existence: the full integration of the components of the human, the soul and the material body. We have said that humans understand and accept that love is a driving power of existence. These two components, yourself as energy and matter, will merge into one, and the spirit and the body will coexist in the dimension of spirits and in the material dimension simultaneously: This is true uniqueness. And pure love will unite the two. Not that the body material can float and travel through time to other places. Actually, the human doesn't need that faculty.

Trues.—*Let's clarify this topic. The fusion of soul and body energy and matter in one does not mean that the human body floats and travels time back and forth. It is enough if they eliminate tribulations and live satisfied, conform with gratitude to the goodness of the universe.*

Robert.—*Trues, it doesn't mean that the human knows everything either, and can do anything (like a superhuman). No, it's not that.*

Sexies.—*It means that consciousness, wisdom, then humans will not think and act under selfish impulses, but will behave based on the truth and love and the general good of all humans. Then they will get into the order of harmony of the universe. And humans will behave according to truth and love; but they won't act driven by feelings and emotions. At that moment humans will control their ambition, their greed, hatred,* *avarice, prejudice, envy, and egotism; humans must tame AGHAPEE, the ogre within the ego.*

Wow, that state would be paradise, heaven, Shangri la, Nirvana. It would be a perfect state of human love, affection, and sharing. But can humans get this before they destroy themselves?

A question appears on the window screens.

Persona M.—*Please, you can tell us how, and what tools and procedures we can use to achieve this oneness.*

Guide.—*Oneness is the harmonious coexistence of a spirit and a material body (or matter).*

Sexy.—*Achieve oneness by cleaning up your ego. By killing the AGHAPEE Ogre that exists inside you, using mental weapons like love, sharing with and caring for your human neighbor, and suppressing material consciousness. [xxv] AGHAPEE's death is slow and prolonged, but the more you hit it with love and kindness "sharing and caring," AGHAPEE becomes weaker, until your love and goodness are so strong this Ogre cannot manipulate your ego.*

A spirit listening raised a hand, and the guide nods in consent.

Spirit Listening.—*By then your will and discipline grows and becomes strong, defending, protecting you and protecting you against the recovery of AGHAPEE. You already have a soul in you to protect yourself from within, and that soul will work through your mind with spirits around you to protect yourself from the outside; this is when the spirits coming to help you become protective spirits. Then your soul and your mind will work together to perfect your oneness.*

All four screens on the stage turn on. The rear-left is for spirit A, the rear-right is for spirit B, on the front left and the front-right is the global spirit moving above the man sitting in a chair in the front center of the stage, in front of the audience. The music plays. Ten spirits dance together on stage around the man, waving their colorful scarves, transparent: purple, blue, orange and red, while the lights follow each.

THE CODICIA (Dialogue of Uniqueness)

An angels' chorus sings.

Spirit A.—*Here he is, the blind man, right?*

The man.*—Where? I can't see him; it's not me; please point him to recognize him.*

Spirit B.*—Blind, your foolishness is everywhere showing the theme of your whim. It's you. Why did you ask for cognition? Don't deny what you said.*

Global spirit.*—Silly, sickening; you have left your honesty behind; you do not need that excessive desire to possess or gain material wealth; your delight is the gluttony of abundant things; and whatever happens for you that is or die. Ignorant, blind man, do you know your greed?*

Spirit B.*—Your selfishness: That desire to gain more than necessary. That avid desire for wealth is sin. I see your face, anxious and greedy, angry, capable of anything for money, power and fame. Blind, greedy old man, you have no love.*

The man sitting in the center-front of the stage in front of the audience gets up and says.

The man.*—But everyone does, why don't I?*

We all compete 'and whoever has more is better'. I'm just trying to get ahead. What's wrong with that? I want to be richer than the rest. They must bow before me, lowering their heads.

Global spirit.*—But you deny others their basic needs, accumulating wealth beyond your needs; and you still want to snatch their survival resources; you know that is your obsession to take away others' food and you do so without remorse. You even use your wealth to gain power, denying others their sacred rights; you build, at the expense of others' welfare, your empire, the tower of your kingdom to increase your influence, glory and fame; your greed is unjust, blind, and immoral.*

Spirit B.*—Shame on you, blind shame; you must change to return to Eden. Abandon your greed, envy and lust, and share your medal of fame. Stop the gluttony, break the greed you carry hidden in your excessive pride.*

Global spirit.*—Until you give up all that for the better and let your hunger for wealth fall, your desire to accumulate possessions, and change to share and care, in a state of honest mood for the health of your brother and sister, you will not gain oneness.*

A thunderous lightning strikes the man; the theater darkens and lights up again. Two spirits drag the inert man. The debate that concludes paints the picture of the human mind infested by its corruption. The AGAPEAE inspires the greed in him and corrodes his ego-this is the specific argument. There are other tentacles of this ogre that you must also amputate. Remember what the tentacles are-ogre's heads? The stage darkens as the audience stays in the twilight.

The situation in Arriaga, Chiapas MX - 2000.

Robert.—*The situation in Arriaga is an example of greed, violence and corruption, a battle of selfish misbehavior against the peaceful way of love for life. Life need not be hard and rude, sometimes impossible; life must be sweet and soft, delightful.*

Trues enters the stage and intervened in the speech says.

Trues.—*The library of omniscience records all information, or evidence, of human behavior, selfish or not, that creates deviations from what life should be. Humans, and only humans, are responsible for the consequences, corrections and or redirects of their intentions and purposes. Souls in humans and the spirits do not interfere, nor intervene, in the free choice of humans. They define the attribute of free will after inflection—when minds integrate—and the ego of the human develops. Humans must change by their own free will, desire and choice, and in no other way.*

Sexy.—*The conditions of poverty and human abandonment are the dangers, risks and threats to the mind and life. The ruthless Sinaloa cartel and drug lords and poverty are reason enough to emigrate to a nation that offers the opportunity to live a safe and fruitful life. People do not emigrate on a whim; They leave their loved persons behind by living or death.*

Robert's thoughts appear on the window screen on the right.

Robert.—*A bit of information in the library of our omniscience contains the following. Some beauty of nature placed. It is a rainforest and green vegetation maintained by the humidity of the climate typical tropical areas. But business, agriculture and livestock have eradicated its beautiful and rich vegetation. Chiapas is not a prosperous state; it's a very underdeveloped area of Mexico. Chiapas' economy for years depended on agriculture that provided a stable source of income for the working* *population but is no longer there. People have moved their occupation to other activities, such as fishing in the Pacific Ocean.* [38],[39]

But people continue to work or cultivate their lands, but above all for their own consumption, just to survive. One factor that impacts is drug smuggling by a ruthless cartel, assumedly headed by Joaquín El Chapo Guzmán (detained and in custody), in the United States.

Stacey.—*Their economic situation is difficult, and farmers work for survival wages. This justifies leaving the area in search of a better life: it is a human right. The United States government does not understand that if conditions in Third World countries were hospitable, its people would not risk their lives to emigrate to rich nations. Another factor is that rich nations exploit poor nations, creating more poverty and the will to emigrate.* [40]

Trues.—The public knows Joaquin (el Chapo) Guzman. Well, around the early 1990, he was very active in drug trafficking so close to the border with Guatemala. People live days difficult in Chiapas because the Sinaloa Cartel kidnaps people for *organ and drugs trafficking.*

Joaquin "El Chapo" Guzman, the man called by the America, the most powerful drug trafficker in the world, was captured in the coastal city of Mazatlan, a senior mexican prosecutor said. He had escaped, but eventually captured on January 17, 2016, and is currently in jail following his conviction, trial and sentencing.

---

[38] https://en.wikipedia.org/wiki/Chiapas,Wikipedia, 2006, par 2)

[39] Chiapas, https://www.history.com/topics/mexico/chiapas

[40] Declaración Universal de Derechos Humanos Naciones Unidas. www.un.org/en/universal-declaration-human-rights/index.html

The left front screen shows a photo of the Chapo for 15 seconds. The situation, and the conditions in Arriaga, Chiapas is a justification for forced emigration in search of better chances of survival. However, human corruption is even worse than drug trafficking through Arriaga. The total population of the municipality called Arriaga is 38,572 citizens, 18,815 men and 19,757 women. Many escape the drug cartel and organ dealers. The four screens show breaking [41] news: Final screenshot of Chapo Guzmán, [42] showing a photo of El Chapo.

Sexy.–*The omniscience of the spiritual dimension contains and preserves all the knowledge in the universe. The thoughts, decisions and actions of all living beings in the tangible universe are visible in the spiritual dimension. Please don't worry, you can keep thinking. We maintain and protect your privacy; it's your sacred right. We do not sell your ID or personal information to "WikiLeaks" or cyber thieves. Spirits do not traffic or profit with your information, and spirits know everything. Our information system is a lot, but very controlled and secure, that Facebook, Twitter, WhatsApp and any other medium on earth.*

Sergio Maltes is now ten years old, but he is much older than that, perhaps not because of his years of life, but because of his intense experience of self-preservation in a constant struggle of survival. The economic situation degraded by the continuing war between the DEA and the drug and human organ trafficking, making incursions into specific locations, especially around the site and farms where the Sinaloa Cartel operates. This is one reason the farmers community loses its desire to invest in productive efforts.

Guide.–*Now, a dual being, Sergio, is ten years old, and knows the calamities of the people of Arriaga. At a young age, he also works on nearby farms, picking products, tomato, chilli, and onions, etc. Children have the constant threat of the cartel, which kidnaps them for clandestine organ extraction, trafficking and speculation. We see the truth and we know the truth.*

---

[41] www.bloomberg.com/news/2014-02-22/-el-chapo-guzman-mo...

[42] https://www.nytimes.com/2016/01/17/world/americas/Mexico-el-chapo...

Sergio with his friend Pedro walks back from school one afternoon; Pedro is also ten years old and goes to the same school as Sergio.

Sergio.–*What a pain in the ass is to be poor, like us; you don't even feel as going to school.*

Sergio's friend Paul comes running, almost exhausted, screaming. Police vehicles, Ford Ranger vans, run on the streets, sounding their alarms at full volume. They travel in a hurry, transporting armed national guards.

Paul.–*Hey, the DEA and local drug agents are raiding the Rancho Grande farm, people say that's the place where they take the children, they kidnap for human organ trafficking. There was a shooting confrontation and four organ traffickers. The DEA captured one of them after they shot. An officer dead.*

Sergio.–*Yes, all that can be good, but what good does it make you know that; it doesn't help us. What's the point of believing, having faith, and praying, when no one hears our prayers? In reality, everything we do in human life and its consequences is and is our responsibility.*

Pedro.–*Only we must resolve or suffer. You and I are children and we work in the field in out of school time, in the evenings. Our vacation is when we go to school. The rich don't work the fields, they go to private schools; they have good parties, food, toys and so on.*

Obvious; life is a vortex of misery, offering unlikely chances of escaping that force that sucks those who fall there. The spectrum of poverty to wealth shows the majority in poverty and the minority (the few) in the rich extreme. So, if this line were a beam on a fulcrum like an up-and-down, the poor is down while the rich are always up. Similarly, the greatest wealth is at the top and below there is little.

Children's thoughts and words are a reality of all societies. They are children, but they tell the truth and suffer equally or more. Their frustrations and pains, the agony in poverty, kills them in hopelessness. And the wind brings his words of anguish to an empty horizon. No one, nothing, is around here to help them, except their own willingness to live or die in their efforts.

Paul.—*For me, that's not a joke. We always serve justice always. History says Pancho Villa's troops fought for the justice and a better situation for the poor and hardworking.*

Sergio.—*So, what did Jesus Christ and Pancho Villa do? This isn't fair. We're as we are because we have done nothing, you see? Poverty brings people to the brink of despair, the twilight of the mind when moral values lose their values, and the need to survive makes them potential criminals. For them, everything goes if it's to survive. I maintain that sharing and caring is how to reduce crime and crime.*

Pedro.—*I've heard people say that in the United States any asshole works an hour and earns a lot more than an adult here wins in two days. I'm thinking, get out of this miserable town and go to the United States from there if I could help my family.*

Sergio.-*But they also say that those who carry them, those coyotes, are the ones who really make a lot of money, passing illegal immigrants at the border, they say, there for Mexicali, to the north. They say that mothers and fathers disappeared their organs and sold clandestinely for thousands of dollars. They say there's a big organization dedicated to child trafficking and organ trafficking, and border-watchers are in that ring.*

But the struggle is in the human soul. The discords or fights that pass through the minds of humans result from the selfish behavior actions of other humans.

Paul.—*When I finish school, I get out of this town. The risk is worth it. I want to go where I can work, study, be a good person, and help my family.*

Humans living off waste feel abandoned. It is the game of souls and minds, a game that conscience and ego make in daily life. Life is not material; it is spiritual (non-religious). What's the difference? The difference is in the wide social gaps. Other living creatures do not experience societies, especially in modern societies, making these struggles or discords, because they fit and live with what the environment provides. Humans have not yet learned to live with the power of their souls and minds. Humans have not yet figured out how to balance their egos with their consciences, to live in peace with the order of harmony of the universe. This balance will eventually come when humans understand what love is, care for and share. This is when the elements of human society will contribute their part to the common goal of life: oneness.

So, you see these guys, ten or eleven, look at the reality as reality is. They call it what it is. But the forces and actions in the background are darker than what we see on the surface. Corruption is profound at all levels of the ladder of dishonesty in government, church, free enterprise, free market and societies; they are partakers in a common promise: exploitation for selfish advantage. It's all about excessive ambition, greed, hatred, prejudice, envy, greed and egotism. The AGHAPEE that advises and manipulates human egos.

Sergio.–*However, as long as you cross the border alive. Those coyotes, they don't like to take old people; they prefer young people; old people get exhausted on the way–from here to the border. I'd rather stay with my family.*

Perhaps organs and human trafficking are a broader illegal regime used to abuse people in miserable conditions. They, Cartels, organize large caravans of families and individuals, offering secure access to the United States. But the goal is to separate children from their parents or relatives for the source of organs; they never return them to their parents. They use young women in forced prostitution. Could this be the total plan? The plan is in the hands of wealthy and powerful individuals helped by people in positions of authority. How can people get rid of these criminals and their corrupt schemes? It's a nut that's hard to crack; a lot of money is at stake fueled by hidden interests.

Peter.–Hey, my uncle knows a guy who knows the move; I will dig in.

Paul.–*Well, boys, I'll see you in the afternoon; are you coming to the square?*

Sergio and Pedro answered yes. But like those things that happen in life, no one went to the square; maybe their spirits kept them away, or they had a better plan. Completed events show the actual plan; and humans can't see results until they're done. So, humans can see the purpose that what happens now is because of what happened before. However, the next day they met again at the end of school in the afternoon. Free spirits don't have these problems like humans. But notice that the souls of humans with similar tribulations cling or come together. Human problems attract souls and spirits by groups or categories of tribulations. For example, rich people hang out with rich people, celebrities hang out with celebrities, people with a power look for other people with power. Will souls need to solve their tribulations, pains, sorrows, groups and categories? Is this why they hang out together? We'll see.

Paul.–*Hey, Pedro, what did you discover? About that trip.*

Peter.–*Yes, discover. Discover that the Coyote charges two thousand five hundred dollars, and they don't guarantee the pass.*

Sergio.–*That's a lot of bucks. Who can pay so much?*

Omniscience records the history of all the resulting plans, thoughts, activities, and events, present, and future. All knowledge is there; nothing is unknown. Free spirits know what is in the journal of human behavior, but souls cannot enter the past or see the future. Human minds can only see the future by analyzing all the activities, conditions, situations and circumstances that play a role in the realization of an event. I will ask the spirits to explain how spirits see the future.

Pedro.–*No, asshole, I learned that those who have no money work in ranches along the way to pay for the trip.*

Sergio.–*I don't believe in all that, you can imagine how long you have to work to pay for that money. I have to go back; I see you later.*

Once again, the three friends went their way, saying the typical farewell. They didn't talk about this company anymore. The mystery of life is that the wheels of moving existence in the material universe. The law of causes and effects is active. Therefore, for each synergistic set of topics, activities, conditions and situations, there is a definite result. Conditions and situations organize and accommodate to give the expected result; human souls cannot avoid the natural sequence that leads to an event. Human minds can say, it is what it is, or what it will be, it will be. But it is not, it is not a random causality; the laws of combinations and permutations, in this application, dictate that for a certain group of issues, conditions and situation there is a specific event, and only, one expected result. We know the results before they happen, if we knew the issues, conditions and situations that cause an event. Humans, however, have only a small control over their thoughts, decisions and activities. And by changing their action, they also change the result of the synergistic set. Spirits know this and often come to help the souls of humans make the changes that avoid the impact of results.

Three months later, the three friends headed to a neighborhood store; when a middle-aged man, the messenger, approaches them.

Messenger.–*Hey, I knew you're interested in venturing abroad; I have the key, and I can help you. The boss knows you inquired about a trip. He sends me to propose a way, and you need not spend anything. What do you think?*

Pedro.–*But you are of the police; I have seen you in command.*

Messenger.–*No, I'm not in the police. But Francisco Cantoreal is the boss's quaint. He's your relative.*

Pedro.–*And what did your boss tell you?*

They talked, sitting on the floor in the corner. After a while, Sergio got up and says.

Sergio.–*I'll go, I'll see you tomorrow.*

At that moment, everyone got up and left. But when they walked, the messenger says.

Messenger.–*See you later, think about it.*

Back to the present, 2018.

Guide.–*Let us continue our dialogue: they show existence in tangible and intangible dimensions. We study two in this research, spiritual and material–life cycles. The universe is full of only two elements, energy and matter, they are the same–they exist in a continuous state of transformation–energy to matter and matter to energy. This notion is very important if we want to understand these two dimensions; but even if they separated the dimensions of spirits and matter, they share the same space; and spirits merge into living matter anywhere in the universe.*

A question appears on a person's screens in the audience.

Person N:–*Could you explain the operation of the living spirit in our bodies? Besides, how can oneness be possible?*

Trues.–*Sure. Every human behaves or realizes his life, and no one else does it for him. All souls are independent. But there is an important superior function of the soul you have; that's your mind. Humans could* *say that the soul is their mind. The soul manages the human with the mind, and two main components, conscience and ego.*

The mind connects with the omniscience of the global (not sacred) spirit to through the soul. The mind thinks and or reasons the realities observed considering the truth of existence. This is how geniuses have discovered laws of existence and applied them in practical uses for the good of humans. For example, penicillin, electricity, electro-encephalogram, EEG, and many others. Consciousness and ego use the power of mind thinking for their own purposes. The mind sees beyond the materiality of the universe and human materialism. It reaches the pure essence of Truth and Love. The mind of the soul belongs to the dimension of spirits, and spirits belong to the global spirit. So, the thought is spiritual; it is not material. The ego is a function of the soul, the expression of the human character and personal identification; like a permanent program embedded in the brain. The ego runs open, manipulates your mind, and so it also influences your soul. He is the link between the soul and the physical world, reality.

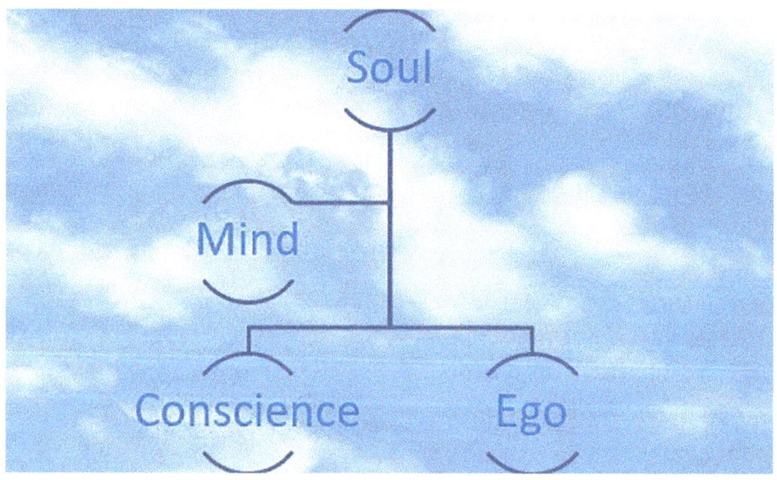

Figure 10: Structure of the Soul

The ego manipulates the emotions, feelings and feelings of humans to their desires, purposes and advantages, transforming thoughts into bodily actions in the material dimension.

Stacey.–*The other component of the soul is consciousness; it manages your emotions, feelings, feelings and moral values. The moral values of consciousness include good and evil, right and wrong, and just and unjust. Wisdom and reasoning don't handle feelings or emotions. Love is an attitude that can also generate logical and ideological actions through the mind. And the mind can analyze the truth of existence and the universe.*

Robert arrives raising his hand or asking permission to speak. And the guide makes a sign of acceptance with her hand.

Robert.–*But I have one more problem; this is how the components of the soul interact within the mind. Components of the soul can use mental functions. First wisdom, a function of the mind, analyzes logic, truth, reality and consequences, providing its findings to consciousness and ego. And second consciousness is the party that oversees the ego's behavior; and with willpower, as an implementing agent, he strives to change the motives and actions of the ego. And conflicts flourish between the different perspectives of consciousness and ego.*

Guide.–*Wait, guys, let's stop our forum. We received permission to go back in time to Richland Mansion in Manhattan, NY. We have breaking news.*

More in Manhattan NY–2016.

The two rear screens of the stage turn on. A MZNDC presenter is on the left screen: Breaking News.

Presenter.–*Victor Richland, the billionaire's son, Mr. Richland, fainted at the graduation ceremony at Harvard University. The faculty of Harvard University and its classmates consider Victor a genius. Victor graduated last semester with the highest honors and two years in advance. His father, Mr. Richland, bought a law firm for the young Richland to run. It is a corporation called 'Richland and Associates, based in Manhattan, New York.*

Presenter.—*ZMN International: reporting from the hospital where Victor arrived earlier: Preliminary information shows that the young lawyer suffers from a strange bronchial-pulmonary condition, draining his energy. We are now waiting for the chief doctor, who will provide additional details. Victor's story has had important episodes. In 1990 Victor's mother died in the hospital and baby Victor almost failed. Witnesses said it was a miracle victor was born alive. Victor has advanced his time, completing his education two years earlier than normal.*

The hospital's chief doctor takes to the podium: all the journalists run to locate their microphones close. The chief physician, Francis Francini, an Italian-American physician attends to Victor.

Dr. Francini.—*Ladies and gentlemen, after long and careful examination, diagnosis and emergency tests, the medical staff of our hospital has concluded that the patient, Victor Richland, suffers from a rare lung bronchial disease caused by a strange bacterium sometimes found in decaying trees. We have requested tests of old logs of trees lying on the beach in front of his waterfront mansion in Boston, where Victor will meditate, study and rest.*

MZNDC reporter.—*Has the medical panel found a treatment for Victor's disease?*

Dr. Francini.—*The panel, fortunately, concluded that the patient should move for a while to a dry or semi-desert environment that can help fight bacteria. We suggest the Richland family move Victor somewhere in Southern California. That's all the time we have for now. We will send newsletters to the press as new evidence and/or information is available and allowed by Mr. Richland. Yes, thank you.*

Back to the year 2016.

The MZNDC network moves to the presidential campaign where Donald Trump, a New York billionaire, and Hillary Clinton, a former secretary of state under the Obama presidency. Several polls predict with a high expectation that Mrs. Clinton will be the next 'President OF AMERICA'S UNITED STATES! The window screen turns off.

I have discussed the situation in Santa Tecla, El Salvador, and the situation in Arriaga, Chiapas, Mexico. Corruption is the same in the world. Manipulative governments, businesses and societies. We hear that Russia became deeply involved and influenced or manipulated the presidential election's result for Donald Trump. Meanwhile, the Trump campaign deployed a brutal attack on Mrs. Clinton, calling her *crooked Hillary* to tarnish her character. The intelligence community claims this based on their search started shortly before.

Return to the present–2018.

Guide.–*Stacey, when we went to Manhattan, Robert was explaining the concept of ego motives and actions please continue after his statement.*

Stacey.–*Spirits foresee the results because they see the future, the present and the past. The human ego is impulsive and does not reason its thoughts and actions. Human egos are weak and cunning, demagogues manipulate people's thoughts, feelings, and emotions. Politicians know it, but people, the believer in sincerity and honesty, bite the hook of politicians. And people become fished, blindly following a (supposedly leader), ignoring where they take them. Analyze what you learn, and you will see the truth through the curtain of lies you hear.*

Guide.–*We advise you that Stacey's comments only emphasize how the human's egos and souls work. Stacey's comments have nothing to do with political divisions or the results of Robert Mueller's investigation or congress. We have seen the result, and we will see more in the short future; but we can't reveal what it is. They'll find out soon or after 2020.*

A question from someone in the audience appears on window screens.

Person O.–*Will they dismiss President Trump? Will he leave the White House?*

Guide.–*Wait a minute. Our forum is a deep theoretical discourse on uniqueness, it is not a political town hall; we have a play in this theater. We reiterate that our mission, as spirits in their bodies, does not allow us to interfere with their decisions and actions: you are responsible for what you think, say, decide and do. What you read, hear and see* *here is the composition of what lives in your mind. Our field of work is the management of their minds, while their ego manages their personal emotions and attitudes. This is regarding the sacred specifications of the universe that establish human freewill, or free choice. Perhaps the truth trail will respond positively to those three questions. However, we say that your rule of law, constitution and form of government of your country can continue and not perish from the land, if you preserve all this.*

The lights flash on the stage and on the audience side.

Guide.–We'll take you back to Irvine, California.

The Irvine situation, CA–2001.

ZMN International.–LAST MINUTE NEWS!

ZMN Presenter.–*From Irvine, California, at the Richland family mansion; and we're waiting for Victor Richland's arrival. We remember that young Victor with having a rare disease in the bronchi. Dr. Francini prescribed that Victor move to a dry or semi-desert area. Dr. Francini suggested a place in Southern California. Its recommendation is accurate; the Richland family owns a large real estate in the Irvine Hills. Mr. Richland, Victor's father, has organized the purchase of a famous law firm in Newport Beach, California for his son, Victor.*

The screens show photos of the Richlands mansion in Irvine.

ZMN Presenter.–*A large crowd, cinematographers and television reporters run towards the entrance of the property; two limousines enter through the elegant iron gate, behind a luxurious white ambulance that looks more like a limousine, and another limousine behind that ambulance enter the property. There's no siren sound, everyone goes silent. Four nurses dressed in flawless white uniform, with matching gloves and shoes roll a sleek and luxuriously padded stretcher out of the ambulance; the wheeled legs automatically extend below the stretcher. The stretcher has computer screens and monitors, apparently showing vital signs and signs of body condition. The nurses rolled the stretcher to the front of the large high entrance door to the mansion, taking Victor inside the mansion. No one can enter the mansion.*

A man dressed in a black tuxedo comes out and announces.

The man.—*The Richland family announces that Victor is ok, went to his room to rest, tired due to a long flight on the family's private jet, from New York. Mr. Richland has hired a medical corps to care for Victor. Assigned doctors and nurses will remain in the mansion for as long as necessary. The Richland family thanks them for their interest in hearing about young Richland's health, and for their prayers. At the right time, the family will issue reports of Victor's health.*

Four guards armed in dark blue uniforms, muscular strong as competitive athletes, each hold a black pit bull dog of developed muscles, asking the crowd and news reporters to leave the property.

Security guard.—*Please, there is nothing else to see here, you must leave the property now, thank you. Please go out through the main gate.*

The crowd and the journalists leave, but they stayed off the property for some time, talking and commenting on the situation.

Guide.—*The American constitution says that all men are created equal; a truth that remains in existence. Human beings have a soul (part of the total spirit) and a body (material part). Irregularities in the matter that forms the body introduce differences that humans cannot correct; in the structures and capacity of their brains. Souls have no imperfections. Humans are born with certain inalienable rights inherited from the universal spirit; this is true, as written in the laws of existence. But on earth the situation is different; wicked egos build differences and social gaps to gain advantages over others. Those who accumulate wealth and power control government, legislation and justice, the best opportunities and conditions in the free market and enterprise.*

Humans aren't the same, and they may never be. The AGHAPEE ogre deeply rooted in egos creates differences in humans and gaps in their societies. What the spirits say is true. And trying what they've been explaining. Spirits become souls into human bodies and work to guide humans, their egos, towards oneness. This is for the harmony and balance of the universe, the purpose of life cycles, and the endless journeys of spirits to the material dimension. The souls work, guiding humans towards oneness. Just see your stages; Scenarios freely share their natural content with living beings supporting their existences. The living creatures contribute to maintaining the ecological balance of their environment, except humans. What a great truth is the concept of uniqueness. As the Encarta dictionary stated;[43] *oneness (a noun) meaning, (1) uniqueness: The quality of being one rather than many; (2) uniqueness: The quality of being unique; (3) Agreement: The condition of being united or agreed; and (4) equality: The quality of being the same.* This is the true meaning of oneness that suited in the three Latin words is *E Pluribus Unum–all in one.*

In the author's theory, the oneness is the mental state, quality or condition in which humans live in harmony with their soul, other souls and spirits, and in perfect harmony with the universe, according to the laws of existence. This state of mind makes our souls have consciousness, wisdom and will, following the purpose under indisputable principles of existence. Then, and only then, will our souls and bodies all be in one, in harmony with the global spirit in the dimension of spirits–in universal oneness. Man must eliminate AGHAPEE's influence, specifically, excessive ambition, greed, hatred, prejudice, envy, greed, and selfishness to attain uniqueness. To achieve that state, man must educate the ego to behave according to the order of harmony of the universe.

Back to the present, 2018.

The lights flash on the stage and in the audience.

Guide.–*Please do not get comfortable, we will take you to Chiapas, Mexico.*

The situation in Arriaga, Chiapas, Mexico–2001.

Early in the morning, two buses full of people: children, teenagers and adults, men and women, arrived at an isolated farm, close to the city of Arriaga. People were sweaty, tired, hungry and showing signs of long hours of insomnia, without bathing for over two days. Two drivers arrived on the bus as they spoke; it seemed to take turns driving on a nonstop journey. The driver 1, Tulio, arrogantly says.

---

[43] Diccionario Encarta: inglés (Norteamérica–Definición de unidad).

Tulio.—*We are in Arriaga de Chiapas, Mexico. Pick up your belongings and follow me this way. Settle here as best as you can; there's grass that the cattle eat, use it to make your beds. There's a shed outside, you can use it to wash, and on the other side of the house there's another shed to pee and shit. Sleep what you can, tomorrow we'll go out early to work in the country.*

The place is a large barn used to store grains, hay, products and agricultural tools. The place to do your biological needs is a deep hole in the ground with a wooden seat. Around the seat above the hole in the floor, there is a wooden cabin with a door. No toilet paper, no water, no hand washing soap. The smell is nauseating and the flies are unbearable. The morning came; the time is about seven o'clock. People are eating what they brought and their few bags. Some people brought pots and made coffee. And they all shared what they could. These people understand that only to achieve their commitment by taking care and sharing among everyone along the way. They don't know what the next stop is; only the destination, the border with the United States. Moses is here among the people in the caravan. He's alert, but lost, not knowing what to do or what to say. No one knew him, and he knew anyone–a kidnapped child forced to travel. Everyone is in the same situation, without identity. But they all had the same dream, the same purpose of crossing the U.S. border, and with that they all have the same risks of death.

The second driver, Tomas, arrives, is a little more compassionate.

Tomas.—*Hey people, this man is Ramiro, the crew foreman; Ramiro will tell you the work you have to do. We'll be here twenty-eight days, and when we finish this job, we'll go north.*

What an experience for the soul, what agony for the body. Humans are *mentauros,* creatures with animal strength and spiritual intelligence, material bodies on earth, and souls with minds of the spirit dimension. The omniscience of existence nourishes their thoughts, and they act in earthly scenarios. The journey of humans is brutal, and the expectation of success is uncertain. One day at a time is all travelers have. There is no tomorrow until tomorrow; and there are no days without work, pain, fears and worries. Migrants have lives, but are theirs? Their lives belong to the Coyotes or the people who promote caravans. Migrants only know they are going to the United States, but their fate is unknown and their successes uncertain. Spirits know the result; know the conditions, problems and situations.

Ramiro.—*Here we have a lot to do, we collect vegetables, tomatoes, onions, chili, green chili, etc. We clean the land of old crops, prepare the land for the new planting, activate the irrigations, tend the cattle and horses, clean the stables. We all work here, all of us, even the kids. I'll tell you who will do what, okay?*

Everyone said yes, they had no choice, and around eight o'clock the supervisor took them to work. They work seven days a week. And twenty-eight days passed. Every morning they'd get up at four in the morning and return to the warehouse at six o'clock in the afternoon. They didn't have time to do anything else. It was like a forced labor camp, worse than being in prison; here on earth they may be free, but they cannot leave. Living creatures are prisoners of their environments, always. Two drivers stand to Ramiro's right.

It's the afternoon of the 28th.

Ramiro.—*Well, I'm glad you were good these days, you achieved a lot; but among you there's a bunch of lazies, if you keep going like this, you won't be doing well in America.*

There you go, can you see? This is the continuous threat, the threat of failure. Life is like this in the physical world of human; this is their reality. But is this situation because reality is a threat or because the certainty of truth for them is uncertain? No evil egos create conditions or situations, and uncertainty in human minds creates threats. There is no uncertainty in the physical world where everything is or is not. Humans, and all other creatures, live on the verge of risk, facing conditions and situations in this world of probabilities. This is a world of reality, but nothing is certain until it happens. Therefore, in this material world certainty is not in the outcome of the matters, conditions and situations that end, but in the certainty. It is the same in the dimension of spirits, with a difference; spirits know that results depend on a set of conditions, situations and or circumstances given. They know what happened, the conditions, the situations, the results-based activities they see.

Therefore, knowledge of conditions, situations and activities give the spirit the vision; the ability to see the past, the present and the future. And while human minds might have the same ability, the structure and disposition of their brains place constraints and or limitations. This is how spirits can see the future and the past, while humans cannot. Spirits apply the precise mathematics in the laws of causal and random events. The human mind is part of the soul, and the soul is a spirit with reduced powers; so, we also have a spirited mind. But they don't see the future. The difference between the mind of a spirit and the mind and a soul is in the limitations of the human mind. The human mind cannot see or keep up with all the themes, conditions, circumstances and activities that make up an event.

And a non considered issue, condition and situation can destroy the certainty of the outcome. The precision of human thought marks the precision of your vision for the future. And when something goes wrong, we blame the unforeseen, but the unforeseen is something we don't consider because we can't see beforehand. Therefore, a soul and a spirit differ only in the ability to include infinite affairs, conditions, situations, and circumstances that make a perfect result. Seneca's Latin phrase "erring is human, but persisting in error is diabolical" shows the situation of the human soul. The human ego is in this vortex of errors, but the purpose of the cycles of life is to train the ego to leave this vortex by itself in the light the order of harmony of the universe. Don't blame the soul for the wrongdoings of the ego; blame the ego for its selfish attitudes and the suffering it causes his soul and others' souls.

The third driver, Francisco, Frank or Pancho, comes and says.

Frank: Hey, pick up your things and walk to the truck, take the seats you came in. Ramiro will give them a portion of what you earned here, but most of it is to pay for your trip, roof and food. We need to leave here and we have eleven hours to get to the next stop. Driver 4, Raul, comes, gets on the bus and in front of the passengers says.

Raúl.—*We have six more passengers, take your things off empty seats so they can sit down. On the way, we will make a stop so you can take care of your needs.*

Moses, take his black backpack, which he didn't lose in Santa Tecla. A young man his age puts his yellow and green backpack on the top shelf and sat next to Moses-Moses suddenly felt cold and trembling noticing that the boy sitting next to him is also shaking. No one else on the bus has those symptoms. Maybe their souls recognized each other, but they can't define where, when, or how. One problem is true, their minds are part of their souls; and their souls are part of a global spirit that belongs to the dimension of spirits. The boy sitting next to Moses, friendly way.

Sergio.—*Hey, I seem to know you. My name is Sergio, which side of Arriaga do you come from, have we been in the same school?*

Moses and Sergio seem very surprised, and yet happy to be together. It's strange, but it's real; is happening. Why is this meeting? What's a causal chain of events behind this meeting?

Moses.—*I also had that same impression, but no, I am not from here; I come from Santa Tecla, El Salvador, my name is Moses Suarez. And you go north to the same place?*

Sergio.—*I still think I've known you for a long time, but forget it, no more, it's just a hunch. Yes, I'm going north, you know where; I didn't want to, but they forced me.*

However, premonitions, forebodings, hunches, intuitions are real; they are not delusions, desires or whims. Humans have them occasionally, but they don't understand them. They even think these feelings are evil, like premonitions. But are they? Why do humans deny spirits send messages to human minds this way? What happens comes from beyond the material world; what if it is? It's evidence that there was a warning, a communication.

Moses.—*It's the same, but as you say, it's better to let it happen, and that's it. Now we sleep if we can; this trip is a pain in the ass.*

The roar of the bus engine, some people snore, others fart, the windows tarnished with dark curtains. The same sound for hours and hours that doesn't end. It's hot, stinky and wet. How can anyone sleep? I have felt what Moses and Sergio feel; It's strange; it's something we can't explain and we can't set the point. But is it the encounter of two spirits? Maybe the spirits explain this phenomenon of encounter. It would be nice if they told the public. Wait, here comes the guide.

Guide.–*It was a strange encounter, like many curious events in life. At some point you have seen things or people you think you have seen before; sometimes, you're in a place you think you've been before. Spirits have the extension of existence to communicate with souls and minds in humans. Spirits, souls and minds have access to that great channel of communication. Most people call this "things of fate," such as the encounter of Moses and Sergio, but they are not. Most of the time those events are part of the covert plan and spirits continue to unite and work together the rest of their journey. It is a phenomenon that souls within human bodies do not understand. Humans should follow the reasons and sequence of events that unite them, paying attention to those experiences and/or visions that show signs of knowledge and/or trends in past cycles.*

The two boys settle the best they can and fall asleep, despite the noise, the roar, the bus engine, crying babies and some snoring. The strange encounter of Sergio and Moses is just one phenomenon that humans do not understand, but they have their meaning and a purpose. The situations, events, and circumstances Moses has been through are neither casual nor random. Two spirits are together at this location. The lights flash on the stage and on the sides of the audience, again. If we followed these events–as we call them–we would see they have consequences (cause to effect) later on.

Back to the year 2018.

A voice in the theater.–*Spirits now may take the public to Beverly Hills, California.*

The situation in Beverly Hills, California–2017.

It is 2017 at the Residence of Rex Martin: the screens show an expensive and upper-class residence. A ZMN Reporter enters the network's stage on TV.

Reporter.–*Rex Martin, aka Ricky Martin, celebrates at his residence in Beverly Hills, California two important events of his life, tonight; these are his birthday and a recognition as a scientific pathologist and surgeon specializing in cancer treatments and rare diseases. Dr. Martin's discoveries in human organs elevate him to the top of the world's specialists. Dr. Martin a scientist rather than a physician; and he will speak at the National convention of Medical Research on Rare Pathological Diseases at the University of California, Irvine on May 15.*

Dr. Martin, son of Rocky and Vicky Martin, who died in a strange case; a love triangle and an adventure of infidelity. Vicky Martin had an affair with Jeff Anderson, the family accountant, over 27 years ago in Henderson, Nevada. The mansion where Rex Martin lives is part of the heritage he received from the Martin family a long time ago. Rex has it all, wealth, fame and youth and future.

It's not only the poor but also the rich suffer great problems, but they handle their situations easier with their wealth and power. Existence has its laws, such as the law of mutual compensation, to balance. For each action there is a reaction, and there is balance.

Back to 2018.

The lights flash on stage and in the audience again.

Guide.—*Well, we just returned and we must travel back in time to the past, to the next place. We now may take you to Tijuana, Baja California, Mexico. We hope you will appreciate how busy spirits are, most of the time. As you can see, we dedicate to generating, protecting, and keeping the lives of living creatures safe.*

The situation in Tijuana, Baja California, Mexico -2001.

The migrant caravan.[xxvi]

The place is the central bus station in Tijuana, Baja California, Mexico. It's the end of summer in North America, but California tourists still pour into the city. A four-bus caravan from the south arrives, one bus at a time at a different time between 11:00 p.m. on a busy Thursday, and 2:00 a.m. on Friday. The first bus enters the station and parked to unload passengers, cargo and luggage. The two boys, Moses and Sergio, came out talking. As for the end of the long journey, humans have a saying this is where rubber finds the road.

Sergio.—*Look, Moses, this city is big. I've never seen so many lights and buildings this big, I think we're already in the United States. This city is big and beautiful.*

Moses.—*Yes, it's huge, but it's not the United States. A coyote in Santa Tecla told me all about this blessed journey. He said the hardest thing is to cross the border. And we haven't crossed that yet.*

No one can compare the cardboard houses in the ghettos with the huge buildings, streets and other big cities. But for those who haven't been out of a poverty belt, this city, and the streets, is a spectacular sight. It is a sense of power and wealth, and also fame, such as Rome, Paris, London, Los Angeles, New York, San Francisco. They're so big they're intimidating. I live in Los Angeles in a neighborhood that looks more like a city within the big city.

Sergio.—*I think you're right; you seem to know more than I do. Hey, let's go to the parking lot, as we were told, it's over there, and…*

Moses.—*Wait for a little, Sergio, I can't find my backpack.*

Sergio.—*What? Did you have two; dumb. Is it not the one you got on your back?*

Moses.—*Hey, sorry buddy, I'm nervous and scared. But tell me, why do they call people ox (buey)?*

Sergio.—*Now calm down silly and let's go to the parking lot. The ox is a spaded bull (have their testicles removed) and becomes meek and timid; he doesn't think; you know?*

Moses.—*Yes, I understand. I'm glad they left us in the same group, everyone else. I feel at peace with you; you're my buddy.*

Guide.—*The spirits of Moses and Sergio met; the boys feel something strange, but they don't realize it. Perhaps their physical conditions and circumstances kept them concerned about immediate survival. This journey is beyond terrifying; and it could be fatal.*

I think now souls synchronized their mental level and identified themselves, and the expression is the evidence,[xxvi]

Moses.—*I feel at peace with you. Just like you feel about a brother and or a sister.*

Sergio.—*Three closed vans with long cabins for 14 passengers, with windows covered, wait for us in parking area C.*

Jacinto is by the sliding side door of a locked van, waiting a little worried. This is a covert or clandestine operation. Moses and Sergio run to the van.

Jacinto.—*He calls them and says, hurry kids, this is not the Rose Parade. Come on in now, quick.*

But before closing the door, Jacinto quietly tells Moses and Sergio.

Jacinto.–*Good luck, guys, and thank you for your help along the way. Here Henry, he'll take care of you, pay attention and listen to him. And don't worry about knowing it's the Rose Parade, you'll notice when you're on the other side, this is if you pass the border alive.*

Henry.–*It is 12 night, do not turn on a light in the cabin for nothing, we will go through the city center to a safe house. You will stay in Tijuana, studying the plan, as long as the opportunity to jump the wall arrives. I don't know how long you'll be here, but meanwhile; you have to work on whatever you're told to balance the cost of your trip.*

No one said anything, perhaps, they were too tired or too scared, or wondering about the final step. Nothing is free in the material world. You always pay with efforts for what you want or get. This is a law of existence; you pay for what you take from life. The raw materials that humans have used to manufacture their products were, are and will be a property of all living beings–no one should sell them to humans hidden in products forms. The purpose is to care for and preserve the lives of living creatures. Perhaps this is the lesson that human egos learn to work for oneness, share and care for one another. Existence, the universe and spirits teach humans, at least on this planet earth. The van turns to the sidewalk. An old lady is standing outside a house. The vehicle stops, and everyone jumps out of the van.

The old lady.–*Quique, just these kids, where are the other three they told me?*

Quique.–*Don't hurry old fart, wait for the other van, come after. Don't shout. You better tell the border police.*

The old lady answers.

The old lady.–*How can't I worry, stupid? A shit of yours and this dam operation can go to hell, you miserable fool... Over here, boys; or will you just stand there staring at the stars?*

The two boys come in the house, following the old lady. The house is large with four bedrooms, a study, the living room, the kitchen, the dining room, and a huge family room. The house is on the hills of Tijuana.

The old lady.-*Hey, muchachos, there are two beds in this room, you will sleep here, tomorrow I will wake you up at four a.m.*

Moses and Sergio's souls can't see what tomorrow brings. All they know is that they're at the threshold of the greatest opportunity of their lives. Humans only live one day at a time, hoping that their hopes will be real the next day. We'll see. For the spirits, maybe this situation is boring because they know the contents of tomorrow. For the souls tomorrow is an uncertainty like the decisions and actions of his ego.

Sergio.—*Fuck man, a bed where I can stretch my legs, buddy.*

The bed is a foldable frame with springs, like a bunk bed, but for the boys these beds are awesome. They had been sitting in the vehicle for so long that their body almost have the shaped of the bus seats.

Moses.- *Shut up, you fool; don't take your things out of your backpack, don't even take off your cloth, we have only three hours to sleep before we wake up; you fool.*

The old lady woke them up on time, four o'clock in the morning. A man in the late forty years, came to pick them up around five-thirty. Francisco parked a black double-cab van on the street. He waited; three young girls, perhaps in their teens, leave a room in the hallway across the boys' room. Jenifer, with blond hair, blue eyes with a body like a model or a candidate for Miss Universe; she was about fifteen. She spoke Spanish with an American accent. Karla, about eighteen, also well formed, tanned skin, brown eyes, reddish hair; speaks Spanish cut with a rare European accent. Luiza, white complexion, green eyes, beautiful dark hair, speaks Spanish with a light Portuguese accent. Jenifer looked at Sergio and he looked at her too. For the first time in several months, the kids had breakfast served at a table. It was even better than the breakfast they had at their homes. But sometimes the changes are transient; and a change has a meaning and a purpose, that humans can only see when the chain of events is complete.

Francisco.—*Hey, kids, you will work cleaning up a night-club that's on Revolution Street, and you girls, I will take you to meet the owner of a cabaret on the same Revolution Street. So, let's get going... Come on.*

Time passed and three months later, the guys are still on the southern side of the border, Tijuana, Baja California, Mexico. All this time, the boys worked as a cleaning team. Jenifer worked as a servant, while the older girls worked entertaining men. It's three weeks to Christmas. At night in that room, Sergio and Moses study English on their own–well, Jenifer helped them–and they had learned so much that the restaurant owner had let them serve tables. The guys worked hard and were very courteous, so the tourists who visit the restaurant gave them good tips in dollars. Each had raised more than a thousand and three hundred dollars. They've never seen so much money in their life. Time passes fast; Sergio and Moses are still in that safe house, at the end of Boulevard Aguas Calientes, northeast of the twin tower hotel, in the hills of Tijuana. One night, when they were returning from the restaurant, they saw a man waiting in the living room. Moses and Sergio.

The old Lady.–*Hey people, this is Cornelius, they call him 'Cornel'. He will take care of you on what's left of your trip. Pick up your things, tonight you are leaving. You know, you know nothing about us, and we know nothing about you. Your life with your silence, if you speak you die.*

One rule of scenarios is that life is episodes that might show an endpoint. But the law of causal events can clarify their link.

Cornel.–*Don't forget your Mexican or home country IDs. If you get caught and then deported, the "migra" will know where to send you. Let's wait for the girls and we'll leave as soon as they get here.*

Here are again the threats and uncertainty of life. The girls come; they gather their things; they go out and get in a black, closed van. Cornel ties a bandage on each, making sure they don't see where they're going through the city. Cornel took them to a house about 300 feet from the line. They came in through the back door. A family lives there: a man, Rudy, a woman and four children live there as a normal family. In the back, there was a new Ford, a four-door car. There was an annex to that house with a bathroom, shower, toilet and sink. In the house, the two boys and the three girls remain with the blindfold. The man says.

Rudy.–*I want to tell you you paid your debts, including what's left - need to cross the border. The boss sends you a hundred bucks for any expenses when you cross. You have three twenty-dollar bills, a ten-dollar* *bill, a five-dollar bill, and five one-dollar bills. A marked twenty-dollar bill will be your password.*

This is it. You make it, or you don't. There are no more opportunities. Time clicks. The boys now face the line, the last step of a long journey to the land of equal opportunities, the land of the free and the braves.

8:30 p.m.

Rudy.–*Hey, at nine o'clock, you'll enter the tunnel. The tunnel joins with a sewer on the other side, and you will exit at a round drain in a dark parking lot next to a house, about 30 feet; notice when leaving just in case, there will be an old car parked next to the drain blocking the view to the street. Do not make a noise with the metal of the drain grate. When you leave, do not wait for the other, run to the left to the back of the house and enter, the sliding door is open. The house is a house in green there is no other with that color around the exit. The time in the tunnel should not be more than an hour. Don't be late for nothing, we have measured and time counts.*

8:40 p.m.

Rudy.–*Don't be afraid, there's no danger there. Someone's waiting for you. They're going into that house in green, and whoever is there will tell you what to do next.*

A vehicle reaches the rear; Rudy looks out the window.

Rudy.–*No problem, it's Cornel. He brings three more guys here. Who knows what happened at the other crosses? We'll see. Now there are eight, five men and the three women. There's one more coming in a few minutes, he's still dropping a few people at other points.*

Cornel.–*Hey Rudy, I brought you three more, there are many people in the other crosses, and also the border patrols are on alert; there are many police cars patrolling, suspecting many people may try to cross on those sides. The scheduled time is always nine o'clock, pm. You must not be late for anything. See you later, and good luck.*

8:40 p.m.

Rudy.–*Let's go over this lesson again, at nine o'clock...*

They go over the plan five more times and in the review, Rudy says.

I want you to understand what you have to do.

8:45 pm.

The ninth passenger hasn't arrived yet, Rudy continues the rehearsal; The key questions are (1) How long does it take to pass the tunnel, (2) What is the password object, (3) What color is the house at the end of the tunnel, (4) what direction do you take when exiting the tunnel, to the right or to the left? The litany continues; it's a matter of success or failure, life or death. In a few minutes, they'll be alone. Everyone's blindfolded and the house is lit with candles.

Crossing the U.S. border.
8:50 p.m.

The ninth emigrant has not yet arrived, but it is time to begin the process of entering the tunnel.

Rudy.—*Well, let's go, it's time, when they get to the other side. They're going out in San Ysidro. But first they come into the house. Kentucky Fried Chicken Restaurant is across the street. Santiago, he'll be there eating. One of you asks him if he has change for a twenty-dollar bill, the others wait outside. That's all. Come on, hurry.*

Everyone's still got the blindfold since they left the safe house. Rudy tells them he'll take them off just when they're ready to go into the tunnel. The ninth passenger is still missing. Rudy tells them to form a line by placing both hands on the person's shoulders in front. The woman of the house helps them and guides them along a hallway to the door of a room.

8:53 p.m.

Rudy.—*I want two to help me, here in this room, you, "muchachos", Sergio and Moses, come. You guys go in the tunnel first.*

Rudy takes the blindfold off them and tells them what to do, and among the three they lift a heavy bath tub and put it aside. Under the bathtub there is a large hole in the floor. On the side, Rudy has a lot of small flashlights and portable oxygen bags with nose adapters.

8:55 p.m.

Rudy.—*Five minutes left. This is the tunnel entrance, it's dark. Before you go in, take one flashlight and a bag of oxygen. If you lack air in the tunnel, put the mask over your nose, press the button on the bag and breathe three times. Moses and Sergio go first, and the three girls go right behind about four steps, and behind the other three. Goodbye and good luck.*

Rudy removes the blindfold from the girls, one by one, as he enters the tunnel. They pick up their flashlights and oxygen bags. The other three go through the same process, one at a time. And just before the last one is ready to enter the tunnel, the woman screams.

8:58 pm.

The woman.—*Rudy, Jacinto's here, don't close the rabbit hole, yet.*

8:59 pm.

The last traveler left. Jacinto runs to the room, takes a flashlight and an oxygen bag, like the other migrants, and enters the tunnel. They're all gone.

9:01 pm.

The woman, Rudy, and the other man work together to close the tunnel. Everyone leaves the house after putting the heavy tub in place. The house had been with candlelight all this time, and now it's dark.

They crawl on their hands and knees; one hour later, Moses touches the drainage grille at the end of the tunnel. It is a heavy cast iron grille, but lifts it and slide it out of the way. Following the instructions, Moses goes out and runs to the back of the house in green, just behind Sergio does the same. The girl behind looked out and saw a police car slowly passing through the street, the girls waited, they went out, but they didn't go to the house; went straight to the restaurant "Kentucky Fried Chickens." The other three went out, but they went the wrong way. The border patrol vehicle slowly passes again, focusing a searchlight on the dark parking lot. All three guys hid behind that car. The patrol car continues to roll; one of the three frightened, gets up and runs through the parking lot to the corner, looking for the restaurant. The border policemen got out of their car and chased him; a few seconds later, Moses heard three gunshots: his heart throbs like a pile hammer. The last guy, Jacinto, was in the tunnel, but he waited there; heard the gunshots. Two guys are dead, one injured and surrenders. The cast-iron sewer grille is in place. Everyone left the lights and oxygen bags in the tunnel at the exit. Border police are out there looking for more, and after 45 minutes, they left. Two ambulances had arrived, collected the two bodies and left, while the police questioned the wounded young man; dies in the ambulance before saying anything. Everything's calm again. A woman, Nora, tall and heavy, old American-looking, in the house in green, and told them.

Nora.–Go wash, change your clothes and come back.

After a few minutes, they return, looking like typical teenagers.

–well, you guys look like American kids.

Sergio.–*What?* [in Spanish].

Nora.–*Oh, what did I say, well, you look like American boys.* [in Spanish].

With a clear American accent. It's almost 11:00.

Meanwhile, at the Kentucky Fry restaurant, the three girls arrived; they went to the bathroom, cleaned themselves and changed clothes. Santiago was sitting there, eating at a table near the entrance.

Jenifer politely asks the man in the "Kentucky Fried Chickens," speaking perfect English.

Jenifer.–*Excuse me, sir, do you have change for this bill?*

Jenifer shows the marked twenty-dollar bill. Santiago checks it out.

Santiago.–Yes, I will give you change; come with me.

The three girls followed Santiago outside, but did not return to the restaurant. After two minutes, Santiago returns to the same table and continued to eat. In the meantime, let's go back to the house in green.

Nora.–*Hurry, go to Kentucky Fry Chicken and change that $20 bill, you remember?*

The boys come out the back door. A border policeman is hiding behind the trees in the shadows, waiting in the dark backyard. Jacinto, who waited in the tunnel, went out and hides behind the old car; then, he walked to the back of the house with a gun ready. Sergio leaves first, followed by Moses, and descended to two steps, out in the backyard. Jacinto sees the policeman and (bang) shoots once. The cop shoots twice, bang, bang. Jacinto falls to the ground. Sergio and Moses jumped to the ground and looked up; Moses remains immobilized on the ground; Sergio got up. [Bang bang], Sergio falls to the ground, shot in the right thigh. Nora comes out holding something in her right hand, which looks like a gun. Three shots are heard–[bang, bang, bang]–Nora falls to the wounded; one of the officer's shots blew Nora's hair dryer to pieces. The policewoman checks the man; He's dead. Nora still alive, rises and runs to the front of the house and falls on the street, about 30 feet from the house, apparently dead. The police officer goes to Moses, pulls his arms and handcuffs him. Then she goes with the other boy and handcuffs him and checks his wound. The officer pulls a rope out of his belt bag and ties the wounded boy's leg by stopping his bleeding. The cop returns to Moses, picks up his backpack, maybe looking for drugs, opens it and pulls out some papers. A small photograph falls to the ground; the officer picks it up and looks under the light of her flashlight, first the paper and then the small photograph. The officer, covering his mouth, yells.

–OH MY GOD, OH MY GOD. This can't be. Oh no, oh no. She cries. THIS CAN'T BE POSSIBLE.

There was no one around. The policewoman walked in circles, thinking about what to do; she was crying. She walks to the dead man in the parking lot and searches him. It's clean. But she found a note, a curious note, in the pocket of her shirt. She keeps it. The policewoman returns to Moses and asks him, showing him the little picture, speaking quickly and her voice shaking, as if she was about to cry.

The policewoman.–*Do you speak English?*
Moses.–*What?*

He understood, but he didn't want to show he understood what the policewoman had said.

The policewoman.—*Look, whose picture this is, who is this girl. She comes with you; where is she hiding, speak you bum?*

Moses.—*My name is Moses. She doesn't come with me; she's my Aunt Isabel and she lives here in the United States. But she doesn't know I'm coming. They kidnapped me in Santa Tecla near my mom's house, Juana; they locked me up for a few days because they would take a kidney from me to sell it, but then they left me and forced me to come. They marked me, burned a little x on my arm. I heard they planned to kill me to sell my organs. That's the truth.*

The policewoman gets up, walks a few steps from Moses and cries, cries, and cries, until she finally turns around and returns to that boy.

The policewoman.—What's your grandfather's name? Who are your relatives?

Moses.—*Yes, I have another aunt; it is my aunt Mary, my grandfather's name is Joseph and my grandmother Celia, she is dead, and I miss her much. I wasn't there when she died, but she died asking for me to come to say good bye, so I was told by a man who works with the Coyote. I couldn't see her.*

The policewoman.—*Get up, now. Come with me. Come on.*

Moses.—*No, I can't, kill me if you want. My friend Sergio is dead and I can't leave him here, lying like a dog.*

The policewoman.—*Your friend is well chamaco. Maybe he's passed out, but okay, believe me.*

Moses cries.

Moses.-*Please help him, help him, I cannot return to my land if he is dead.*

The policewoman.—*Quit giving me that story. I told you he's fine. Now, stop crying and get up, walk kid, hurry, lets hurry, come, help me up your friend.*

The policewoman calls headquarters and reports the dead man in the parking lot across the street from the Kentucky restaurant and asks for help. Police officer nearby arrived and took over the situation. The police woman walked to her "Big Cherokee" which she parked around the house in green and took with her the two boys waiting in the vehicle. The next day, the policewoman, Isa (Isabel), woke up early, called the border patrol.

The policewoman.—*Good morning, who's there. Yes, yes... but I can't go to work today; I'm not feeling well, and I have to do something very important. I need permission to take two days off... Yes, I'll wait... Hey, okay. Please thank the boss for me, will you? Hey, thank you ... what? Seriously, believe me; I don't feel good... Hey; you know what I look like... I've never taken days for sickness... Yes. Ok. See you in two days, bye. That morning Isa, as everyone calls Isabel-the policewoman-she goes to the kitchen and prepares breakfast for the boys.*

Isa.—*Hey guys, come on, bathe later, there's two bathrooms, soap and towels, you change your clothes, and we go. Hurry.*

Isa.—*Once the boys were ready, check Sergio's wound, put a new dressing on his thigh and fix it with tape.*

Isa.—*That, those clothes, you don't have another one?*

They just looked at the policewoman, lowering her head in positive response.

—*It's okay. Come; we're leaving.*

She took them to a law office in Santa Ana, CA. Isa carried her police badge with her, as always, Isa says.

Isa.—*Good morning, I'm Officer Suarez,* [shows her badge]. *I have an appointment with Mr. Clark, Ted Clark.*

The secretary.—*Yes. Officer, I'll let you know.*

He lifted the intercom.

—*Mr. Clark, Officer Suarez is here to see you. Yes, sir, I'll take you to your office.* [Returning to Officer Suarez said] *Officer, will you follow me, please?*

The police woman moving her head instructs the boys to follow her and says.

Isa.—*Come on, guys, come on.*

The officer had the two boys handcuffed, with their hands in front of their bodies.

They go into the lawyer's office.

The lawyer.—*Hello, Isabel! How have you been? It's been a long time since we last saw each other.*

Isa.—*It's true, isn't it?*

Lawyer.—*You're as pretty as ever. Well, would you like, and the boys, something to drink, water, coffee? And what urgent case do you want to talk about?*

Isa.—*No thanks, we're fine. Well, I stopped these two boys across the border in San Ysidro...*

Isa and Ted chatted for over twenty minutes alone. The two boys waited, a little scared. The boys didn't understand most of what they were saying. Isa and the lawyer's language were complex and too quick for their knowledge of English.

The lawyer.—*I will get custody of these two boys for you this morning. Stay in Santa Ana and come back after lunch. It's not a problem you're related to one kid. The fact is, they kidnapped the boys and forced them to come involuntarily. What I see as a problem is that the government may send them to their country. I have to resolve this with the court. OK. I'll see you after lunch. I advise you to take them to the authorities and report the arrest, appointing me as their lawyer. I will apply and file a formal asylum-based petition for criminal persecution and danger to their lives if they return to their countries.*

After she denounced the arrest with the authority in Santa Ana, she negotiated the release of the boys based on the legal case on behalf of the boys brought by her attorney, Ted Clark. The boys completed the corresponding paperwork and were registered as victims of a kidnapping act in international territory and brought to the United States. Authorities release the boys under the responsibility of Officer Suarez. The authority representative removes the two boys' handcuffs and hands them over to Officer Suarez. The boys are free; they made it to America. Officer Suarez called the Ted Clark.

Officer Suarez.—*Hi, Ted, we've done everything here, how are you doing there (pause)... that sounds awesome (pause)... "hey" let's meet for lunch with the boys, and we talk about all that (pause)... Well, I'll see you there–"Las Brisas Restaurant" in Santa Ana near Orange County Court? OK. All right, I'll see you there, bye, anyway, bye.*

At around 12:30, Officer Suarez and the boys found Ted, his lawyer, at the restaurant.

Isa.—*I am forever indebted to you, Ted. I'll never forget this.*

Ted.–*Don't worry, Isabel; after all I will charge you for my services, and you will pay me capital and interest.*

–Well guys, [the lawyer says.]

Isa.–*[Interrupting] Ted, they don't speak English, let me translate what you want to tell them.*

As the lawyer explains the case, Isa translates simultaneously.

Lawyer and Isa.–*I filed and filed a claim-demand, a restraining order, against several people in the Sinaloa cartel for drug trafficking, human trafficking, organ trafficking and illegal smuggling across the U.S. borders in Tijuana and Mexicali. The file includes a permanent "in-situs" asylum petition for boys based on the existing danger of life that such people mean for boys if they ever return to the countries where they come from and from where they abducted.*

The lawyer continued his explanation for over twenty minutes. That night, at Isa's house, just after dinner, Isa spoke to Moses. Sergio was there, sitting on the sofa in the family room, somewhat dazed by the whole sequence of events. It was like a dream.

Isa.–Moses, why do you carry this photo of your Aunt Elizabeth?

Moses.–*I always carried that picture with me, it's my good luck charm and the beginning of my dream to see it one day. But she left a few days after I was born, so I didn't know her.*

Moses thrilled, as if he were about to cry, and confused, processed strange, recent events.

Isa.–*What would you do if you found her.*

Moses.–*I don't know, madam, I'd die of such joy, but I will find my Aunt Isabel, I swear; although I don't know how. Today I feel in a great debt to you and I do not know how to pay you; I'll pay you, somehow, I will.*

Isabel.–*So, here, I'll give you back your picture, but now let me show you a picture like yours, but bigger.*

Isa goes to her bedroom, takes the picture on the bedside table by her bed, brings it and shows it to Moses.

Isa.–*Look Moses, here it is.*

He looked and looked and looked at the big picture of the female police officer who arrested him. He was so surprised, so much he couldn't speak. It took a few seconds, but for Moses, every second seemed like hours. Until Moses sighed loudly and broke the silence with a heartbreaking cry. The emotion was so intense that a child's body trembled like a blade shaken by a strong cold wind. The thick tears in his eyes did not allow him to see, and the lump in his throat was suffocating him. Elizabeth approached slowly and when she embraces Moses, Elizabeth also let go of her crying. The emotions in waves, vibrations that other souls receive. And when Moses could speak, he asks Isa.

Moses.—*Are you my aunt Isabel?*

That strong policewoman, Isabel, also shaking emotionally, says.

Isa.—*Yes, Moses, you are my nephew. Thank God you're alive. I could have killed you last night.*

Minutes spend a long embrace of pure love. Looking at all this great miracle, Sergio can't stand it either, and swallowing hard too will burst into tears. Isabel sees Sergio's suffering the emotional experience and called him to join them in a single embrace of love. The lights on stage go out, and in the audience at a twilight moment, emotional sighs. Stage light come back. Twenty silhouettes of spirits dance together to music while a tenor-voiced man sings on the four screens of the song "*Love is a splendid thing*". Humans do not understand the behavior of spirits and can judge what happened as the force of destiny. But is it fate? Maybe it isn't. In this story, the sequence of activities and events shows an intent. An intention rooted in the humble desires of souls in humans. The intense longings Moses had to see his aunt, and Isabel's soul yearning for her family in Santa Tecla, are evidence of the intention to gather their souls. The chain of events had a purpose to bring Moses to Isabel. This is how spirits work supporting human unity; with gratitude, satisfaction and rejoicing. Now we see Isabel and Moses together; But for what? What is the purpose of this union? What's next? A man-like spirit standing in the center of the stage sings the song: "*The Sea of Love*" while 15 spirits dance in rock style to the rhythm of the song.

Come to me, my love, to this sea;
The Sea of Love.

I want to tell you how much I love you.

Return to the present of 2018.

The nature of human beings.

Guide.-*Some people may say that what has happened–the miraculous encounter of Moses and his aunt–is just a coincidence. But the rules of existence specify the laws of causal and random events. There are events that occur only if certain events occur before, as in the chain of intent events in this story, however, there are causalities–conditions and circumstances–or events that occur, randomly, changing the course of causal sequences. The sequence or chain of events that united Moses and Sergio, also Moses and Isabel, have a clear purpose; cannot be random events or the force of fate. Spirits seem to gravitate around the force of their commitment or intent and thus unite for that purpose. Souls behave like magnets or charges of electromagnetic forces.*

Trues:–*So when a sequence like these interdependent events happens, it leads to events or results that reach the end of the string. And the causality of events, but the resulting event is not random. Similarly, a constant causal sequence sometimes random events that occur in or out of the brake the causal sequence. You may remember what happened to Alfonso when his friend delayed Alfonzo's sequence of deliberate activities; Alfonso could have bought the baseball cards at any other time.*

Stacey.–*Yes, that's right. Yes, a purpose. The encounter of Moses and his aunt Isabel cannot be random. It is a chain of events that occurred causally in time and space to reach the meeting of the result do. Humans experience these phenomena, but do not pay due attention to their signs or meanings. These are the signs of the actions of the spirits. What else can it be if there is no physical explanation?*

Trues.–*The work of spirits becomes obvious, now that their spiritual actions are visible or real. The power of spirits changes the conditions and circumstances to produce a desired event. This is how spirits work on their mission to protect and sustain life. Some humans understand it, but most do not, perhaps ignored it because it involves them with their material interests, or perhaps they find no value in their experience.*

Stacey.-*We witnessed how Sergio and Moses met on that bus in Arriaga, Chiapas. The timing had to be perfect to get such a meeting. The spirits of Moses and Sergio knew their whereabouts. The commitment these spirits made at that exit station is now visible, and the spirits worked simultaneously to create conditions and circumstances that would change the causal events specified in passing life. Spirits constantly communicate with each other because they are part of the supreme spirit. That's how spirits work. His actions do not fall within our physical consciousness. Now, three of the cast spirits met and now they travel together on earth. There's no doubt about that, they've met again. However, we must observe how they remain together from this moment on.*

Guide.—*The AGHAPEE that humans carry in their egos kills the goodness they receive; how will they change and choose love instead? Oh, human, how wicked and ruthless they have become.*

I understand, from what spirits say, that the greatest opacity in reality is the reality of the purpose of spirits, or materialism within the egos of humans. What would life be if humans thought and acted in the light of truth, and only the truth? What would life be like if humans were 100 percent honest and sincere, with zero selfishness? Would life be boring? Perhaps not, because the challenges of reality would continue; but people's souls would share the burden of solving their tribulations as common problems. The lights flash on the stage and on the sides of the audience, again.

Guide.—*Spirits, let's take the audience to Newport Beach, California. It is our spiritual devotion to fulfill without a doubt the plan of the global spirit—our plan—especially the activities related to our missions on earth. Let's pause our conversation for a moment. We must travel back in time, back to Newport Beach, California.*

The situation in Newport Beach -2003.

At Ted Clark's home a small ceremony was taking place, close friends from the legal and police communities. Approximately, there are about one hundred and sixty guests. Ted Clark (31) and Isabel Suarez (26) married. Ted touches a glass of wine to make a toast.

Ted.—*For all my friends and friends of Isabel, it is a great honor to have you here to witness our wedding. You know me and Isabel. We're finally married.*

Elizabeth was standing next to him in a long, beautiful white dress. She looked beautiful, like a movie star.

The guests.—*Good for you, Ted. You stole the princess from the border police association. We'll be watching you…*

Laughter is everywhere. It's a happy time. The party continues until midnight, when the wedding couple climb into a limousine that takes them to John Wayne Airport, who were on their honeymoon in Las Vegas, Nevada. Moses and Sergio stayed by the pool after Ted and Isabel left. It was an elegant and beautiful party. Moses and Sergio speak improved English, now.

Sergio.—*I never dreamed of being here, ever. It looks as if the path to an established destination. I remember when my father couldn't repay a loan to a rich man in Arriaga. I was about to lose my little house there. The hard days, my suffering, when the people of that rich man came and told me I could pay my father's debt. They said it was the only solution: I had to give one kidney. I said no. However, they kidnapped and they removed, anyway. They never let me go back to my family. Six months later, they brought me back to the place where I met you in Arriaga.*

Moses.—*I feel sorry for you, Sergio; you deserve to be here. More than me. Did you say all that in your statement?*

Sergio.—*Yes, I did, Moses; That's right. I also gave them a detail of where they kept me all that time. I told them I heard someone say take that bag of dollars to the mayor of the city… and say it's the last month's share.*

Moses.—*Your case is bigger than mine. Can you recognize the people in that cartel?*

Sergio.—*Yes, Moses, I could if I saw them.*

A few minutes later Virgil, Ted's driver, came and told the two boys.

The driver. *Well guys, this party will continue until morning, I'm supposed to take you home no later than midnight. It's 12:30 a.m. Are you ready?*

The two guys respond simultaneously: Yes, we're ready.

Sergio.–*You know, Moses; I feel like I've known you all my life, and I have full confidence in you; you're my buddy.*

Moses.–*The same goes for me, Sergio. People say that spirits have an affinity and seek or seek each other, so they walk together, they stay together in several lives. We know it may not be true, but I'm glad you're here; maybe we both have spirits that have walked together in previous lives.*

Sergio.–*Moses, I cannot forget the situations, the circumstances, that we passed by to get here. I can't forget how coyotes exploit and take advantage of people in need, immigrants. I think of Jenifer, the blond-haired girl from Tijuana, I liked her–she helped us with our English. We talked a lot; he told me the things that made him go through and then to serve the men, tourists in that brothel. She was a pretty, lovely girl. She didn't deserve that life. I wonder what happened to those three girls; I wonder if they crossed the border.*

Moses.–*Don't think about it, Sergio, it doesn't do you any good; it's sad and depressing. Let us try to live with what God has given us and hope that other people will do well in life. In addition, let us try to help others with what we can so they can also achieve better living conditions in this selfish and unjust world of men.*

That's it; that who has not had the experience cannot describe the perception of the experience. In 2006, three years after Ted and Isa married; Isa left the border patrol commission and opened a private investigative agency in Santa Ana, California, working for the public, and with the law firm of Ted Clark and Associates. Isa studied criminal law. The agency built an excellent reputation in California.

Return to the present, 2018.

Contacts

Guide.–*Spirits in human bodies contact other spirits in two ways: Voluntarily and non-voluntary.*

Two groups of spirits arrive on stage. One group dressed in light blue with pink and the other in light peach and blue, all transparent garments. There are men and women, and boys and girls, in both groups. Dance the ballet near you (*"Close to you"*).

Robert.—*Voluntary contact—When humans face a situation for which they see no way out of their own knowledge, thoughts and actions; they yearn for help, and they want someone or something to come to help; they seek help from the global spirit through prayer; they meditate and reason problems to find a solution for themselves. This contact usually occurs through meditation and prayer. It must be vehement mental communication when a soul seeks help. Mental anguish becomes distress signals that travel into space and remain dormant in the cosmos. Meditation takes advantage of omniscience where knowledge of all problems and solutions is eternal. Contact can occur when the human wants to contact or communicate with a spirit. The human spirit focuses on that spirit and invokes its presence. This can be an individual decision or the intervention of a psychic or medium. Be assured that an answer will reach you soon.*

Spirits dance around and kneel to the left of the stage, join hands and pretend to meditate or pray.

Stacey.—*Involuntary contact: These contacts come outside the souls of humans. They come as visions, dreams, forebodings, premonitions, inspirations; as a surprise. Humans startle; these contacts can arrive at any moment, unsolicited, and in various degrees of urgency. It can happen when a free spirit tries to contact our soul, say, as a deceased loved one.*

The dance of the spirits changes to simulate the invocation of both spirits, expressing a positive result with joy. Robert and Sexis return to the stage.

Sexy.—*Involuntary contact: (1) Souls in human bodies communicate with the souls of other humans through mental vibrations or frequencies transmitted by their feelings. Spirits recognize each other mentally and cling and stay together, somehow, during their stay on earth, perhaps because of their missions. This contact can be transient or continuous stay. Crying, fearing, loving, trusting are typical cases of transmitted feelings that other souls capture and respond to. These contacts are involuntary.*

The spirits simulate this contact, showing surprise of the affinity of their personality or character, thinking they have known each other for a long time. They mutually attract each other and create a strong bond and a relationship or any kind.

Robert.–*Contact involuntary: Sometimes humans find themselves in critical situations, even perhaps life or death and unconsciously send distress signals to the universe: In times of tribulation, anguish and suffering, despair of humans, spirits that roam nearby, in any form of living creature, can pick up these signs and rush, as protectors, to help the troubled human spirit.*

The dance changes and the spirits simulate this contact, showing the despair and anguish of their situation longing for help from any source.

Sexis.–*Involuntary contact: When humans face problems, situations of material life, they unintentionally send distress signals to the omniscience of the universe yearning for a workable solution. Then, through unconscious contact, solutions flow to their minds until suddenly a problem fit. It is the answer of omniscience, providing solutions that can solve the problem.*

The dance changes and the spirits perform is a simulation of mental anguish, showing frustration and hopelessness, dancing and raising their arms to the ceiling crying for the help of any source, and when they receive an inspiration, they show their joy and happiness. Stacey's back on stage.

Stacey:–*Involuntary contact: It can occur when humans feel strong impulses, spontaneous, urged speaking or act to help, care for and or protect another human in distress, in situations of life or death, even walking in a step to danger. This action may not require the thought or analysis of your decision; it's a spontaneous action. This is a case when we become a guardian spirit (guardian angel).*

Spirits come off the stage. The lights go out and the curtains close.

The situation in UC Irvine, CA.

May 15, 2017.

The lights flash on the stage again and the curtains open.

Guide.–*Well, we just got back, and we have to go back one more time. Spirits, we now may take the audience to the University of California at Irvine where Dr. Rex (Ricky Martin) gives a lecture on* *pathological disease research, today May 15, 2017. The conference deals with rare diseases sponsored by the National Medical Research Association of the University of California, Irvine; this is an important conference we wouldn't want to miss.*

The conference room is full. Perhaps, near 750 prominent, well-known and famous personalities, pathologists, doctors and psychologists reunite in the place. The Host, Dr. Heisenberg, Dean of the university's medical research team on the podium, introduces Dr. Rex Martin.

Dr. Heisenberg.—*I am honored to introduce young Dr. Rex Martin this afternoon; some people* gave *him* the *nickname Ricky Martin. However, he won't sing for us today. Dr. Martin is more than a doctor, at his young age he is a scientist; their great work and discoveries are major factors in medicine. With you, Dr. Rex Martin.*

Dr. Martin.—*Thank you, Dr. Heisenberg, thanks to the National Medical Research Association and the University of California, Irvine. Thank you to all the professionals in Psychology, and to the public. I'm not wearing Ricky Martin's suit; so, I will not sing. However, if I sang, I would sing a classic song titled "What I Did for Love," by MARVIN HAMLISCH lyric, EDWARD LAWRENCE KLEBAN. What we do in medical research we do for love.*

The conference lasts an hour and thirty minutes, and before finishing, Dr. Martin mentions a patient Victor Richland, the billionaire who lives in Irvine, California.

Dr. Martin. *I waited until the end of all the technical introductions of our subject to present a patient who has caught all my attention, Mr. Victor Richland.*

Victor stood up and the audience also stood up and burst into loud applause.

—Victor Richland, born in Manhattan, New York, developed a disease that dismays our medical advances. My preliminary review of his medical records suggests that delayed birth and lack of oxygen in the brain that affected certain areas of neuron development, causing an imbalance in the respiratory system. Tonight, I'm meeting him and his medical staff right after this conference. I thank you for your attention and presence. Have a good night.

At the end of his lecture, Dr. Martin left the stage and Victor Richland and his personal physician went outside the audience. In a large meeting room inside the medical research ward, Dr. Martin and Victor meet for the first time, and shake hands. Hand contact, a visible spark, like an electric shock, jumped from Victor to Rex. This strange phenomenon. They look like two brothers who haven't seen each other for years. Still surprised, Victor says.

Victor.–*Dr. Martin, it is a great honor and a pleasure to meet you, but I must tell you, Doctor, that I have known you for many lives. Thank you for your attention. I'll always remember this hour.*

Dr. Martin.–*Mr. Richland, I must also confess that I am surprised by this encounter with you. I share our feelings. I feel as if I am meeting my twin sister; a feeling I would have if I knew my twin sister who died when I was born. I feel like I've known him for more than the time of this life. This innate feeling of intimacy can help us in our medical work, and I hope its recovery.*

Both men walked a few steps and each sat in a fluffy armchair and talked about Victor's medical condition; it was a long friendly conversation as two friends who meet after 27 years... it was almost 9:15 pm when they shook hands as in a case of not wanting to end the conversation; however, they did. They had agreed to meet again in two weeks. Both men left the meeting thinking about that strange handshake. As he left the ICU campus, and once in his car, an involuntary impulse struck his mind, that strange handshake phenomenon with Victor. Dr. Martin orders the driver.

Rex.–*Please drive slowly, I'll make a phone call... Good evening, Sam, how's it going? Oh, well... No, not really, I have to check with you something when you have time, can you tell me when? What? Are you sure? Ok. I'll take your word for it. I'll be in 15 minutes, okay? Thanks, Sam, I'll see you in a little while.*

At Sam's.

Dr. Sam Wells.–*Welcome Rex, it's been a while, hasn't it? Go ahead; would you like a drink?*

Rex Martin.–*Ok. Martini with two olives, please. Yes, thank you.*

Sam (behind the bar).–*You haven't given up your olives in your Martini, huh? Tell me, Rex, what happened that's bothering you?*

Rex tells Sam what happened when he met Victor at UC Irvine.

Rex Martin.—*That's what intrigues me, and I want to study paranormal phenomena.*

Sam.—*Well, Rex, I'm researching spiritual encounters, because there is a spirit in every human. I am inclined to accept that spirits are beings of light and formed only of energy without matter. However, as we know, energy converts into matter and matter into energy, but both are the same substance in different states. Matter and energy; these are attributes of a superior, omnipresent, omnipotent entity. That is why we maintain that, if spirits are energy, they must be part of the total energy and matter of the universe. Our theoretical research continues that spirits in humans are a small part of a global spirit, which cannot destroy or create for the same reason. So, humans do not die; energy imbeds in human bodies as souls. Later, a human spirit returns to the spiritual dimension for a new cycle of life. This is a breakthrough because according to scientific discoveries, we can now prove that humans, as spirits, are eternal or never die.*

Rex.—*That is very interesting, and I understand it; however, what I need to know is how we can detect if the spirit in one person can connect with the spirit of another person. I want to advance tests of connecting our spirits to spirits in their dimension. I need you to study this and tell me two things, one, install a complete lab and the cost for your services; and I'll be very grateful. Well, Sam, it's late, so I have to go now. I'll let you rest part of tonight.*

Sam.—*I need an expert in radiology and low-wave frequencies to experiment with the five brain waves. I'll keep in touch with you soon, good night, Rex.*

Rex.—*I will find the best and let you know, soon. Good night, Sam, and thank you again for having me so late tonight.*

Guide.—*We will continue the dialogue between the spirits and the public we were talking about.... Wait, wait.*

The light flashes on the stage and on the sides of the audience again. Mr. Spirits, we now may take the hearing to Newport Beach, California. We'll travel to Mr. and Mrs. Clark's house.

The situation in Newport Beach, California -2017.

At the Clarks' residence. The two boys, Sergio and Moses, they are talking in the library of their house. *Let's listen to their conversation.*

Moses.—*It seems as yesterday, but it has been twenty-six years since we met in Arriaga. So much has happened in these years, but here we are. How could I have known this tough and tough cop was my Aunt Isabel? Less so she would save my life and your life. We're here today. You have a law degree from the University of Southern California, and a licensed attorney in California. And I got a PhD in Radiology. I feel that in my life there have been three great miracles to be in America, (1) My birth, (2) my kidnapping, (3) finding my Aunt Isabel. The sequence of events happened for a reason and expressed by the spirits.*

Sergio.—*What happened to us is evidence that what Donald Trump says about immigrants is not true; not all immigrants are rapists and criminals, many with the right opportunity and support can contribute to the greatness of this country. Check what Trump has said during his campaign and what he is doing now as president. Here we are enjoying everything we did with a little help to catch great opportunities. In addition, we are contributing to the rise of this nation—now ours. Hey, do you believe in guardian angels?*

Moses.—*Yes, in a way. I think and say that certain events follow a causal sequence, while others are random or lucky (random) events. But the sequence of events we passed or happened so we are here amazing me more. It was a miracle for me to find my Aunt Isa the same day I entered the United States. It's a miracle I'm alive. She could have killed me in the that dark yard. But it could also have been the way spirits in humans connect and ask other human spirits to come together.*

Sergio.—*And I'm sure these are miracles. I remember I'm here because the organ dealers took a kidney from me. And because of that, they couldn't let me go back to my family, and they brought me to Tijuana. I thank you and your aunt for taking me as part of your family. You have a relative here, Moses. However, I can never forget it.*

Truly, thoughts, feelings, fears, emotions, etc., are vibrations of the soul that travel and remain in the space. All the mental vibrations are in, and only in, this space. Other spirits and/or souls can grasp and react to these vibrations. This explains why we laugh and cry when we see others laughing and crying. We trap the moods of spirits near us, and we become happy or emotional like them. So, sadness saddens, and happiness makes you happy.

Mental waves are contagious.

Moses.-*Sorry buddy; I didn't mean to make you remember that part of the past.*

Sergio.-*No, Moses, it's not your fault or mine, but look at the stark chain of events since our birthdays, or even after the cartel men kidnapped me, they extracted my kidney and deported me from my country. The importance of this sequence is its purpose or the consequences of its results that lead to specific objectives. Isn't it funny that the cartel got us both for its criminal purpose? The curious fact is, why we came together we don't know right now. So, I think back to then; I was better off dead than alive. Why they didn't kill me; I do not know. I remember a day after the operation, I tried to run away, but I got caught at the outskirts of town. They thought I'd talked to someone, and they tortured me to find out who I'd talked to. They took me out once at midnight, to kill me, but I don't know why several things in a row they stopped short. First, when the guy pointed the gun at the back of my head, I was kneeling with my hands tied behind my back. At that very moment, an ambulance or the siren of a police car rang. They quickly took me back to their barracks. About two hours later, they pulled me out again, and I felt the gun in my neck again; at that moment a guy from the cartel stumbled into the dark and rolled down the hill into a stream bed. They took me inside again. The next day they came and told me that if I ever talked about what happened to my kidney, they would kill my whole family in Arriaga. So, I've kept your crime all this time.*

Moses.-*You need not remember all these things, Sergio. Maybe it is better to forget it.*

Sergio.-*No Moses, it is better to talk about it and get it out of my system; it is healthy to get it out of my mind, doing something about it. When Ted started our case, I thought of running away. When your aunt mentioned that the Sinaloa Cartel had killed my family, I told everything.*

Today, I have no family, except you, your aunt and Mr. Clark. I'll have the courage to go back to Arriaga someday to see if they killed my family. I want to do that, but I don't know why; I just feel that impulse. It is what I felt before those guys tried to kill me, someone has been protecting me, but why and for what?

Moses.—*I think it may be possible for you to do that—to go back—that is. You and me, we are American citizens now. Maybe a channel or diplomatic protocol could help, you can legally find out what happened.*

It was about 7:30 pm. when Ted and Isabel returned from a visit to nearby neighbors. Moses and Sergio had been talking and working on common projects in the house library.

Ted.—*Hi guys, are you still working?*

Isa.—*Hello, aren't you tired?*

Sergio.—*Yes, Isabel, we had the beef stew you left us. Did you say work? No, we've been going over everything that happened in our lives before we came to America.*

Moses.—*Sergio said he's thinking about going back to Arriaga to visit that place and maybe find someone he knows.*

Isa.—*But Sergio, think twice. Is it a safe place to visit?*

What do you expect to find there?

Sergio.—*I don't know, Aunt Isa. However, there is something calling me, something I need to see there. I hear a voice in my mind telling me, come back, come back. Maybe it's something I need to know to free my soul and mind from the ghosts of the past.*

Those are the signs, the messages, the voices that come to our minds, that we often ignore. Maybe we should pay attention to these messages.

Ted.—*If you go there, you need diplomatic protection and travel with official credentials.*

Moses.—*I just mentioned that of a diplomatic protocol.*

Ted.—*I could talk to Governor Brown or the FBI and get diplomatic credentials for you.*

Sergio.—*Thank you, Ted, that would be wonderful, let's talk about it on Monday. Ted suggested he was fine, nodded, and Isa looks at them nodding the idea.*

Isa:–*Hey, let's go see a movie in the living room, what do you think? Come on, guys, let's go have a drink, will you?*

Everyone said yes, it's a good idea. They got up and went into the living room. But what are these impulses in Sergio's mind? Why do you feel like there's something calling you? It's funny and strange. But who can tell us that their feelings are not premonitions, forebodings created by spirits or their soul knowing something that their mind does not know? Could it be this is the origin of his mood? No one can say unless one knows the reality in Arriaga; only the spirits that induce his soul to act now. Your feelings won't go away. They'll come back again and again. Maybe if we review the itinerary of Sergio and Moses, we can see clues from the chain of events that led them both to this point, and in doing so, we can see the reality of Sergio's premonitions.[xxvii]

CHAPTER 6

Fight against evil

Abstract

What is the devil, a religious belief, or an evil of the human soul? But if humans only have one spirit in their bodies, then evil is in the ego. Is ego the main evil spirit with its autocratic human attitudes? If this is the case, humans do not need an army of archangels and angels to fight evil. Because the soul is perfectly structured with its consciousness, wisdom, morality and willpower to contain its ego. The spirits, the soul, do not intervene, nor interfere with the thoughts, decisions and actions of the ego. The ego has the power of his free choice and will. And because the ego is the only link to reality, human beings are at its mercy. The fight against the evil of the human ego is a long battle. And spirits fight for one goal, "oneness." A state where humans achieve the order of harmony of existence, a condition of conformity, satisfaction with gratitude; that's the goal of life.

The Delegation of Intelligence.

Five days later, on Wednesday of the following week, Ted returned to work around 6:30 p.m. Sergio was already home. Isa and Moses were still in their work. Ted looked for Sergio in the backyard; Sergio was sitting at a patio table, under a yellow and gray umbrella, covering that table, He was by the pool reading a pile of documents from past stories of the Sinaloa Cartel.

Ted.–*Hello Serge.* [that's the way Ted used to call Sergio, sometimes.] *I got the answer from Governor Brown. The credentials will be here for this coming Friday. The governor suggested forming a group that travels as a diplomatic attaché of our Embassy in Mexico City with the assignment to visit the area controlled by the Sinaloa Cartel and Chapo Guzmán, with an extension to Central America. The investigating judicial mission is to test and collect evidence of ongoing cases against that cartel filed at the Federal District's ninth Circuit of the Federal Government in the State of California. Two representatives of Clark and Associates make up the Diplomatic Attaché, Ted Clark and Sergio Maltes, a representative of the Private Investigators of Suarez, LLC. and a living witness, Moses, besides the head of the investigation, Agent Isabel. Ted mentioned that he asked Victor Richland to take part in this investigation by providing two of his lawyers.*

Just before the departure Fred Stern and the group departed for the countries of Mexico and Central America. They agreed and divided the delegation of two fronts, one group to visit Santa Tecla, El Salvador, and the other to visit Arriaga, Chiapas, Mexico. They left Los Angeles International Airport in a hurry. They also contacted and communicated with the embassies and consulates in their plan, including their work schedule.

Return to the present, 2018.

Guide.–*There are keys for humans to capture the signals of spirits in their minds. Do you want to know how to do it? Answer gently and with a single word yes or no, all at once, to the count of three: 1, 2, 3.*

The TV screens floating in space in front of the audience go on, but they turn off. During this, the audience urged their response with thoughts and voices, and the sounds of muttered voices filled the space of the theater room. Everyone wants to know how to communicate with the spirits.

Guide.–*Yes... but for you to receive them, your being has to be in tune, or in harmony, with the global spirit: Relaxed, calm, peaceful, and* *your mind focused on yourself and your longings, with humble vehemence. Think about how often you've met someone you've never seen before, and you feel a sense of security, relief, at ease, that you've never had. Possibly, the spirits of the two people have been together in the material dimension. Think about how often you have longed with vehemence and humility something and that something appeared or came to you.*

Trues.—*When your mind yearns with vehemence and humility, to get and or bring an object or subject, your mind generates certain low frequencies that standard radio receivers cannot capture, but your soul and mind filter these frequencies into the global spirit. There, your longings bounce all over the universe and mingle with all the other longings waves. Over time, your mind captures frequencies back in amazing ideas, inspirations or thoughts, answers to your longings or longings, or guide you to find your goal. Pay attention to these signs—it's easy to perceive them.*

Stacey.—*Then an answer can return to your soul and your mind lights up with surprise when you see your longing realized. This is how your spirit and mind connect and work with the global spirit. Practice this technique until it's a positive habit. Thinking this way, it is valid for people to believe that praying connects a person to the universal spirit; apparently, it does.*

Guide.—*there is nothing that humans cannot do in the material dimension, but they need to focus, think carefully, decide and act. Who wants to connect with spirits?*

All four screens flash again, receiving signals from the public's minds; but before the spirits respond, a man suddenly interrupts, entering the stage on the left, hurried and staggering, holding a bottle of wine in his right hand.

Person P.—*[Surprised and excited]. Yes, me, me.*

A woman's voice screamed off stage.

—*Come back, dirty rat, come back; give me my money back.*

The woman enters the stage waving a broomstick, running after the man; but when she reaches the edge of the stage, she realizes where she is and stops quickly. Surprised and embarrassed, she quickly turns and leaves the stage. The man is on the stage, looking for the woman. The woman hides behind the curtains, watching angrily occasionally.

Guide.–*What's your name, good man?*

The drunk.–*My name is Joshua Jimenez…*

Guide.–*What did you say? Jose Jimenez?*

The man laughs and says, lifting his bottle above his head.

The drunk.–*No, Not José Jiménez. I love spirits… I have, I have spirit in my bottle. You said, who wants to connect with the spirits? I say, I. I. Show me spirits.*

Guide.–*Yes, Joshua. You have a spirit within you, which they assigned to you before he was born.*

The drunk.–*No, no, no spirit in me, yes. I don't drink spirit when I, baby or child. I drink spirit from bottle. I buy spirits in liquor store… Many types… Tequila, Vodka, Bacardi… make me happy. 'The spirit in the bottle helps me forget life that is not good, ha, ha, ha.*

The music plays the famous song from the film 'Zorba the Greek'. The man tries to dance like Anthony Quinn and falls and can't get up. Two police officers arrived on stage and pulled the drunk off the stage. He sings that song.

The drunk.–*la, la, la, la, la, la, la, la, la; spirits love me, spirits love me.*

Stacey.–*What humans do to themselves we, the spirits (but not Joshua's), cannot amend. Human beings have the sacred attribute of freedom of choice, their free will–freedom to think, to speak, and to act –, for which human beings are fully responsible for the consequences of their behavior. As we said, our mission is only to protect, protect and sustain life, if there is time for us to act. Joshua drinks or not for his own reasons. He is a good man; he doesn't see solutions to his problems or realize what he does about himself.*

Existence does not punish those who misbehave. The law of mutual compensation maintains the balance of morality, right and wrong, good and bad, just and unjust, pleasant and unpleasant. And those who violate this law pay a price for their bad behavior, thereafter. Trues enters from the back of the right, walks like a military cadet, while speaking with authority.

Trues.–*In existence there is only one global spirit, it fills the space and carries all the power and knowledge of the universe. The beliefs and faith of religions call it God, Ala, and so on. The definitions of the* *global spirit are consistent in all religions, according to these attributes: Almighty, omnipresent, omniscient, love, mercy, justice, and absolute benevolence. Love and mercy suggest that the global spirit is truth and absolute compassion, it's existence. Human religions are correct. There is a global, and only one, spirit. He's all-powerful, he's everywhere, and he knows everything. Therefore, the global spirit does not intentionally harm any object or subject, never unfailingly possible. The souls that live in you are a molecular representation of the universal spirit with all its attributes. Therefore, if there are opportunities to improve their lives, there are opportunities for Joshua, if he takes them.*

Stacey.—*The Love of Existence rule applies to life and establishes the mission of spirits that penetrate human eggs. Their mission is to protect, guide and sustain human lives. All living creatures receive a molecule of knowledge, power, and the absolute presence of the global spirit, all in proportion to the innate category of their consciousness.*

The four screens blink again, and we hear a voice in the echo.

The light flashes on stage and in the audience again.

Authorization to investigate.

The spirit's voice.—*Spirits may take the audience to Santa Tecla, El Salvador and Arriaga, Chiapas, Mexico.*

The group into two delegations: one group will visit Santa Tecla, El Salvador, and the other will visit Arriaga, Chiapas, Mexico. Both offices leave the international airport from Los Angeles, California soon. They organized to maintain constant communication between the two groups. Each member of the delegations carries diplomatic credentials allowed by the intelligence agencies and the United States Department of State. Members carry the corresponding official authorizations of the Governments of Mexico and the Central American Countries required by the members.

While delegations in Mexico and Central America, the dialogue of spirits continues.

Guide.—*that humans cannot see from the present to a second does not mean that their souls cannot expect the events to come. Evidence comes in premonitions, visions, feelings, anxieties, worries, fears, etc. They are the intuitions of their souls.*

Trues.—*Yes, humans can see the future through the fog of their mental constraints or limitations. The key to solving these limitations is to observe and understand the patterns of the universe and the behavior of a surrounding scenario: the human environment. The causal sequences of events draw future results on the canvas of reality enough. The process requires intense, deep and tedious meditation.*

Stacey.—*That is the reality of the spiritual dimension where spirits can see all future events. While human tribulations, emotions, fears, and concerns block that human attribute. Clear your minds and follow what's about to happen.*

Research in Santa Tecla, El Salvador.

Fred and Isabel presented their credentials, and the international legal purpose of their mission, to the government authorities of Santa Tecla. The delegation speaks to Commander Ruiz, Colonel Osvaldo Ruiz himself, who was in charge of the disappearance of Moses Suarez.

Isa.—*Commander Ruiz, I'm Officer Isabel, and this is Ted Clark, and diplomatic protocol officer. We have permission from your government's "International Relations" to investigate and collect evidence of the abduction of a minor to extract the child's organs for profit, and subsequent disappearance of the same subject.*

A translator translates that statement into Spanish for Commander Ruiz. The translator repeats what Commander Ruiz says in his answers.

Commander Ruiz.—*Officer Suarez, I remember that the case was closed a long time ago because of insufficient evidence to make it meritorious of an additional investigation, as given by the court soon. We have sent to the central archive station in San Salvador. However, with the utmost pleasure and responsibility we will provide you with all the documentation you request in about three days. Do you have another matter to deal with?*

Fred.—*Yes, we ask for respect and protection as we search and interview potential witnesses who may still exist in and around this city.*

The translator translates Fred's words into Spanish as he speaks.

Commander Ruiz.–*Understood, and to support the permission granted by this nation, please wear these badges on a visible part of the clothing at the height of your chest. I'll order an officer to accompany you in your investigations. And if you have no more business to deal with, please allow me to continue my occupations.*

Fred.–*Commander Ruiz, we thank you for your accompanying officer, but that violates our reciprocal international rights to investigate crimes against our nations. We want to carry out our work on the privacy of our own research.*

The delegation stood up; they shook hands, left the commander's office, and went straight to the crime site. Isa anxious and eager, she went door to door asking about the disaster of the old House of the Suarez, without success. The rumor of this investigation had spread everywhere, and people feared what the commander can do after the delegation leaves.

As they walked through one dirt street, a few blocks away, a light illuminates Moses' mind and prays for something. That place wasn't the same as it was all those years ago. Now there are more houses and paved streets.

Moses.–*Aunt Isa, I remember something about this place, follow me.*

Walking a half mile down the street, Moses guides the delegation through backyards open to a small house in dense large trees. It was his old neighborhood with quite a few changes. Pigs, ducks and chickens wandering around and Moses warns others.

Moses.–*Be careful not to step on pig droppings; it smells very bad.*

There were four people in the house, an old and one old woman, a young man and a middle-aged woman, and three children who fled to the backyard when they saw the people approaching the house. One child, about seven years old, stood at the door. The time is around 1:00 p.m.

Moses.–*Hello, good afternoon. Is your mom here?*

With a typical Salvadoran accent, the child responds.

The boy.–*Well, no, she's not. So, she requires it?*

Moses.–*No, boy, I'm not looking for your mom, I'm looking for Mrs. Esperanza, and is she here?*

The boy responds with a child's innocence.

The boy.—*So, what do you want her for… if it's to attend a delivery, I tell you, sir, my granny doesn't work on it anymore. She hardly sees desde hace tiempo and hardly hears, she's old.*

Moses pulls out a chocolate bar and moves it in front of the child and says.

Moses.—*Look, tell your granny Esperanza that Moses, the son of Juana Suarez, her neighbor, is here.*

The boy looked at the chocolate bar for a minute, said nothing, took it and ran to the backyard. A few minutes later, four adults and three children entered through the back door, dawdling. They all look suspicious and scared.

Ms. Esperanza.—*Look, are you from the government? No one here lives by that name of Esperanza. That lady left for Honduras, uh, a long time ago. We've been renting this little house for many years. I'm sorry, but we can't help you.*

The old lady's trembling voice pointed out that she was not telling the truth. But that is normal behavior under the threat of drug traffickers trafficking human organs, and corrupt authorities. No one can blame these people. His behavior is his instinct for self-preservation. They are afraid; they fear for their lives, especially for children. Moses, he knew this behavior; he lived under this threat and insisted on question and identification to earn his trust.

Moses.—*Look, Mrs. Esperanza, I am Moses Suarez, son of Juana Suarez. We lived in the last house of the cul-de-sac. My grandparents were Lina (Ma' Lina) and Papa Joe (Joseph). I was born in 1991, you, Mrs. Esperanza, attended my mother, Juana Suarez.*

Looking through the corner of his eyes, looking at these well-dressed people, doubting everything she heard, she says.

Mrs. Esperanza.—*I tell you; I don't remember anyone with those names.*

The old man bends over and says something in the old lady's ear. The delegation was already coming out of the door when the old lady says something.

—*Wait, come back, and tell me, do you come from Commander Ruiz? And if you don't, can you identify yourselves?*

Moses.–*Mrs. Esperanza, I bring with me my graduation certificate from the school here in Santa Tecla that confirms my name.*

The obvious fears of cartel criminals are clear in the intelligent responses of the people in that house. They know that a misguided answer is a matter of life and death for them. Moses gives his school certificate to the boy still chewing the chocolate candy, and the child walks and gives it to the young man standing behind the old woman. The delegation did not ask to enter the house; they are still standing outside the door. The young man looks at the document for a minute and then says something to the old lady and the others together, then, the whole group, they look at Moses. There was a deep silence for a moment, until the middle-aged woman, standing on the old woman's side, broke into sobs and tears. The members of the delegation don't know what's going on. But the screaming young lady says.

The young woman.–*Oh my God, ay, ay, ay. If it's Moises, my nephew.* She ran to hug him, crying.

The young woman.–*Oh, ah, ay, son, I am your Aunt Mary; I have dreamed so much that you were alive, ay, ay, ay. Nephew, something in my heart told me you weren't dead, ay, ay, ay.*

The man next to the old lady can't hold either and screams.

The young man.–Ah, I am Carlos, Moses. I knew the cartel people hadn't killed you, man. Carlos rushes to hug his best friend from those school years. Moses, also crying as he hugs Mary and Carlos, pulls Agent Isa, covered in tears, trembling; turns to Isa and says.

Moses.–*This is my Aunt Isabel.*

Mary turned to look at the elegant and well-dressed woman, and overcoming her emotions she embraced Isabel, and says.

Mary.–*Oh, my God; ay, ay, ay, ay sister, Isabel, tell me I am not dreaming. Oh, my dear sister, I've missed you so much. Oh, ay, ay. How I wished our mother and grandmother were alive to live this moment, Isabel, ay, ay, ay.*

The emotions of this encounter continued, and the woman, Esperanza, overwhelmed by emotions, sitting in her rocking chair, could not say anything. The drama covered that house that afternoon;

and nothing could have stopped the deluge of emotions that fell hard into the minds and souls of these relatives who loved each other so much and separated for a long time. There is nothing more damaging than misery and necessity. These are the consequences of forced family separation caused by people in human organs trafficking, as well as by precarious situations in poor countries. All this happen when cosmic forces were at play influencing the minds of Moses, Sergio and Isabel. There must be a reason all these souls come together again.

Back to 2018.

Returning to the theater for a moment, as people in Santa Tecla go through the emotional episode of their encounter, we can continue our conversation.

Guide.—Humans can say these strong emotions distinguish the human species from the lower ones, but is it true? Spirits have no emotions like that because the attribute of omniscience removes the element of surprise, and or ignorance of the future, and therefore the wow factor. Is this state of certainty better than the uncertain state of humans? In addition, the omnipresence that allows spirits to be during an event, present, or future provides spiritual minds with details of future events. The caveat is that a spirit attached to a human body does not have the ability of the mind to expect future events (except under certain mental and emotional conditions).

Trues.—*There is an important theme in the history of Santa Tecla: it is the sequence of activities and events that lead to the emotional outburst. In a physical world where causality processes predominate, the actions of spirits expressed or precipitated the chain of activities and events that led the diplomatic delegation to where they are now in that city.*

Are these random events? No, they're not, they're causal chains that deliver expected results. Do spirits manipulate these sequences? No, they do not, because causal chains obey the law of cause and effect; and the effects are the product of conditions and situations integrated into specific events. This is how the existence established life; and this living creatures must endure.

The four window screens capture a question in the mind of a person in the audience.

Person Q.–*What does the thinking, the mind or the brain?*

Stacey.–*This is a good question, raise your hand if you have thought about this question. Let me say, the brain does not think; the brain is a material organ that starts and processes gnosis, fragments of information, captured through perceptual function to generate images. The mind is the operating system, like a computer, and its processes are like computer applications, programs and or instructions; the mind makes the thought, assembling reality with perceived images. The mind creates images through its conceptual functions, too. While the brain is material, the mind is spiritual. Mental connectivity through an attribute of soul's conscience. This conscience occupies a point within two extremes along a spectral line, total consciousness to full unconsciousness.*

Trues.–*That's right! The mind handles certain functions in three states, (1) Consciousness and (2) subconsciousness, and (3) unconsciousness that are parts of operating the mind on the spectrum of consciousness. These are three levels of the mind awareness.* [47]

Stacey.–*The mental realm has two executive sub-domains, (1) Ego and (2) Conscience. The conscience contains, (1) Morality, (2) Wisdom, and (3) Will Power; while the ego has (1) Character, (2) Internal-external awareness and (3) Personal identity. The ego attaches to material objects and subjects. The wisdom in the conscience reasons and meditates, while the willpower; rational and or irrational, controls the materialistic behavior of the ego. Remember that ego is part of the soul and has freedom of choice. Because of the free choice of ego, humans behave capriciously without regard to the natural order, often irrational, and often ignoring the consequences.*

Screens capture another question from someone's mind in the audience.

Person R.–*Can humans control the behavior of our ego?*

Guide.–*Yes, humans can reduce, change and or suppress the ego's unwanted behavior, but it requires strict procedural discipline: The process is self-inductive meditation or hypnosis that leads to the suppression of material consciousness, until we automatically handle a routine or reaction to stimuli. Like the management of anger and temperament.*

The light flashes on the stage and on the sides of the audience, again.

Guide.–*Listen, we now may take the hearing Arriaga, Chiapas Mexico.*

The investigation in Arriaga, Chiapas, Mexico.

Ted and Sergio, and a representative, Chris Sanders, of The Private Investigators of Suarez, LLC work in Arriaga. The delegation learned the details of the capture of Joaquín Chapo Guzmán on January 16, 2017. The danger of the Cartel remains eminent in the Chiapas area.

Ted is reading files at police headquarters, he says.

Ted.–*Look, Sergio, I think we found a witness. It says here that Antonio Morales, then 18, said that the fire that burned your parents' house provoked and started at the back of the house around 3:00 in the morning. The city's fire department found burnt persons but could not recognize the bodies.*

Sergio.–*Let me see. Look right here in the back pocket of this folder.*

These addresses are of Antonio (Tony) Morales and Diego González.

Ted.–*Who are these people?*

Sergio.–*I don't know about Diego Gonzalez, but Tony was my best friend at school; he used to find baseball cards for me. Let's go find them.*

The three members of the delegation departed in a hurry. The delegation found Diego and immediately questioned him with simple questions. Sergio serves as a Spanish translator. The translation from Spanish to English appeared on all four screens of the stage. Diego is a local photographer and video producer in Arriaga. Diego responded in Spanish, but Sergio translated into English.

Diego.–*It's been many years so, perhaps, I miss the details, but I can tell you this: One day, early in the morning, I would work at Virgilio Vegas' farm and as I passed by Mrs. Ophelia's house I saw two men behind the house each with a red can. I hid, and I saw the house bursting into flames. The men ran down the open yard in the back.*

Chris Sanders.–*Did you recognize the two men?*

Diego.–*No, I couldn't see their faces, but the vehicle they were driving to escape was a black suburban like the one driven by the cartel* *people. I had my movie camera with me, and I filmed a clip of the men, their black suburban near the burning house. Anyway, when they left, I screamed fire, fire, fire to wake up the neighborhood. We all tried to put out the fire, but it was impossible; everything caught fire. By that afternoon, the house was still hot; the fire department worked carefully; and the fire returned several times in the rubble. They found four bodies, but they couldn't identify them. I saw the bodies. That's what I told the police. Neighbors said two children were missing. The rumor was that the cartel people took them, but nobody confirmed.*

Sergio cried, but tried to keep his composure.

Sergio.–*Did you ever talk to them?*

Diego.–*No, I never met them; I was new it the city, but the neighbors talked about the family. They recall that about six months before the fire; the family informed authorities that one of their sons had been kidnapped by the Cartel. That kid never showed up, and the police didn't solve that case. I work as a contributor to the local newspaper and I can retrieve information about that case.*

Sergio had moved away from the team and had remained alone. Many thoughts went through his mind, but the idea, by this evidence, is that the Cartel had eliminated his entire family.

Ted.–*Diego, do you know Antonio (Tony) Morales?*

Sergio comes back and keeps translating. The rage on his face was obvious, but he kept his thoughts to himself.

Diego.–*No, I don't know him, but I think Ms. Ramona can meet him, she knows all the people of this city.*

Ted.–*Thank you, Diego, please find the film you took from the fire and the black suburban; we would like to have a copy for the evidence, also if we come up with other questions, can we see you again?*

Sergio walks away from the group.

Diego.–*Yes, you know where to find me.*

Ted talks to Chris.

Ted.–*Chris, go get Sergio, we're leaving.*

They all left and a few minutes later they arrive at Tony's address; however, the house was empty, no one lives there. Suddenly Sergio remembers that he heard Diego mention Ms. Ramona and says.

Sergio.–*Let's go find Ms. Ramona.*

They found the house where Ms. Ramona still lives, but her health and memory are not well; she forgets a lot.

Sergio.–*Ms. Ramona, do you remember Teresa, the daughter of Ms. Ofelia?*

Ms. Ramona.–*Let me see, son... isn't she the one who lived in the burned house at the end of the cul-de-sac? Yes, she is... You know, son, I helped her in the birth of her son Sergio who was stillborn, but God gave him back his life as a miracle. The poor thing, her life so painful, lost her son Sergio; the cartel people killed him a long time ago. Well, but why are you looking for?*

Ramona, Sergio tells you this.

Sergio.–*Ms. Ramona, I am Sergio, Sergio Maltes, the boy you say was stillborn and revived.*

Mrs. Ramona.–*Oh no, God help me, this can't be.*

The poor old lady looks at him and faints in that chair: a man and two women there run; they bring some strong-smelling substance, and give it to smell, while the other man rubs the alcohol mixture with camphor on her arms, and the other man blows her face with a large hat. Everything seemed as if this event happened often. The old lady came back and herself.

Mrs. Ramona.–*Please tell me this is not a dream, and this is not the ghost of Sergio dead, oh my God. I think it's my time to submit the account book of my life and travel to heaven.*

Sergio.–*I'm sorry, Mrs. Ramona, forgive me, I didn't mean to cause you this.*

Sergio walks to the old lady and Ms. Ramona scared faints again. She thought Sergio's ghost was coming to take her away. People know what to do and after two minutes Mrs. Ramona returns. After the commotion and all the identification, with all the emotions under control, Ramona says.

Mrs. Ramona.–*Sergio, Son; your grandfather Julian, your grandmother Ophelia, Teresa, your mother, and Alfonso, your brother, all burned in the fire of your house; it was horrible, son; it was horrible. That property is yours, son, I have the deed of ownership and I will give it to you now. And I have more that I will give you back right now.*

Sergio's mind stops, shocked, thinking about what Ramona might give him back. The delegation learns that Sergio's house caught fire, and they discovered four bodies of reconnaissance, the neighbors assume that the dead were the whole family. The old lady with a head-to-side movement tells one man to go somewhere. The man returned with a young man and a young woman walking behind him. They came in and stood, particularly frightened, by Ms. Ramona. She calls Sergio with her hand.

Ms. Ramona.—*Come here, son, come closer.*

Sergio walks towards her, and she takes his hand and pulls him towards the young woman and the man by her side, saying.

Mrs. Ramona.—*Sergio, hug your sister Clarita and your brother Jorge.*

Once again, a world of deep emotions comes upon Sergio and his brother and sister. Tears flowed like rivers coming down from their hearts, and their long-repressed sobs and tremors of love silently shook the land of Ms. Ramona's house. Time goes unnoticed or ignored, and Ted and Chris, also emotionally affected, witness the drama that unfolds from this encounter.

Mrs. Ramona.—*Sergio, when the fire burned your house, Jorge and Clarita were spending a few days here at my house while Ophelia and Julian repaired the roof of their house. When we learned that the men in the cartel set fire to the house of Julian and Ophelia, we hid Jorge and Clarita. I sent them to my sister Hortensia's estate, because we knew the men in the cartel were looking for them everywhere. We even changed their names and passed them as Hortensia's children. Two years later they were still looking for Peter, your friend, your schoolmate; They grabbed him and tortured him to get information about Jorge and Clarita, but Pedro didn't sing. He ran away and went to relatives in Nicaragua. Sergio, two days ago my soul wouldn't let me be calm. I had a need for the children to come; and I sent for them, to bring them from Hortensia farm, with Emilio [A man near her], Hortensia could have taken them to Belize's Belmopan tomorrow; they would be safer there; here they have no life.*

What a horrible story of a place where human lives make sense, just the greed of traffickers. There are important points of spiritual work here. First, Sergio goes to America, we know. Second, Ophelia and Julian fix the roof of their house. Third, Clarita and Jorge go to Ms. Ramona's house because of the roof work. Fourth, the people of the Cartel burn down Sergio's house and kill part of his family. Mocha saves Clarita and Jorge. Fifth, Sergio needs to know what happened to his family; something was calling him in his mind. Sixth Ted organizes a research team and travels to Mexico and Central America. Seventh Ramona has a feeling and sends the children into hiding. Eighth Sergio shows up at Ramona's house and finds his sister and brother. Ninth Ramona reveals to Sergio the whole truth about his family's tragedy; this is a clear chain of events with a purpose, satisfy Sergio's premonition and/or forebodings. They couldn't be random coincidences. There's a purpose in this story. It is a fantastic application of the law of cause and effects we should all study. Ms. Ramona still talking endlessly. Until Ted suggested it was late, and they had to go.

The delegation flies to Managua, Nicaragua and locates Pedro Pietro, Sergio's friend, and after another emotional encounter, Pedro agrees to return to Arriaga to identify the crime site and testify before public authorities. The delegation spends over two weeks searching for sources and witnesses. They found no further witnesses, but the team found in the police records in Arriaga, a council that leads the delegation to discover a defined pattern by which the abduction and trafficking of organs out. After completing their investigation, Ted, Sergio and the three witnesses fly to Mexico City. Ted filed an asylum petition for Jorge and Clarita and Pedro, based on the danger of life by the Sinaloa Cartel, persecution with intent to kill them.

While in Mexico, Sergio discovered that an American girl, about four years old named Jennifer, in Acapulco around 2001. She was the daughter of an American couple named Armstrong. Through further investigation, Sergio discovers that the Cartel had sent her to California, circa 2001. Two days later Ted talked to Isa.

Ted.—*Isa How are things there? Excellent ... how is Moses and his brethren? Oh, that's unbelievable. Here, Chris and I arranged all legal proceedings for Pedro, Jorge and Clarita at the American Embassy in Mexico City. No... No... we had no problems. We'll stay in Mexico*

City waiting for you. Yes, that's right. Ok. I love you too, bye. Oh, wait, I've got something else; we discovered that the daughter of a Brazilian diplomat in... Hello, hello, hello. Damn this communication. What a fucking service.

The investigation in Mexico City.

The next day, Ted went to pick up Isa, Moses and everyone at Mexico International Airport and they return to the Hotel. That night they had dinner with the U.S. ambassador. The embassy was celebrating a more year of service in Mexico City, here. A medium-sized Mariachi from Garibaldi came to perform at the embassy. The ambassador gave Sergio certain documents about Jennifer Armstrong, an American girl taken from her mother at a resort in Acapulco, and information from other girls also abducted: one in Rio Janeiro, and the other in Mexico City. Amid the tables, in the house, the Mariachi de Puebla performs several songs for the celebration, and a choreographic group of dance Mexican folk music for the ambassador and her guests.

The next morning, the entire delegation returns to Los Angeles, California. On arrival, Isa said.

Isa.—*It's so nice to be at home, happy together.*

Ted.—*Isa, what were you saying when our telephone communication broke down in El Salvador?*

Isa.—*Oh, yes; I was telling you we discovered that, in the lobby of the Camino Real Hotel across the road from the international airport, in Managua, Nicaragua, the people of the cartel kidnapped a Brazilian girl. And when we returned to El Salvador, we investigated the kidnappings there. We discovered that another girl was abducted in downtown El Salvador in the same year. Now we know that the Brazilian girl is Luiza Pinheiro, and the other, a German girl, is Jenifer Heisenberg. These abductions occurred in 1991.*

The entire group, Ted Isa Moses with Maria and Carlos, Sergio with Pedro, Clarita and Jorge, is safe in California. The private agency Isabel investigated the whereabouts of Jenifer Heisenberg, and then communicates with Dr. Karl Heisenberg, dean of medical research at the University of California, Irvine. Isa's suspicions were correct, Dr. Heisenberg lost his daughter Jenifer while traveling to El Salvador with his wife and other son. Isa arranged for Jenifer's reunion with her family a year after Isa's return from Central America. Jenifer, Sergio and Moses are very good friends; they meet as often as their time allows them. Jenifer shows interest in Moses, while Sergio found a girl. Isa also researched and found Karla Armstrong's and arranged a meeting with her parents living in Kentucky.

Return to the Present 2018.
Meeting the Four Spirits.

On stage, three spirits sit in the air chatting about human situations. So much has happened and we have seen the participation of the spirits and souls of humans.

Guide.—*So many things, so many activities and events, and as you have seen them, life seems like a normal life on earth. It is curious to see us, the spirits in the human bodies involved in their stories, actively taking part to realize the events of their lives. The actions of spirits contribute with humans to walk to their destiny: not death—there is no death, only the return of spirits to the spiritual dimension—because matter, the human body—the human body is eternal matter.*

Stacey.—*Let us understand that even when the human mind is an element of the soul, like conscience, humans have an ego with freedom of choice. Spirits do not intervene or manipulate human actions. The ego manages its decisions and actions, and so spirits only act to preserve the safety and lives of people.*

Trues.—*About spiritual encounters, yes, spirits communicate with, even when they speak or think through a human body; for example, when two people coincide strangely in the same thought or physically take the same action, simultaneously. They say gee; "you guessed my thought, or you're doing what I thought I'd do.*

Inter-dimensional connectivity.

The guide takes advantage of the time left by the effort of the research delegation. He thinks that the connection of spirits is a topic to understand what happened. The lights flash on the stage and on the audience side again.

Guide.—*Spirits, you now may take the public to Beverly Hills, California. We will travel back in time to the Residence of Dr. Rex Martin.*

Dr. Martin had invited a select audience and several experts to a meeting at his Home Research Laboratory to hear Dr. Samuel Wells talk about dimensional matter-spirit connectivity, CIMS. He also invited a team of lawyers to certify procedures and results that protect intellectual property, led by Ted Clark and his wife, Isabel Suarez-Clark. The stage is a huge entertainment room, like a small home theater, with a small stage, but big enough for a small band or acting cast. The sound system is excellent.

Dr. Rex Martin.—*Good evening, distinguished guests and audience; Let me introduce Dr. Sam Wells, a world-renowned psychologist. Sam has been studying the fusion of spirits and bodies for a few years now. He will explain how spirits connect our souls with human minds. Let us welcome our special guests to Mr. Victor Richland, Dr. Moses Suarez, Dr. Rex Martin, and Mr. Sergio Maltes, a partner attorney for Clark and associate lawyers. Besides Mr. and Mrs. Clark. And now, with you, Dr. Wells.*

Two guests enter from the right stage and the other two from the stage-left. They come to sit a table covered with white linen, a jug of water, glasses for guests. The table with two vases with flowers to the right and left of the four guests.

The stage light shines over the guests and the table, while the rest of the stage remains in the twilight. There's soft music in the background.

Dr. Wells.—*Thank you, Dr. Martin, guests and the public. The subject of contacts with spirits is not new; it has existed since the homo genre appeared on earth. Our souls are not material; belong to the dimension of spirits. The soul of mind, consciousness and ego, which are not material. The mind is the voice and represents the soul. These three components define and manage the identity, character and behavior of humans. As a psychologist, I work with all three, and you deal with them as humans every day. Human minds generate all ideas, all thoughts; and* *from these, the human body executes the actions ordered by their minds. We are "mentaurs" this is a creature with half spirit and half a material body. The ego follows "AGHAPEE", which feeds on power, wealth and fame. The ego blocks humans from their own spiritual nature. We need to free our minds from the influence of the ego to enter the dimension of spirits. We have two procedures: one natural and one induced. In both cases, we must separate the mind from the material world. I will divide this presentation into two parts: The suppression of Consciousness and Connectivity. We will use kaleidoscopic light refraction to suppress consciousness; and Inter-dimensional spirit and matter connectivity—to connect. I'll work with Dr. Suarez, with a PhD in radiology. He is an expert in low-frequency radiological procedures that capture the attention of the mind, suppressing material consciousness; this effect reduces stress.*

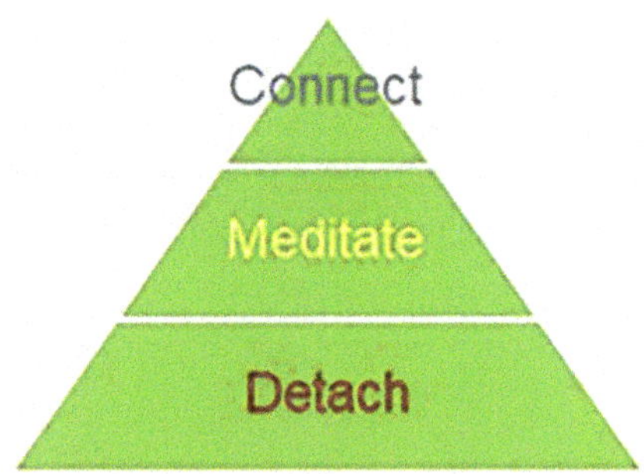

Figure 11: Mental Separation.

The topics are:

1- Connectivity with lower beings;
2- Interaction with spirits (called guardians);
3- Strange sensations;
4- Strange visualization of the spirits;
5- Visualization of strange phenomena.

Sam.—*First theme: The function of a spirit embedded in a creature of inferior intelligence is simple. Moses performed a procedure to prove a spirit in living creatures of lesser intelligence. The result was blunt. Moses, please.*

Moses.–*Thank you, Sam, I am honored to be part of this great research team led by Dr. Wells. My medical radiological research team recorded an episode related to spirits in a living creature a year ago.*

As Moses explained his case, the stage gradually darkened, and our minds go back to the time of Sam's experiment. The curtains close for a moment; and when the curtains open the lights return and the audience sees on stage a surgery room with tools, equipment and instruments. The surgery team: Dr. Martin, two nurses and two assistants, all dressed in proper surgical suites, ready for an operation procedure.

The spirits in inferior living beings.

Dr. Suarez.–*Room manager, turn on the equipment.*

Room manager.–*All equipment turned on and ready. Frequency generator group ready. Gamma wave range set to its lower range (40 Hz); Beta waves set in their lower range (12 Hz); Alpha waves set in the midrange (10 Hz); Theta waves set to 5 Hz; and the delta waves fixed at 2 Hz.*

Dr. Suarez.–*Quality controller, turn on video and audio recording devices.*

Quality controller.–*Revised video unit and list; a set of audio recorder, configured and ready. Devices configured and ready for activation.*

The surgical team voice gradually dims as the meticulous preparation of the room continues if you leave no steps unregistered and checked for high quality. This includes lighting, room conditions, recording equipment, audio and video. Oh! Also, the environmental control of a room with zero bacteria and zero dirt particles, including humidity and temperature that should be precise: 60 degrees Fahrenheit, the air flow laminate at 100 feet per second. Same with sterilization of people and dresses. Now the O.R. is ready. But for Dr. Suarez, they're not ready yet. For example, staff should prepare to enter the clean operating room, and the sterility of the equipment and operating tools. We hear voices almost imperceptible in the background.

Operations Wizard.—*Instrument carts in place and ready, connected and ready intravenous solutions feeder. Various items and materials ready.*

Dr. Suarez.—*Operational personnel prepare for operation. Start. Turn on the live recording devices, turn on the air lights. Activate the robotic arms. Prepare and establish the radioactive substance. Turn on the gamma-ray projector. All right, bring the patient.*

-Recording on, take 1, come on. Dr. Suarez explains the purpose.

For Dr. Suarez, quality is a real factor in the success equation. The spirits have said that the precision of existence—as seen in the universe—shows what life is or should be like.

Dr. Suarez [to the staff].—*This operation proposes to establish a connection between a soul or mind in the brain of a living creature with other souls within other living beings and or the global spirit. The procedure involves the implantation of electronic devices in the patient's brain to establish communication with the soul through their mind.*

To the staff, doctors and nurses, they answer yes when Dr. Suarez asks if they understood the purpose of the experiment. But the procedure was not as important as the result. There is proof of the soul's communication of a less intelligent being with other more evolved souls. The patient, still covered with white surgical sheets, becomes restless and resists, as if conscious and frightened of the outcome of the operation. The voices in the background almost inaudible show the despair and chaos in the operating room.

Dr. Suarez.—*Nurse Chief, reassure the patient.*

Julie.—*Injection ready, sterilizing firing point, airing flask and ready to inject.*

The patient moans and squeals aloud as he tries to escape the straps that tie him. The nurse request help to keep the patient stable; there are difficulties with the patient. Two assistants hold the patient. Voices in the background continue.

Julie.—*the patient stabilized, ready for injection.*

The patient is desperately shaking, discovering, and detaching from the straps, jumps from the surgery bench to the floor and runs, avoiding getting caught. The public is eager to see who the patient is. The images of the patient on all four screens of the stage. It's a big

180-pound Duroc-Jersey male pig. The public can see the struggle with the patient. The patient runs under the tables, nurses and staff chasing the patient. They stumble, they slip, they fall. But they catch the patient after about five minutes of pursuit. The audience laughs and laughs.

Dr. Suarez.—*Abort the procedure, abort the procedure.*

Everything stops. This is strange; it shouldn't happen like this. The patient behaves as if he knows what this means and knows the result. Using your body at the end of the experiment.

Dr. Suarez.—*Call the University of Iowa and ask about the patient's mental and behavioral history.*

Pausing momentarily, Dr. Suarez says.

—There is a remote possibility this patient may be...

Stop your phrase and redirect...

—wait, I think I better confirm my suspicion.

In the background, you hear certain sarcastic comments.

Julie.—*Well, it looks like we're not have squeaks or carnitas. The patient resists the process.*

Sam [a little worried] intervenes by asking about the activities of the spirits in this process.

Dr. Suarez.—*Julie, keep your comments and call Victor and Sergio to a closed spiritual session with Sam, and I; right now.*

Dr. Wells runs an impromptu emergency meeting and asks the following on the operational audience side. Moses remains in the procedure room, communicating through an internal telephone system with the outside team.

Dr. Wells.—*In our previous session on the starting platform, do you remember any spirits programmed to enter a pig? Moses, Victor, Rex and Sergio have been working on spiritual contact, communication, and memory of experiences.*

Sergio.—*Yes, Dr. Wells, I vaguely remember there was a spirit not so enthusiastic about its mission on earth. This is Bochar commissioned to enter a pig, but delayed its departure for several years. I propose that we do a session to confirm this thesis.*

The four spirits agreed to pass the radio-kaleidoscopic and inter-dimensional connection test. They've done that before.

Dr. Wells.–*Moses, I installed light scattering equipment. We must establish why the pig; I mean, Bochar resists the experiment.*

The audience sees images of the chase of that patient in the surgery room for a while with tremendous, chaotic and destructive results, but with humorous and risible actions. And the pig did not resist anymore, and they brought it back to the lab. Rex has set up a changed EEG machine; A pig's brain waves differ from human brain waves. This can be difficult.[xxviii]

Rex talked to the patient. The patient was calm and cooperating voluntarily with the tests. Then they resume the experiment.

Dr. Wells.–*Bochar, if you hear us move the tail, and when we ask something if you agree move your right ear. If you don't agree, move your left ear. If you don't like what you hear, squeal, and if you like just tilt your head. We'll call you Bochar from here on out.*

Moses.–*Bochar, you can hear us.*

Bochar did not answer, but moved his big eyes, frightened and surprised.

Dr. Wells.–*Operator increase the intensity of the Beta waveform by 0.1 hertz and refocus.*

Moses.–Bochar, can you hear me?

For the second time, the subject didn't respond.

Dr. Wells.–*Operator, decrease Delta beam intensity by 0.5 hertz, and refocus.*

Moses.–*Bochar, you can hear us.*

For the third attempt, the subject did not respond.

Dr. Wells.–*Operator decrease the intensity of the Delta beam another 1 hertz and refocus.*

The main operator.–*Dr., yes, but if we increase the frequency will come out of the patient-spirit reception frequency range. However, I will keep the transmission within the brain waves.*

After two minutes. A little heartbroken, Dr. Wells understands that the connection to Bochar was impossible, and he says.

Dr. Wells.–*I'm sorry, folks; we seem to have failed our experiment. There's no reason to go on. Remove the connections and release the patient. Abort the experiment.*

Staff and nurses begin discontinuation when Rex speaks.

Rex.—*Wait, wait. The subject is responding: the patient moved the tail. The patient is red; it turns cold and blue. Did you see that?*

No one answered.—*They looked down, sad and disappointed.*

The phenomenon surprised everyone to see what's going on. An electric green aura appears around Bochar's body.

Dr. Wells.—*Operators, maintain the last frequency and keep the transmission running.*

Moses.—*Bochar, you can hear us.*

It takes a minute, frustration and despair add up, but Bochar moves his tail. The theater lights go out and lightning hits the pig. The lights hit the lab floor. In the dark, the right back of the stage lights up. A green halo forms around the patient's body. A ghostly image slowly appears on the screen and jumps on the screen making the strange sounds look as if they come from above, inaudible to humans and spirits, thoughts or voice is unclear, and continues. Gradually the words become clearer. This situation lasts about 3 minutes.

Moses.—*Rex, don't turn off the beam, leave it on. Give the image time to synchronize with this transmissible frequency channel.*

Dr. Martin.—*I will keep the light diffuser projector running, Moses, I understand what you're thinking.*

Moses.—*Keep transmission stable, stable, stable... increase the Delta 0.2 hertz wave... Hold it steady.*

Bochar is apparently going through a strange trance. After nearly 4 minutes, the ghostly guttural sounds continue to fill the theater space. After that, finally, a voice comes clear from above; a dark, deep, cracked, metallic voice.

Bochar.—Brothers spirits, I saw myself coming out of my body to prevent you from committing an act of disgusting violence. You shouldn't have tried to use me for your experiments; you shouldn't try to make carnitas-burritos or pork out of my meat. I struggled to get out of my body to communicate with you is; but now the problem is that there's no way I'm going back to the pig's body. I went out and left. Soon I will cross the interdimensional boundaries back to the dimension of spirits. I'm doing this on my own. None of you is responsible for my abrupt return; it was my decision. After I leave, you can get rid of my pork body to make tamales, bacon, ham, or whatever you want; you can have a party with my carnitas. I can't use that body anymore. My mission is over, I'm going back to the spiritual dimension. Then, go ahead ask your questions, quickly; I have enough time to answer a few in a hurry, please.

Moses.—*Bochar, do you remember our conversation at the departure station before you enter some come back cases?*

Bochar.—*Yes, you made a joke of my lodging in a pig's brain. I suppose my mission was to complement and support your mission. Now I understand why I waited several years before entering eight earthly months ago. I have to go now; I'll see you when you get back. Try to contact me when you arrive to the other side. Enjoy your stay on planet Earth, because I learned quite a lot.*

The image on the screens turns off. Rex stops the experiment to turn off all the equipment and lights. We recorded for further analysis.

Guide.—*This phenomenon is not abnormal; it is only that the conditions and circumstances for integrating into a lower living creature differs from an integration into a human body with a higher developed brain structure. I ask Trues and Stacey to explain it more.*

Trues walks in his unique military cadet style and says.

Trues.—*The life cycle after integrating a spirit into a lower living creature is a normal process. It's simpler. Their brain structure is simple, and their extent of mental capacity is for the basic functions of life, even though they have intuition and instinct for preservation. They're also afraid and they get scared. But they don't think or reason like humans.*

Stacey.—*There are categories of living beings, as recorded and explained in earthly biological writings, from a single cell to more complex animals such as a lion, a horse or a pig, which is in hand. The "life cycle" of a living creature has only these three functions, entering, living, and dying. There is no complex life in the middle. They live with fundamental sensations and/or instincts.* [xxix]

Guide.—*What happened here is that Bochar's action exemplifies the consequences of killing a creature of inferior intelligence. They involve humans in the natural process of the life cycle of an inferior creature. There is an abrupt release of their souls because there is no procedure for instant separation, and their spirits lose sensitivity to certain frequencies* *that promote their development. It can take time to reset the sensors in the mind for later adventure, especially in a human body. But the soul-body connection broke. Their brain functions break down quickly to where their souls cannot re-enter their bodies.*

Dr. Suarez.—*We understand and know the outcome of this exercise. Yes, there is communication between the souls and minds of inferior intelligent creatures with human souls and minds. For example, the love and affection of dogs towards humans. It is not because of the food they give to the canine, but because of the feeling of attachment, or affection, that the dog feels for his master. The dog's soul cares for and protects its master with its life.*

The fundamental sequences.

I tell you, as a soul of a human, that because of the law of cause and effect life in existence follows an established forward process. Spirits understand this process. Existence and the entire universe follow a pattern that we cannot change; live matter undergoes a continuous transformation, returning to its existential balance. Material life has its beginning and has its end. The course is logical; life moves in one, and only one direction, which is the balance of the energy level in matter. And energy flows from higher to lower level of energy content. But the issue is not the content of the universe, energy and matter, the point is its balance. As in the principle of communicating vessels, the liquid in the vessels achieves the same level; so does the ideal human confort state. That is, the human's soul steady state of satisfaction, conformity and gratitude. This is the sustained state of harmony with the existence. In that process, things and living beings spend their energy in life. There are reversible and irreversible processes in existence that we cannot change. The unique process of life is irreversible, including the life of the universe. Let's see, the guide is back.

Guide.—*After you have finished this contact with Bochar; He moved on to the spiritual dimension. Therefore, we can continue with the rest of Sam's presentation of Spirit-Matter Connectivity, Inter-Dimensional.*

The experiment in kaleidoscopic decomposition of light is a simple procedure. Light scatters through the crystal (this strange kaleidoscopic effect) creates random, colorful images that act as a strong attraction to thought, inducing the imagination to focus on amorphous images. These images induce the brain to produce optimal Delta waves, while reducing the other waves. The result is that the mind blocks its awareness of existence in the environment of its material body, which relaxes the ego, easing the path to a subconscious or unconscious state. A frequency generator, at the level of the five brain waves, transmits voices at low radio frequencies that the minds of spirits can tune into. The transmitter-receiver is an Electro-Encephalogram, changed EEG, equipment. The goal is to convey thoughts or voices that spirits can capture, decode, and respond with their signals. The device does not capture the soul or its mind, but captures its attention and concentration in the imagination–the state produced by the images. On stage, the projector tube behind the screen, invisible to the public. The tube has three cameras at the front, which rotate in the opposite direction. We fill them with loose colored crystals, or prisms, and the cameras rotate freely. An intense white light shines on the front of the glass of the first glass chamber. Crystals refract light and as they rotate forward or backward; they create kaleidoscopic images. The device projects these images onto an 8-foot-high 10-foot-wide screen placed at the back of the stage. This screen approximately five feet above the floor in the center of the stage. The mediums sit in a row (parallel to the screen) in the center of the middle stage, in front of the screen. Subjects wear a helmet built to transmit, receive and adjust the five brain frequencies. Patients see the images without thinking of anything, with a blank mind. [44] The system has a set of microphones to talk to patients through their headphones. Therefore, they can receive messages and or questions and answer through their audio-microphone. Transcendent music, soft, and low relaxing volume, sounds in the background. [45]

---

[44] Read endnote xxviii (Human brain waves)
[45] Lea sobre el efecto de las ondas gamma en esta misma nota final.

Sam.—*Audience, kaleidoscopic effects can also induce their minds. But don't be afraid; several spirits among you can return them when necessary. Please focus on what's going on stage. As spirits separate from their bodies, their minds will appear on window screens on stage.*

A blue-green glow appears around the silhouettes of the four patients, Victor, Rex, Sergio and Moses concentrating on the screen. The stage light dims slowly and gradually, while the glare around the subjects becomes more intense. The stage darkens. You hear a high-pitched sound.

Dr. Wells.—*Subjects respond to stimuli and sublimate to space. They're not out of their bodies states yet. Their minds can still connect to their bodies. Spirits remain always connected to their bodies, even in an experience of outside the body; it's just that they're free to travel in time and space when they separate from their bodies.*

The green light shining around the subjects is intense and then the stage lights go out, and the green light turns gray, darker and darker, the lights come on at the front of the stage and I see four clouds of smoke rising from the ground and disappearing. The body of the four guests remains in their seat with their heads down. Four silhouettes appear behind the chairs and bodies. They state their names in distorted voice-from left-to-right line up-on the screens.

front left, I'm Victor Richland.

right front, I'm Moses Suarez.

back left, I'm Rex Martin.

back right, I'm Sergio Maltes.

In unison, they say, we are in *spirit's form.* Four women-shaped spirits walk in a row, each takes a chair and pushes the bodies to the back of the stage that remains dark. The minds of the four spirits appear as images from on the screens. They are ready to narrate the fundamental sequence of events that bring them to the present moment.

Individual sequences.[xxx]

Sam.—*If the audience thinks of a question regarding this work, it will appear on either front screen.*

The front screens turn off, the rear-left screen on the stage will show the questions and the rear-right screen will show the spirit response. The four spirits explain the path, activities, and events, starting with Moses.

Moses.—My sequence is direct, (1) I wanted to help my family, (2) I wanted to go where my Aunt Isa, (3) I heard the conversation of the trafficker, (4) the traffickers kidnapped me, (5) they sent me to USA., (6) I met Sergio on the bus, (7) I crossed the border; they captured in San Isidro–I found my Aunt Isabel, (8) I met Mr. Clark; litigated my asylum in the United States, (9) I got a PhD in Radiology at UCLA, (10) I met Dr. Rex Martin, (11) I met Victor Richland, and (12) I met Sam Wells. Don't confirm it, but I heard that Toad ordered to kill me if I gave them trouble, after they kidnapped. So, I kept silent for a while. But I said they burned a little x mark on my arm, which means for organs. I don't know what would have happened if I'd gone with Santiago, the man waiting in the "Kentucky Fried Chickens." I always thought the spirits were saving me for something I had to do. Look. He always longs to come to America. and find my aunt; I feel like someone made the way or walked to come cross the border and find my aunt. I found her, but I guess my mission isn't over yet.

Another question from the audience. This question is for Sergio:

—*How come the people of the Cartel didn't kill you, and how did you end up in the U.S.?*

Sergio.—*That's a big question, even for me. Before my abduction, I lived my childhood years in fear, in Arriaga, because I heard of many Cartel's activities, as kidnapping children for organ trafficking. I even dreamed they were tearing my body apart, taking out one of my kidneys. In real life, they cartel people kidnapped me from the street one rainy day evening, and took one kidney and sent me to USA to disappear me. For many moments I doubted that God was there for the poor, but I still thought love and hope are all around us, always saving us. I never thought of coming to America, that idea was not my purpose. I remember my conversations with Peter and Paul; He used to say that what the 'coyote' asked for the trip to the USA was too much. After they removed my kidney, they tried to kill me several times, but something always came* *up to save me. I realized someone was taking care of me for some reason. After taking my kidney, the cartel people had no choice, they couldn't let me go back to my family; so, either they killed me or disappeared far away; they tried to kill me. My guardian angels protected me or saved me for something I didn't know. I have no other explanation. The sequences of events inevitably drove me away from my hometown, and my path is (1) I dreamed that the Cartel kidnapped me, (2) the traffickers kidnapped me, (3) they took one kidney, (4) did not kill me, but they sent to the USA, (5) I met Moses on a bus from a caravan of migrants, (6), I crossed the border; Officer Suarez did not kill me in San Isidro, (7) I got asylum in the United States thanks to Officer Suarez, (8) I met Ted Clark, (9) I met Rex, (10) I met Victor (11) I met Sam. I don't see the final results of my mission on earth.*

Another question from the audience. This question is for Mrs. Isabel Clark, even though she is not on the panel.

—Your life has also been much easier than that of Moses and Sergio; but it's not like Rex or Victor's; When did you notice or realize your cripple to leave Santa Tecla?

Isa.—*I didn't understand why I became obsessed with my idea of coming to California around 1990. I had no valid reason, but I couldn't get it out of my head, I had to go. When I came here, I needed to prepare, and I studied criminal processes and psychology—I graduated in less than academic pensum demands. I had a good job, but my longing to be a policeman led me to quit my job, and my career in criminal law, and register with the police academy; they assigned me to the border patrol force. Why the border patrol? It made little sense. I don't know what forces dragged me into that. The sequence of events was not under my control, and not intentionally aimed at waiting for Moses' arrival. I'm sure everything guided me to the final results we now know. I'm sure my desire to come to America was to be prepared for what would come next. My spirit and the spirits had anything to do with the purpose of this plan. The perfection of this plan is impressive, to a second of time, so, if had I delayed my engagement at the border, I would have lost the events near that green-colored house. With what I know now, my haste to come to the U.S. and study a career and enroll in the border patrol force had one purpose: I had to be ready for Moses arrival to this country. The events* *in my path are these, (1) Moses was born: I saw the misery of our lives in Santa Tecla, (2) I came to the United States as an illegal immigrant in 1992, (3) I became legal by the amnesty of section 245, (4) I studied psychology and criminal law, (5) I enrolled in the force patrol, (6) I met Ted Clark, (7) I captured Moses and Sergio in San Isidro, in 2001, (8) I asked Ted to seek asylum for the boys, (9) I married Ted Clark, (10) I met Rex Martin, (11) I met Victor, and (12) I met Sam. The latest results, we all know now.*

Another question from the audience. This question is for Mr. Ted Clark, even if he is also not on the panel.

—What do you think is your role in this whole chain of events?

Ted Clark.*—I think everything happens for a reason, even when what happens hurts us a lot. When my wife died in a car accident, I moved to Southern California. Three months after I arrived, I met a young police officer in a legal immigration case. She returned my desire to live again. I was shy for several years and never told him anything. He was just a good friend of hers. We met frequently during the asylum cases of Moses and Sergio, and when I finished these cases, I asked her to marry me; and she agreed. In this universe, nothing happens or appears in vain. My wife had to die, and Moses and Sergio had to come to the US so I married Isabel. This is how our spirits came into contact and united. And the sequence is clear, (1) my wife dies, (2) I move to Southern California, (3) I met Isabel, (4) the boys cross the border, (5) Isabel asked me to take their asylum cases, (6) I met Moses and Sergio, (7) I married Isabel, (8) I met Rex, (9) I met Victor, (10) I met Sam. And now we are all together, the spirits from the exit station in the spiritual dimension some time ago. These events are like knots in the fabric of a fishing net, but the goal of a spirit has a purpose, the purpose of the entire group of spirits.*

Another question from the audience. This question is for Rex.

—Your life has also been much easier than that of Moses and Sergio; like Victor's; When did you notice or hear about the need to find your fellow spirits?

Rex.*-My spirit was the least connected with the other spirits in this group, but the sequence of events aroused my curiosity why certain events happen the way they do. For example, my mother and father. They were rich and lived in Beverly Hills, California. But my path changed when my* *mother escaped to Henderson, Nevada, assisted by the family accountant. The forces created the situation so they would take a convergent path with the paths of the other spirits of the group. Now I know that my father's financial books showed large sums of money for expenses attributed to my mother's purchases she claimed she didn't do. The chain of events is clear. She escaped with the accountant, but my father's detective found where they went. My father went to get her, found out she was having a baby, and assumed it wasn't his. You know the rest of the story. This incident changed the course of my life to a different sequence than I would have if my parents hadn't had family disagreements. I am glad, however, that I had found the group of spirits who came with me to earth. The sequence of my path was like this, (1) Jeff, the accountant, takes large amounts of money from my father's banks and assigns them to my mom's purchases. (2) my parents argue and dislike each other, (3) my mother leaves my father, advised by the accountant, (4) my mother escaped to Henderson, Nevada, after arguing with my father, (5) I was born in Henderson, (6) my father and mother die, (7) I move in or return to my parents' house in Beverly Hills, California, (8) I met Sam at the University, (9) I met Victor who asked me to treat his illness, (10) I met Moses as a partner of Victor's medical treatment team, (11) I met Ted and Isabel through Moses, and (12) I met Sergio.*

Another question from the audience. This question is for Victor.

—*Your life has been easier than Moses and Sergio's, but when did you realize your spiritual affinity with others?*

Victor.—*I didn't think fellow spirits waited or looked for me. My life was too complex to think about that. When I discovered my condition and needed to get specialized medical care, I discovered that an advanced researcher was in California. I didn't enjoy leaving New York anywhere in the world, less yet California. The conditions and circumstances left no alternatives to choose; I think someone forced me to go there. It was as if fate left me no choice. Rex Martin, a pathologist, a rare disease specialist. Later, I met Dr. Moses Suarez, a scientific researcher in radiology. When I met Sergio and Moses, I felt I knew them for a long, long time. I now know that Dr. Martin and Suarez are fellow spirits committed to seeking my spirit, just as mine pledged to find his and other spirits in this group, on earth in any material and spiritual way possible. I owe my material* *life to Rex and Moses–thank you Dr. Martin and Dr. Suarez–. The events of my journey were like this, (1) I was born in New York, and I lose my twin sister and my mother at birth. This tragic event established how to find the spirit friends, (2) my illness developed, (3) I moved to Southern California, (4) I met Dr. Rex Martin, (5) I met Dr. Suarez, (6) I met Ted Clark and Isabel Clark, (7) I met Sergio Maltes as a lawyer, and (8) I met Sam, a doctor in psychology, a specialist in paranormal phenomena. Accumulating wealth is not the true purpose of life, but making life worth living–that's the reality.*

Another question from the audience. This question is for Dr. Wells His spirit traveled alone for a while.

–When did you join the group?

Dr. Wells.-*My participation seems to be waiting for a call when they needed. I felt strong attractions to their spirits. Because of my research on the behavior of spirits and encounters, I thought and confirmed that they were fellow spirits. My path is this, (1) I was born in California, (2) I studied at USC, (3) there at the University I met Rex Martin–my first meeting), (4) I received Rex after his encounter with Victor, (5) I met Moses a few days later, (6) I met Ted and Isabel, (7) I met Sergio, and finally (8) I met Victor. Am I part of this spirit group? I say yes because of the strong attractions of common interest in a subject I love. If I look at the configuration of their group sphere, I say, the group needed my knowledge and experience to resolve and confirm their spiritual identities. We are all compatible spirits in this mission. I thank you all for your attention and interest in the subject of spirits.*

The four spirits will return to their bodies in a moment.

This session is over.

Well, it's not over, not yet. Humans cannot control, prevent, or block the reunion of spirits. It is an event that results because of an earlier event. The sequential results of one or more decision chain of actions paint the Intent and purpose. The kaleidoscopic images on the screen seem not embedded, but they are. It's like the behavior of spirits; it does not follow an organized pattern and has intention. The five brain waves are a great human discovery. Perhaps they work harder on these and control the transmission and reception of them. Because the mind is a spiritual element, we communicate between souls. Humans are near to discovering the rules of telepathy. And finally, the proven sequence is a consequence of the law of cause and effect: the intentions of the spirits.

CHAPTER 7

• • • • • • • • • ● • • • • • • • • •

Spirits' Experiences

Abstract

We have within our bodies a soul representing the spirit; a structured mind with two components: ego and consciousness. We think, make decisions and take action every day. We imagine objects and themes and situations. We have emotions and feelings; we have illusions and inspirations; and everything that comes from our mind is from our soul or spirit. Our mind is an intangible function; it is invisible; it's a force. Therefore, if we put aside our physical actions, all those other functions are not material; are of the spirit within us. The soul that impels our being while we live leaves us when we die. These are our experiences with spirits, or, rather, these are the experiences of our spirits within our human bodies. Without soul and mind, humans are as other inferior animals or creature, inferior o of less inteligencia. Solo somos animales instintivos.

Reflections

Guide.—*Spirits can travel in time and open up omniscience. We know that humans carry a spirit within their inner being. We also know that spirits in humans have attributes or abilities of limited scope, and limited access to omniscience. We also know that our mind thinks, reasons, or ponders; however, the ego chooses, decides and acts in this material* *dimension. The spirits of our four guests are still in a state outside the body; but they will soon re-enter their bodies to take on their duties on earth again. Therefore, let us test our guests to witness what they know beyond their material consciousness; Before they were born. Please ask your questions with your thought.*

The four spirits sit at the back of the stage in their chairs, semi visible to the audience. The back of the stage is in a natural twilight. First question from the audience. This question is for Victor.

—Can you tell us what happened before or at birth?

Victor gets up and floats on his chair.

Victor.-*First, I see myself floating adrift in time, quickly. I'm in Manhattan, New York, in 1991. Two nurses by a wheeled stretcher wait for a helicopter to land on top of a skyscraper. They run under and unload a woman on that stretcher and run to an elevator door. It is my mother in labor, and my authoritarian father takes over, giving instructions and orders, as usual. The door opens and they come in. The elevator goes down to the fifth floor. In the delivery room, I see the baby in my mother's womb. Dr. Gentile and nurses have problems; the baby lays crosswise and cannot align his body to come out normally. My mother and baby, they're worried and scared, and they're transmitting signals for help. A spirit captures these signals, sees the situation, and prepares to act. Another close spirit picks up the signs, and rushes to help, connecting with the first spirit. Both spirits know what to do and move on without hesitation. Spirits cannot grasp or take matter, but their energy beams stimulate the baby to turn and line up; but with a series of small contractions the baby comes out. Martha, the nurse, calls Dr. Gentile to take the baby and complete the procedure. Humans outside call this result a miracle, but it's not. It is a regular activity of the spiritual mission. That spirit that came to help is a supporting spirit. My mission on earth, otherwise I would have returned to my point of origin in the universal spirit. I heard my mother's distress signal. But she agrees to change her material existence to that of the baby. The supporting spirit and I saved the baby. Any spirit can be a spirit that helps, the closest to the point of anguish.*

This question is for Moses.

—Can you tell us what happened at your birth?

Moses [remembers].- *My situation differs from Victor's. My family is poor, having only what nature provides. My mom's suffering severe pains and my grandmother is desperately running and ordering us tasks. Esperanza, the midwife, sweats, helping my mother with the delivery. My birth ends smoothly; we thank the midwife, for delivering the baby to this material world. My aunt Isabel sits outside the room, thinking. Poor people complain about their miserable conditions and situations. They live by grace of the global spirit, and they do what they can with what they have every minute to survive. I hear my aunt, Isabel, thinking about how she could get out of poverty, be someone in a position to help her family. I hear her decision to go to America. The baby cries. My mother is out of work, taking care of the baby, my grandmother works washing and ironing clothes. Grandpa makes hammocks and straw hats. All that to survive. My aunt Isabel holds me and changes my diapers several times. One day, she left telling no one, months after I was born. Poor people behave according to their poverty conditions and circumstances, suffering the consequences. Poor people depend on the universe's mercy that delivers them from harm and evil; and humbly ask for their daily bread. Poor people live alone, but not by their choice. I was born among these people; I had nothing to say about that, but I see the differences and injustice. Injustices do not come from existence or the universe, but from humans who create social gaps. Powerful people as those of a cartel or government abusing of people in their countries; and the rich conspiring to keep people in poverty and ignorance, or close to that, because it is easier for them to manipulate poor people, while gaining greater wealth, fame and power. I see many people and families asustadas y escondidas.*

This question is for Rex.

—Tell us what happened at birth?

Rex.—*I'm a lucky individual after all; I've been lucky since before I was born. I started my journey with horrible events. Jim and Ryan are in a casino; Ryan tries to cash in his coupon, and the cashier who has problems with the system delays Ryan; it's almost 2:00 am. The situation is critical. A protecting spirit captures Vicky's distress signal, and this spirit transmits its energy upon Jim. It could have been anyone else anyway. Jim feels the need to go to the hotel lobby and walks to wait in the hotel lobby. He feels as leaving the casino. In the lobby, Jim sits on* *a couch away from the exit, but then a spirit makes him feel restless and Jim gets up and walks. Jim sees my mom, Vicky Martin, suffering on the couch in another lobby and feels the need to help her. My twin sister in the womb, and I see her spirit waiting in transition. My sister does not reach this material dimension, but her spirit enlightens Dr. Spencer to perform a C-section operation to save me. I see and hear my father, Rocky Martin; he says stupid bitch how you could fool me with Jeff–now he pays for your stupidity. My father shoots and kills my mother–*[Rex swallows hard and weeping continuously]–, *my father says, "I have nothing to live for"* [and commits suicide in the hospital].

Rex trembles and cries, but despite her great continuous pain.

–I can't do anything to prevent that, and it happens; it's the human's decision. If this event had been an hour earlier, he would have killed my mother before my birth. Then, the omniscience of the global spirit clears my doubts; I'm my father's son. My mother had nothing to do with that man. Jeff took advantage of my mother's fight with my father, keeping her in Nevada, against her will.

Rex turns his back to the audience; he's crying... [a long pause]. After a long time, this question is for Sergio.

–Tell us what happened before or at your time of birth?

Sergio.–*I was born dead, but luckily a guardian spirit wandering nearby, collects the distress signals of Ophelia and Chana and is quick to help, perhaps, this is the great value of praying: aspiring vehemently to receive help. I see spirits working patiently and quickly, coordinating their efforts to save the baby (me). I wanted to stay and complete my mission on earth. Human beings do not understand these situations, and they call it miracles. In fact, they are so close to the impossibility that the event cannot trace any other description, but they are natural to the spiritual dimension. My mission was stronger than death, and I survive the test. I see the situation in Arriaga; I see poverty and fear. I had to do something about it. I was aware of the Sinaloa Cartel's control over the people in that area: the cartel men keep people afraid. Poor people only think about surviving one day at a time; just like in the city of Moses, Santa Tecla. Even though we, the spirits, do not adhere to specific conditions or situations; these conditions annoy us because they hinder our mission.*

This question is for Officer Isabel.

—What do you see around the time of Moses' birth?

Isabel.-*I am not in a state outside the body; but I can describe my premonitions or forebodings that come from my soul. The birth of Moses was a wake-up call for me; made me realize that our family was growing and the financial situation was getting worse. I thought I should help my family. This baby made me think about his future, my family's and mine. I felt the need to go north to the U.S. A need that got stronger and stronger every day. I wanted to do it on my own, not give in to the cartel network. So, the time came, and I left telling none, just my sister Juana. I used to write to her until one day I stopped getting her answers. Nobody knew where he was, except he was in America. I wanted to get ready, but for what? I wasn't sure; I just felt a constant impulse; I wanted to help my family. It was very difficult at first; but now I know the reason, as this story says.*

Moving forward in time.

Robert and Sexis are back on stage. The guide asks Roberto to continue the dialogue of the theme connectivity inter dimensional, of spirit-matter.

Robert.—*Humans know that their souls and minds have no power to see the future. But we have said that according to the law of cause and effect we can study what has happened recently and what is happening in the present tense. With this it is possible to establish trends and trajectories of what can happen. The accuracy of our predictions depends solely on the accuracy of the study of the conditions and circumstances that support the outcome of these conditions and circumstances. Casual events (stochastic events) are unforeseen events over which we have no physical controls.*

Based on the above we see a possibility, or need, of developing inter-dimensional connectivity spirit-matter.

Sexy.—*humans may develop their telepathic functions, assisted by devices configured to capture and transmit human thoughts by private frequencies. If this is possible soon, we can see on private networks its first impact. I can see that the transmission of thought through controlled channels is of military interest in the United States, and elsewhere.*

We cannot say that experiments are already being carried out in inter-dimensional communication, but we see by 2030 the first steps.

Robert.–*Free spirits–those spirits not housed in somebody of living beings–can communicate with souls in human bodies. And souls can communicate with free spirits, anyway.*

A voluntary contact is the prayer or meditation of humans. During prayer or vehement meditation, the mind reaches a state detached from the influence of matter or materialism. In this state, the ego does not take part, and isolates, from these two processes. Emphasize that attachment to matter and materialism absorbs the mental capacity to maintain and preserve this attachment.

Sexy.–*At the moment, humans can only use their connection to spirits and the global spirit through meditation and prayer. But even these two processes and more efficient results.*

Guide.–*Let us hear what spirits see in the past and future of humans.*

Victor (Ariel 12010).–*Entering the library of omniscience, I see that a political catastrophe is approaching, helping to restore government as imagined by the founding fathers. They catch Trump in many lawsuits and cases and lose most. Trump does not have a second term affecting his immediate family. Democracy and the rule of law survive.*

Moses (KETA).-*I am at the departure station, 28 years before the present with the term spirits. We are happy with our assigned mission and eager to stay in a human body. Our conversation is hopeful and optimistic and sometimes humorous. We know the future, but we don't talk about it; we know when we'll be back, just as an actor in a movie or play knows his or her script and we know what will happen, we (spirits) know what's coming and we still play our role. However, when we enter a human body, we can no longer see the future. Being out of the body, we can see results. We have a long life ahead of us. Looking to the future, I see a political change in the United States from the 2020 election in November. Trump leaves the presidency and faces legal proceedings as a private citizen. There's a bad time for Trump's family. Russia is still trying to gain control of the world. The Middle East is almost under Kremlin control. The United States is winning cyberwarfare, which runs until 2024. On other issues, humans can communicate with spirits by the end* *of 2035. Artificial intelligence never replaces human minds and brain functions, but it will become a source of cheap labor.*

Rex (TZZS).—*Going back in time, I see Bochar at the exit station upset because he would get into a pig. He stayed on the platform after we left and finally traveled to Iowa State University many years later. He went to an experimental farm. We must try to tune it into our frequencies; energy and light frequencies. Those frequencies that impact us the most as we travel the earth and can stay with us, in our spiritual minds, after leaving the material dimension. These frequencies can appear in any of our next life cycles, unrecognizable. Looking to the future, the technology to communicate with other spirits can be reliably functional by 2040, soldiers will wear special helmets to communicate telepathically.*

Sergio (Cenia).—*I am at the departure station: we are chatting; and we will look for each other on earth. That was a figure of thought, as you say on earth (a figure of speech) because spirits are energy that cannot create or destroyed. However, the frequencies of vehement thoughts, desires, longings, and humble desires are strong frequencies that penetrate and remain in the spirit. These frequencies can cause "action-of-forces" in the material dimension. I see humanity entering an intellectual change, leaning towards global fraternity where social networks. Social institutions in Silicon Valley, California, lead the integrated wireless programming of instant audio and video. Advances will help the development of devices used in mental telecommunications. The government will adapt this technology in soldier's helmets for instant communication, IFC. The world will be in constant communication because of more capable and affordable communication devices. Every person can become a news reporter and people coordinate their actions against repressive, illegal, human rights violations that occur anywhere on earth.*

Encounters with spirits.

At the Dr. Wells' private research laboratory.

Dr. Wells.—*Let us move on to the phenomena of encounters with spirits. Are they premeditated, spontaneous or random? Rex originated the investigation, and I must mention that Victor is a patient of Rex and Moses. So, let me call Rex to share his experience.*

Rex.—*Spirits behave differently while in human bodies than they behave in the spiritual dimension. Spirits are part of the global spirit of the universe, and they seek each other as they travel in the material dimension. They group together and travel together because their vibrations of thoughts, feelings, sorrows and longings are similar. In our case, we committed ourselves at the departure station to look for each other on earth; and that increases the attraction between them. At the end of my lecture for the National Medical Research Association of the University of California, Irvine, last year 2017, I met Victor. Before I met Victor, I received a strange feeling, as if something was about to happen that I could not understand. When I saw Victor, I felt a deep state of happiness, as if you meet a relative you haven't seen in a long time. I knew Victor for life; when I shook his hand, a spark leaped from his hand to my hand and I trembled. I saw his eyes, questioned my thoughts. Where have I met him before? Now his illness was the means of communication that his spirit followed to find me and the rest of the spirits of the group. I see Victor will have a long life. I felt the same way when I met the other fellow spirits.*

Dr. Wells.—*Victor, what was your experience?*

Victor.—*I didn't want to come to California; I considered moving to Texas or Arizona, but not to California. My experience was as Rex explained, and I felt the need to share my thoughts and feelings with Rex. I felt I had no secrets from him, feeling safe and protected. When I saw Rex's eyes, I felt he knew what I knew and felt what he felt, as if he knew my experiences. I felt I had always shared my thoughts and experiences with Rex. It was strange for me to feel spiritually discovered. I kept thinking about Rex, my meeting with him, and my feelings, often for a few days afterwards. I confirmed that we are spirits of the same group that departed and entered human bodies at about the same time in 1990. This encounter experience was typical for all encounters with my other fellow spirits.*

Dr. Wells.—*Moses, can you share your experiences with the public?*

Moses.—*but first let me say I am a radiologist and part of Dr. Rex's team who studies Victor's clinical case. In my work I have detected green glows, like halos, engulfing human bodies; I have seen these green glows coming out of a human body in a spiral like cigarette smoke, but not* *upwards, but horizontally next to it, disappearing at a short distance. I could not explain the strange phenomena at first, and for a few years I have been experimenting with these strange glows, leaning towards a theory that glows are spirits, or spiritual energy, imbued in the bodies of humans. They leave the human body during states of deep concentration, induced suppression of material consciousness. Our experiments at reproducing these states* at will.

Dr. Wells.—*Moses, do you have personal experiences you would like to share with the audience?*

Moses.—*I am a refugee who came to America unintentionally, I was the victim of criminal acts perpetrated by the Sinaloa Cartel, led by Joaquín (el Chapo) Guzmán in the years 1990. The Cartel abducted me to remove my kidney and other organs; they thought I had heard a conversation about their human trafficking and drug activities and wanted to silence me. That I have not understood. They did not kill me and on the contrary they brought me to the border of the United States. I crossed the border illegally; I got caught. I learned on this trip that part of the operation is to make it easier for immigrants with children to come to the border; then, when they cross, they take their children away from their parents. They deport the adults to their countries, keeping children for human and organ trafficking. This is an old clandestine operation they've done for decades.*

Dr. Wells.—*Sergio, please get up.*

Sergio stood up for a few seconds and sat down.

Moses.—*Sergio got on the bus as the last person and sat next to me. I felt a sense of security as having personal guards, and I turned around to look at Sergio; That was when we met. I looked into his eyes and saw he was a good person; someone I could trust. I shook his hand and felt a strange feeling that the handshake was familiar, or that we have had other adventures together in the past for a long time. How could that be? He was just a 10-year-old from another country. Truly, I thought I would die and would never make it to America. I never knew why I felt that way.*

Dr. Wells.—*Sergio, please tell us your version of this meeting.*

Sergio.—*Yes; the way Moses explained it represents my experience. It was strange, as many strange things happen in our lives. I didn't think* *about the spirits, because my mind and soul couldn't disassociate from the people in the cartel having kidnapped me and had taken one kidney to sell it. However, Moses' presence made me feel protected, somehow, but I didn't know how I could be. I am also a refugee, an illegal immigrant who came to the USA because the Sinaloa Cartel wanted to send me away from my birthplace. I heard President Trump say that all illegal immigrants are criminals, rapists, etc. That's not true. Trump can't see, he'll never see, or understand the depth of poverty, or the meaning of life when that life is one day at a time. Trump wants to build an impenetrable wall to stop illegal immigrants, but I ask, can Trump stop hunger and or desire to survive? That's the point of illegal immigration. This great nation is a promised land, the freedom of the world, and the salvation of all lives. Recalling America's history, I discovered that the greatness of this nation lies in the cultural diversity of its immigrants, who come to find better opportunities. This desire emphasizes work, inventions, cultural development and economic progress. California understands this evidence and therefore supports and welcomes immigrants. Oh, one thing I forgot; this is a dream I often have. In this dream someone pursues me with the order to kill me; but a hand always comes to get me out of danger to safety.*

Dr. Wells.—*Thank you, Rex, Victor, Sergio and Moses, their experiences are intriguing and glimpses of the mind. Let's take a little break and come back in ten minutes. You can now return to their respective bodies. The music in the background played an instrumental arrangement, "Our Day Will Come)" sung by a spirit in the work. The panel returns, and Dr. Wells is on the podium. The stage is dark and the theater room is with twilight lighting. The curtain opens, and the forum arrangement is exactly as before. Ten seconds later the four window screens turned on, flashing, and the spirits were visible as before. Everything is ready to go on again. Just before the legal case against the people of the Sinaloa Cartel ended, Ted Clark and Associates received a report of the shooting in San Isidro, where Isabel. This police report provided evidence collected from the dead individual's backpack, named Jacinto. Jacinto carried a written note, however, "Jacinto, cross the border with Moses and Sergio, take care of both on American soil and go back to base." This note, or contract, never opened in court, it was no longer necessary.*

Perhaps Moses feels this and Sergio dreams; it's information they'll never know unless they open that report. The court returned the case documents to Ted, including all discoveries. The note is in this package.

Remember that spirits do not communicate directly with souls in humans. Souls do not have free access to omniscience, and information comes through those other channels. But the code is to provide all knowledge in omniscience to all spirits, including souls. And spirits send signals and messages to souls in other ways such as dreams, feelings, visions. Therefore, Victor has his dreams and Moses has his feelings that will persist until they know the truth about Jacinto order to kill them.

One afternoon while Isa felt a decided to reorder the file system in Ted's office. By apparent chance, she finds that sealed crime case package against the Sinaloa Cartel. Isa intrigued opens that bag and innocently rummaging finds Jacinto's note. Isa realizes there is an order to kill Moses and Sergio not fulfilled. Isa, warn Ted, and order her team of detectives to provide protection (security) for Moses and Sergio. Ted contacts and alerts Moses and Sergio to his situation. And from that time on, they protected the boys. Detectives discovered and tainted two murder attempts against the boys about two years after arriving in the U.S., but there were no more similar incidents later.

CHAPTER 8

• • • • • • • • • ● • • • • • • • • •

Awareness of the material.

Abstract

The universe represents the material side of existence and all living beings in it. There is no life if there is no energy and matter in the universe. And this way of life, even thinking, is based on the materiality of living concepts, objects, and creatures. The notion that nothing exists and is not real if it is not tangible and visible, is all we think. But will it be true? Maybe it isn't; we pay no attention to the fact that we perceive and conceived reality from an invisible and intangible realm: the mind and soul. Our ego is part or element of the soul, but it lives tied to materialism, conditions and situations, seeking possessions, power, wealth and fame, at any cost. We live chasing these three things; and we forget what it is. We market everything, including love; but life is simpler, more fruitful, and more beautiful if we change ambition, greed, hatred, prejudice, envy, greed, and selfishness, out of ourselves, caring and sharing with others.

Suppression of Consciousness.

The human is dual: Soul and body. Human life has two simultaneous phases, a spiritual life and a material life. The soul exists in the spirit world. The body exists in the material world, the universe. The soul is immaterial and takes up no space; it has a mind, a consciousness and an ego and all these are invisible and intangible–they are the spirit. The body is matter; it has volume and weight; it is three-dimensional; it is tangible and visible; it takes up space. The soul (and its three components) is energy capable of producing movement, change, and work–as electrical energy does. The mind is the thinking function of the soul and is available to both consciousness and ego. Identity and personality are individual attributes of the ego that have freedom of choice and visible; with physical reality. The body executes the will of the ego; does nothing else, except for involuntary reactions. The three sub-functions of conscience, morality, willpower, and wisdom work to guide the ego according to the purpose of existence–which is to live within the order of harmony of the universe. The purpose of existence for living beings is to lead a life coupled with the soul. The ego contributes nothing. Their observable actions pursue or seek to produce physical results to satisfy their selfishness. The interaction with material affairs, objects and creatures reflects attitudes towards possession, power and appearance; three objects that translate into wealth, authority and fame. Ego ambition, greed and selfishness lead the ego towards maximizing its power and wealth, and gaining maximum admiration. Ego is the big problem of the human. The ego welcomes any knowledge, concept and discovery that have the potential to support that maximization, and uses them for its selfish benefits. All the tribulations of human life are because of the behavior of their ego. But life is frugal and not, or has not conceived to have excesses, but to reach a comfort zone. That zone is a stable state where the human living, while working to achieve a better situation. But humans complicate their lives by leaving this comfort zone, feeding resentment, protests, and arrogance. The content of materialism exalts and stimulates the ego. This encore binds the human ego to the materialistic world and separates it from the consciousness of the soul. And the more he sticks, the more materialistic he becomes, losing his moral values. But everything typically associated with moral values, justice and injustice, good or evil, right and wrong. Constant consciousness to the ego shows that passing life does not agree with the behavior of the ego. And the willpower of consciousness works on guiding the ego on earth back to the harmony of existence.

We achieve this order controlling attachment to materialism–the suppression of material consciousness. Suppressing consciousness does not mean that humans ignore the internal and or external realities, consequences and eminent dangers. But it is impossible to eliminate awareness of the environment while being in a wake state. The soul needs a body and the body, because it is matter, can only exist in a material world. Suppression of consciousness means that humans must know how to handle object and subject stimuli. Humans should reach the psychological-mental point where their own physical problems, thoughts, words, decisions and actions, and those of others do not cause feelings, stimuli or emotions that take them out of their comfort zone–tranquility. In this state humans are alert, but they control their excitement and attachment. They are not spiritual zombies; they are human spirits. To be human spirits, humans must reduce their attachment to materialism to where it does not alter the purpose of life. What is the purpose of life? and how do you reduce materialism attachment?

Guide.–*Existence has a defined general purpose. This purpose is to create, protect, maintain and perfect life in the universe. Robert, Trues and Sexis return to address these two topics.*

Robert.-*We have seen, but emphasize the concept of the purpose of life. We'll give a preamble.*

When some energy became matter–with the Great Explosion or otherwise–the invisible and intangible and invisible became tangible and visible; but this matter remains part of the same substance, energy. But before this conversion appeared the laws that regulate the universe and the situations and conditions that allow organic life, including the great explosion itself. But a Great Explosion did not create life. And when the conditions and situations occurred, the different life forms appeared.

Sexy.–*Understand that conditions and situations are the property of scenarios that become environments of entities that enter or exist in them. The characteristics and appearance of the inhabitants conform to the conditions of the stage.*

True.–*Then, the conditions and situations to permit life in the universe. They establish the laws that give way to life, and the laws that* *protect and regulate her behavior. These laws involve love that maintain and protect existence, the universe and organic life.*

__Robert.__—Trues have cleared it all up! But I must add and redefine that the purpose of life is not only to "create, protect, maintain and perfect life in the universe," but also to train the ego of dual beings in using their free will within the order of harmony of the universe. And this training includes reducing or eliminating the influence of the monster, AGHAPEE the ego they bring within themselves.

__Sexy.__—Regarding attachment to materialism, materialism, we must begin with the nature that originates it. In the configuration, the ego component receives the right of free will and the duty to connect the soul with the physical reality of the universe. Besides this, it also receives the responsibility of establishing the character and personality of the human dual being. It's the executive power of the soul. The ego knows what the purpose of life is. But he becomes a lifetime autocrat and does not listen to advice from the other elements of the soul, mind, and consciousness.

__Trues.__—All these rights, which upset the autocratic ego, give you the power to do what you think is appropriate. It sticks to the splendor of matter that increases its power, its presence, and property. The ego changes the goal of life with its own selfishness. The soul that is not material adheres to the material through its ego. This is the origin of attachment to materialism and materialism.

__Roberto.__—Yes, it is! The soul represents the governance structure of the dual human. Here the mind, the thinking element, is the part that interprets the laws of existence and plans rules of behavior. While consciousness is the judging element, on the one hand, and it punishes the ego for its behavior.

__Sexy.__—The answer to the big question, how do you control the attachment to the material? It is a conscious, simple and difficult action simultaneously. This action requires a partly unconscious change of consciousness. It requires dedication, constancy and discipline. As we know, consciousness has three levels, consciousness, subconsciousness, and unconsciousness. The first maintains a direct perch to reality, internal and external; the second keeps and saves information that we do not open at will; and the third keeps functions and knowledge to which humans do not have conscious access. The third level saves routines of involuntary *behavior that the human cannot handle in a conscious state, such as breathing, heart palpitation, and certain defense actions that the body performs automatically.*

Trues.—*Fortunately, you can program that third level of consciousness, unconsciousness, from the conscious level. Let Sexis explain programming the unconscious, after presenting certain examples. One.—riding a bike, swimming, driving a car, etc., are routines that require no more thought. Learning done at the conscious level becomes an unconscious routine. Two.—habits like smoking or alcoholism are unconscious routines, such as addiction, that run automatically—without thinking. Three, automatic functions such as native language learning, typewriting, operating a adding machine, and others, are functions of the unconscious; the operator need not think about them. In the above context we can create unconscious routines to manage our thoughts, decisions and actions according to patterns programmed from the conscious state.*

Sexis.—*Trues! The mind is the thinking function of the soul. Therefore, it also supports its three levels, conscious, subconscious and unconscious. The principle of unconscious programming has one unconscious and one conscious method. Conscious routines are those that the human consciously embeds in the unconscious. For example, a scheduled physical exercise routine, or garden maintenance routine, for which the human dedicates a specific plan at an exact time, for a defined time, in an order, with specific objectives; and repeats them until it is a routine in the unconsciousness. Another example, the morning routine to prepare for work. We do a sequence of actions we execute without thinking of doing an unconscious routine. For example, work routines learned in service and production jobs. The unconscious routine formed executes outside of our ego's awareness of why, when, or where we perform the routine without thinking.*

Trues.—*Those conscious routines involves the ego; the ego knows what the mind and consciousness is doing, and does not resist if it thinks it does not cause it any harm, or does not go against its purposes. The programming of the unconscious is the highest potential of the mind's capacity. And the programming procedure to brain waves.*

Robert.—*Yes, Trues, Sexis, you are right. Of the five waves of the brain, the Theta [46]wave suspends the mental activity of the ego and reduce the attachment to the material reality in which it lives.*

Sexy.—*True, Theta and Delta waves predispose consciousness at the unconscious level. The first puts the mind in a susceptible, semi-hypnotic state. The second leads the mind to a deep state of relaxation that involves the unconscious level of conscience. The human can use the Theta wave to condition the mind to a receptive state and then use the Delta wave to schedule the new desired action routine. [47] The new routine with conscious actions and repeated for as long as necessary until the mind automatically executes that routine.*

Trues.—*The question is, how do we train the ego? Actually, it's hard to train the ego because of its selfish nature. It is easier to train the unconscious through the brain waves, Alpha, Theta and Delta, while exercising conscious actions and reciting messages that sublimely unconscious. These messages must predispose unconsciousness to support and execute the action instructed by messages.*

Experts recommend studying the effects for and against brain waves that are used to reach the Delta state. [48] There are three starting with Alpha state, across Theta state, until it reaches Delta state. The goal is to prepare the mind to receive new conscious routines and leave them in the unconscious for automatic execution.

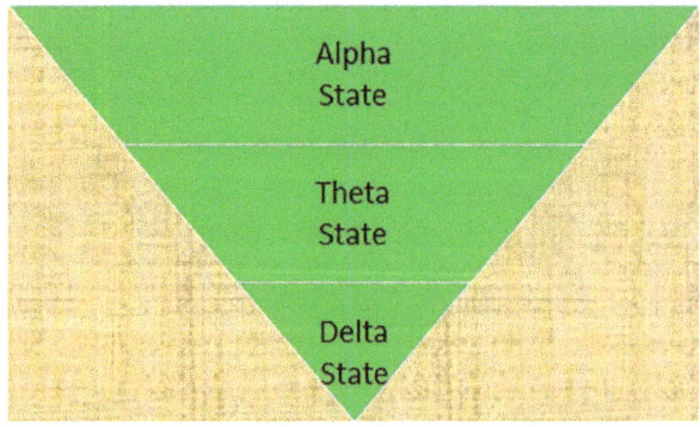

Figure 12: Main Brain Waves

---

[46]   htps://mentalhealthdaily.com/2014/04/12/ theta-brain-waves-4-hz-to-8-hz/

[47]   https://mentalhealthdaily.com/2014/04/14/ delta-brain-waves-0-hz-to-4-hz/

[48]   https://www.binauralbeatsfreak.com/brainwave-entrainment/9-things-you-should-know-about-delta-brain-waves

Robert.—*In each state (while running the wave with musical accompaniment) recite the instructions you want your unconscious to accept, respond to and or execute. Sexis may give you certain examples of instructions.*

Sexy.—*After listening for about 15 minutes the alpha brainwave music recites with a soft, slow and clear voice something like this: breathe deeply and exhale slowly; you are concentrating on your mind and your body becoming more relaxed; breathe softly, deeply and exhale slowly. Now you reach maximum relaxation of your mind and body, take a deep breath and exhale slowly.*

Repeat this as often as you want until you feel relaxed. Now switch to Theta wave music and after listening to it for about fifteen minutes, repeat and repeat the instructions. Take a deep, gentle breath, exhale slowly, slowly, think of only relaxation; breathes, breathes, deeps, exhales slowly. Your mind is leaving behind its connection to material things, you are calm, quiet, without emotions, without thoughts. Take a deep breath and exhale slowly. Repeat this step until your mind no longer thinks only of what it perceives without giving it thought or meaning. The mind ignores the physical meaning of what the senses perceive. Perceptions do not cause mental or psychological effects. The mind is neutral in its spiritual state. Now switch to Delta wave music and prepare your mind to receive instructions for your new routine. For example, let's say your routine is to live in a spiritual state. In this state, although you know material issues and things, these or that, do not affect you, mentally or psychologically. Repeat and ponder repeatedly on each principle! Just as spirits do as they dance to the music of brain waves!

It's your soul!

Spirit A.—*The greatest evil in the world is the inequality galloping over your deep feelings, and flies with breathing selfishness. It is not the intention of existence; it is the demand of my untamed ego.*

Spirit B.—*I will let out the love of my soul and open my eyes to reality. I will discover the reason for the pain and sadness of humanity.*

Spirit C.—*I am the spirit that cares for them, walking freely, I am the pure soul; the being of light that with its flashes illuminates the peace of this madness.*

Spirit D.–*My mind perceives physical reality and everything has a meaning that comes from existence, from pure love absent from evil; or from that purpose, that existence has given you.*

Spirit A.–*Nothing has psychological, mental meaning, or material; even if it has for others. The fundamental principle separates my soul and body, while running free in this fleeting life.*

Spirit B.–*Wealth, power, and fame do not affect me, they are material things; and for my soul, they are secondary things. Because in my being there is only the flame of love, but not of banal things, and for my spirit, they are ordinary.*

Spirit C.–*Every moment of my life I control my thoughts, emotions, and feelings. It is the clear mission granted for my moments and moments: It is my rule of behavior.*

Spirit D.–*I am satisfied, conform, and always gratefully alive with what I have achieved and have. I don't need anymore; I am spirit and so I exist. I'm not materialistic like humans.*

Spirit A.–*I do not let the profane ego or his AGHAPEE destroy my soul; for power is in my hands; I let my will build my dual being, soul and body.*

Spirit B.–*Nothing will ever overcome my pure and beautiful soul; it is my spirit; so, will my conscience be the star, sword and shield against the attributes of AGHAPEE;*

Spirit C.–*I do not have:*

Greed.–*eagerness to hoard for pleasure;*

Greed.–*vehement desire to possess;*

Prejudice.–*negativity towards something or someone;*

Envy.–*desire to have the others;*

Ambition.–*desire to have and possess everything;*

Selfishness.–*the thought that everything is for and for me.*

Spirit D.–*And from this moment on, I will live by these rules. My confort zone is my state of conformity, satisfaction and gratitude.*

Spirit A.–*I promote and care for the truth of the universe and existence; so, I will have oneness in form and presence.*

Spirit B.–*I am in harmony with the universe. I, in my conscious state, remember these rules when my ego acts. I take care of my life in all its forms.*

Spirit C.—*I will embrace those I have offended. I will free myself from what amasses my sad, confused ego.*

Spirit D.—*I will do with all my peace and then I will take care of everything I do.*

Trues.—*The poem that the four spirits recite represents verbal instructions from a routine that your soul can learn and keep in your unconscious. But there is another method to program the unconscious directly with conscious actions. You can register a routine executed consciously, with definitive steps at a certain time, shape and sequence as the individual wants to perform it. Conscious actions must repeat until the mind does not think about the steps of the process anymore. At this point the routine stays programmed in the unconscious, and the mind will execute it automatically—without thinking when or how. They programmed everything.*

Robert.—*The individual can program his consciousness to do what we detailed above: an act of living life without attachment to material or materialism. The sequence of actions differs from the instructions the spirits recited earlier. But it depends on those instructions.*

Meditate on the reality of ordinary human life.

1. *I list things I don't like and set in my mind my moral model without the Ego's AGHAPEE.*
2. *I live without attachment to materials and or materialism.*
3. *I know I will not die if you give up superfluous things that only satisfy my vanity and pride.*
4. *I eliminate everything that feeds my ego—my selfishness, and what makes me feel great, powerful, above others.*
5. *I know I need material things to care for, feed and protect my body and mind.*
6. *I think of those material things I can replace.*
7. *I control the vagaries of the ego.*
8. *I recognize that I can do without materialism.*
9. *I know the basic things I need.*

10. *I lay the foundations of the sequence of my conscious behavior; to justify your action s before the ego. My decision is essential to my mind and conscience's balance.*
11. *Eliminate doubts or reservations of what you want to do.*

Sexy.—*Recognize that your inner peace is not in a position of power, wealth and fame. Peace is in the order of harmony of the universe—oneness. It's really your soul that is at stake and not that of others. Now meditate, reason on the thought of the poem "It's Your Soul." Recite the poem slowly in your mind, analyzing the words of each verse. Memorize the poem; let your wisdom take it with you to go over its sentences. This action will place it in the unconscious plane.*

Robert.—*Now it is time to act the thought. Practice this example or similar example of your liking. A daily routine after waking up.*

Wake up at 5:30 a.m.

Open the curtains in your windows.
Put the coffee in and turn on the coffeemaker.
Make your lunch.
Go to the bathroom, get ready for work.
Have your cup of coffee and breakfast, while you
Watch the news on TV.
Brush your teeth.
Take the key to your car and 7:10 a.m.
Drive to work in 40 minutes.

After doing this routine for several days without failure, you will record it in your unconscious mind, and you will automatically perform it without thinking.

Understand that if you repeat this daily routine the day comes when you no longer have to think about these ten steps. So, you will never be late for work. And there will come a time when you don't need the alarm clock because the unconscious will wake you up at the right time and guide your steps without mistake, no hesitation. All this depends on your discipline, organization and commitment, even if it goes against your desires, tastes, preferences, attitudes, and ego.

Trues.—*Now let's look at the routine of suppression of attachment to the materialism. Let the willpower of your conscience work. Direct the ego mind to the opposite side of material attraction during its day awake. For example, every day on way to work you stop by the Corner Coffee shop and buy an iced coffee. This time don't; save your time and money. You will have the impulse and the desire of the ego might dominate you and end up in the coffee shop, but little by little, you will dominate the ego, and you forget that habit.*

Sexy.—*The highlight in what Trues says is the meaning of things. Meaning is the source of attachment to material things and to materialism. There are two meanings, a natural meaning that existence assigns to each object and to each living being, and the meaning (values) that the ego gives to these same elements. And with each meaning goes the value of the object or of the living being. And there are two values, the existence's value and the value that the ego gives them. Often altered by the whim of the ego. In reality, living objects and beings have no other meaning or value than that which existence gives them. These are not only for material things, but they apply to subjective factors such as power, wealth, and fame—selfish attitudes.*

Robert.—*Trues, Sexis, we see other meanings and values in the relationship of humans. These are two, one strictly mental or concepts and one psychological. In both cases, the meanings are intangible and invisible and the value they think the meaning deserve.*

In the dimension of spirits, the relationship have the value of love. On earth, the ego gives them meanings according to their selfishness.

Trues.—*That's how it is. There are also differences in concepts among humans because of their different levels of knowledge. The ego translates these differences (of time and space) as of superiority and inferiority. Within these mental concepts we see differences in physical form and appearances. We also see differences in beliefs. Likewise, the ego translates them as of superiority and inferiority or as of certain or uncertain. One example is racism and a sense of supremacy. Within psychological concepts we see selfish differences reflected with hatred, disdain, rejections, etc. We* *also see the differences in capacity, and here we find envy. We can expand these observations to other differences.*

Sexy.—*The emotion for the material and materialism is because of the mental and psychological differences we mention and the artificial meanings and values that the ego gives to the material elements. The monster, AGHAPEE, who lives in the human ego carries most of those meanings, values and differences. The more humans attach to those meanings, values and differences, the further they are from the order of harmony of the universe, and the more materialistic is the ego.*

Gee, that's amazing! The suppression of consciousness is not to transform itself into spirits, but to act as spirits while living as humans in this material dimension. In this state, nothing material affects our souls. Is that Nirvana state? Ego tastes and preferences do not affect us, they do not provoke mental or psychological reactions in our behavior. From this viewpoint all we perceive are natural issues and events that do not alter our state of satisfaction, conformity and gratitude—this state is tranquility!

Robert.—*Then if the verbal routine we install in the unconscious can reduce, or eliminate the attributes of AGHAPEE, the ego loses its field of influence. The soul lets out the love that leads inside. And managing meanings, values and differences is possible and easier. Then the human stops judging in vain and only acts according to the truth of reality. The soul sees the truth as it is without tints or mental and psychological arrangements that change the truth.*

Trues.—*This procedure reaches the potential of the mind and expands the limits of thought. In that state of Nirvana, we mentioned, the mind does not react to negative stimuli by material, mental, and psychological meanings, values, and differences. It does not change by consequences or actions of the ego—AGHAPEE. So, anything is possible. There is no argument if the illogical is logical.*

Now I understand that, if we ignore the meanings, values and differences that the ego assigns to living objects and beings, and only take the value that existence gives them, the selfish attitudes that AGHAPEE executes disappear. Those mental and psychological values fade away because, in reality, they have no material basis. And they cannot harm us unless we give them materialistic meanings, fake values, and false differences ourselves, as we do to this day. This is the state of Nirvana that Hindus expect and yearn for, or the earthly paradise that Abrahamic religions preach. According to spirits, with increased knowledge and wisdom, understanding tells us that levels of knowledge of humans obey the influences of a lifetime, and exposure to experience. Likewise, the mission of existence is to promote, protect and maintain life, and the rule of love, care and sharing, which commands us to help raise the level of knowledge, skills and experiences of others. I understand that if we remove the seven attributes of ego (ambition, greed, hatred, prejudice, envy, greed, and selfishness) we unleash the forces of the soul to achieve oneness. Then I live with love, for love and to love.

A voice in the audience.–*What is the procedure for achieving this state?*

Sexis.–*The procedure is simple and difficult. The strategy is to suggest the ego indirectly. The goal is to program the unconscious level of consciousness, creating a personal action plan to eliminate AGHAPEE and eliminate the meanings, values and differences with which your ego operates. For example.*

1. *I seek and get what is necessary—no avarice.*
2. *I have no greed.*
3. *I forgive those who offend me,*
4. *I don't harbor hatred and I love others.*
5. *I'm not prejudiced.*
6. *I bless who achieve more than I do without envy.*
7. *I ambition the order of harmony only.*
8. *I care and share with everyone, I'm not selfish.*
9. *I protect the existence and life of the universe.*
10. *I seek the uniqueness of existence.*
11. *I don't stick to material things or materialism.*
12. *I take the real meaning of things and living beings.*
13. *I don't add unfair and unnecessary values.*
14. *I receive all with equality, and have no differences.*

Then read, review this commitment every night before bed while listening to music with the Delta wave of the brain to achieve a deep sleep and meditate on these points. It relates to your conscience to confirm what you say and do. Copy of this covenant with the unconscious level of your soul conscience and take it with you. Read your covenant during the day each time you see the ego thinking, deciding, and or acting. You will see how little by little your being changes the behavior of your ego to the point when you no longer need to read this covenant.

Gee! What surprises existence has, isn't it? She has her mysteries; and the problems bring the solutions and are in the view. For example, the order of chemical elements that make up matter. Also, the categorization of species. And even more so, the structure of the soul and the brain. It's a fantastic thing! But this unconscious programming shows the simplicity of the difficult. I ask... Will be possible to be a human spirit, as they say. Will it be as simple as mounting routines on the unconscious plane of consciousness? And so, can the behavior and identity of the human change? It can be, according to spirits, Robert, Trues and Sexis. My experience creating automatic behavior routines supports this theory. Unconscious knowledge does not come out to the conscious, but we use it without thinking. For example, when we make a soft drink or make a new cooking recipe, we already have in mind the taste and aroma we want to achieve. And then we compare the mixtures of the ingredients that satisfy the taste and aroma we have in the unconscious. But after making those mixtures often, the person makes the soda or recipe to taste almost without measuring the ingredients or thinking about the result, but the taste is accurate. My experience is that after doing a new routine and doing it for a few days, the next day the unconscious brings it to the conscious level, casually.

One person asks.—*So, you can train the ego?*

Robert.—*That is true... But if you commanded it to what it must think, say and do; the ego rebels. The method is as the spirits suggest, repeating a routine of action at the conscious level (of the ego) until it is automatic. The ego needs not think, decide, or act consciously. The ego* *abides by the will of the mind; like creating an exercise routine at the time of a football match.*

Guide.–*Well, we've heard Sexis, Trues and Robert talk about the possibility that humans can reduce their attachment to materials and materialism, controlling the unconscious. They suggest a simple, though difficult, method that humans can practice. We warn that younger children do not create unconscious routines without adult supervision. We recommend, however, that parents instill behavioral routines in children to remove AGHAPEE from their egos. Now let's go back to the play, "Life Cycles."*

Trues.-*There was a fatal accident at the beginning of this play. Five humans died and the spirits forcibly separated from their bodies. It was a shocking experience for bodies and spirits. Of course, the spirit, the energy, goes on, not the body. But the separation of spirit and matter goes through a process. The screens show a life cycle diagram.*

Trues refers to the normal process mentioned above, but to benefit the public, I repeat the interpretation of that process.

Step 1.–When the body enters its process of death, the body experiences an initial spasm or stiffness, and the soul leaves the body. Outside of the body, mind and soul can see the body, continuing mental functions as if they were in the body.

Step 2.–The soul wanders near his body for about 8 to 12 hours, which is the approximate time of this step.

Step 3.–Between 12 and 24 hours, the muscles of the body relax, and the stiffness disappears, becoming flexible again. The body is not yet dead, and the soul continues to roam around its body.

Step 4.–The body hardens again between 24 and 36 hours. The soul continues its process outside the body still connected to the body through the mind and brain of the body. At the end of this last step, the body has lost all its energy, and the soul collects it. The body becomes inert and the soul let the body go. This is the point of no return; the soul becomes spirit and can go. But it can't stay if it decides to stay; it must leave just as it concludes its mission on earth. The concept that spirits roam around the body for over 36 hours is undefined. However, the spirit that returns to the spiritual dimension can keep certain material frequencies; other spirits on earth have spiritual and mental attachment to the spirits that left the material world. Spirits active in their material mission may have real contact with the deceased spirit. This connection depends on the time people on earth vehemently remember and miss a deceased spirit. That's true! Your emotions and feelings, such as love and affection, are not material questions; come from your soul and or your mind–they are spiritual themes. And as spiritual matters, they remain in the cosmos in mental (energy) waves. Your emotions and feelings and fears and anxieties, desires and longings are vibrations or waves of your soul. Every thought and word that your soul generates and pronounces through your mouth has specific frequencies floating in the cosmos. These waves are intense and have purpose or direction. They impact definitive parts of souls. And its source is not important; because they can come from your reality or virtual reality. These waves excite consciousness in specific areas; and human reactions are predictable. Their effects are the same no matter where they come from. Some of these vibrations can change the way you perceive and conceive your environment with humans, and your soul transmits these vibrations to the cosmos. Other spirits can capture these waves and react to their frequencies. You know, humans cry or laugh when other humans cry or laugh next to you. Pain and suffering are strong waves easily sent and or received by other spirits as strong signals. So, a connection between the spirit dies with the souls left on earth. It is a union not lost, even if the remaining people's minds forget the deceased.

Stacey.–*During the fundamental separation cycle, you are not dead yet. You're not here, but you're. The mental processing unit, the mind, still works; connectivity codes remain with the soul; if you get excited, the soul can go back to your body and continue to live in this material world. Your soul waits until your body releases all its energy; this is its condition of rigor mortis. The soul collects all the energy of the body and takes it with it back to the spiritual dimension—energy recycles. And your mental waves leave with their code in space and omniscience.*

Guide.–*Humans claim that airlines do not allow too much baggage (weight) on their flights. Well, our spiritual dimension specifies that spirits do not bring material substances to the dimension of spirits– they do not allow it. The perfection of this mandate alone is evidence* *and proof that a higher, or supreme intelligence establishes universal, infallible laws: there is a perfect separation of dimensions.*

Know? If you understood death as a condition of life, real and inevitable; you could free yourself from many feelings and emotions, including the fear of death. This fear is not to death itself, but to the feeling or notion of losing the presence on earth and of all possessions, power and fame, attained, no matter how great or small. The dimension of spirits does not take or store matter, only energy.

Person U at the hearing:
–How was the end of the murder case in Henderson, Nevada?
–What about the Sinaloa Cartel in the cases of Moses and Sergio?

Guide.–*Regarding the case of the murders in Henderson: The investigation concluded and the case was closed. Jeff had fallen in love with Vicky, provided her with a place to hide from her husband after a fight, while she filed a divorce lawsuit. Detectives found irrefutable evidence that Jeff held Mrs. Martin locked up against her will at his residence in Henderson, from where she escaped. DNA evidence confirms that Rex is Rocky Martin's legitimate son. Jeff's autopsy reveals that he regularly took opioid and had fallen into severe addiction, suffering delusional trance.*

Stacey.–*about the Sinaloa Cartel. Joaquin (el Chapo) Guzman in 2017 and taken to court for trial. Guzman is in a U.S. jail. They arrested and prosecuted him in court; he now serving long-term sentence. Detectives of the Suarez group corroborated evidence, witnesses legal files, and assisted the courts against the Sinaloa Cartel.*

Guide.-*Dr. Wells will ask the spiritual panel a few questions before we finish our forum.*

Dr. Wells.–*Gentlemen, what do you see beyond 2020?*

Victor.–*The future of humans is in crisis with large burdens of social, economic and environmental inequalities. By 2030, food and energy available will achieve critical shortage conditions.*

Moses.–*The cure of cancer is at hand by 2030, longevity reaches 100 years by 2040. But diseases are increasing because of a lack of pharmaceuticals and because of high and rising prices. By 2040 we* *will break the barrier of the spiritual dimension and various advanced attributes, such as telepathy may be available.*

Rex.—*The political situation by the end of 2020 will undergo major change, students, women, minorities and green peace marches crippling the United States. Stores suffer heavy losses because of consumer shoppers from selected stores only. People add to the list of prohibited businesses, banks and loan sharks and stores that manipulate prices and the availability of goods, during critical a situation.*

Sergio.—*The big factor for voters is the disappointment of President Trump's goal of dismantling the strong democracy in America that helps Russia's political and economic status, benefiting Putin. Trump's actions discredit the United States in the eyes of world leaders. The 2020 general election shocks the Republican party. Donald Trump and his family face legal cases in court after leaving the White House. The country achieves peace in mid-2022, under the control of Democrats.*

Stacey.—*Guests, now you can go back and look for the image of your body, concentrate, slowly come down and return to it. They can do it on their own, slowly.*

Guide.—*That is a simple process; we warn the audience not to experiment with this process without understanding what you are trying to do. Thinking about the concept of introspection [xxxi] we can apply it to human mental analysis and or study to find, perhaps, what our consciousness cannot determine with good or evil standard, or good or bad comments. Now, let's go back to inter dimensional connectivity. The key that, if all four steps, you will be out of the body. Whatever it is, your mind focuses on outside the body. Seeing other places, those you haven't seen before, letting your mind make the map for you. Humans ignore how to induce a spiritual state outside the body without losing connectivity to their body. In reality, the soul never loses the connection with its body, only when the body dies. So, a state outside the body, it only means the mental state freed from all influence of the material world that surrounds it. The soul may think and fly within the spiritual world. For starters, humans regard spirits as dangerous and mysterious, prone to harm; And that's not true. Living humans fear the dead and close their minds, avoiding thinking of death.*

True.—*humans think this life in the material dimension is singular, long and there is no more; but for the spiritual dimension material life is a micro bit of existence. Humans must understand that life in existence is spiritual, and material life is only an occasional point in eternal existence. Therefore, it is a blessed event to cross the border to return home, the spiritual dimension.*

Stacey.—*The day when humans understand that life is in the spiritual dimension and that material life is nothing more than a brief passage or adventure, as acting in a play, then humans will see material life as something less important. Just imagine that in a play actor work to be rich and famous, and they do whatever it does to achieve their goals. In the play some do, others do not. But they leave the scene, with nothing achieved in their performance in the play. Likewise, humans are immigrants of the spiritual dimension who come on an adventure in the material dimension: they bring nothing and they take nothing with them. Later, when the curtains close and the cast leans to receive generous applause from the audience, everyone knows that the work is over—audience and artists. The actors leave their costumes, dress up, and leave the theater. Outside, the spiritual dimension awaits you, that is your true reality. They know that they are returning to their normal existence and bring nothing from the earth (the work), except, perhaps, certain waves, low frequency memories, which stay in them, the spirits.*

The stage darkens, and the images on the screens disappear, the screens are off and the curtains close, just after the souls return to Victor, Moses, Rex and Sergio, sitting at the forum table. The lights return to the stage, and the audience sees them as humans. Souls who mingled with the audience left, and the guide, Trues and Stacey.

Back to the present,

The curtains open; we are in Dr. Wells' laboratories, in the living's life.

Dr. Wells.—*Well, ladies and gentlemen, and people in the audience, our panel guests, now they return as dual beings, soul and body, ask your questions if you have any, but please don't ask who to win the presidency and the Senate in November 2020.*

There was a long silence in the audience.

Dr. Wells.–*Well, I thank you for... an interruption. Someone raised a hand.*

Person V at the hearing.–*Please wait and see what happened to Victor, Moses, Rex and Sergio.*

Dr. Wells.–*Oh, yes, let* the guide answer your *good question.*

The public no longer sees the spirits, but even the spirits remain present and can hear us say. I keep narrating this production for you. On screens you can hear what spirits respond to in their minds.

Guide.–*Looking to the future of Victor, Moses, Rex, Sergio, Ted, Isabel, Stacey: Then, Victor, finally healed from his illness after the treatment prescribed by Dr. Martin. Victor married Isa's sister, Mary, and had three wonderful children. Dr. Martin found cancer cells around his lungs and after several years of radiotherapy treatment Victor returned to the spiritual dimension at 65 (2056). Moses perfects his radiology machine that works at low frequencies and can hear voices and images of spirits. Moses married a young German scientist, Jenifer Heisenberg; together they are developing the theory of spirit-body, inter-dimensional connectivity. They have a boy and a girl. Moses died and moved to the spiritual dimension in 2079 at 88. Rex continued with his medical research lab, famous worldwide for his discovery in rare diseases, including paranormal projections. Rex married a Mexican doctor in April 2010 and had two beautiful girls. Rex died in a car accident on the Pacific Coast Highway near Santa Barbara while driving to the University of Santa Barbara, where he expected to give a lecture on advanced pathology. Rex was 81 years old (2072) on the day of the accident. Sergio became chairman of the board of directors of the law firm Clark and Associates, right after Ted passed away. Sergio, who lived with only one kidney, had a remaining kidney infection and was on dialysis and after three years, Sergio dies in 2076. Isa, Ted's wife, dies in 2048, 10 years after Ted; Ted and Isa had two children, a boy and a girl. All the spirits of the group were great friends close and occasionally under the device brain waves and kaleidoscopic, and travel to the spiritual dimension for intellectual research.*

Guide.–*Although our four souls are very young and will not return to their spiritual dimension. They still have a long life ahead of them, so let me call your voice and assistants back on stage. As you humans can say* *"hey"; emotions are high, and it's good to digest events. Let us focus on the last topic of our previous conversation, how to manage your conscience. The conscience is what keeps you united and focused on physical reality. For us spirits consciousness is not a problem; our omniscience does not allow us to ignore anything; we know everything unless we're housed in a human body.*

True.—*Sometimes human face tribulations, difficulties, problems of social, economic or political origin. Sometimes, they want to get out of their material dimension, and may want to escape the spiritual dimension. Most of the time it is to see and talk to a dear deceased. There's nothing wrong with that longing. The process is easy, but their discipline is difficult because a person's material or physical attachment is strong.*

Moving forward in time until 2075. We now see nine spirits conversing about their new assignment to the material dimension at one of the exit stations. They are talking about experience with illegal immigration, human organs and drug trafficking in the years 1990 to 2017 in the nations of America.

Guide.-*Thank you for being a splendid and understanding audience. We have concluded this forum on Life Cycles. Be careful when you leave the theater good night.*

The applause of the audience is intense and noisy. The curtains open and the whole cast of spirits come in and with courtesies and parsimonies to thank the audience. The lights went out on the stage, and the spirits disappear from the stage. The curtain closes. The theater lights go out. At this point the stage is empty. And in the closed curtains a projection shows the following.

LIFE CYCLES.

The work of the spirits:

Truth and Love.

End

Cast of Spirits.

Diana Van Sander (DEANNE) Los Ángeles, CA–1996
Samuel Wells **(VRTL),** Los Ángeles, CA–1970.
Ted Clark **(LEEGAHL),** Santa Ana, CA–1972.
Isabel Suarez **(AGNT),** Santa Tecla, El Salvador–1977.
Victor Richland **(ARIEL),** Manhattan, New York–1990.
Moses Suarez **(KETA),** Santa Tecla, El Salvador–1990.
Rex Martin **(TZZS),** Henderson, Nevada, USA–1990.
Sergio Maltés **(CENIA),** Arriaga, Chiapas,
México- 1990 **(BOCHARS),** Iowa–2017.
Espíritus corroboradores.
Stacey
Robert
Trues
Sexis
Humanos
Josue
Esposa de Josue.

CHAPTER 9

The Evidences.

Abstract

The truth is one and only one, when the premises of support are all true; regardless of the difficulties encountered in testing those premises. Physical tools and procedures may not be appropriate for humans to capture, observe, and explain non-material phenomena, such as the existence and behavior of spirits. Perhaps the law of cause and effect can guide humans back to the origin of such phenomena, walking from the visible and tangible to the invisible and intangible. And perhaps then humans can claim that intangible reality exists because tangible reality exists. Perhaps, then, humans can demonstrate how a spirit enters a human body and acts in synergy, living as two separate components of a single dual being in the same space and time. In this way, these dual beings, the mentaurs, will be on the way to oneness—the order of harmony of existence.

Closing comments.

Everyone left, back to their material, materialistic world, the dimension dominated by the human ego; where truth hides in the gloom of lies and deceptions–a selfish world. And now, I'm alone in front of the curtains, in front of the audience, the theater. I'm going to the left side of the front of the stage, a meter from its edge. I still hear the applause, the murmur, the noises of the seats; are signs of reality that returns to material normality. The applauses last a long. Now people are going out, but I'm still here, standing on stage, more no one can see me anymore. They do not have the spiritual attributes granted temporarily. I turn around and still sit in front of people leaving the theater. My mind detects confusions doubts in people's minds. The concept of "Life Cycle" is strange, a hypothesis which needs deep meditation. As a writer, I want to explain to you, reader, while you are still reading my book certain points, arguments and evidence. I'll take the mic from the guide's podium and talk to you about this.

I am Diana Van Sander, the spirit of the girl stricken by an object launched that day of the tragic accident that forced the separation of five souls. I was deeply thinking about the mysteries of existence, love, light and life: the book of Miguel Soto, written in Spanish. I was trapped in his thoughts when I fell unconscious, with my mind attached to his mind. My body also died because of that same accident. But I am here to give you–I feel I owe you–an explanation of spirits and "life cycles" from a human viewpoint. I'm still attached to the author's mind.

The Premises.

Almost everything starts with assumptions or premises that require verification. I follow the words and spirit of my book; I wrote it in the author's mind. And now, I say, only truth can prove the truth; but if truth is reality and certainty, then truth belongs only to the visible and tangible realm. This notion does not imply that everything else is false just because we cannot prove it; intangible and invisible matters and entities–that too–can be true. But truth builds on truth; just as the calculation of the structure of a bridge has to be true, because any error makes it false, the calculation is not true, the bridge will collapse. There is no unreality, there is only truth; and what is in the spirit dimension is also true–a truth we cannot see or touch, we cannot perceive, although we can imagine it. It is a truth like the truth of thought, mind and soul. Existence is bipolar so that if there is reality there is also unreality, and just as visible substances invisible substances exist. More than a tool or method of reality, truth is inadequate to prove unreality as the dimension and behavior of spirits. Here, I confirm nothing we read above in this book about spirits. And we cannot prove the existence of spirits because they are invisible and intangible. So, the conclusion they do not exist is not valid; well, we cannot deny or assert beyond reasonable doubt. And maybe we should keep looking for that truth. Do we have enough evidence to establish its existence? I observe strange patterns and phenomena that point to the existence of spirits. We realized there is a law of causal events and a law of random events. And by these laws, we can trace the origin of an event already held, and we observe the sequence of steps, topics and activities that made that event possible. Because of these observations of causes and effects, we can define the reality of the effect to its cause even when the cause originates in unreality. So, walking back from reality, you are to think what you have observed in the universe so far is true; for example.

The global spirit of existence.

Energy is the spirit of existence, true. What else could it be? Energy causes movement and change, movement and change are a sign of being alive; therefore, energy generates life, keeps it moving, always changing. This energy fills the universe. And if we now see energy in the universe, it was before the universe; because we cannot create or destroy it–and it existed before the universe appeared. We don't see or touch energy, it's invisible, it's intangible. But the results of their interaction with reality lead us to accept that it exists and is real. We recognize and accept the existence of energy, invisible and intangible, for example, the four forces of existence, electromagnetic, weak and strong nuclear, and the force of gravity. These forces of existence, according to scientists, caused the great explosion that created the universe. Is love the force or spiritual gravity that attracts two souls? It may be, because love is an invisible, intangible force, attracting or mooring two souls into one; forever love is spiritual, it is never material; it is not of the ego.

Reality and unreality.

Two dimensions are parts of the spectrum of existence. Their ranges range from zero to one hundred percent in reverse. When one component is one hundred percent, the other is zero percent. One end is unreal, invisible and intangible, and the other is real, visible and tangible. Our imagination offers evidence that unreality exists; for example, when we create thoughts and images of subjects, conditions, and situations that don't pass reality tests. Children live in the fantasies of their imagination, and adults support their creations. Elders tell stories that fit unreality, and the adults think they're losing their minds. Great writers like Dante went down to unreality and brought it to reality in his narrative. Beliefs and faith are unrealities that exist in human minds, but they do not make them a reality with any material action.

This book deals with concepts and themes of unreality, trying to explain them with the language of reality and logic. But are children and elders wrong? Or is it possible that the hidden components of existence are also real? No, it can't be in reality, but are they really in unreality. The obvious component is the observable space with all its contents, which we call the universe. It's the reality, or the certainty we observe. And reality is the truth with its logic we know. But truth and logic are elements of reality. The knowledge of humans has come from the observations of their environments, which are part of the obvious dimension. And we do not know of the non-obvious part. And so, the logic within the universe only applies to questions, objects, situations and conditions within this reality. There's no other space outside the universe. Because if space is infinite, anything left outside is part of infinite space. The information on Google's website says that the space of the universe is spherical with a diameter of about 93 billion light-years (8.8 x 1026 meters). A universe that appears about 13.8 billion years ago. [49] However, we cannot measure, and any measurement of infinity is only part of infinity.

---

[49] https://en.wikipedia.org/wiki/Observable_universe

Invisible and intangible dimensions.

I observe an invisible dimension that coexists with the visible and tangible dimension in the space. And these two are the two great dimensions of existence.

1. There is no other dimension of space; because this is the whole content of existence;
2. Energy exists and is within matter; matter exists and can transform into energy by physical means;
3. And energy and matter always go together, side by side;
4. Energy applied to energy remains as energy; but energy applied to matter causes transformation or change. And that change is life.

I know the world around me; but if there was no reality there would be no universe, and this world would only be in our imagination. My conscience and or imagination, however, confirms there is existence, evident-reality or hidden in unreality. Therefore, I exist and am real and unreal. I have no arguments against or objections to the previous four concepts. And the separation of matter and energy in the two dimensions is clear; matter is visible and tangible and energy is invisible and intangible. There is a warning, however, energy coexists with matter in the material dimension, but matter does not exist in the spirit dimension. Matter carries energy, and energy is in matter. Life is the union of the two dimensions. So, I'm energy and matter, and I'm part unreal and part real, all in one entity. Existence has both dimensions. To be and not to be, and so we exist both ways.

Infinity—a single space.

The concept of containers, sets, and subsets makes the subject of infinity doubtful. Humans think if something exists, something else must contain it. So, for them, the space of the universe exists. But in the concept of an infinite set, this one is so vast that anything inside (infinite time) would never come to the awareness of what could be outside. What's in the space? Infinity contains everything and what is outside is part of infinity. The infinity includes what is inside and also what is outside. And what is within infinity exist accounted in infinity, but it is part of the inventory of infinity. And in this infinite space is the obvious reality, the latent reality, and the unreality.

Energy is in relative situations of the different atoms of matter, in the physical atomic structure, in the molecular affinity of substances. And there is latent energy at rest, and dynamic energy in motion. But normal matter and energy are in a stable state, sustained relationship; physical and chemical balance. And energy causes changes in matter, including the growth of human consciousness. This space existed before the matter scattered in the universe existed. I mean, space existed before the universe appeared.

Knowledge and intelligence.

These two words don't mean the same thing. Knowledge of existence–which is not equal to human knowledge in quantity or quality–was present before the universe appeared. And the intelligence of existence shows how, when and where existence applies that knowledge. For example, knowledge of what would happen if the four forces of existence apply to matter existed before the great explosion. We derive knowledge from the omniscience of existence; and intelligence is the property of the mind. Human knowledge is therefore only what we know from reality to a moment in time. Intelligence applies to that knowledge–how we use that knowledge. So, existence has a mind with the knowledge of omniscience. But (1) All knowledge belongs to the existence, and we cannot do anything to it. It is as eternal as the existence itself; (2) And existence passed this knowledge to the universe and its content, according to the requirements and intrinsic characteristics of its scenarios.

All knowledge is in the libraries of the omniscience of existence and is always available to the intelligence of living creatures, but we cannot alter it–it is the truth. The intelligence of existence shows in the laws, in order, the logic and behavior of the universe. This is the purpose of existence: Life, Light, and Love for All, the universe, and living beings.

Knowledge is critical to life. It's in the universe and is the real part of existence. Humans learn, you know, they use it. It's a matter of fact, and we need no more evidence. Scientists, architects, engineers do what they do because they borrow knowledge of the universe. All mathematics, science and so on, were present in the existence before man. Humans don't create knowledge, they don't own it, they can't take it. They only realize (awareness of learning) knowledge and keep copies of the images in brain memories for mental use; this whole process is your learning and knowing how. Knowledge is outside the soul, mind, ego and consciousness; and only conscience values knowledge. Knowledge is an intrinsic part of matter, reality and unreality. Humans can't see or touch knowledge. Knowledge is a descriptor of observed reality. It describes the identity, origin and constitution of substances, objects, creatures, thoughts and themes, in the dimension of reality. Even in the unreal dimension, why not? Any human action only results from knowledge in the world. It is part of the spirit dimension; and spirits have full access to omniscience. Knowledge is the muscle of existence and the universe; and the force moves them from the mind of the human soul.

There is an hidden but latent reality. The universe only shows knowledge on the surface of observable reality, or in what humans perceive. This is the evident reality. Most living creatures go through life aware only this reality. But other reality exists beneath the perceptible surface. This is the latent reality, and we only discovered with reasoning, using inductive and deductive logic; assumptions or assumptions, hypotheses and theories. All objects and creatures have an innate information within themselves, a reality that is not available to simple perception. Spirits know all this hidden information because they have access to what omniscience records and stores in its libraries. Humans don't know it, for them it's intangible and invisible, and they discover it only with their logical reasoning. Latent reality is the great mystery of light (knowledge) because it belongs to omniscience, and yet invisible and intangible, the human mind can surely attain it. This is evidence that the human soul is in constant contact with the mind of the global spirit.

Existence is specific.

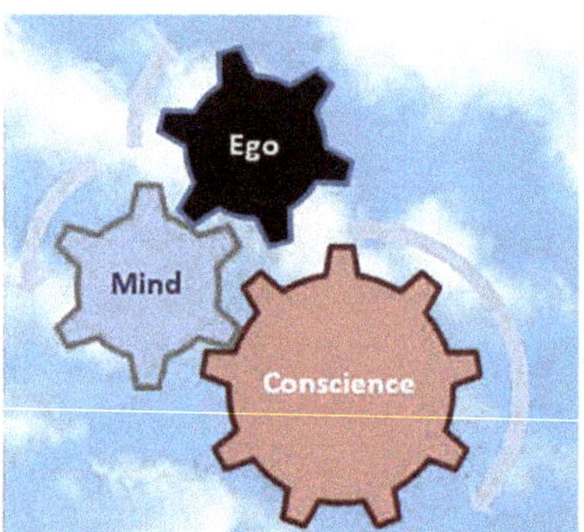

Figure 13: The soul's gears.

Spirits gears. energy and living objects and creatures are matter; they are eternal and infallible. These are two forms of the same substance, the spirit (energy) and the tangible form (matter). And this substance is the global spirit of existence with overwhelming attributes: omnipresence, omnipotence, omniscience, and absolute love. Thus, these four attributes are the power of the great spirit. This substance has a myriad of molecules, and each molecule keeps the characteristics and attributes of the whole substance. The spirit (energy) is eternal, but the body (matter) is transient. Humans know that when the body ends its lifetime, the body returns to matter. But they are not sure that the soul will return to the spirits' dimension after the soul separates from the body, or of what spirits do thereafter. A spirit can return as often as existence allows and enter new living creature (or body) every time they come. The soul of a human can communicate with souls in other human bodies, and with other spirits molecules of the global spirit. Three elements in a single real being. This is the global configuration of the soul—the spiritual gear of the soul in the human body.

The ego in the soul.

How do spirits enter the body of a living creature? The global spirit is omnipresent, it is in everything. A functional molecule of this spirit enters a living beings at its conception. This built-in spirit transfigures into the soul and mind of that human: spirit (energy) and body (matter). Only one soul impels every living creature, forming a dual being. And every human and living creature has an innate soul. A directive function of the spirit is the mind; and the mind is the operating system of the soul. But the soul and mind are invisible and intangible. Humans imagine, think, decide and act; and it's a spiritual operation in the real world. For example, feelings, emotions, love, thought are functions of the soul in the dimension of spirits projected to the reality of the material dimension. The soul is a generator of strength, and the mind is the creator of thoughts; and thoughts are forces that induce actions that the body executes. The soul has three main components, the mind, the ego and the conscience (see Figure 10); they are independent components of each other, but they intrinsically synchronize. For example, the author's mind writes my book, but his ego and conscience do not intervene or take part in writing. Conscience can judge ego conditions, situations, and behavior without ego intervention or participation. The ego has free will and behaves regardless of conscience and mind. But there is a caveat, conscience and ego use the mind thinking function. The mind does not intervene with thoughts, decisions, decisions, or ego actions.

The Ego.

The ego assumes the relationship with material thoughts, decisions and actions, since it inherits the attribute of free choice, or free will.

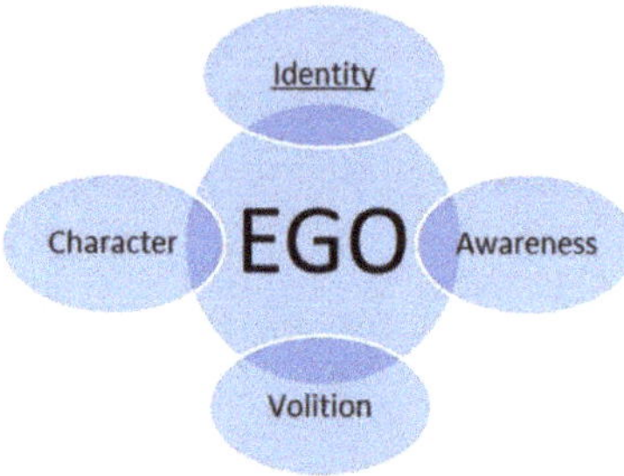

Figure 14: Structure del Ego.

The ego is solely responsible for all the consequences of their thoughts, words and actions. He handles four sub functions: Identity, (2) character or personality, (3) awareness, and (4) volition. The ego personalizes its individuality and with its character represents the dual human. It also assumes how this being acts and behaves, showing its character and personality, attitudes, tastes and preferences, interests and values. The ego is aware of itself and of its surrounding. It is the connection between the soul and is aware of the reality of the universe. It facilitates the social, political, mental and emotional relationship with other entities in its environment. The ego thinks, decides, defines its plan of action to satisfy its whims, desires, and this is its will. The ego handles its free will (volition).

The Consciousness of the Soul.

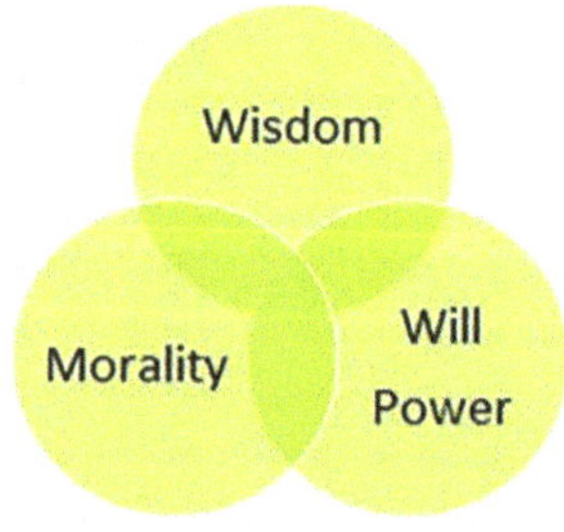

Figure 15: The Conscience

Conscience has three sub-functions: (1) Morality, (2) Wisdom, and (3) Will Force. Morality is automatic; while the conscience manages the other. Morality is the innate function that tests the ego's ideas, decisions, and actions automatically: right and wrong, good and bad, right, and unjust.

Morality is a voluntary function when conscience studies the thoughts, problems, conditions or situations of humans to determine their values. Morality determines what is right or wrong, good or bad, including the just or the unjust. [50] Conscience tests or asses the ego's thoughts, decisions, and actions, and provides a moral and logical judgment, and the alternative action it can take. The ego takes it or ignores it. The wisdom of conscience, meditates, provides logical reasons in support or rejection of the thoughts, decisions, decisions and actions of the ego and for conscience. Wisdom is the ability—the primary cognitive function of conscience—to see the world, the thoughts and actions of humans from the perspective of truth. But it requires knowledge, capacity and experience—human capital—and moral quality to judge problems and the situation in search of unbiased conclusions. Humans don't always do this; it's voluntary action available when consciousness requires it. Willpower[51] is a function that conscience uses to control the impulses and actions of the ego. The willpower of conscience carries a dialogue with the ego, trying to convince him to think, choose, decide and act according to the councils of conscience advice. Humans say it is their self-control or the ability to control themselves, which can control their emotions, desires and greed, or expressions of these, especially in difficult situations. [52]

Fundamental premises:

There is an observable order of universal unity; Existence has only two dimensions: spiritual and material. These two dimensions share the space of the Universe—there is no other space—and one does not interfere with the presence and activities of the other. There are two forms of spirits: free spirits and spirits housed in living beings.

---

[50] https://www.dictionary.com/browse/morality
[51] https://www.dictionary.com/browse/willpower
[52] https://en.wikipedia.org/wiki/Self-control

Free spirits inhabit their dimension, invisible and intangible; Spirits housed in human bodies are souls, invisible and intangible; Souls remain integrated with humans until when the body ends, and at that moment, the spirits return to the spiritual dimension. A human is a dual being: spirit (energy) and body (matter). Spirits occupy human bodies according to established life cycles and for a short time. The spirits return to their dimension to start a new cycle when the body passes away. Spirits (or souls) and the bodies of humans (as energy and matter) are eternal; (1) the spirits (energy) never die, and work in eternal cycles; (2) humans are immortal; but their presence only exists in a life cycle–in the cycle of matter. Spirits communicate with each other at various levels through their minds: (1)the hosted spirits communicate with the other hosted spirits; (2) hosted spirits may communicate with free spirits in the spiritual dimension. Spirituality is not religious, but religions are spiritual: (1) Religions consider or depend on faith and belief; (2) Spirituality is a life separate from material life and materialism. The souls exist and actively participate in humans' operation; we have evidence. The actions resulting from the above premises are visible through the normal behavior of humans and reflected through institutionalized religious groups or churches. Do they prove the existence and spirits functions? Perhaps not, but their existence and their participation in human lives prove their real presence, even though they will remain like this, a mystery and secret until we have evidence to prove this theory. Religious groups deserve honorable mention in this speech. Most of the world's religions; therefore, it is appropriate to read fundamental concepts of the major religions in the world. The impact is considerable if you look at the world's population. Global population growth shows these statistics: 7 billion in 2012, 8.4 billion in mid-2030, and 9.6 billion by mid-2050. This book mentions five important religions down here. [53]

The spirits' purpose.

There are many notions for or against spirits, but do we know what a spirit is? Maybe we know it or not. The general knowledge

---

[53] https://www.bing.com/search?q=Total+global+population

is that humans and living beings have a part that is not physical, bringing emotions and character or personality, including[54] thoughts and attitudes. The general belief holds that spirits make humans alive or animated. Spirits drive the lives of humans and unite the body and mind [55] (soul). [56] Obviously, a spirit in a human body is not material; and it's the seat of emotion and character... including quality and mood.[57]

General beliefs broaden ideas of spirits; there is a supernatural spirit, and often, but not only of a non-physical entity; such as a ghost, fairy, or angel. [58] Obviously, the popular notion of spirit includes a supernatural being, God; yet this notion also identifies other forms of spirits, which have ranks and duties. A more general and important belief is that the spirit remains or continues its existence after the death of a human body, as they say, A Force... and often to suffer after leaving. From the above information we see that the concept of spirits is critical and consistent with the way of being of man, or human life. However, can we interpret a credible definition, or confirm the existence of spirits? I don't think so, not yet, and the question Do spirits exist? It may be, but this question opens up three choices about spiritual existence, (1) denying it, (2) accepting it, or (3) not caring about it.

First choice: The thoughts that come to our mind are that, if the 'existence of spirits, we would also deny the existence of invisible and intangible parts of human beings, which are naturally of spirits: Mind and Soul. Religions have for centuries preached there is a supreme spirit; the foundations of religions would crumble under the weight of this opinion, that of the existence of spirits. Second option: If we accept that spirits exist, we accept the possibility of the identity, attributes, functions and interaction of spirits with the universe and the world of living beings. If we define universal existence by absolute knowledge as the omniscience that defines places, and maintains the

---

[54] https://www.merriam-webster.com/dictionary/spirit
[55] https://www.dictionary.com/browse/spirit
[56] https://dictionary.cambridge.org/us/dictionary/english/spirit
[57] https://en.wikipedia.org/wiki/Spirit
[58] https://www.biblestudytools.com/dictionary/spirit/

universe together (laws and rules of the universe), a spirit exists within and outside of everything, subjects, and objects, in the universe. Certain humans don't like to rely on beliefs because beliefs don't give them the sense of security they'd like; so, they argue and fight to make their beliefs the prevailing reality. Besides the above, the interaction of spirits with the universe and living beings, logically, must have rules of coupling. Third option: The position of remaining neutral regarding the existence of spirits is to allow science, thinkers and philosophers to study or seek evidence of the existence and operation of spirits. Being neutral destroys humans' sense of loyalty to a faith, allowing the free thinker to shatter their beliefs. But isn't it better to know the truth instead of continuing in the gloom of beliefs?

Every option has problems, but humans would like to establish their belief as an infallible reality, beyond doubt. That human beings cannot see, hear or touch spirits implies that spirits may not exist. A definition of spirits, the spiritual dimension and their dimensional interaction; the theme or concept is not beyond their reach, because there is evidence of functions or spiritual elements already within our human bodies, functional, critical and vital elements for our existence, which are neither faith nor beliefs. This evidence facilitates the definition of the dualism of humans: part spirit and part matter. And this dichotomy divides the existence of humans into two distinct and separate dimensions. Evidence of spirits and their dimension includes: A Soul with a mind, ego, and conscience. What role does the human body play? Only the physical execution of actions that follow mental thoughts and ego decisions, but the body has no intention, cannot reason, and has no goals. The body has no thoughts, decisions, emotions or feelings; these are attributes and functions of the soul. The human body is not aware of reality, looking beyond sensory perception; the human body has no capacity to think, reason and decide for itself. So, what should we study? Let's review some basic assumptions or hypotheses, which may depend on a viable or verifiable theory of what spirits are and how they work.

The Oneness.

The information of the world provides abundant evidence that the universe–it has an established order–is not a chaotic system, but follows a pre-established rules, or laws, that hold the universe together and in balance–these laws are infallible. They organized and detailed with categories and classes of objects and subjects given by the order of oneness; for example, the periodic table of chemical elements, not arranged or organized by human intelligence. The periodic table naturally organizes the elements by their atomic weights, from the lightest to the heaviest. The four fundamental forces and their intrinsic interactions or reactions in juxtaposition, gravity, electromagnetic, weak and strong nuclear, are not a human effort. The laws of motion, chemical balance and defined proportions, and even the theory of relativity have existed before humans discovered them. Everything exists in perfect balance, and each part, object or subject, plays its role with the intensity that the Universe requires. There is no waste; everything has just what it needs to exist in the order of unity of the Universe–there is no excess. That's the law of balance. I declare through the author's mind that the physical universal balance is constant: the forces that pull the universe in one direction is equal to the forces that pull the Universe in the opposite direction, integrated from zero to infinity. Therefore, the system is always in a static and dynamic balance state or balance, however; the system is always changing. The universal spiritual balance–the order of the oneness of the universe– is equal to the optimal state of good, the right, just and pleasant. Poor, incorrect, unfair and unpleasant conditions and circumstances, is the situation which the universal system seeks to overcome: when good, right, just and pleasant reach the level of one hundred percent. Universal disorder comes when a dynamic system (the universe, or a human) enters chaos while the existence rearranges its contents to maintain or regain its balance. Reorganization of the system content calls for the time required to organize all the disturbed parts. This is because of waves of controversies of the pairs–good (B) or bad (M), right (C) or incorrect (I), fair (j) or unfair (I), and pleasant (a) or unpleasant (d) of existence.

The maximum universal harmony is when the difference of the sums of these opposite pairs is zero, (B + C + j + a)–(M + I + i + d) is equal to 0. Chaos, perhaps, is when forces are returning the system to their command. An observer trapped in the wave (vibration of the universe) sees disorder, but not forces restoring order. [59] Humans have a short lifespan, and it doesn't last long enough for them to see a change—and for them life in disorder seems permanent.

Beliefs and the great religions in the world.

Religions usually address the subject of spirits and spiritual issues. Therefore, it is appropriate to learn what higher religions believe and preach about spirits. For example, most religions believe there is a God. This book studies five major world religions, which gather about one hundred percent of the world's population.

Abrahamic Religions.

There are three Abrahamic religions spread throughout the world, Christianity (33%), Islam (24.1%) and Judaism (between 14.5 and 17.4 million followers worldwide). These religions belong to a family of monotheistic religious beliefs derived from Abraham; a prophet in the ancient testament of the Bible. About 52% (about 3.85 billion people) of the world's population are in an Abrahamic religion, and perhaps this percentage may grow more than the world's population grows. However, the millions of people do not believe in a supreme spirit, angels and archangels that make the existence of spirits true because it is only a belief. We are not saying this number of people is wrong, but it is necessary to provide evidence of the spirits. Let's look at these religions to find common reasons for their spiritual beliefs.

---

[59] Orden Divina del Universo –El Universo tiene significado, propósito y orden inteligente-http://paulbrunton.org/notebooks/26/1

Christianity

Christianity is the religion based on the life, teachings and supposed miracles of Jesus of Nazareth, known to Christians as the Christ, or Messiah, which is faith. Christians believe that Jesus is the Son of God and savior of mankind whose coming as the Messiah (I prophesied in the Old Testament. [60] God the Father is a title given to God in various religions, more prominent in Christianity. [61] In Christianity, God the Father is regarded as the first person of the God, followed by the second person God the son (Jesus Christ) and the third person God the Holy Spirit. Creed Christians include the affirmation of belief in God the Father (Almighty), mainly as his capacity as Father and creator of the Universe. However, the concept of God as the father of Jesus Christ goes metaphysically beyond the concept of God as the Creator and father of all people, as stated in the Apostle's Creed, where the expression of belief in the Almighty Father, creator of heaven and earth is immediately, but followed separately in Jesus Christ, his only Son, the Lord, thus expressing both senses of fatherhood. In monotheistic thought, God is conceived as the Being and the main object of faith. The concept of God, as described by theologians, commonly includes the attributes of omniscience (all-knowing), omnipotence (unlimited power), omnipresence (present everywhere), and as having an eternal and necessary existence. [62] Depending on the theism, these attributes are used either in analogy, or in a literal sense as properties other than God. In agnostic thought, God's existence is unknown and/or incomprehensible. In atheist thinking, there is none, and they lack of belief in any god.

Comments on the beliefs of Christianity.

The previous discourse is a definition of the spirits, God, and attributes of God. [63] A supreme spirit capable of dividing into three people who coexist according to the belief of fatherhood considers a

---

[60] https://en.wikipedia.org/wiki/Christianity).

[61] https://www.history.com/topics/religion/history-of-christianity

[62] https://en.wikipedia.org/wiki/God

[63] https://en.wikipedia.org/wiki/God_the_Father.

trichotomy of God. This is three spirits, father, son, and holy spirit. In reality, the parental relationship of the third person, the holy spirit, we do not know. These three entities are intangible and invisible, including Jesus, who in his accounts lived as a human on earth. Followers speak with these three spirits in their prayers, and spirits respond according to their time or terms. There is nothing wrong with believing that spirits can take forms of a human person; there is nothing wrong with a person to claim he had a contact or vision with spirits. Since, according to the author's theory, the spirit housed in Jesus did so in the same way as other spirits housed in human bodies. The big difference is that, according to the narratives, Jesus attained high uniqueness with the order of harmony of existence. Thus, he lived independently of the influence of materiality and materialism—this was his struggle against the power and wealth of the Romans, protecting the underprivileged in misery and oppression. What is a child of God, it is a question with its answer in Catholic belief? The other two religions of the Abrahamic group have different beliefs. The other two non-Abrahamic religions think of the Catholic Messiah. Christians believe that God created from clay (earth) and the woman from a rib; however, the genesis does not define how or when a spirit enters a human body—perhaps this happened when God blew life in Adam's noses, when he encouraged him. One fact is that men and women are dual beings with a spirit and a body; then, showing how a spirit integrates with a human can prove the existence of all spirits.

Islam:

This is the second Abrahamic monotheistic religion teaching there is only one God (Allah) and that Muhammad is God's messenger. Islam teaches that God is merciful, almighty, unique, and has spoken to mankind through prophets, revealed scriptures, and natural signs. This belief does not differ from that of Christians. [64] For the followers of Islam, Ala is a merciful and powerful spirit, supreme, communicating with a prophet, a human messenger of God. The

---

[64] https://en.wikipedia.org/wiki/Islam

primary scriptures of Islam are the Quran, seen by[65] Muslims as the literal word of God, and the teachings and normative example (called Sunna, composed of stories called hashish) of Muhammad. Regardless of when and why they created, the important issues are beliefs.

Commentary on The Beliefs of Islam.

God speaks through prophets, and Muhammad is his greatest prophet. Islam teaches that man was created from a blood clot while creating the spirit of man, which is like Adam's rib to make Eve. This spirit is a supernatural being that enters a human body that influences Manon's problems regarding good or evil (which supports the inflection of spirits in humans.) As in Christianity, he has Christ. Islam has a Prophet Muhammad transmitting messages to Almighty Ala (God), [like the Christian God]. Christians have their Bible, Muslims have their Quran, which in both religions are scriptures of the word of God, directly. Islam believes in spirits, Ala and his prophet Muhammad. Muslims converse with Ala and the Prophet in their prayers, exemplifying direct communication between humans and spirits. Is there really a communication, or is it an eager illusion of the loneliness and hopelessness of humans? The existence of spirits and the possibility of communicating with them is here in their belief.

Judaism:

Judaism is the third ancient monotheistic Abrahamic religion with the Torah as its founding text encompasses the religion, philosophy and culture of the Jewish[66] people. Judaism is regarded by religious Jews as the expression of the covenant that God established with the Sons of Israel. Judaism includes a wide body of texts, practices, theological positions and forms of organization. The Torah is part of the broader text known as the Tanakh or the Hebrew Bible, and the supplementary oral tradition represented by later texts such as the Midrash and the Talmud. God is understood as the absolute,

---

[65] https://en.wikipedia.org/wiki/Quran
[66] https://en.wikipedia.org/wiki/Judaism).

indivisible and incomparable being who is the ultimate cause of all existence. Traditional interpretations of Judaism emphasize that God is personal, while some modern interpretations of Judaism [emphasize that] God is a force or ideal.

Comments on Judaism beliefs.

The covenant or covenant, according to the Jews, is between God and the children of Israel. How is this covenant translated for the rest of the world who are not children of Israel–how do Catholic, Muslim, Buddhist and Hindu believe? Judaism hasmain beliefs: (1) the law of God, (2) equality and justice, (3) the existence of the soul and (4) the existence of free will.

The author states there are laws of existence present before reality appeared and necessarily before the conditions of the universe allowed life, in any form. This belief does not differ from that of Christians. God is a spirit, invisible, intangible, an incomprehensible Spirit, the ultimate cause of existence. The Jew believes that God is personal (it is a human), while Judaism interprets God as a force. Being absolute... Indivisible... the ultimate causes of existence is an important vision; therefore, there is no God other than Him, and existence is because of Him. However, for his belief of the soul and free will is support for the discourse of this book. The author suggests that God is not an ideal, and agrees with Judaism's belief that God is a force–it is energy, the spirit of existence.

Non-Abrahamic Religions.

We know there are two other great religions that have similar, if never equal, beliefs. Perhaps the difference is because of developing human knowledge in different areas of the world. Maybe humans in different settlements gradually changed their beliefs–in the way they pass them on from generation to generation.

Buddhism

The Buddhist religion–the fourth largest religion in the world, 520 million followers–consistently rejects a walking deity. Buddhism does not believe that a supreme God has created the universe for man. Buddhist ontology follows the doctrine of "Dependent Origin", whereby all phenomena arise in dependence on other phenomena that occurred earlier, therefore, no primal immobile (event)–fixed in time and space or originating–could recognized or discerned as the beginning. Buddhism teaches the concept of gods, heavens, and rebirths in its Sasara doctrine, but regards none of these gods as a creator. Buddhism posits that worldly deities like Mahabrahma are misinterpreted as a creator.[67]

Comments on the beliefs of Buddhism.

So, for them there is no principle–that is, no god, the reality, the universe. Buddhists believe there are spirits. They suggest that Buddhism is true; unlike Abrahamic religions that believe that a god-created heaven and earth, man and woman. Buddhists suggest a polytheistic approach or belief. In addition, they present the concept that a phenomenon arises in dependence on another phenomenon that happened earlier–Dependent Origin. This belief (dependent origin) is in line with the law of cause and effect, so everything that happens today depends on other events that occur in their support and support; so, there couldn't be an originator of things that don't depend on previous phenomena. The Buddhist belief of dependence on origin fits into the law of cause and effect, so an event occurs because one or many other events happen earlier, but the mysterious question of a beginning: how the chain of phenomena originated. For them there is no primary still origin, which they interpret as not having a stationary entity that starts the universe. For them, Buddha [68] is a title of nobility, but not a prophet; still, a first Buddha attained the fourth truths, [69] attaining a higher state of universal harmony-spirit and matter. The author similarly suggests that oneness of spirit and matter, the order of harmony, of existence, It is as fourth truths are, (1) Life is suffering, (2) suffering is because of greed and desires,

---

[67] http://en.wikipedia.org/wiki/Buddhidm).

[68] https://en.wikipedia.org/wiki/Gautama_Buddha

[69] www.thoughtco.com/the-four-noble-truths-450095

(3) the cure is to let go, and (4) to go through passing the eight virtues (wisdom, ethics and discipline to mental). Free thinkers can take these truths as internal, spiritual or mental attitudes, not material–the body (matter) does not intervene in a determination. The author suggests that AGHAPEE influences the ego selfish behavior. It also mentions that eliminating AGHAPEE creates control of the human ego and consequently get to oneness.

Buddha taught that the skandhas are dukkha. Skandhas are the components of a living human: form, senses, ideas, predilections and consciousness. The author's theory suggests that the human living soul within him has a mind, a conscience and an ego. According to Buddhism, the animated body that identifies itself is dukkha because it is not permanent, and eventually perishes. In Western philosophies the living body (or matter) perishes about a hundred years–and it is a live dual being with a soul.

In Buddhist terms, Skandhas (Sanskrit) or khandhas (Pali) means lots, aggregates, collections, groupings. This refers to the concept of five aggregates, which states that five factors make up and explain the mental and physical existence of a sensitive being. The five aggregates or heaps are: <u>form</u> (matter or body); (rupa), <u>sensations</u> (or feelings, received form); (vedana), <u>perceptions</u>; (samjna), <u>mental activity or formations</u> (sankhara), and <u>consciousness</u> (vijnana). Here we can see a similarity in the configuration: a body, a conscience with all its emotions, sensations and feelings, and the mind with its production of ideas and thoughts. But los skandhas reflect the integration of spirit (mind) and matter (body), and in this dichotomy we can see (1) the form of skandhas (such as the body of living beings), (2) perceptions, (3) conceptions, choice, and (4) consciousness and preferences. Point 2 is sensory–it is the capture of reality and the process of images of reality; point 4 is self-awareness (inner being) and awareness of the surrounding environment. This follows our discourse, the spiritual structure in mind and soul, as we explain in this book. However, we must understand the four truths of Buddhists. For Buddhists, suffering is also self-inflicted and because of unsatisfied desires, as defined in the four skandhas–the components of a living human.

They say that life is suffering (dukkha). Is dukkha a truth? No, it is not.

Can we remove our feelings? Yes, we can! Life is not synonymous with suffering; and we can live without suffering. But when the ego doesn't satisfy its desires or has a stressful situation, he can't solve right away, he creates his own sufferings. Desires emanate from the human ego and reflect in their attitudes towards life. Often the ego cannot get what it wants; and he creates his tribulations. The ego is so miserable this suffering is its agony. But suffering is attitudes, ideas, and or selfish actions that humans do not do. Maybe they're broken dreams, and or dead hopes, failed longings, unfulfilled aspirations, and so on. But humans have the power of the mind to reduce or eliminate their sufferings. Buddhists say that the suffering is due to greed and *desires*: Maybe this is thirst or whims as Buddhists say it is thanha. The context of this book addresses self-inflicted sorrows, anguish, misery and suffering for the choice of ego (free will). This is the concept of AGHAPEE, seven attributes of the human ego. [70] AGHAPEE is the integrated attitude of the human ego. The seven attitudes that unite dual humans with the illusory charms of material affairs, fame, power and wealth.

For Buddhists, the concept of skandhas is (in) contrast with a unified being or individual and complements the anatta doctrine of Buddhism that affirms that all things and beings are without (a) self. The anatta doctrines and five aggregates are part of the liberating knowledge in Buddhism, in which one realizes that being composed of a temporal grouping of five aggregates, each of which is not me, and not me, and each of the skandha is empty, without substance.

The author furthers that the ego decides and acts; thus, the ego creates its tribulations. But the suffering comes from AGHAPEE's influence on the ego. The author takes sensations, feelings, mental activities and consciousness as functions of the soul. These functions do not mean the human inner self. In the discourse of this book, the body–the non I–is only a vehicle, and the other four skandhas are functions of the soul. The soul is the mind, ego and conscience

---

[70] www.thoughtco.com/why-do-buddhists-avoid-attachment-449714

housed in the human body. The visible self is the behavior of the soul we must perceive as the true individual. The inner self is the composite image of thoughts of sayings and actions carried out over time–that is the true me.

In Theravada tradition, suffering arises when one identifies or clings to the aggregates. This suffering extinguishes ceding the attachment to the aggregates. Mahayana tradition states that the nature of all aggregates is intrinsically empty of independent existence. The self agrees that it is possible for the soul to stick to its material part (the body), but it does not agree that the soul attaches to its mind, thoughts, consciousness because these belong to the soul, so there can be no attachment to what is already of the soul. However, if you agree that the ego is part of the soul, it can stick to the material and materialism. This attachment of ego causes human suffering.

In Buddhism, I use the concept of skandhas to explain the self is unique among the major Indian religions. It contrasts with the premise of Hinduism and the Jainism that a living being has an eternal soul or a metaphysical self. Perhaps to renounce the annexes or aggregates is not at all possible. But if we think of AGHAPEE and the human ego, we may find common ground. AGHAPEE comprises seven ego attributes, (1) ambition, (2) greed, (3) hatred, (4) prejudice, (5) envy, (6) greed, and (7) selfishness. For example, the body is the soul's vehicle. Humans wouldn't be able to see their inner and outer reality if they didn't have a perception. Mental function is how to communicate with other minds. We came to know our inner self and our surrounding scenario through our conscience. This book proposes that humans must first control their egos. And so, humans must get rid of AGHAPEE that manipulates their egos. So, we can take the "ties" of Buddhists as the bonds of humans with material things. John Daido Loori sees the belief of Buddhists from an inclusive view of all things in a total unit.

Zen master John Daido Loori says that non-attachment should be understood as a unity with all things: according to the Buddhist viewpoint, non-attachment is exactly the opposite of separation. You need two things to have attachment: what you are attaching to and the entity to which it is being attached. In the no attachment there is no unity. There is no unity because there is nothing to adhere to. If you are part of the total universe, there is nothing outside of you, so attachment becomes absurd because you are part of it. I mean, my hand can't feel an attachment to my body because is part of my body. But my soul can stick to my body because it's not part of my body. But the soul has no attachment to the global spirit because the soul is a molecule of the global spirit. Who will stick to what? Living in no attachment means we recognize there was never anything to attach to or cling to.

In relation to spirits and the spiritual dimension–in the discourse of this book–the concept is that a global spirit, energy, is in everything. It is in the sperm and in the egg and automatically passes to the zygote that forms during fertilization. We can consider that a molecule of the global spirit enters the matter, implying detachment; and when the spirit passes through its functional separation from a human body, when the body reaches rigor mortis, the soul becomes spirit again and returns to the global spirit. This is non-attachment because the molecule was, is, and will be part of the global spirit; The spirit molecule has nothing to adhere to because it returns to the body to which it belongs. In addition, the molecule of a spirit housed in a zygote never binds to the human body; and despite the functions that the spirit configures in the human brain remains in association and dependent on the function of the soul and mind: The mind and the body are two components that maintain their full identity while functioning as a single dual being: spirit and matter that make up humans' *mentauros*.

The cure is to let go.

There is a condition or state in which a human dual can reduce, eliminate and ensure the non-occurrence of subsequent sufferings; a genuine adoption of the order of harmony of the universe and oneness. A human dual being reaches the order of uniqueness when the inner self is in the optimal state of satisfaction, conformity and gratitude; it is within the order of harmony of existence. As the soul struggles to achieve a higher level or better conditions.

The Buddha also taught that it is possible not to suffer. This is fundamental to the joyful optimism of Buddhism: the recognition that the cessation of dukkha is possible. We achieved by giving up the illusion and ignorance that feed the attachment/clinging and the dislike/hatred that make life so unsatisfactory. The cessation of that suffering has a name well known to almost everyone: Nirvana. The meaning of Nirvana: In the spiritual definition, nirvana (or nibbana in Pali) is an ancient Sanskrit word that means something as extinguishing, with the connotation of extinguishing a flame. This more literal meaning has made many westerners assume that Buddhism tries to destroy themselves. But Buddhism, or nirvana, is not about that. Liberation implies the extinction of samsara's condition, the suffering of dukkha. Samsara defines it as the cycle of birth, death and rebirth, although in Buddhism this differs from the rebirth of discrete souls, as it is in Hinduism, but a rebirth of karmic tendencies. Nirvana is also said to be the release of this cycle and dukkha, stress/pain/life dissatisfaction.

Samsara (Sanskrit), is the repeated cycle of birth, life and death (reincarnation), and actions and consequences, present and future. Nirvana is not a place (it is more like a state of existence) Nirvana is beyond space, time and definition, so language is inadequate to discuss it. You can only experiment.

This book holds there is a repetitive cycle of life and the purpose of perfecting the integration of spirit and matter (body) into the unit of spirit and body. The life cycle for all human dual beings until each being reaches the universal order of oneness—conformity, satisfaction, and gratitude as it strives to achieve better conditions. Perhaps this is the concept of Nirvana in Buddhist beliefs. When dual humans reach that final state, a state of unity appears: the integration of spirit and matter and both will be in both spiritual and material dimensions simultaneously. This could be Nirvana, according to Buddhism.

The cessation of dukkha is possible... we achieved by giving up the illusion and ignorance that feed the attachment/clinging and aversion/hatred that make life unsatisfactory. Nirvana is not a place... it's beyond space, and time... Some also say that it is the release of this cycle and dukkha, the stress / pain / dissatisfaction of life... Liberation implies the extinction of samsara's condition, the suffering of dukkha... Samsara defines as the cycle of birth, death and rebirth... can life cycles extinguish? It's not possible. Buddhists believe there is one path humans can follow: it is the eight-lap path.

The eight-lap road.

Finally, the Buddha taught rules and practical methods to move from a condition of ignorance/attachment/aversion (dukkha) to a permanent joy state (Nirvana). Among the methods is the famous eight-lap path, a set of practical recommendations for living, designed to move practitioners along the route to the state of Nirvana. Yes, a nirvana state is possible. [71] The author mentions that the state of uniqueness is to be within the order of harmony of existence–an optimal or sublime balance. In this order they satisfy the soul and body, conforming, and in complete gratitude. But it does not mean that humans do not work to reach a higher level in the same three conditions. It implies only that, in each level achieved, and in the transition between levels, the human is in uniqueness with existence. Nirvana is a state of existence where there is no longer any sorrow or suffering. In oneness there are no sorrows or sufferings either, but In addition, the human stay in conformance and satisfied with what he is and has, feeling gratitude for his condition–then he has no suffering or sorrow. The hypothesis of this book is that the universe always exists in an infallible order of oneness; humans can attain the universal order of oneness by controlling the ego to (1) eliminate its attraction to material objects and subjects: wealth, fame and power, (2) subdue the seven ego's attitudes, ambicion, greed, hate, avarice, prejudice, envy, and egotism. The hypothesis of this book suggests that by eliminating AGHAPEE, humans can attain oneness, the spiritual condition that fulfills the universal order of harmony. The author argues that the best you can get is satisfaction with your achievement, while trying to achieve better condition, not allowing effects attempting to disturb his state of satisfaction, conformity, and gratitude. Buddhists believe they logran Nirvana following attitudes, thoughts and practical physical-actions, mainly with correct human behaviors, applying all of the following correct actions.

---

[71] www.thoughtco.com/the-eightfold-path-450067

1. perspective or understanding of true reality.
2. intention and selfless desire for enlightenment.
3. speech, using speech compassionately.
4. action, using ethical behavior to manifest compassion.
5. lifestyle; earning a living through ethical and non-harmful means.
6. effort; cultivating good qualities and releasing bad qualities.
7. living in the present properly, without tortuous consciousness of the body and mind.
8. concentrated, meditating, or some other dedicated and concentrated practice.

The author argues that oneness is beyond an understanding of reality. Oneness is in the recognition that the human is spiritual; and the composition of a dual being is the integration of a soul and a body. But the soul through its three components, the mind, the ego and the consciousness, impels the material human. And ego control is the way to oneness. And oneness is to live as a spirit in the material world, without attachment to material or materialism, seeing beyond reality to avoid sorrow and suffering.

Hinduism

Hinduism is an Indian religion and dharma, or a way of life, widely practiced in the Indian subcontinent. Hinduism has been called the oldest religion in the world, and some practitioners and scholars call it Dharma of Sanstana, *eternal tradition, or the eternal path beyond human history.* Scholars consider Hinduism to be a fusion or synthesis of various Indian cultures and traditions, with diverse roots and no founder. Although Hinduism contains a wide range of philosophies, linked by shared concepts, recognizable rituals, cosmology, shared textual resources and pilgrimage to sacred sites. Hindus classify in Aruti (heard) and Smáti (remembered). These texts discuss theology, philosophy, mythology, Vedicyajna, Yoga, garnomic rituals, and temple building, among other topics. The main scriptures include the Vedas and Upanishads, the Bhagavad Gita, and the Agamas. Sources of authority and eternal truths in his texts play an important role, but there is also a strong Hindu tradition of questioning authority to deepen understanding of these truths and develop tradition. Prominent themes in Hindu beliefs include the four Purusarthas, the goals or objectives of human life, namely the Dharma (ethics/duties), Artha (prosperity/work), Kama (desires/passions) and Moksha (liberation/freedom/salvation); karma (action, intention and consequences), Samsara (rebirth cycle), and the Yogas (paths or practices to reach moksha). Hindu practices include rituals such as bidding (worship) and recitations, meditation, family-oriented rites of passages, annual festivals, and occasional pilgrimages. Some Hindus abandon their social world and material possessions and then get involved in Sannyasa (monastic practices) for life to achieve Moksha. Hinduism prescribes eternal duties, such as honesty, abstaining from boiling living beings (ahimsa), patience, tolerance, self-content, and compassion, among others. The four largest denominations of Hinduism are Vaishnavism, Shaivism, Shakism and Smartism. The three deities: Brahman (the greatest god and his work was creation), Vishnu (he is the protector of the world and the restorer of the moral order (dharma)) and Shiva (Shiva is the destroyer of evil and the transformer; the Supreme being who creates, protects and transforms the Universe).

Hinduism believes in a deity, Brahman, held responsible for creation. Vishnu protects the world and maintains moral order. Dharma and Shiva take responsibility for destroying evil and what drives the change or transformation of the Universe. They include the concept of good and evil. Hinduism suggests the existence of the deity, (Spirit). Hinduism focuses on the way of life known as the eternal tradition or the eternal path. Interpreting this could be that the universe has a truth, an established order, pattern, or laws, which regulate the behavior and performance of its living contents, objects, and creatures, and that it develops and maintains tradition. Hinduism believes that the proper goals of human life follow four main premises, (1) ethics and duties, (2) prosperity and work, (3) desires and passions, and (4) liberation, freedom and salvation. In addition, humans are responsible for their actions, intentions and consequences (karma). Hindus believe in a cycle of rebirth, and in paths or practices to get that liberation, freedom and salvation. A personal god is a deity that relates as a person rather than an impersonal force, such as the Absolute, the All, or the Land of Being.

Comments on Hindu beliefs

We note that deep down Hinduism believes that the universe was created and that a deity protects the world and the moral order. And two other gods or goddesses fight evil and driving the change of the universe. This book suggests that, because it is existence, the universe and the dual being–spirit and matter–all this is the product of a higher intelligence, which has omniscience, omnipresence and omnipotence. This intelligence is energy–the spirit of existence. And the soul, the human ego that is the source of all the sufferings and tribulations of the dual being. But consciousness must guide the unruly ego with the power of the mind of the soul. Mention that conscience, besides its trichotomy-Morality, Will and Wisdom-operates on three relative levels regarding the awareness of reality. Those three levels or planes are (1) the conscience of being and the environment–this is the plane of consciousness for the ego, (2) subconsciousness is the automatic action of certain activities within reach of the conscious ego; and (3) unconscious. The last one is the most distant level of the real awareness and to which the ego has no access. Hinduism believes in eternal duties while this book emphasizes that the ego's freedom of choice is the source of the tribulations of the human dual being. The dual beings are responsible for their thoughts, decisions and actions. As for eternal authority and truths, the author's hypothesis suggests, (1) the universe establishes and maintains the universal order through its eternal and infallible laws, which we cannot alter, changed, or exchanged by any means, unless such alterations, modifications, and/ or changes are an intrinsic part of these laws, (2) there are two main laws governing natural events and sequences, causal and casual. The first handles the sequence of *directional dependency* by which no event occurs if required events do not occur. The second handles events that occur randomly and do not require other previous events to occur. These random events may change the course of causal events; (3) living beings, dual beings, have a spirit (energy) and a body (matter);

(4) the spirit and/or the body are eternal; (5) knowledge is universal, absolute and we cannot create or destroy. Human knowledge is part of the universal knowledge held for a lifetime and returned when the body dies; (6) all conditions; circumstances and events exist if the laws of existence allow them; (7) causal events occur when the conditions and situations support them; (8) human are responsible for all humans activities. Living beings possess full freedom of choice, within the laws of existence, in the universe; (9) a soul, and only one, manages a human body, thoughts and behavior. These regulate the lives of living things.

CHAPTER 10

The Structure of Spirits

Abstract

We observe that existence has its omniscience from which man derives his knowledge. A spirit (soul) and a body (matter) form humans. Spirits have no physical structure. And when spirits enter humans, it becomes soul. The soul-made spirit organizes mind, ego and consciousness. The conscience receives feelings, thought and awareness. The conscience and ego use the functions of the mind. The conscience focuses on morality, wisdom, and willpower; while ego assumes character, conscience and identity. The soul and its components are neither visible nor tangible; belong to the dimension of spirits. However, its elements drive human beings. Without the mind there is no human being; without the ego there is no representation in the material world; and without conscience there is chaos, no wisdom, no willpower, no morality. Without wisdom humans do not apply knowledge. Without conscience, humans cannot see what is good or bad, good or wrong, just or unjust. Humans would be completely selfish animals.

The purpose.

That everything must have a purpose may come from repeated observations that something happens only if something else happened earlier. They must have taken many observations, reasoning and evidence to conclude that life is a chain of events, in which some events happen so other events can happen. For example, it was necessary for our ancestors to plant an apple tree so we now enjoy its fruit. This is the law of interdependent events: Causality. This law is part of absolute knowledge, and the duality of humans also has a definite purpose. The purpose is in omniscience, absolute knowledge, which maintains all knowledge of existence. Omniscience: is the ability to know, object and hold, causes and reasons, why, when and how of all that is within existence; so that there is no additional knowledge outside of omniscience. We understand that what we perceive is only the tip, or the surface, of reality, truth and knowledge–this is the evident reality–while, below the tip and or the surface, there is an encyclopedia of knowledge related to perceived reality–this is latent reality. And our consciousness grows. In this sense, purpose is not a secret; it's just that we humans don't know. In addition, there are random events (random events that occur without relying on previous events) that occur, and they can alter the sequence of causal events–in human terms these are unforeseen. A causal chain change takes place to realign your path without changing your goals. That's the purpose. For example, the river is to flow downhill and fall into the sea; and no matter how many natural or artificial obstacles it finds in its course, it will always fall to the lowest level on its path. The natural phenomenon, such realignment, reveals the intention of the causal chain and the firm desire to achieve its objectives. A classic example is life with its purpose, end or death, in the upper causal chain of a living creature, 'born, live and die'. It doesn't matter what we do while we live; the end is to die and fate is death–when the time comes. This is the inevitability of purpose, a purpose loaded with thoughts, intention is, the decision and actions; why matters seem to disappear? The dual-spirit and material state–living beings, including humans–must have a definite purpose; but what is that?

Perhaps the answer is not in the chain of events of life, but in the history of the achievements of each event. The results of each event can define what must have taken place for it to happen; therefore, we can follow the alignment back to its origin, and from there draw a straight line to future results, at least we would know its path and the trend of that path. By studying the current conditions and circumstances we can see the realignment, if there is one chain built towards its goal. The mystery of life is its way, but if we follow the knowledge back, stopping at each stage, we can see that life is to improve it at every stage, with greater integration of humans with their environment. Living in harmony with the universe is the apparent goal. Is this why spirits travel to earth in life cycles? It may be to put dual beings in harmony of energy and matter: spirit and bodies.

We now understand that the reality hiding in the gloom of consciousness clarifies a little more with new knowledges. The total image exists, and it is there or there it is, but we don't see it, not yet. The duality of humans (spirit and matter) is real. We cannot deny that, even if the mind can see what truth is, spirits and functions are still hiding in the dense fog of human ignorance. Knowledge is to open the mystery of life; so, the more knowledge we have, the closer we get to have the code of the secret of life, and it opens, little by little. We have observed in human history, from the days of the caveman to the present day, that humans have improved considerably as knowledge increases. The improvement comes based on accumulated knowledge, without obstacles. We have also observed that certain human attributes ambition, greed, hatred, avarice, prejudice, envy, and egotism have also grown in the light of growing knowledge. Perhaps the solution is to understand these attributes can destroy human life with the same life-enhancing knowledge. Spirits entering human bodies work to push their egos the right way on each journey to the material dimension until egos behave in harmony with the natural frequencies of universal existence. But they do not intervene or interfere with the ideas, decisions and actions of the ego. Spirits respect the right to free choice and ego thinking. So, the responsibility to improve and walk right is the decision of the human dual being. The impartiality of existence and supreme justice–equal treatment for all–implies there is no preferential treatment for any living being, because applying the laws of existence we cannot violate.

We cannot say that the attributes of AGHAPEE disseminate in all human souls because there are millions of people who have reached higher levels of understanding, realizing that the preservation of humans is through mutually caring for and sharing their resources, including human capital–knowledge, skills and experience–with their fellowmen. If this path as we follow it, perhaps, let us see that the ultimate purpose is to cleanse our minds of selfish desires and attain oneness–the state in which matter cleanses and harmonizes with its spirit into a single individual, exists in both dimensions, spiritual and material, simultaneously.

Is this crazy, like an impossibility? Maybe, but walking on the moon was an impossibility in the past. And then it became a reality. The purpose is to achieve together a harmonious life and not just a few; for humans need other humans to have a sustained life on earth. And as a social, political and economic system, each individual has an equally important duty as the duty of others. So, the goal is to cleanse our inner self of all material preferences and dependencies to achieve the oneness of spirit and matter here on earth.

Living beings: Eternal energy and matter.

We know, the sciences tell us, that matter and energy. We know the dichotomy of a human reveals two components, a spirit and a body. Our spirit is energy, and our body is matter. Therefore, the notion that living beings, humans never die, is true. If we recognize our dual being, spirit and matter, then death is nothing more than a simple separation of the soul from our material form (body). And while our spirit lives on alive when our bodies return to matter, the body continues to live in different forms.

Energy and matter are phases of the same substance, which according to science are present in a finite amount in the universe. However, a thermodynamic law states that when an energy balance, when there is no more energy flow, the ability to produce work, matter and energy will remain latent without encouragement. Then there will be no more movement or changes of state or shape. The universe will be in a floating or latent suspended animation in space, i.e., that's his thermal death. There are no more thoughts or actions, or anything that requires energy exchange or flow thereof. Even if existence can continue, the animated life ends. Therefore, life is in the changes and movements of the energy and matter, phases of the same substance, which according to science are present in a finite amount in the universe. What appears shows its presence, reacts with its surroundings, and then disappears, finally fulfilled. However, the notion that energy and matter cannot implies that both keep their future resuscitation capacity when an event or events restore the energy differential to make their flow happen. We are humans not because we have a material body, but because we have the mind of a spirit capable of being conscious, having feelings and emotions, thinking and creating thoughts, and aware of the internal and external environment. But these functions of the mind are intangible, invisible, spiritual, and do not belong to the material dimension. This quality defines our mental and moral character; and we are living spirits in a material body only for a short time in the material dimension. When we die our body ceases its functions; our spirits return home to the dimension of the spirits. But our spirit communicates with other spirits, and with the environment through the operational functions of the mind. Is there an internal reality beyond our material body?

Duality of human beings.

For example, an article on the definition of 'spirit' published on the Internet includes two important points, *(1) the non-physical part of a person is the site of emotions and character; the soul. 2) the qualities considered definitive or typical elements are in a person's character.*

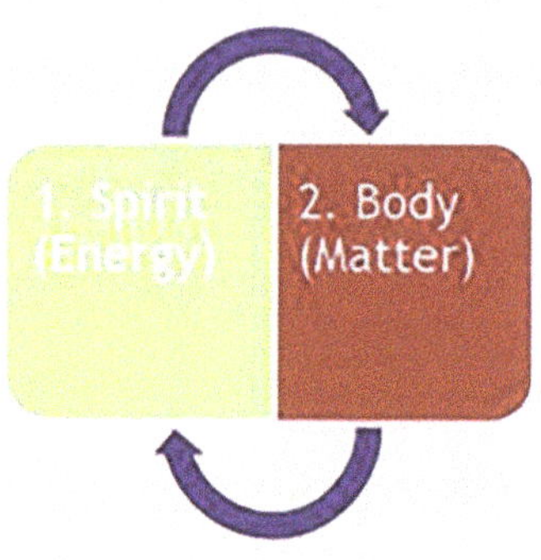

Figure 16: The Dual Being

Accepting a component part of the spirit dimension is a good[72] start. This article defines or adopts that a spirit generates the soul, and the soul has emotions and character. "Bing" defines the character, *the distinctive mental and moral qualities of an individual."* This definition implies that the mind is present in the soul and contains the mental and moral qualities of an individual. From here we confirm the duality of humans. In addition, "Bing" defines the concept of 'moral' as the *"principles of correct and wrong behavior and the goodness or evil of the human character."* In addition, the Merriam-Webster dictionary defines' consciousness' as the sense or awareness of moral goodness or merits of guilt of an individual's "own conduct", *"intentions or character along with a feeling of obligation to do good."* Statements may seem like a contradiction, but there is no contradiction; these two statements imply that consciousness is another element, or independent function, of the soul. "Bing" defines *"The Mind"* as *"the element of a person who allows it to be aware of the world and his experiences, think and feel; the faculty of consciousness and thought."* This says that realizing, thinking, feeling, are functions or attributes of the mind; however, the spirit (the soul) has the seat of *emotions, and the character of a person.*

The conclusion is that humans have two defined components, (1) a spirit that is invisible and intangible; but it is a force that moves the body

---

[72] bing.com (definición de espíritu)

to measurable action, (2) the body is an organic matter with specific biological functions to keep the body alive. In our standard human behavior or performance, we recognize, or will accept, that each human comprises two main components, a soul (energy) and a body (matter). The mind (soul or energy), is the element that thinks, creates thoughts and drives the body (matter) to action in this material dimension. But spirit or mind is an element of spirit dimension. The soul and mind are the same; the mind is the soul or the higher function of the soul.

If we observe all knowledge exists in the universe from before man existed and before man perceived reality and accumulated knowledge. There is no knowledge not included in the universe. And we can conclude that we cannot create or destroy that knowledge because it is part of the material and spiritual dimension; and stays there even after the man disappears. Is there prior knowledge? Maybe not on the initial tabula rasa as a mind. But if we consider that all human knowledge comes from perceived discoveries, conclude that all knowledge existed a priori. The Universe is frugal; there's no excess. Nothing exists in the universe if it doesn't have a function or a role. Existence and the universe depend on the contribution of each party.

The duality of the human exposes that humans comprise two parts: a mind and a body. The dichotomy of the human is not a division of good or evil. The mind is a thinking component, and the body is material with biological functions. The thinking function of the mind, the process of thoughts through brain functions, causes the body to act or react. The body is a tool of the mind.

The mind.

The human has a mind: The question is, is the mind the soul? The theory proposes that a spirit penetrates the fertilized egg, becoming its superior management function: The mind represents the soul itself. Does it integrate with matter? I propose that when a zygote moves into its period of embryonic gestation; the soul structures the functions of the mind in the brain. What is the mind? It's a power generator, feeding on omniscience. Humans do not understand the power of their minds, and evil spends it on trivial material issues, objects or subjects, such as wealth, fame, and power. Where's the mind? Science has not yet determined where it is. The mind is the aura or energy involving the brain and the material body; it is not in one place: the mind is ubiquitous or ubiquitous in a human.

The lack of information or evidence allows us to study and hypothesize likely explanations; and like any other hypothesis, its explanations are subject to revisions and evidence. We accept that we have a soul and mind capable of conceiving realities and unreality. The mind has energy-like powers, and thoughts that come out of it are invisible forces that excite measurable actions. The mind can produce physical, visible work that can measure. It is an energy generator; it produces thoughts that are forces, which push humans into actions; thoughts are driving forces with intensity, direction and purpose. There are no actions if there are no thoughts to support them, except for automatic reflexes, and thoughts implanted in the brain to trigger reactions. And the body (matter) carries out actions according to instructions of thought. This is how the spirit or mind expresses itself, with thoughts, and interacts with the surroundings through the body. Figure 17 shows a hierarchical diagram of the structure of a spirit that shows and distributes the mind in two main functions, The Ego and conscience.

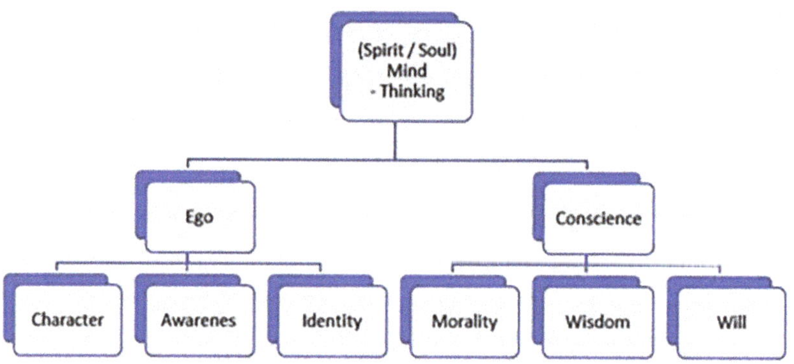

Figure 17: Structure del alma human.

The duality of the human is obvious; it needs both components. We know the body, but do we know the mind or the soul? Maybe so, but we can't explain it, or maybe we're afraid to talk about issues, physical tools and methods. However, if we recognize and accept there is a soul within us, why cannot we openly accept there is a dimension of spirits? A dimension to which all spirits return when our bodies fail. It may not be heaven as many believe, but it must be a dimension where spirits dwell eternally. We cannot display images of the elements in the structure, as shown in Figure 17, because these elements are invisible and intangible. We see the mind and soul in action because we feel and have feelings and emotions. We show their functions through actions and sentimental results.

Table 1: Structure of the Soul.		
Spirit (or Soul) (Non-material part of a human): (1) the non-physical part of a person who is the headquarters of emotions and character; the soul, (2) those qualities considered forming the definitive or typical elements in a person's character. The distinctive mental and moral qualities of an individual. Source: Bing.		
2-Alma (or Spirit): (1) The spiritual or immaterial part of a human or animal being, considered immortal, (2) Energy or emotional or intellectual intensity, especially as revealed in a work of art or an artistic representation. Source: Bing.		
	2.1-Mind: The element of a person who allows him to think, and feel, to know the world and his experience–an attribute that the ego uses regularly; faculty of conscience and thought. Source: Bing.	
		2.1.1-Thought (thought creation process): The ego is the conscious mind, the part of your identity you consider yourself. The part of the mind that mediates between the conscious and the unconscious and is responsible for the evidence of reality and the sense of personal identity. A person's sense of self-esteem or self-importance. Source: Bing.
	2.2-Ego (controlling of reality): The ego is the conscious mind, the part of your identity you consider yourself. The part of the mind that mediates between the conscious and the unconscious and is responsible for the evidence of reality and the sense of personal identity. A person's sense of self-esteem or self-importance. Source: Bing.	
		2.2.1-Character: Distinctive mental and moral qualities of the individual. Source: Bing.
	2.3-Consciousness: The function that judges the principles of correct and wrong behavior, good or bad, just and unjust, questions. Source: Bing.	

	2.3.1-Morality: (1) The sense or awareness of the moral goodness or culpability of one's own conduct, intentions or character with a feeling of obligation to do good or be good. (2) The sense of consciousness of righteous and unjust thoughts and resulting actions. (3) The sense or awareness of the choice of pleasant and or unpleasant. Source: Merriam-Webster Dictionary.
	2.3.2-Force of will: (1) The ability to control oneself and (2) determine the actions of oneself. Control of impulses and actions; determination; Self. Source: Bing.
	2.3.3-Wisdom: The quality of having experience, knowledge and good judgment; the quality of being wise. Source: Bing.

Two main functions support the soul and mind. This is a plausible structural provision according to the definitions of various sources as stated on the table above. The structure that integrates a spirit (energy) with the body (matter) of a human seems complex, but the operational functions of the human are even more complicated because of including the Ego in the soul. The Ego inherits from the mind power of thought, of conscience, freedom of choice, from which he develops a sense of personal identity and self-esteem. The ego assumes the role of oneself. In reality, the ego represents the inner self, although it is not in the material dimension. Depending on the scenario the beginning of the life (environment or habitat), ego builds its personality, tastes, preferences and goals, its formula of victory, for life. It is not inappropriate to have an ego, but what is harmful are the seven human attributes, AGHAPEE, included in the ego. The functions of other souls cannot easily control the ego. [73]

Figure 18: AGHAPEE—Hydra-Ego

---

[73] Foto tomada del internet Google.com/searcj?q=

The hypothesis that spirits penetrate living matter, in a nanosecond when fertilization occurs, requires research and physical evidence. But if we affirm that they create the spirit during the gestation period, then we deny the existence of a spiritual dimension. And we also deny the concept of heaven, and the existence of free spirits roaming around a paradise. The author presumes that there is a global spirit that fills existence and all universal space, and organic beings and inorganic objects and creatures that inherit parts of the attributes of that spirit. The molecules of this spathe create the spirit spread into living beings at the time of fertilization. A consideration of the idea that a spirit housed in a human egg in the millisecond when fertilization occurs follows the understanding and duality of humans: soul and matter. The soul leaves its mental function and configures the mind in a fixed process in the following way, (1) starts a process of compatible integration, (2) starts the creation of the functions of the human mind, (3) establishes the soul and its structure (4) establishes consciousness, (5) configures the structure of the ego according to its DNA, (6) installs the will power, (7) configures the wisdom, and the connections of the neural system. It seems crazy, but all this takes place during embryonic development.

The Soul.

The soul is not a component of the spirit; it is the soul, the nucleus of living beings, like humans. For others, the soul is the emotional and mental part of humans, charged energy–often confused with conscience–that we express in different ways, such as interpretation, writing and recitation of poems, painting, sculpture. Sometimes you're also confused with feelings. In some ways, the soul is a controversial concept as we can see in the abundant information about the soul, and anywhere, for example, the following. In many religious, philosophical and mythological traditions, there is a belief in the incorporeal essence of a living being called a soul. The soul or the psyche (Greek: psyche, psyche, to breathe) are the mental abilities of a living being: reason, character, feeling, consciousness, memory, perception, thought, etc. Depending on the philosophical system, a soul can be mortal or immortal. In Judeo-Christianity, only humans have immortal souls (immortality discussed within Judaism and Plato may have influenced). For example, the Catholic theologian Thomas Aquinas attributed the soul (anima) to all organisms, but argued that only human souls are immortal. Other religions (especially Hinduism and Jainism) argue that all living beings, whether smaller as a bacterium to a very large being like humans and animals, are souls (atma, jiva) and have a physical representative (the body) in the world. The real me is the soul, the body is a mechanism to experience the karmas of that life. Some teach that even non-biological entities (such as rivers and mountains) possess souls. They called this belief animism. Greek philosophers, such as Socrates, Plato, and Aristotle, understood that the soul must have a logical faculty, exercising which was the most divine of human actions. In his defense trial, Socrates even summed up his teaching as nothing more than an exhortation for his Fellow Athens to excel in matters of the psyche, since all bodily property depends on such excellence. [xxxii] Anima mundi is the concept of a world soul that connects all living organisms on planet Earth.[74]

To disambiguate the purpose, the word 'soul' in the previous article deserves some clarification, as follows, the statement, the soul is *the mental capacity of a living being: reason, character, feeling, consciousness, memory, perception, thought, etc.* (1) closely resemble the Definition of Bing/dot/com of spirit given in Table 1, suggesting semantic concatenation of meanings for spirit and soul: Spirit and soul are the same. But the soul is a spirit captured in the human body.

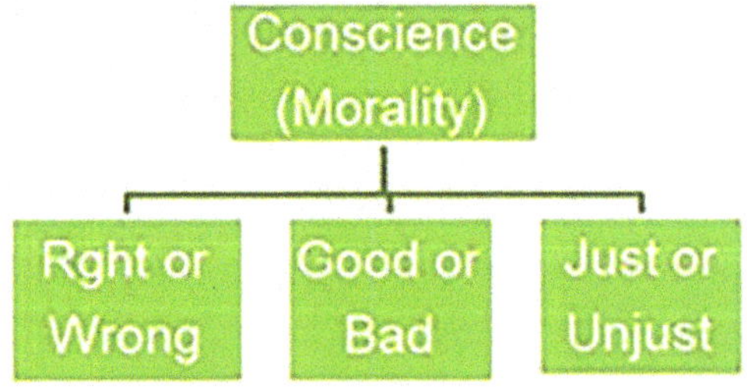

Figure 19: The Soul's Morality.

---

[74] Wikipedia (fuente: https://en.wikipedia.org/wiki/Soul)

The sciences say that energy and matter are two phases of the same substance that no one can create or destroy. Science also states that energy is a force capable of producing work or movement. This evidence is critical and important for explaining the concept of spirit (soul). The author suggests that spirits are forces–invisible and intangible–or a molecule of a total spirit; such as the anima mundi that can generate actions, work, changes and or movements. The definitions given here advocate that spirits in human bodies are immaterial, are part of a universal animation and can communicate with each other.

The author argues that a global spirit (or mundi animates) fills existence, the universe, or is in everything, inorganic and organic, structured in a fundamental scheme configured to adapt to the characteristics of objects and subjects. Its static force and or internal dynamics promotes and maintains the creatures and objects of 'existence: And so, creatures and objects carry their own intelligence that by the object or creature reveals its purposes to the world. We know that spirits are energy; we know that energy exists in matter (at the atomic level); then, spirits are in everything, like the soul of everything, including the universe. The omnipresence of the spirits shows that; and the global spirit is around, in and out of all the inorganic things and organic beings of the universe, including space.

The mind- thinking function.

The mind handles the function of thinking: using the mind to consider or reason about something, using intelligent thought or rational judgment, produces thoughts independent of logical or illogical applications, negative or positive, true or false. [75] This thought function is available for all components of the soul. Thought is an invisible and intangible process, and thoughts come out through words, becoming progressively decisions and actions that materialize through physical activities. Thoughts have a purpose or intent directly related to the motive that drives them, consciously or unconsciously. Ego and consciousness freely use this function, even

---

[75] www.bing.com/search?q=thinking&form.

simultaneously. The thought process includes comparing ideas or thoughts, performing reasoning, analysis and synthesis, conceptual deduction and or induction. We cannot deny this mental process; it's obvious. Ideas or thoughts produce decisions and actions that can be benign or malignant. Those decisions and actions are ego-like. But ego and consciousness are separate and independent components, and wisdom is a function of mind-driven consciousness. All functions, mind, consciousness, ego, wisdom, willpower are part of the soul and work in the dimension of spirits. Conclusively, the soul and mind live in the dimension of spirits. And the ego drives the actions of the body in the material dimension; but humans can't see or touch mental activities. Humans can only see the results in the physical world. Therefore, the ego runs and handles the human.

The Human Ego.

The ego is responsible for the evidence of reality and a sense of personal identity. [76] The ego inherits from the soul functions such as consciousness and awareness, get, freedom of choice and decision, from which he develops his sense of personal identity, self-esteem and self-importance. It assumes the role of inner self and depending on the nature of the initial life scenario [environment or habitat] builds a human personality, tastes, preferences and goals—its winning formula—for life. It identifies the individual presence in the material world to which it is closely linked. From all of the above derives his arrogance. Ego is a module of the soul that operates seven main negative attributes, (see Figure 16), attributes related to physical or material life, as well as fame and wealth. These seven attributes exist in all human beings, but, depending on the willpower and discipline of the individual, education and enculturation—consciousness gains control and power over the attributes of the ego. Psychologists claim that ego handles individual self-image and personal identity, which are combined with the seven attributes mentioned. Freedom of choice makes the ego overbearing, arrogant and indomitable. Maybe spirits

---

[76] www.bing.com/search.

come here to train and tame ego behavior. In the end, consciousness, wisdom, and reasoning build a corral to control ego behavior.

Consciousness

Why do humans have a conscience? Was it the result of a large explosion or the result of an intentional specification of greater intelligence? An explosion cannot or does not produce living beings; particularly living things with emotions, mental, psychological or intelligent attributes. The immediate implication of the above is that the delicate order or arrangement of the human mind is not chaotic, but follows the order of uniqueness of the universe. There's an attempt at purpose! Figure 17 presents an info-graphic structure, a dichotomy, of the soul in a human body: Ego and Consciousness. Human consciousness has three components; one of them is 'Morality'. Table 1 shows a breakdown of consciousness where the primary function is to discern human moral matters, and correct or incorrect deliberation, good or bad, etc., is paramount. Conscience has no power to reduce or suppress selfish thoughts and actions wrong, evil, unjust, and unpleasant; it only points to the moral state of human thoughts and actions.

Looking for answers to the initial question, we find one that says: *Consciousness is a cognitive process that provokes rational emotions and associations based on an individual learned moral philosophy or value system. Consciousness contrasts with emotion or thought provoked because of associations based on immediate sensory perceptions and thoughtful responses, such as the sympathetic responses of the CNS; where CNS is the central nervous system.* This mental process causes emotion and logical deliberation, or judgments, according to people's system of moral criteria. [77] Conscience debates or tests whether thoughts and actions are right or wrong, good or bad, just or unfair, and pleasant or unpleasant. This comparison is most often made based on a set of pre established moral standards, which may be personal or group standards. Moral norms may differ from the global principles of the universe, and may impose it by acculturation, social rules or traditions,

---

[77] en.wikipedia.org/wiki/Conscience

religious habits or beliefs. Perhaps the spirits housed in humans strive to discipline the human ego to conform to the order of established uniqueness of the universe: In the eternal balance or balance there is only creation, not destruction, under the true components of the triangle of existence, love, light and life. The universal order of oneness requires higher moral standards that, conceivably, humans are not yet close to attaining. Perhaps, the traveling spirits are this trying to achieve by occupying human bodies. It is not the spirit or mind that needs correction, domestication or education, but the autocratic ego enabled by free will, freedom of choice, and other rights. The conscience points out what the ego should do, but it has no power to force the ego to abide by what the conscience tells it. Willpower is the function that forces the ego to follow wisdom counsel according to the order of uniqueness.

The function of conscience integrates four main elements, morality, wisdom and willpower; and morality divided in four sub-functions, as shown in Figure 17, discerning (1) what is right or wrong, (2) what is good or bad, (3) what is just and unjust, and (4) what is pleasant or unpleasant. Conscience tests the material and moral realities of thought, actions and consequences. Think of conscience as the place where the mind creates and tests thoughts, and or integrates words and decisions, according to the natural and moral norms imposed by man. Two results come out of the debates; satisfaction and gratitude, guilt and remorse. Conscience automatically tests every thought and acts, storing the result of each judgment in the memories of the brain; however, the ego follows, regardless of the consequent decisions and actions that arise thereafter. A common concept or attitude of selfish individuals is that they must be right or win each time; However, this is not true; the results or consequences of actions are subject to conditions and circumstances beyond the person's control, most of the time.

Can humans ramble about this fundamental question, does conscience work before or after the thoughts, decisions and actions of humans? The mind is open and free. And conscience and ego use the cognitive functions of the mind. Then the conscience and the ego instantly see what the other thinks. People see and judge situations, conditions and circumstances following rules that benefit them most of the time. The final decision of the ego favors its own intention, conveniences and purposes. Conscience works before, during thought, decision and after the actions of human testing situations, conditions and circumstances. Sometimes a person does not feel well thinking or doing something that he knows is wrong, bad or unjust, and they build a remorse on conscience; However, the individual does it any way. Remorse remains in consciousness forever. Does the soul intervene? Well, it does so indirectly, because its mandate is not to interfere, or not intervene in, the thoughts, decisions and actions of humans. The ego, as we mentioned earlier, has the attribute of free will. But conscience acts simultaneously with the ego; and its moral function reviews the thoughts, decisions, and actions of the ego, using its wisdom and the thought function of the mind (Table 1). This is unbelievable! Conscience determines what is right or wrong within the surrounding scenario, individual thoughts, words, and actions, according to standard criteria set by nature, the individual, and or a group of individuals. But these standards are for each individual and are questions of individual preferences, taste and choices. Therefore, what is right or wrong for one may not be for another, but the order of uniqueness of the universe always shows what the right choice is, and what we should take: that is the universal balance. The second sub-function of conscience, morality, deals with determining good or evil, carrying out an analysis and or a synthesis of deeper assessments of what is good or bad, providing truth to the intentions and consequences of each thought, decisions and actions, especially, according to established moral concepts, human, religious, social, etc. Everyone chooses the moral standards that can be good, or bad, for everyone. Again, what is good or bad for one may not be for others. Similarly, the third sub-function of conscience, justice, determines what is just or unjust. This is the mechanics of conscience; perhaps the function results and learning of how to behave according to what conscience calls is the main goal. However, facts imply that a choice can be false because truth is only one, and individual selfish decisions can be wrong, bad, unfair, and or unpleasant.

Conscience is the awareness, knowing of something inside or outside our inner self; consciousness is not an attribute of ego, only. The mind is aware not only of the obvious reality but also of the hidden reality that exists behind the obvious reality. Therefore, the mind has deductive and inductive logic and reasoning attributes; but these functions are intangible and invisible, typical reality of spiritual activities in the unreal dimension. Ego knowledge depends on what the mind learns and or discovers. The ego feeds on the wisdom of conscience and knowledge of the mind. The human perceives reality, but the mind processes the image of reality.

Sometimes awareness or awareness of our own incapacity or deficiencies alters our competitive behavior, making us shy and introspective. But there is a level of consciousness through which an individual can move at will. For example, noticing our dual being, soul and body, frees our minds to consider the concept of spirituality, accepting the presence and behavior of spirits in and around us. Some people know material things, power, fame, and wealth they may not consider their own feelings or feelings, problems, failures, or successes. The path to spiritual life depends on the conscious level of material, problems, objects and or living creatures. For example, the lack of awareness of human spirituality increases awareness of the end of life or death. However, if we realize that that our spirits (energy) and our bodies (matter) we cannot destroy, our fear of death would not be essential.

Moral and mental quality.

We know our feelings, such as emotions, feelings, love. We live with them every minute of our days, even during our dreams, in our dreams. Our conscience also serves as a judge, and or as an evaluator of our mental and moral qualities: Good or bad, right or wrong, just or unjust, so we learn of our position on issues, conditions and circumstances. These mental and moral qualities are intangible and invisible if we don't let them out. The moral element of conscience that weighs on these moral spectrum must have a code of ethics and moral standards by which the conscience makes comparative assessments. Conscience may have no power to make the ego fulfill any moral conclusion about its behavior, but it advises the ego, and conveys its verdict to willpower, a function of conscience. Willpower can then try to convince the ego to behave according to the conclusions of the conscience. The ego decides and acts; the body takes the consequences. This is like the belief in Karma (intention and consequences); but this results from causation. The soul (as a spirit) does not interfere with the decisions and actions of the ego.

Wisdom

Humans know they have a sub-function called wisdom, a component of conscience, but most do not know how to use it, which is just ignoring it. What is wisdom, really? Dictionaries and institutions provide valuable leads on this term, for example. *(1) Wisdom is the ability to discern qualities and internal relationships: insight; in addition, insight is common sense (1.1): the accumulated judgment of philosophical or scientific learning: knowledge.*[78]

The author says that wisdom is the attribute of chasing, seeking and finding the truth of reality; and of unreality, why not? The wisdom function controls nothing, it studies the realities life only according to the laws and logic of the universe; i.e. meditation. Wisdom is non automatic function for any level of consciousness, consciousness and unconsciousness. Wisdom relies on data, information and knowledge stored in the brain, doing an in-depth analysis, looking for the truth of reality for the three sub-functions of conscience. The location of the ego is not essential, but the storage function is critical. Wisdom sees the world and the reality of the universe of what something can or should be: truth and reality is the lining of the channel of a right step of human life.

Good and bad.

Theoretically, the spirit of the universe is a totally 'good' set and everything that happens within it is just and necessary for the existence of it and its order *of oneness*. In addition, good and bad exist simultaneously because if there is good the opposite there is also

---

[78] Fuente: www.merriam-webster.com/dictionary/wisdom dice

at least the possibility of taking the wrong because of the awareness of the existing good. What is good or bad is still so, because the two cannot be good and bad; their spatial relationship is one state or one of the two. The image in a plain mirror reflects these two terms, as if they were identical; they're not identical. These two situations are not equal in size, the set of good is always greater than its subset of bad. Even if existence were and going through a necessary sequence of "quasi-balance", the set of good and subsets of bad movements and changeover. Every occurrence or phenomenon in the universe happens for a reason, and therefore these are always good, even with including random occurrences or phenomena. Good is an element of truth, and evil is part of the false; so, because truth prevails, good does; but maybe in a latent state. If they left alone the universe, its order of uniqueness would be in a stable state forever, absent humans. However, when humans enter a scenario, the scenario turns red-bad because of the free will of the human ego that carries errs and choose the bad.

Good or bad depends on the desires and desires of humans, and what is bad can now be good a few minutes later. In the first case, good or bad thoughts or actions are of the individual character that reflects their attitudes towards the environment, and external objects or subjects. Reciprocally, an environment, object or subject, can be good or bad for an individual, depending on their tastes and preferences. What is good or bad when almost everything follows motives and desires that fit personal egos in this material world? Good or bad results from individual selfish judgment. Good or bad is a matter of convenience and satisfactory characteristics of a problem, subject or object, for an individual; and choosing is opportunistic. And, yes, choosing the good or the bad is a matter of individual judgment. For the universe, good is all that preserves its order of natural harmony, and evil is all that destroys it. Comparison of these terms, good or bad, applies to categories such as social, moral, religious, political, economic. The concept that evil wanders around to tempt humans to have bad thoughts or to do evil deeds is a fold of reality, perhaps a paradigm. The benefit of bad thoughts and actions is a paradigm. Evil does not come from outside, but from within our souls caused by evil egos that can harm and or put others on the path of harm despite judgment and the counsels of conscience. The old phrase, the end justifies the means, includes personal considerations for doing wrongdoing for profit. Is this good? Not because the universal order of oneness exists under the principle of goodness, which must always favor truth.

Right or wrong.

The laws of the universe are infallible, and the simultaneous application of all laws produces a perfect existence, always suitable for the universe and life. If the laws of the universe and existence are perfect, all phenomena that occur are necessary and correct. The etymology of concepts, however, reveals that what is right is not the 'right' label, but the contribution it makes to perfection. "Thesaurus" states that right is all that is right, true, accurate, true and more. This is so, because of the causality and casualty laws that govern the reality of existence. Therefore, if performance of the universe is correct, then what is wrong is the performance of human life; the attitudes and behavior of humans towards and towards the universe. What is right or wrong in material dimensions where almost everything follows the interests and purposes of each who's ego? It's just the attitudes and actions of humans. Doing good or evil is a matter of moral and ethical attitude unless a thought or actions we inadvertently mistake it–"errare humanum est". However, even if what we say and do is a mistake, the wrong thoughts and actions carry the corresponding consequences. An implication jumps from the above; good or evil represents a comparison of a thought or action in relation to a baseline; therefore, above the line is fine and below the line is wrong.

We must define the parameter baseline for the comparison before we compare; and such a definition could be moral or physical. If the line of comparison is moral, then thoughts and actions fall into the spiritual dimension of emotions, feelings, and/or sentiments; whereas, if the line is physical, then the thoughts, actions and consequences belong to the material dimension. Regardless of the comparators, the dividing line is ethical, and is a set of pre-defined standards with which we compare thoughts and actions. The laws of the universe and the laws of man are different; the former is infallible, but the second ones are fallible because "errare humanum est." An example of this view is the laws of nature and the laws of men. We present good or evil within an argument of physical or moral ethics. However, belief or faith does not define them; we improvise good or evil because its nature. However, right or wrong is not a matter of belief, because the very nature of the terms reflects truth, which we cannot bend. The comparison reveals a conditional relativity of the two terms regarding the creation of the human ego provided with free will and little knowledge. We condition good or evil regarding situations and in relation to the intentions and purposes of humans at a specific time, conditions and circumstances. Here, what is right or wrong for one person may be wrong or right for another; and this may also be true for the same individual later on. Therefore, good or absolute evil belongs to the spirit of the universe, but not to the egos of men.

Fair or unfair.

These two terms refer to justice, which is a relational concept; it is typical of the interrelationships between (1) two individuals, (2) an individual and society, (3) the individual and the environment. Fair and unfair are terms not necessarily opposite to each other of good or bad. These terms concern the fairness of mutual treatment between interested parties, including mutual or mutual respect for the rights and attributes of others. The term just or unjust falls within the realm of justice and peaceful coexistence; the ancient saying, "Give to Caesar what is Caesar's and to God what is of God's" means respect for the rights and properties of others in the way they will probably respect our own. What is just or unfair in the material dimensions where almost everything follows perspectives of equity, ambition, selfishness, means and ego methods? This goes for any relationship, social, political and economic; when most people go out to get the deals that favor their purposes and desires. Capitalism is a trading system in which the concept is to obtain or maximize the return with minimal investment; this could mean getting the greatest return on zero investment. There is nothing wrong with this concept; what is wrong is the greed of few who manipulate the free market; Is it free? No, it's not. We manipulate the free market, just as we do with the law of supply and demand.

Pleasant or unpleasant.

We relate these terms to pleasure or membership in the category of giving or providing pleasure or satisfaction, conducive to satisfaction, and or happiness. Among these pleasures are the conditions that please desires, often selfish. While unpleasant is the opposite side of pleasant. What is pleasant or unpleasant in the material dimensions where almost everything follows the emotions and desires, tastes and preferences of egos? Pleasant or unpleasant are, most of the time, outside factors or parts of the immediate environment that might alter the state of an individual's pleasure or satisfaction. The pleasant and unpleasant belong to a category of human preferences, but not necessarily the result of choice. Humans prefer pleasant problems, conditions or situations; However, pleasant atmosphere or situations attract, and unpleasant environment or situations repel. Humans can categorize pleasant situations and or conditions as good and unpleasant situations and conditions as bad.

Morality: Faith and Beliefs.

Morality is conditional and relative; depends on the moral character of each, even if the individual exposes and learns certain moral standards. The ego of the person has the last choice, and such a choice may not meet the ethics and/or standard learned early. That we can only get morality through the teaching of religions is to deny the components of the mind of humans to attain the universal order of oneness by themselves. Human beings can, because it is always an individual decision, to follow or not follow any established moral standard. Therefore, if people do so base on faith and belief, they can also do so because of their free will.

Ethics in religions: *Ethics involves systematizing, defending, and recommending concepts of behavior, correct and wrong. A central aspect of ethics is the good life, the worth living life, or the life satisfying, which many philosophers argue is more important than traditional moral behavior. Most religions have an ethical component, often derived from supposed revelation or supernatural guidance. Some claim that religion is necessary to live ethically. Blackburn states there are those who would say we can only flourish under the umbrella of a strong social order, conceived by the common adherence to a particular religious tradition.* [79]

A thought, word, or act can be harmless or offensive; thoughts, words, and acts have intrinsic consequences. We can categorize morality; and an article on the Internet provides the following.

Morality and religion are the relationship between religious and moral views. Many religions have value frameworks for personal behavior intended to express followers in determining good to evil. These include the Triple Gems of Jainism, Halacha of Judaism, Sharia of Islam, the Canon Law of Catholicism, the Way of eight turns of Buddhism, and Zoroastrian good thoughts, good words and good concept of deeds, among others. We sketched and interpret these frames by various sources such as sacred books, oral and written traditions, and religious leaders. Many of these share principles with frameworks of secular values such as consequentialism, free thought, and utilitarianism. [80]

Human beings need ethical values to think, speak, and act morally correct, and or to behave morally correct. However, each religion proposes its own principle. For example, the quote in the previous article lists four value *frameworks,* which can inform our discourse: *Secular, Consequential, Free Thought and Utilitarianism.*

Secular: *Secular is the state of being separated from religion, or not being only allied with or against any religion. A dichotomy between religion and secular originated in the 18th century European Enlightenment. Since religion and secular are both Western concepts formed under the influence of Christian theology, other cultures do not have words or concepts that resemble or equal them.*

Consequentialism: *Consequentialism is the normative ethical theories that argue that the consequences of conduct are the ultimate basis for any judgment on the accuracy or injustice of that Conduct. Therefore, from a consequential viewpoint, a morally correct act (or*

---

[79] https://en.wikipedia.org/wiki/Ethics_in_religion
[80] https://en.wikipedia.org/wiki/Morality_and_religion

failure to act) is one that will produce a good result, or consequence. The consequentialism is not primarily prescriptive, so the moral value of an action we determine by its potential consequence, not by whether it follows a set of written edicts or laws. [81]

Regulatory Ethics: *Regulatory ethics is the study of ethical action. The branch of philosophical ethics investigates the set of questions that arise when considering how one should act.*

Free thinking: *Free thinking (or free thinking) is when we form a philosophical view that holds that position on truth based on logic, reason and empiricism, rather than authority, tradition, revelation or dogma. Free thinking strongly links to the rejection of traditional systems of social or religious beliefs. The free-thinking cognitive app known as freethinker, and practitioners of free thinking we know as free thinkers.* [82]

Utilitarianism: *Utilitarianism is an ethical theory that states that the best action is that that maximizes utility. We define utility in several ways, usually in terms of a sensitive entity well-being. Jeremy Bentham, the founder of utilitarianism, described utility as all pleasure that results from an action, minus the suffering of anyone involved. Utilitarianism is a version of consequentialism, which states that the consequences of any action are the only standard for good and evil. Unlike other forms of consequentialism, such as selfishness and altruism, utilitarianism considers the interests of all beings equally.*

This book praises religions for moderating and or guiding humans to behave according to ethical canons. The caveat is that their differences over beliefs do not reconcile, though the innate logic of the universe states there is one and only truth of existence. This notion states that only one religion and belief is true, or all religions are not. We all know that the egos of humans behave according to selfish attitudes, tastes and preferences, and perhaps the willpower of the consciousness of humans is not strong enough to discipline their egos. However, for justice for all, this book offers equal opportunities to all beliefs. Secular does not mean enemy of religion or religions; it is just a non-alliance with one or all religions. There are laws of

---

[81] https://en.wikipedia.org/wiki/Consequentialism
[82] https://en.wikipedia.org/wiki/Freethought

the universe, not created or specified by humans, developed and implemented before the universe arose to reality; because otherwise they could not implement or achieve the universal order of oneness. The theory of this book holds that the universal order of oneness is dynamic, it is not a sustained state, by which the universe and all objects and subjects, material and spiritual, are always in balance. The result of thoughts and words does not cause harm to the universe, the immediate environment, or any object and subject in an environment: the entropy of the universe remains unchanged. Is this state sustained? Maybe not, but human interaction with other humans and the environment can establish and maintain offensive relationships. By observing the spiritual structure and organization, one can conclude that the evils of human character or personality are part of the ego's actions, freedom of choice, and its attributes. That idea that we cannot tamed the ego is a paradigm we must break. We're missing, yes, an educational program that has at least three training phases for infants, teens and adults. The goal is to control the monster, AGHAPEE, who lives in the human ego. How to tame the ego is to follow norms of consciousness under disciplines implemented by individual willpower: think about what you say and decide before you act. We can undo any habit, bad or good, that we create or set. They say that winning heaven, Shangri-La, paradise, or Nirvana, through moral ethics and religion, is a spiritual yearning that secular could call a paradigm. We have read the opinions of the religions of the higher world; all these beliefs have deep moral objectives despite their philosophical controversies. (1) Catholics follow the ten commandments of Moses, and later the teachings of Jesus Christ. (2) Islam provides normative teachings and sunnah–a way of life based on the Mahanese interpretations of the Koran–and the hadeeth, which is the embodiment of the Sunnah tradition, the words and actions of the Prophet and his family, the family of the house, the twelve political and spiritual successors of Muhammad in the twelve branches of Shia Islam, and the prophet's daughter, Fatima). (3) Judaism does not accept Jesus as the Messiah, but it has its code of ethics common to all these meanings. [83] the Torah consists of the origin of the Jewish brotherhood: its call to God, its trials and tribulations, and its covenant with its God, which involves following a way of life embodied in a set of moral and religious obligations and civil laws: *Halakha (Hebrew: the Way of Walking), the collective body of Jewish religious laws... and ordinances that have evolved since biblical times to regulate religious observance and the daily lives and behavior of the Jewish people.* (4) Buddhists believe in a path of eight folds: wisdom, ethics, and mental discipline. Deep down, these religions care about good, and human moral behavior.

Volition and willpower.

The author proposes willpower. What is volition or willpower? Is it sub function of our conscience? I think so. Willpower is the conscious application of the purpose of disciplining our ego to think, decide and act in the preservation and improvement of the universal order of oneness. All that is right, good, fair and pleasant for oneself is for everyone else, simultaneously. We know that we have volition in ego and willpower in consciousness. Willpower is a superior function of consciousness. It's a control for ego behavior. The freedom of choice at will, free will, is a mystical function of the human that is born when the soul structures the mind. Free will is not willpower, but freedom of choice at the will of the ego, volition. The change of man must be genuine and by his free will or will. Let's read a definition on the Internet broken down into various attributes or sub functions, which it says. The ego is the third component of the soul, but willpower is *self-control, an aspect of inhibitory control, is the ability to regulate emotions, thoughts and behavior in the face of temptations and impulses. As an executive function, self-control is a cognitive process necessary to regulate one's (ego) behavior to achieve specific goals.* But willpower is a function of conscience, not ego; and by this force the ego can change its attitudes and behavior. [84] *Volition is the cognitive process by which an individual decides and commits to a*

---

[83] https://en.wikipedia.org/wiki/Jewish_ethics
[84] en.wikipedia.org/wiki/Willpower

course of action. We define it as a purposeful effort and is one of the main human psychological functions. Others include affection, motivation and cognition (or thought). We can apply volitional processes consciously, and we can automatically make positive habits. Will is that faculty of mind that selects, the now of decision, the strongest desire among the desires present. The will does not refer to any desire, but to the mechanism for choosing between desires. Within philosophy will is important as one of the distinct parts of the mind—along with reason and understanding. We consider it fundamental in ethics because of its role in enabling deliberate action. One of the recurring questions discussed in Western philosophical tradition is that of free will—the related notion, but more general of destiny—that asks how will can be free if a person's actions' natural or divine causes determine them. We can directly relate it to discussions about freedom itself and the problem of evil.

I suggest that the will may be the tool the ego uses regularly in its decisions and actions.

The power of your will.

What is willpower? [85] Willpower is the human determination to think, decide and do the right thing, well, just and pleasant, always, even if its consequences can cause suffering in the individual. Also, it's a popular wisdom term, but it has a lot of power in our culture and psyche. People with will power are strong, competent and in control. But I consider people who are of weak behavior are devoid of willpower. We can associate problems of all kinds (about eating, promiscuous sex, debt, poor school performance, or work) with a lack of willpower. But what makes us fail? Kirsten Weir, a psychologist and researcher, has identified two characteristics that seem to affect the behaviors we would attribute to willpower: intelligence and self-control. Self-control is a quality that can develop and run out. The same approach and energy needed to exhibit self-control (resist impulses) that we can associate with decision-making. He refers to Roy Baumeister's work that found that after deciding, people exhibit less self-control and resort to simpler solutions to a problem. The phenomenon, called decision fatigue (Baumeister calls

---

[85] https://motivationandchange.com/what-is-willpower

this an ego exhaustion), can wreak havoc on our ability to make decisions that help us towards our goals. They point out that we can alter intelligence. logic, also point out that willpower (or the ability to resist impulses) is used to control other things like emotional reactivity and task performance. Why do we care about this? The author argues that discipline and/or the will to power is a human attitude that we can develop at a high level of self-control, which can suppress consciousness, pain, suffering, fears and more. This high self-control depends on knowledge, logic, and exact reasoning. This it's the point; the best way to tame the ego is to suppress material consciousness using willpower.

Emotions

As for the concept of spirits, emotions are reactions to conditions, circumstances and or situations that alter the comfortable psychological state of each person's being. Emotional outbursts are spiritual manifestations (it has nothing to do with the body). The causes of emotions, as we know, can be several; such as (1) threats and fears, (2) disgust and controversy, (3) love and hatred, (4) doubts and/or ignorance of situations. Most of the time these outbursts are perceptions of the ego of external situations. Sometimes bursts are the result or reactions to fair or unjust damage and undeserved damage from external sources. Perhaps we can better handled emotions with wise considerations absent from personal pride. Current emotion definitions can provide support for the above; however, an example may lead the reader to his own research. [86]

Feelings

Are they sentimental emotions or spiritual (psychological) attitudes? Besides, is this question critically relevant? Most scholars attest that feelings are mental reactions or emotional positions of affinity, acceptance, or rejection, or something. Feeling is a thought and feeling expressed in words and actions. [87] A feeling is a spiritual

---

[86] www.dictionary.com/browse/emotions

[87] www.dictionary.com/browse/sentiments?s=t

touch, like an emotion that comes through an unreasoned perceptual reaction. Several dictionaries define feelings, but all are similar, for example, *"a complex combination of feelings and opinions as the basis for action or judgment; general emotional attitude: the feeling of romantic love; a touch, opinion, judgment..."* Feelings are emotions, invisible and intangible, controlled by the mind; they are spiritual.

Can humans control their feelings? Definitely yes; humans have the ability and wisdom to reason, meditate, and find clarity in their feelings. Feelings are within the spiritual control of the mind.[88]

Love

Love is the most popular of all emotions and feelings; but it's a mystery of existence. [89] Its definition depends on the human perspective. We can find samples of this view on the Internet. [90] Love is not a mere emotion or feeling, it is a solid affection of integrated devotion with absolute mercy and total transparency; it always shows its six attributes, solidity, affection, integrity, devotion, mercy, and transparency. All humans possess these loving and spiritual attributes–they are not material. When two people meet, they automatically test the compatibility of their six attributes–consciously or unconsciously. And if the comparison of their attributes is (or almost is) perfect, they reach the highest sentimental attraction. This is the condition of the soul mates. But, although the love of existence is general, absolute, and infinite love in living beings is proper and limited. It is proper because we configure it by each individual's feelings and limited by the free will of the ego.

---

[88] www.yourdictionary.com/sentiment
[89] El autor, Misterios: Amor, Luz y Vida.
[90] www.theguardian.com/commentisfree

CHAPTER 11

Interaction with spirits

Abstract

There are certain phenomena that we cannot explain thoroughly with material or physical tools and methods. Spiritual sensations and visions, for example. It is not wise to deny an event because it cannot be physically tested without creating a paradigm. The fact that we do not understand a problem, or an issue, does not give us the right to reject the legitimacy of its premises. The fact that a vision cannot be proven does not deny the vision, nor does it deny its validity. Existence and the possibility of being true exists, even if it is an ideological reason. How can you know if you pamper? We forget or ignore that we carry a soul within the body. We think we know the body and they don't know the soul. But we can show that we have a mind, an ego, and a conscience in our bodies, permanently, during our lives. The spirit that enters every human body and becomes a human spirit—its soul. And this soul lives in contact with other souls and free spirits through the mind. Human beings are not material, they are dual and totally spiritual beings— a human spirit.

Interaction with spirits.

The author suggests there are actually no contacts with spirits. Since the soul is a part of the global spirit, it is in direct and continuous contact with it and all free spirits, part of the global spirit.

Consider–It is unwise to keep our experiential learning captive and or limited to material reality. Experience is not a daily activity, it is an attribute and right that we get with knowledge, including visions or spiritual interaction. Perception is a human activity, the action of observing, studying, concluding with issuing individual opinions on any observed event. And conception is an innate faculty. Being right or wrong is not the essence of the initial observation of an event; the scrutiny and evidence of reality carried out approves or rejects the validity of an observation. The more observations we report, the clearer the picture of reality will be, understanding there are certain phenomena we cannot explain thoroughly with material or physical tools and methods. But re-observations improves accuracy and creates experience. Therefore, it is not for the wise to deny an event by stating that it cannot be physically proven; this betrays existence and the possibility of its truth, even if the truth may be logical or logical. In the universe, problems, beings and objects, logical or ideological, are equally accepted. Humans are so involved in physical reality they reject anything that does not conform to the facts. It is not appropriate to laugh or mock the experience of spiritual encounters. If a person says, *"I saw a person walking in front of me carrying a child in his arms, singing or crying, dressed in a transparent, bright, white dress, you can see through it, and I could see a clear picture of someone I knew who was now dead."* That one does not understand a problem, or an issue does not give the right to reject its legitimacy. There is nothing wrong with that statement; it's a statement of something that happened, even though we can't test it with physical methods or using physical tools. However, that such a vision we cannot prove does not deny the vision, nor does it deny its validity. We accept that knowledge a human gains initially comes through perception and then new knowledge comes through the study of the cause for effect or analysis and synthesis carried out with a careful procedure. There is no difference between individual processes and scientific experiments, except that their experiments follow orderly and repeatable procedures. But most of what we do begins with assumptions.

Interactions

Whether we know contacts with spirits, humans tell stories of having experienced encounters with spirits in different ways. [91] No one takes these stories seriously, and sometimes they make fun of such a possibility. We forget whether we know contacts with spirits or ignore that we, humans, comprise two elements, a soul and a material body. We can know our material part (our body) well, but we do not understand our spiritual component. Religions preach and speak of sanctified spirits; Catholics speak of a soul Spirit, Jesus, Mary, many saints and souls in one place, all as spirits. However, when we turn to our own spirit and the spirit of others, we stop believing in spirits. Sometimes we associate spirits with the dead and think they are evil spirits that can harm us or kill us; But that's not true. Spirits are invisible and intangible and live in the spiritual dimension where all spirits are. They cannot hold subjects or material objects, such as humans. In our physical world we can show we have a spirit within our bodies, or at least associated and integrated with our material body, permanently during our physical life. Although we can be skeptical of spirits, we talk about protective angels, and whether they exist is not the point. What we think or say when we are in difficult situations–something we don't ask for or ask for–comes or happens out of nowhere to help us.

Presence and activities of spirits.

There may be several signs that reveal the activities of the spirits, but we are not sure that the signs are theirs. If we may not challenge these warnings, but if we are scientific minds–who need

---

[91] http://www.charmingelements.com/spiritual-encounters

physical evidence to assert truthfulness; we subject these warnings to reality tests. Maybe an interaction with a spirit is nothing more than a product of the mind. We have studied that the spirit of existence fills all and the visible and tangible universe, for that global spirit is ubiquitous; It is in everything, space, energy and matter. So, the spirit turned into a soul in a human body–and therefore in all living beings–is part of that global spirit of existence. If ours are parts of the global spirit, we directly connect with the global spirit. We have said that the soul and mind, thought and feelings are spiritual. So, we are spirits and what we think and feel is spiritual. We have also seen that only the body and the actions of the body are of a material or physical nature. The communication between two people, you and I, for example, is from mind to mind and spiritual origin. The caveat is that spiritual expression translates into material or physical sound in the vocal cords producing the words or meaning of spiritual thought. In reality, we have no contacts with any spirit because we are part of the global spirit, to which other molecules of that spirit belong. We can conclude that all human activities are of spiritual origin because we are spirits acting within a material body. We have seen that the soul within us is a limited spirit–we have no omnipresence, omniscience, or omnipotence. From this viewpoint, physical reality challenges our egos, causing tribulations or problems that the ego cannot solve. Then the soul sends signals asking for help from the global spirit. Then a nearby spiritual molecule comes to help the anguished soul. These are the supposed contacts with spirits, which can be perceptible and imperceptible. The author advises you to read the book, *"16 Signs, a Ghost or Spirit Visits You"* (translation of the title by the author), by Taanas Chubb. [92] Chubb explains there are ghosts and spirits. We know that they are normally invisible and intangible, and under these conditions ghosts and or spirits cannot grasp or sustain matter; and so, we imply it that ghosts and spirits are just energy. Maybe the energy is the feeling you feel when someone is watching you. Chubb claims that ghosts and spirits are different

---

[92] 16 Signs a Ghost or Spirit is Paying You a Visit by Tanaas Chubb, published in Foreverconscious.com

beings, the former can be hostile and the second can be peaceful and quiet. The energy of spirits can explain why doors or cabinets someone is; lights and electronic devices turn on and off.

Bing defines ghosts as *"an appearance of a dead person believed to appear or manifest to the living, usually as a nebulous image."* Chubb recognizes that ghost and spirits are different energy and defines them as, usually, *"spirits make you feel calm, comforted and safe. They often appear in dreams or you can see them as an apparition. Either way, the feeling surrounding a spirit is often quiet. Ghosts often leave you feeling creepy and can sometimes make you feel uncomfortable. They can come as an apparition, shadow, or ectoplasm fog. They can also attach to an object or a living person."*

Regardless of the attitudes and behavior of the spirits, spirits belong to a dimension of spirits, and because of the constituent nature, they attach through matter, are invisible and intangible, and cannot take hold and or carry material objects or living beings. Despite the above, ghosts (if they exist) or spirits can be the energy of the universe and cannot be a different energy from the one that fills the universe; hold and ghosts (assuming they exist) and spirits can be in different states of willingness to act or react differently. Anyway, we have said there is no more energy than that which fills the space of existence. So, the energy of spirits is the same as of existence and the universe–the global spirit–and they cannot be harmful, because of the definition of the supreme spirit.

Humans cannot doubt their spiritual nature based on physical evidence and their souls and minds, and their activities in the material dimension. The nature of humans confirms their duality; humans are beings that integrate a spirit (energy) and a body (matter). But a mind manages and controls the human body, its thoughts, sensory perceptions and physical actions. Because of their spirit, humans are in constant contact with other spirits; the thoughts, decisions and actions of humans are spiritual. We have occasional contacts with free spirits, and their apparitions may be intentional or unintentional. Humans live in contact with their soul (a spirit) twenty-four hours, seven days a week.

Signs and categories.

We can classify the contacts of spirits with dual beings into five specific types depending on their nature or roots, for example:

Feelings.–Spirits appear as energy that comes from an external source. Humans feel it.

Feelings.–Spirits manifest the self as energy, stimulate the mind and incite an action–such as love, fear, despair. The signals emitted by our minds and captured by protecting spirits are part of this group.

Apparitions.–Spirits appear for no specific reason, perhaps to communicate something–to protect human life–or to give a warning or give a message or to protect the human dual being.

Revelations.–Response of spirits to mental and psychological requests as solutions to a problem.

Invocations.–Spirit sought by a person or a medium; prayers and petitions.

These five sources are practically spiritual relationships of humans. There are other forms of direct contacts between humans and spirits, which are ingenious procedures. Human minds start processes that expect spiritual knowledge, such as inspiration or imagination. The author's theory is that knowledge of the universe belongs to omniscience and we cannot create or destroy it. Humans borrow some of this absolute knowledge and use it in their material life. And when humans think, they open up and enter the omniscience of existence. They find or use knowledge and are in contact with the global spirit; they read gnosis in the libraries of absolute knowledge and keep copies in their minds. Human knowledge remains in the universe's omniscience. Human beings do not produce new knowledge, they only discover and apply what they learn. When humans get new ideas beyond their cognitive level, it is when humans find knowledge in omniscience.

Imagination

Humans operate with the knowledge accumulated to a point in their lives and combining diverse knowledge produces ideas within the limits of accumulated knowledge. However, when we imagine a new gnosis that includes or combines knowledge not yet learned, new knowledge comes from absolute knowledge. Imagination takes advantage of the omniscience of the universe to get new gnosis. The results of imagination can be logical or illogical, real or unreal, as something that cannot pass the tests of reality, including fantasies or delusions. Some people say that imagining is the ability to form new *"ideas, or images, or concepts of external objects that are not present to the senses."*[93] I say that imagining is a way of working within the content of the omniscience of existence.

Inspiration

They limit human knowledge to the total knowledge learned at a time. This limited knowledge is a constraint and triggers various emotions, such as longing, nostalgia, sigh, and aspiration. Humans bring these emotions to their dreams and perhaps dream of answers to their desires. They walk like zombies thinking of a solution to their problems. Then, one day, a light comes to your mind and you see the answer or solution you were looking for. Humans call this phenomenon an inspiration. If the solution is not perfect, we repeat the cycle in anticipation of a new inspiration. There are scientists who claim that their work is or was an inspiration, or enlightenment, unexpected from a higher knowledge. There are people who believe that inspiration is a divine guide or influence exerted directly on a human mind or soul. The emotion of the mind or emotions at a high level of feeling or activity: A person or thing that moves the intellect or emotions or provokes action or invention, and [94]or the following, being mentally stimulated to do or feel something, especially to do something creative. [95] Regardless of the way we make a contact, the process is spiritual, dealing with intangible and invisible beings,

---

93 https://www.bing.com/search?q=Imagination&form
94 www.thefreedictionary.com/inspiration
95 https://www.bing.com/search?q=inspiration&form

carrying nothing material. Perhaps humans should cultivate a formal relationship with their counterparts, just as they do with their minds.

A life with your soul.

Humans live with a spirit within them. Your mind is spiritual, invisible, and intangible–and omnipresent–; it's a generator of thoughts. Consciousness generates feelings, emotions, etc. the egos of humans think of the spiritual dimension, the brain processes thoughts in commandments of actions, and the·body decides of its ego in the physical dimension. Actually, these are the actions of the soul in the material dimension. Every human does that; therefore, communication between humans is spiritual, not physical. And although humans produce words (the translation of spiritual thoughts) through vocal cords, resonators and articulators (physical devices of the human body), while we command actions from a spirit: the human soul.

The producer says goodbye.
And so it is, my reader friend, the end has come, only you and I remain in the theater in your mind, after the play is over. I thank you for staying with me through these explanations and final notes of my book. I'm sure it was a rewarding reading. I congratulate the author for lending me his mind to write my book; but I leave all the credit to him, as he signs the copyright of this book. Maybe we'll meet some other time in any of the dimensions I mentioned; or I could return to one of your future descendants.

For now, I say, goodbye.

The author.

ENDNOTES

· · · · · · · · ● ● ● ● ● ● ● ● ● · · · · ·

[i]   Death: Death is the end of the material life of an object or living creature. Death is the destiny of life, but not of existence. Existence regulates the same event that occurs in life, according to the conditions and circumstances of the moment. This is true regardless of the causes of death, by accident or natural cause. Death is only the end of a life cycle for humans, the short stage, but not of the material life itself. In other words, death is only the end of that stage, not the end of existence, it is eternal. For example, the dynamic life of the universe ends with its thermal death, the state where there is no more energy exchange. Existence is eternal; will continue forever, even though the inert universe, and all matter in it, cannot move or change any more. What humans lose is just the material or physical appearance.

[ii]   Spirits are energy: Yes, spirits (energy), invisible, intangible, they have no weight or volume; it is safe to conclude that there is no matter in the spiritual dimension, only energy. In addition, because the universe includes all available space, each and every dimension is contained within the same space.

[iii]   Spiritual life: Our life is spiritual, not material: it is eternal. If you think about it. Well, our lives are about biological performance and mental functions. Human biological performance includes nutrition and protection, which, in fact, requires no more than what is needed to stay healthy during the aging process: our lives progress to death. The rest of the things, the attitudes, are just selfish and superfluous whims, which add nothing to the process of life. The real person–individual character–is represented by our mind, ego and soul, who work with or through spiritual functions.

[iv]   Life Cycles: There is one, and only one, repeatable cycle of life, birth, life, death; within this cycle there are many other sub cycles, but all are designed to sustain life for all lives, organic and inorganic. These cycles carry interesting mysteries that humans do not understand yet; for example, the integration of a spirit with the human body sometime before birth and the separation of that spirit into death. In addition, there are other aspects of the duality of the function of a human being (spirit and matter) between the two extremes, the beginning and the end, or birth and death. This book refers to this life cycle: It's a simple cycle. If we accept that there is a spirit within every person,

intangible and invisible, and if we think that this spirit goes somewhere after our body dies, then we accept duality, spirit and matter. Moreover, if we consider that the spirit is energy, and the human body is matter, then the spirit and the body cannot be created or destroyed. Our spirits live forever in eternal cycles of life.

v   Contacts with spirits: There are sensitive people, who act as mediums, claiming that they can see, hear, contact or talk to the spirits. Science has not confirmed any of the experiments conducted; however, we cannot emphatically conclude that contact with spirits, of any kind, is impossible. Maybe we haven't found consistent channels or ways to get in touch.

vi   Spirit Dimension: There is certainly no definite place where the spirit comes or goes, but there is evidence that living creatures are primarily spiritual. There are religious beliefs that claim to know where that place is; they all have a similar concept. For example, there is an opinion that spirits are created as a blank slate and reach the material dimension to perfect themselves. May the author ask what problems the spirits need to perfect when they come to earth? Why are spirits not perfect and pure in their creation? What kind of perfection do you seek when human life is far from perfect? Obviously, according to the definition of an absolute benevolent spirit in addition to the fact that matter does not create spirits, it is appropriate to accept that all spirits are perfect molecules of the global spirit, which inherit attributes of the global spirit. Spirits are like water droplets extracted from an ocean; retain all the characteristics of ocean water, and when these droplets return to the ocean, they mix again with the rest of the ocean water, disappearing. If we regard spirits as drops of ocean water (all spirit), we would realize that every spirit in the bodies of human beings returns to the infinite ocean of the great spirit, mingling with it, disappearing. The obvious question is how can you find a drop of water in that spiritual ocean after it blends? The hypothesis is that all the pieces of the Great Spirit also have access to their omniscience, and therefore communicates with the whole spirit, as it also communicates with individual cells. What we do not know, however, or that we have not cleared, are the means and/or methods that we must use to regularly connect our spirit with other spirits. One thing is perfectly clear; However, there are no spirits that are not part of the whole spirit.

vi   If spirits have omniscience, why is the mind of human beings ignorant? Is it true that spirits have full access to the omniscience of existence? Moreover, if spirits plan their stay on earth in a human body, why is it that man misbehaves? Any written theory about the soul (spirit), existence and behavior must answer all basic questions.

viii   Man's duality: Spirits contact us. If so, why not? This book theorizes that man's duality is made of a spirit and a body–energy and matter. It is a paradigm, God inspired his own spirit in man, yes or no. Our theory is that a spirit, a molecule of the global spirit and lodges itself in a zygote, integrating a dual human being. This spirit transforms into a soul and is housed in the zygote; the soul expands in mind, ego and conscience. The ego is divided into (1) character, (2) conscience, and (3) identity; while Conscience is divided into (1) morality, (2) wisdom, and (3) willpower," (see Figure 15: structure of the human soul, in). We know that Conscience handles (by definition) emotions, fears, feelings, etc. as part of the soul. One of the greatest beliefs is in the context of the Bible that says, "the human spirit is the breath of God and was breathed in man at the beginning of God's creation: "Then the Lord God formed a man from the dust of the earth and breathed into his nostrils the breath of life, and man became a living being"(Genesis 2:7). It is the human spirit that gives us self-awareness and other remarkable, but limited, "like God". The human spirit includes our intellect, emotions, fears, passions and creativity. It is this spirit that gives us the unique capacity to understand and understand (Job 32:8, 18). The words spirit and encouragement are translations of the Hebrew word neshamah and the Greek word pneuma. The words mean "strong wind, explosion or inspiration." Neshamah is the source of life that vitalizes humanity (Job 33:4). It is the intangible and unpublished human spirit that governs man's mental and emotional existence. The Apostle Paul said, "Who of men knows the thoughts of a man except the spirit of man within him?" (1 Corinthians 2:11). When he dies, the "spirit returns to God who gave it. (Ecclesiastes 12:7; see also Job 34:14-15; Psalm 104:29-30). Of course, everything said in this final note must be checked; but his meaning is consistent with the author's theory..

ix   Ego Purification: The general belief in the world is that spirits need improvement and thus reach this material dimension to purge their imperfections. In fact, this is incompatible with the definition of a spirit from a pure spirit. It seems that imperfections come from the fusion of a pure spirit with the function of an imperfect mind, the Ego, created in matter (the human brain): A controversial ego, the component of a mind, makes conflicts behave capriciously with the freedom of choice that is given to him.

x   Soul separation process: A functional separation is a multi-step process of body and spirit, having a set time in hours to complete: During this process, the body releases its spirit following an established process according to rigor body mortis. According to the sciences, this process takes approximately 36 hours. During this time the body becomes stiff in the first 12 hours and then becomes flaccid again for another 12 hours, and hardens in rigor mortis at the end of the next 12 hours. By the end of this time, the body has released all the energy stored in it. The spirit gathers all this energy, the energy of the body, before leaving, leaving behind no part of it. Now, you can understand that spirits should wait for that final moment. During these many hours the spirit remains attached to the body and can continue its interactions with the material dimension. Certain mental images or functional routines may remain in the mind, which a spirit carries with it.

xi Energy Release: The disconnection process refers to a sequence of steps following death, separating energy (the spirit) from organs, flesh, and brain from the body. Obviously, each cell requires energy for its function, energy that must sometimes be released before the rigor mortis is put in. It takes about thirty-six hours.

xii Separation model: The complex way a spirit works through the mind to handle a body requires a step-by-step separation process to exit the body. Figure 4 shows a model of this process. The spirit goes through fixed steps to get its energy from the cells of the body, organs and brain before separation. The ego, the consciousness and the mind, and are the last elements, in that order, to separate from the body. Sometimes consciousness takes longer to close because there may be controversial and unresolved issues.

xiii Eternal Existence: Humans who know a person remember it by the last image and its mentality. This image does not age, but it is just an image of a human being who was once alive, not the real deceased spirit. The deeper the memory of a person in another person's mind is, the closer the connection to the person is. That connection can reach a point of being able to read the thought of the deceased person just by looking that person's eyes in an image. The more you remember what a person was like in life, what that person would say about a problem or how we should do things the more you connect with the person's way of thinking and acting. It is possible, therefore, that you can think and do exactly what she or he thought and did. This way that person would be talking to you through a mental connection.

xiv Awareness: Humans are not fully aware of the immediate surrounding inner self, and outside its body. The image of themselves and or there near environment is limited by the level of knowledge at current time, and their conscious reasoning capabilities. The lack of knowledge–ignorance–causes fears, apprehensions, anxieties or panic attacks. This is the fear of the known. There is nothing like that for the spirits; their omniscience empowers them to know everything in the past, present, and the future. Their mind is always calm and peaceful unlike the mind of a soul living in a human body. Thus, the perceptions and or sensations you experience here in this theater may disturb your mind; but you are fine with us.

xv Limitations of human beings: It is true that human beings have limited minds compared to omniscience, omnipresence, omnipotence, and absolute love. The structure of human minds includes an Ego with free will, free choice (see table in the text of this book). We have seen, however, that humans can observe and learn by increasing their awareness of reality and, improving from generation to generation. It is a superior creature created with power of thought, feelings and emotions, which is perhaps too much for humans to handle by themselves. The improvement of behavior over thousands of years shows that the purpose of human beings is to improve or gain a final understanding of rational life, until the material life of human beings resembles a spiritual life, at that time the unity of spirit and matter, can live in both dimensions, simultaneously. The key to mystery, perhaps, is not the ability to transport, telepathy or telekinesis; however, perhaps the key is to gain enough knowledge to fully understand the intentions of human thoughts and the purpose of actions. If this skill is achieved, we can predict the future, which could be the way to travel back in time. Perhaps another key is to accumulate enough knowledge to be able to see the reality of the universe in all its splendor, and in doing so, begin to learn the reasons for spiritual behavior.

xvi   Structure and laws: The existence defined laws, rules, and specifications to regulate the behavior of the universe–the laws of chemistry, physics, quantum mechanics, combinations and permutations, probabilities, etc. The knowledge we have accumulated in our minds until now is a small part of what exists in the universe since before humans appeared on earth. There is no knowledge outside the absolute knowledge of the universe, and there is no more knowledge outside infinite space. Moreover, knowledge cannot be created or destroyed; because it's part of existence. But we can probably say, at this time, that the universe contains a defined knowledge corresponding to the visible and tangible portion of existence, as well as the invisible and intangible portion. This assumption is not far-fetched, since, from this day on, human beings have gained knowledge, which is neither visible nor tangible. For example, the laws of mathematics, physics, chemistry, astrophysics, quantum mechanics, all of which are invisible and intangible in a material sense, is knowledge.

xvii   Uniqueness: Unity is the concept of merging the spirit and the material body into a single being, considering that the spirit and dimensions of the body coexist in a single scenario. It is possible, perhaps it is, that human beings prepare and condition their being to communicate freely with other spirits, as well as with the global spirit. It is a fact that the mind (soul), ego, consciousness, etc., are spiritual; and for this reason, we already communicate in spiritual terms (mind to mind) through words. So, the removal of words would allow direct switching between souls, in a telepathic form. The use of communication tools and methods are in the human bodies, the rest, the processes of communication are in the mind; and the thoughts are spiritual. Obviously, our mind, being spiritual, cannot grasp or manage matter; therefore, it needs the body to work and or handle material objects and living creatures. Perhaps the goal is not to become spirits that have the three attributes, omnipresence, omniscience, and omnipotence, but rather the dream of being one in unity.

xviii   Meaningless bodies: The expression, "a human body has no mind of its own" means that the body itself or its brain has no thought or attribute to think or reasoning ability. The mind performs these functions, but the mind is invisible, intangible; it's spiritual.

xix   Existence of spirits: The human consciousness that we have mind, soul, consciousness, ego, etc., is evidence that we recognize the existence of a spirit within our inner self. These are elements of the spirit and as such are not materials. However, we realize that the mind produces thoughts and directs the body to perform actions in the physical world.

xx   The spirit of the universe. – This book considers a hypothesis that spirits in a human body are not created at the time their formation, but that spirits in a human being are part of the spirit of the universe that penetrate and are housed in a zygote in it urged when the egg is fertilized. The theory is that the spirit (energy) of existence is ubiquitous; that is, it must be in and out of everything. Therefore, nothing can be created to occupy space if it does not contain molecule of the global spirit. Consequently, the spirit automatically penetrates and lodges in the nascent body at the same instant of the fusion of a sperm and an egg.

xxi   Human beings: Source: https://www.thebump.com/a/difference-between-embryo-and-fetus. According to James A. O'Brien, MD, medical director of obstetrics for inpatients at Rhode Island Women & Infants Hospital. Developing pregnancy according to the experience of obstetricians is "the formative phase of an embryo until it becomes a fetus, about eight to ten weeks," after conception." During the embryonic period, cells begin to assume different functions. The brain, heart, lungs, internal organs, and arms and legs begin to form. Once the baby is a fetus, growth and development are aimed at preparing the baby for life abroad." It seems that the configuration of a dual human being (spirit and matter) begins immediately after conception, during the first five to six days, [Source: https:// www.babyq.com/most-popular/when-does-an-embryo-turn-into-a-fetus/] "After conception, the egg is fertilized by the sperm, becoming a zygote. After a few days of cell division, it becomes a blastocyst, reaching the uterus around day 5 and implanting into the uterine wall around day 6." At the moment an embryo is a fetus, and the configuration of components and spiritual elements is complete: the brain is loaded with data and information fundamental to mental functioning. Sensory perception is activated, and the fetus begins to synthesize its environment. However, it seems that there is still no reasoning. Mental and corporeal development continues over the next few weeks to week 25, when "the baby develops a startled reflex around week 26 a rapid brain development occurs as the mother progresses in the third trimester. In that final trimester, the nervous and respiratory systems develop, the bones begin to form, and the nails and hair grow."

xxii   Guardian Angels: Many people believe that a guardian angel walks around to protect each person twenty-four hours a day for seven days a week. Maybe that's an exaggeration. The phenomena we have to see is the form and time of unexpected help come to help us in difficult situations, unexpectedly. Very often, a guardian angel comes, helps without expecting anything in return, and disappears without a trace. A guardian angel can be an animal, or a person, unknown.

xxiii The work of spirits: The question is how do spirits work within a material body? Obviously, they do not work with all the omnipresence of the spirit, omnipotence, omniscience, and the rest of the spirits. We need an explanation outside of belief and faith. For example, the source, http://www.ministrysamples.org/excerpts/THE-FUNCTIONS-OF-THE-SPIRIT-THE-SOUL-AND-THE-BODY-1. HTML says, Man is made up of two independent types of material: spirit and body. When the spirit entered the body of the dust, the soul was produced. It is impossible for the spirit to control the body directly. Therefore, it requires a means. This medium is the soul, which occurred when the spirit touched the body. The spirit mingled with the body and drew the soul. As such, man became a living soul. Therefore, the soul is the result of the union between the spirit and the body; is a man's personality. The body is the outer layer of the soul, and the soul is the outer layer of the spirit. Before man fell, it was the spirit that controlled his whole being. When the spirit wants to do something, it communicates this to the soul, and the soul motivates the body to obey the commandment of the spirit. This is the meaning of the soul as the medium. Luke 1:46-47 says, "My magnificent soul [present time] to the Lord, and my spirit has exurized [perfect time] in God my Savior." The spirit must first exude, before the soul can magnify the Lord. The spirit first communicates joy to the soul, then the soul communicates to the body.

xxiv How the brain works: Mayoclinic.org: How the brain works - https://www.mayoclinic. org/brain/sls-20077047. Medical information reveals three main components that make up the brain in the complex nervous system. In addition to these three main components of the brain, there is an extensive super road of brain-derived nerves that reaches the entire body. The Brain, the largest portion contains two halves (hemispheres) that communicate with each other through a flat band of measuring fibers (Corpus Calloso). The brain is designed with four main areas, called lobes. The cerebellum controls the vital functions of the body, and at the center of the brain mass there are two twin areas, reflected, that process emotions and memories. These brain areas are divided into three subareas. A review of the information available in Mayoclinic.org, including the functions of neurons, does not reveal how thought, meditation, or meditation is achieved. It seems that most activities are to process and control each process. However, it is important to note that communication between neurons is achieved with electrical impulses that are sent or received by neurotransmitters. It is a highly complex system through which the mind thinks, conceives, selectively analyzes and synthesizes realities and or realities.

xxv   Structure and laws: The existence defined laws, rules and specifications to regulate the behavior of the universe. like the laws of chemistry, physics, quantum mechanics, combinations and permutations, probabilities, etc.

The knowledge we have accumulated in our minds until now is a small part of the implanted in the universe since before humans appeared on earth. There is no knowledge outside the absolute knowledge of the universe, and there is no more knowledge outside infinite space. Moreover, knowledge cannot be created or destroyed; because it's part of existence. But we can probably say, at this time, that the universe contains a defined knowledge corresponding to the visible and tangible portion of existence, as well as the invisible and intangible portion. This assumption is not far-fetched, since, from this day on, human beings have gained knowledge, which is neither visible nor tangible. For example, the laws of mathematics, physics, chemistry, astrophysics, quantum mechanics, all of which are invisible and intangible in a material sense, is knowledge.

xxvi   Oneness: Unity is the concept of merging the spirit and the material body into a single being, considering the dimensions of spirits and matter coexist in one space: the universe. It is possible, perhaps it is, that human beings are prepared and conditioned to communicate freely with the global spirit and its spirits. The fact is that the soul, mind, ego and consciousness are spiritual elements; so that we already communicate in spiritual terms (mind to mind) through words. So, the elimination of words would make a telepathic form of direct communication of the spirit. The use of sensory communication tools and methods is what makes us all human beings; and the processes of thought and feelings makes us spiritual. Obviously, our mind, being spiritual, cannot grasp matter; that's why the mind (soul) needs the body to work and or handle material objects and living creatures. The goal is not to become spirits that have the three attributes, omnipresence, omniscience, and omnipotence, but rather to be one in oneness.

xxvii   Sergio y Moisés secuencia de eventos:

Moses	*Sergio*
1-The soul is 1990	*1-The soul is 1990*
2-Born in 1991	*2-Born in 1991*
3-Meeting with a Coyote	*3-Meeting with a Coyote*
4-Kidnapping by the Cartel	*4-Removing a Kidney*
5-trip to the U.S.	*5-Travel to the U.S.*
—Caravane of Immigrants	*—Caravane of Immigrants*
6-Meeting with Sergio on the bus	*6-Moses Meeting on the buss*
7-Captured by Isa —at the border	*7-Captured by the Isa at the border.*

8-Isa legal action
9-Isa adopts them
10-Get asylum
11-Education

xxviii   Human brain waves
https://psicologiaymente.com/neurociencias/tipos-ondas-cerebrales
The electrical activity of neurons that populate the human brain is at the base of all the thoughts, feelings and acts we perform. That's why it's so hard to understand what neurons do every moment; everything that makes up our mental life consists of that inexplicable leap that goes from the frequency with which neurons send electrical impulses to the transformation of this so simple into mental processes in all its complexity. That is, there is something in the way of coordinating with each other of these nerve cells that causes feelings, thoughts, memories, etc. to appear. In turn, brain waves can be classified into different types according to their frequency, that is, the time that passes between times when many neurons fire electrical signals at eleven. These types of brain waves are received on behalf of Delta waves, Theta waves, Alpha waves, Beta waves, and Gamma waves.

xxix   Instincts: This is a natural form of behavior or intuitive reactions to external or environmental threats. The subject reacts intuitively to preserve his well-being and his life. https://en.wikipedia. org/wiki/Instinct provides the following on the Internet (excerpts): Instinct or innate behavior is the inherent inclination of a living organism toward particular complex behavior. The simplest example of an instinctive behavior is a fixed-action pattern (FAP), in which a sequence of very short-to-medium-length actions, without variation, are performed in response to a clearly defined stimulus. An instinctive behavior of shaking water from wet skin. A baby leather turtle makes its way to the open ocean. Any behavior is intrinsic if performed without relying on prior experience (i.e. in the absence of learning), and is therefore an expression of innate biological factors. The sea turtles, newborns on a beach, will automatically move into the ocean. A marsupial climb into his mother's bag at birth. Bees communicate dancing in the direction of a food source without formal instruction.

Other examples include animal fighting, animal courtship behavior, internal escape functions, and nest construction. Instincts are complex patterns of innate behavior that exist in most members of the species, and should be distinguished from reflexes, which are simple responses from an organism to a specific stimulus, such as pupil contraction in response to bright light or spasmodic movement of the lower leg when you touch your knee. The absence of volition capacity should not be confused with the inability to modify fixed action patterns. For example, people may be able to modify a stimulated fixed-action pattern by consciously recognizing the point of their activation and simply stop doing so, while animals without a sufficiently strong volitional ability may not be able to separate the self from their fixed action patterns, once activated. [1] The role of instincts in determining animal behavior varies from species to species. The more complex an animal's neural system, the greater the role of the cerebral cortex and social learning, and instincts play a minor role. A comparison between a crocodile and an elephant illustrates how mammals, for example, rely heavily on social learning.

xxx Individual sequences: Each human dual being (spirit and body) follows its own way of life; is, in fact, modified by the decisions and actions that each individual makes. On the path that human beings go through; However, his spirit directs thoughts, decisions, and actions toward points, conditions, and circumstances, which produce forces of mutual attraction to the fellow spirits. After all, it is the life of the spirit that we do. The infographics given below show the paths for the seven spirits that navigate the earth in this story.

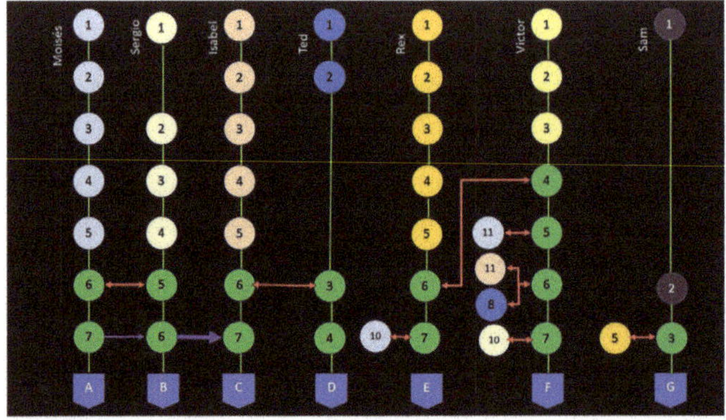

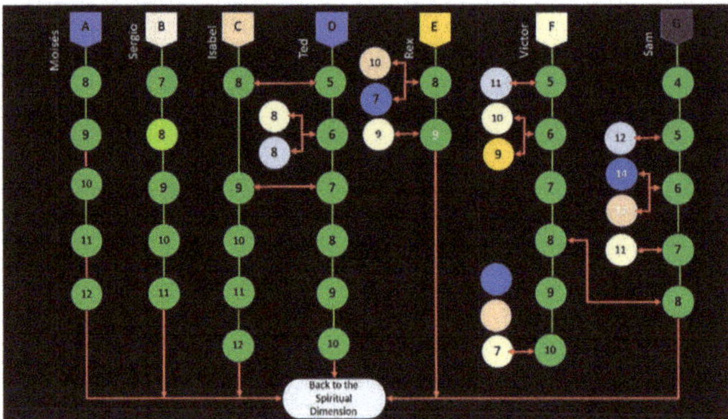

The sequences of events in each story are clear, showing situations and the timing of spirit encounters. The narratives of each dual being complement the events along their paths, helping the reader to understand twists and turns, or motifs, which leads to their encounters. Each sequence has a final physical action, back to the spiritual dimension. Perhaps, humans could build their own sequence of life with their friends to find the purpose of their encounters.

xxxi Introspection: "The examination or observation of one's mental processes and emotionally." It is the examination of your own conscious thoughts and feelings. In psychology, the process of introspection is based solely on the observation of the mental state, while in a spiritual context it may refer to the examination of his soul.

Introspection is closely related to human self-reflection and contrasts with external observation. Introspection generally provides privileged access to our own mental states, not mediated by other sources of knowledge, so the individual experience of the mind is unique. Introspection can determine any number of mental states including: sensory, body, cognitive, emotional and so on. Introspection has been the subject of philosophical discussion for thousands of years. The philosopher Plato asked, "Why should we not calmly and patiently review our own thoughts, and thoroughly examine and see what these appearances really are in us?" While introspection is applicable to many facets of philosophical thinking, it is perhaps best known for its role in epistemology, in this context introspection is often compared to perception, reason, memory, and testimony as a source of knowledge."

Humans can use introspection as an effective support of the soul, and meditate as many times as practical analysis of the four main components and/or attitudes: (1) right or wrong, (2) right or wrong, and (3) just or unfair, and (4) pleasant or unpleasant. The first goal of this meditation is to elevate the soul to higher levels of suppression of the external and internal consciousness. The second goal is to make this introspective meditation a daily habit that aims to educate the ego and achieve uniqueness. Source: ttps://www.bing. com/search?q=introspection+definition&form] [Source: https://en.wikipedia. org/wiki/Introspección] "Introspections the

^{xxxii} Karma refers to action, work or action; it also refers to the spiritual principle of cause and effect where the intention and actions of an individual (cause) influence the future of that individual (effect). Good intention and good characteristics contribute to good karma and future happiness, while bad and bad intention.